It Was Difficult to Know Which of Them Moved First . . .

or if they came together at the same time. Gina held on to him as though she had been cast adrift at sea and had suddenly latched on to a life preserver; Myles held her so hard she had faint blue marks all over her shoulders for a few days afterward.

When he bent his head and lowered his lips to hers, she turned up her mouth to receive the sweetness of his kiss as though it were the most natural thing in the world.

Several moments later, when their mouths unglued, Myles said huskily, hesitatingly, "Gina?" She swayed toward him, her hands flat against his chest.

"Yes," she whispered. "Yes, oh, yes."

One of his arms was under her knees, the other around her shoulders as he lifted her. Gina gave herself utterly to the strength of those arms, snuggling as close to him as she could while she drew her lips down from his jaw and along the side of his neck in one prolonged kiss.

Promise Me Forever

JACQUELINE MARTEN

A CHERISH BOOK
New York, N.Y.

This novel is a work of fiction. Names, characters, places and incidents are either the product of the author's imagination or are used fictitiously, and any resemblance to actual persons, living or dead, events or locales is entirely coincidental.

A CHERISH BOOK
Published By Cherish Books, Ltd.
New York, N.Y. 10018

Copyright © 1981 by Jacqueline Stern Marten

All rights reserved. No part of this book may be reproduced or transmitted in any form or by any means, electronic or mechanical, including photocopying, recording or by any information storage and retrieval system, except where permitted by law.

First Cherish Printing—1984

Printed in the United States of America

For
My husband, Albert E. Marten

(Chapter 34: 1781)

*And for our sons—Richard S.,
Jonathan M., Seth J. and Ethan E.*

*As we are now.
As we were in Williamsburg.*

Grateful acknowledgment is given to the museums, galleries and associates of the Smithsonian Institution of Washington, D.C., particularly to Uncle Beazley. Further appreciation is extended to Colonial Williamsburg, which is wonderful and unique, and where the future learns from the past.

Chapter 1

The dusty red Toyota bumped onto the shoulder of the highway, a small rental trailer jouncing merrily in the wake of its churning pebbles.

Two unkempt men in their early twenties uncurled long legs and staggered out of the rear doors, juggling three backpacks between them. They came over to the driver's side, thrusting bearded faces close to him.

"Thanks for the ride, man," one said hoarsely.

The second voice sounded like an echo. "Yeah, man, thanks a lot for the ride."

The driver barely glanced at them. "You bet," he said briefly, then turned to the passenger next to him, his expression softening. "Are you sure?" he asked urgently. "Baltimore is only an hour away. I just have to stop there maybe forty minutes, then I'm going straight on to Boston. I could have you there by early afternoon."

"I'd love to, Greg, honestly, but I'm so close to Washington now, it would be silly to pass it by."

"I understand. It's just—goddamn! I hate to leave you here like this . . . with them." He jerked his head contemptuously toward the lanky, jean-clad figures that now stood close to the highway, sharing a cigarette.

1

"They're harmless." Gina was unconscious of the equal contempt in her own voice. "Anyhow, I'll be dumping them in a few hours. I promised them a lunch at the Smithsonian—my father bought me a membership years ago. After that we'll go our separate ways."

"Your father!" He said it like a curse. "What the hell kind of father lets his daughter hitchhike alone around the country? My Pat is—"

"The same age as me," she broke in smoothly. "And she'd get her head handed to her if she tried this."

He grinned reluctantly. "Okay, okay, so I've said it before. But, seventeen or not, she'd have a sore a—rear end, and so would you if you had the right kind of father."

The blush which had crept up the collar of her blouse when he mentioned her age disappeared with a sudden swiftness.

"Well, I don't!" she replied tartly. He looked at her with such troubled eyes, her conscience took over. "Listen," she continued, "the next lap of my trek is to New York. How about if I promise to take a plane there? And maybe another one to go to Boston?"

"I'd feel a hell of a lot better if I thought you meant it."

"Okay, then, I promise I will." Gina interpreted his look correctly. "Rest easy," she assured him. "I always keep my promises."

Impulsively, she pushed her oversized sunglasses up onto her forehead and bent toward him. The tip of one breast, unimprisoned by a bra, pressed against his shoulder. He had a quick glimpse of huge, stormy blue eyes and charcoal lashes as she planted a firm kiss on his right cheek before she plunked the glasses back into place.

"Thanks a lot for the ride, man," she said in teasing imitation of her fellow travelers.

For a full two minutes after the girl had slid out of the car, Greg sat, shaken and still. "Jesus!" he exclaimed aloud, starting the motor. "And I felt *fatherly* toward her!"

Gina hitched up her jeans, tucked in her blouse and addressed the two smokers. "Okay, guys. On to Washington."

She shrugged to herself as they all raised their thumbs. Damn! she thought. Greg was great. I really hate to lie, but on the road, telling the truth about my age causes too many problems. Anyhow, it would only have complicated things if he'd found out I'm really twenty-three.

With a last wave of his hand, the driver of the Toyota was

gone. Gina moved farther out into the highway, one hand on her hip, one leg thrust forward. She took off her glasses, stood under the NO HITCHHIKING sign and smiled at the approaching stream of vehicles, nearly causing a four-car pileup. A small truck and a big car, both jostling for the shoulder, stopped abruptly, one just in front of and the other just behind her. Two heads popped out of the drivers' windows.

"Going into Washington?" she asked.

A telephone ring in the middle of the night was one of the more unpleasant sounds he knew. This particular ring not only shocked him awake, it yanked him out of a dream he would have preferred to run its course. Having just unfastened the hooks of Danny-Sue Donaldson's bra—the last article of clothing she had on—he was about to bury his face in the opulence let loose, when Danny-Sue and the delectable offered pillow were both dissolved by that shrill, persistent sound.

Sweating and swearing, he reached blindly for the phone and turned over onto his stomach as he fumbled the receiver to his ear. The hands of the clock stood at five forty-five. Not quite the middle of the night, even though no hint of daylight showed through the open slats of the Venetian blinds.

"Myles, sweet, is that you?"

"No, it's the milkman," he growled. "Who else did you think you'd get at this hour?"

Danny-Sue laughed softly, and he marveled, not for the first time, at how much sex she managed to throw into that sound. "My competition, maybe?" she purred.

"No competition. I go into strict training for at least two weeks before I see you."

"Darling, how precious of you."

Myles winced. Even all that dripping syrup sometimes failed to compensate for the affectations of her vocabulary. Bluntly, he demanded, "Why the midnight call?"

"It's morning," she replied reproachfully, "and I wasn't sure what time you planned to leave Williamsburg. I couldn't risk missing you, because there's been a little change in plans."

That brought him to full consciousness. "How little?"

"Charlotte's going to be at the apartment this weekend after all."

"Hell!"

"And I've been rescheduled. I have a flight out to Dallas late Saturday night . . . well, actually almost Sunday morning."

There went both his dream and his weekend.

"Nice of you to let me know in time," he grumped. "Unfortunately, I have to go to Washington anyway. I'm having lunch with Dr. Strager at the Smithsonian in about seven hours."

"Darling, I'm not calling off our date."

Myles cheered up enormously. "You're not?"

"I told you, it was just a *little* change in plans. We'll have the whole day, from the time your lunch ends until midnight, when I have to report in at the airport. I've already made the hotel reservations."

"Where?"

"At the L'Enfant Plaza."

"The L'Enfant Plaza!" he howled in outrage. "You didn't happen to forget that my next six months are very carefully budgeted, did you? We stay at the L'Enfant Plaza, and I'll be dieting all next week!"

"But you won't go hungry this weekend." The reminder floated through to him on a wave of laughter, deep and intimate, and he started to perspire again, as no doubt the little witch had intended. "Myles, are you still there?"

"Who do you think is doing all the heavy breathing?"

"Aren't I worth the L'Enfant Plaza?"

"Yes, damn it."

Danny-Sue laughed in pure female triumph. "Don't fret, darling. I reserved through the airline. Discount rates. You won't go too broke. See you there any time after two. I booked us as Mr. and Mrs."

She hung up without the formality of a good-bye, and Myles lay on the bed, tossing about, picturing the last time they had been together. He felt a little guilty as he reviewed old memories and recalled the economies practiced by Danny-Sue, who made such an effort not to put undue strain on his wallet.

It was too late now to tell her that pride, not financial necessity, was what made him determined to stay within his fellowship budget for the rest of the year. As long ago as his college days, he had discovered that mention of Grandfather Edward's New England mill shares had brought an acquisitive gleam into even the softest of feminine eyes. Almost thirty now and playing the role of happy bachelor, which for the present he was resolved to remain, Myles Edward thought it was better to be regarded as a struggling archaeologist rather than as a man of independent income, one-third heir to the Edward Fabric Factories.

He'd buy her a scrumptious dinner, Myles decided. "The hell with it!" he suddenly muttered, giving up trying to go back to sleep. He showered, shaved and packed his overnight bag.

Myles had planned to leave Williamsburg at nine for the two-and-a-half-hour drive from Virginia to Washington. Instead, he left shortly after eight. Even with his turning off the highway just beyond Richmond for a coffee break and lingering over a newspaper, he arrived more than an hour early for his lunch appointment.

His first piece of good fortune was to discover a parking spot on the Mall near the Castle. He locked the car and headed across the road toward the Museum of Natural History. Perhaps, thought Myles, his second piece of luck would be that Dr. Strager had arrived early, too.

It was a lot colder in Washington than it had been in Williamsburg, but Myles felt too lazy to go back to the car and get his topcoat. Instead, he plunged chilled hands deep into his jacket pockets and strode quickly along the wide, pebbled path, over which newly budded tree branches danced in a brisk April breeze.

Cold or no cold, he slowed down as he always did when he came near Uncle Beazley, the friendly-faced triceratops beloved of juvenile tourists. Every inch of its twenty-five-foot fiberglass length was awash with kids. There were half a dozen dungareed imps of assorted sizes and sexes astride the dinosaur's back, and several more swarming over its head. On the sidelines, parents called out instructions about looking up, down or over while their cameras kept up a busy clicking.

Myles was about to move on when one tiny gymnast, who was swinging between Uncle Beazley's two long horns, let go, impaled his little backside on the shorter nose horn and tumbled to the ground.

The boy seemed to be roaring much too lustily to indicate any serious damage, but, as the nearest adult, Myles felt called upon to pick him up and make sure. While Myles was patting blond curls and uttering soothing noises, the child's parents joined the rescue party. Myles straightened up, smiled away their thanks and started to move on again.

Then he stopped short, mesmerized.

The neat button behind bumping backward over the dinosaur's left eye belonged to no small child. As its owner stretched out her legs to the utmost in order to get both feet firmly planted on Uncle Beazley's great skull, pale blue suedelike cotton jeans, skintight, outlined every mouth-drying inch of the girl from thigh to ankle. A dirty white sneaker lace belted a waist so incredibly small, Myles's fingers flexed with the sudden urge to dig into her sides and meet across her vertebrae.

Without conscious thought, he left the path and crossed the grass to get closer to her. "Giddyap, there, boy. Come on, my lovely," he heard her say, and his senses reeled under the impact of this second shock. Even allowing for the fact that she was half whispering, her voice seemed to extend all the way down to her diaphragm. Its throaty timbre and lilting quality stirred him almost as much as her figure did.

As Gina reached out like one of the children in a pretense of pulling at reins, Myles felt his first pang of disappointment. Her arms were a bit too thin. In a sleeveless striped jersey, which was a ridiculous thing to wear on a windy April day, she was unattractively adorned from shoulders to wrists with goose flesh.

He must have made some sound—maybe one of chagrin—because her head swiveled around suddenly, and he was even more disillusioned.

Great, round, dark-tinted glasses covered her face from the middle of her forehead to the tip of her nose. The only features clearly visible were a pale, tight mouth—lips compressed and corners tucked in—and a thrusting chin that might possibly pass as firm. Myles wasn't quite so charitable in his estimate. Stubborn as hell, he would bet.

A thick, untidy ponytail, of a light brown color but darkly streaked, had whipped across her shoulder to hang down the middle of her back. It was tied with another sneaker lace, a black one this time.

"A rag and a bone and a hank of hair," Myles muttered to himself irritably.

Her head was still turned toward him. He had a notion she was staring at him as intently as he had looked at her, but from behind the dark glasses it was impossible to be sure. Suddenly, she put a hand to her head as though it hurt.

You win one, you lose one, he decided fair-mindedly. As he moved away, his grimace turned to a grin. It was too much to have expected that her top would equal her bottom.

"April, oh, April!"

He wasn't the only one to stop and stare. There was so much incredulous joy in those few words, such a wealth of love and longing.

He turned in time to see the girl take a breakneck slide down the inner ridge of Uncle Beazley's bony crest and the channel between his horns. She came to grief in the exact spot as the little boy Myles had picked up, but she was off her knees and onto her feet in seconds without any help. She cast one quick look around, then wrenched off her glasses and flung them away.

"April, April, wait for me!"

Then she came running at him.

They wound up on the grass in a mad tangle of arms and legs, he the worst for it because she had landed on top of him. It wasn't that she weighed so much—she didn't—but that he had his breath knocked out in their fall.

Gina made no effort to get off him, merely kept looking wildly about. Then her head drooped low. "She's gone," the girl said in a sighing, sorrowful half whisper.

Myles was too bemused by what the tinted glasses had concealed to attempt to unload her. Under the straight, dark smudge of her eyebrows were the most magnificent eyes he had ever seen. Too dark to be blue, too light to be purple, much too alive and glowing, even shining as they were with unshed tears, to go with that sullen mouth.

Then Gina quite literally shook herself and looked down at him with a slight air of surprise, as though she had no idea how either of them came to be where they were. Faint color crept into her pale cheeks while she said, with apparent unconcern, "Dr. Livingstone, I presume?" She started wriggling off, which gave him, despite the cold ground underneath, a moment's regret.

Slowly they got to their feet.

"You're all covered with grass," she remarked gruffly. "Sorry I was so clumsy." Uninhibitedly and with vigor, she started to brush him off.

Though the brushing was far from unpleasant, Myles

objected for form's sake, but Gina paid no attention to his protests until he was cleaned to her satisfaction. Then they stood looking at each other for a few more seconds of awkward silence, shattered unexpectedly by the twang of the Midwest.

"Hey, chick, you A-Okay? What flipped you out like that?"

There were two of them, carbon copies except for coloring. One was dark and one was fair. Otherwise they were identical—longish hair, straggly beards, dirty work shirts, patched dungarees.

Each carried a knapsack on his back. The dark one had a third backpack dangling from his wrist. Hers, Myles supposed. The dark-haired young man had asked the question; the fair one was holding out her glasses.

"One of the brats nearly stepped on them. You ready to take off now?"

Gina looked up at Myles. He suddenly had the strangest notion that she was asking him for the answer. Just three little words from him—"Please don't go"—and she would say no to them.

He didn't know why he was so convinced of this, and for a moment, looking into those glorious eyes now gone navy blue, he was almost tempted. "Stay with me a while" was on the tip of his tongue, and then common sense came to the rescue.

For God's sake, what's gotten into me? Myles wondered. I've got my appointment with Dr. Strager, and the day and night—my God, yes, the *night*—with Danny-Sue. The last thing in the world I need is even the briefest involvement with this teenaged hippie type.

"Well, thanks for the brushing off," Myles said. He gave her a little nod and a smile that were both dismissals. For good measure, he spoke the words aloud quite firmly. "Good-bye."

"You brush off nicely, too," Gina replied softly, mockingly, and without another word she walked away between the blue-jean twins.

It's crazy to feel this way, Myles told himself bewilderedly, heading once more for the museum. This stab of conscience, as though I've hurt some soft, defenseless creature. Even more confusing to him was the squeeze of pain in his gut.

Chapter 2

Dr. Strager was neither in the Associates' Court nor in the adjoining exhibition rooms, and Myles was too restless to wait around for him. He decided to stroll over to the Hirshorn Museum and check out the current showing.

Some twenty minutes later he was on the Up escalator, nearing the second floor, when a sudden tailspin sent his heart back down to the lobby. There was no mistaking that voice.

"You can have your spatter-paint Pollocks," Gina was saying cheerfully. "They don't do a thing for me. Now, that huge thing—what was it called?—the one where you feel as though you're inside a big ball of knitting yarn looking out. Now *that* was soothing."

"Art isn't supposed to soothe."

"Who put that in the Constitution?"

They stood next to the top of the escalator, bickering amiably. None of them noticed Myles, which was just the way he wanted it, he told himself. As he moved swiftly behind them, his face turned away, the Midwest twang suggested, "All right, what do you think of this one? Step back a little; you're too close for the right perspective."

Obediently, the girl stepped back . . . and into Myles! His hands reached out instinctively and held her upright.

"Oh, I beg your par—"

The apology was cut off in her instant recognition of him. Myles let go of her, inclined his head politely and moved on. Behind him he could feel two eyes boring into his skull like twin dentist drills. He resisted the impulse to look back one more time before he was swallowed up by the white-walled cavern.

He had lost his taste for art. He did a fast circuit around the floor, then took the escalator down and the exit out.

He had been quick, but not as quick as the girl. He came around the corner and saw her balanced precariously on the edge of the central fountain, her back very straight, one hand lying in her lap, the other trailing in the pool. His eyes met the head-on glare of the dark glasses. The closer he got, the more tension he could feel. It seemed to come at him in waves from her straight, still body.

Was she lying in wait for him? he wondered, horrified. She had certainly used considerable speed to shake off her escorts and get into a spot outside the building where it would be hard for him to miss her. The name of *her* game might be involvement.

It was the second time around in their brief three meetings that this thought had occurred to him. He had the uneasy sensation of a trap being sprung, and because of that unease, he made the nod he gave her extra frigid as he passed by.

She slid off the fountain's edge with fluid grace and stepped directly in front of him. It was either stop or trample all over her. He had to stop.

Her voice was low and furious but still beautiful, he noticed. "April brought me to you. It wasn't *my* idea. You can quit worrying. I don't want anything to do with you either."

"What on earth are you talking about?"

But she was off and running, back toward Independence. For the second time he headed for the Museum of Natural History, engulfed once more by that heavy, drugged feeling of loss.

It made no sense to him, no sense at all. He had a sudden wish to get out of Washington fast and back to the safe, snug sanity of Williamsburg, but Dr. Strager would be arriving any minute . . . then there was Danny-Sue. Yes, thank God for

Danny-Sue. She would be a grand cure for whatever it was that ailed him.

Myles waited on the steps of the museum until Dr. Strager arrived, after which they walked into the Hall of Dinosaurs. There, Dr. Strager made a brief note on an envelope. Then they went past the Bush Elephant and downstairs to the Associates' Court.

Busy talking to Dr. Strager, Myles absentmindedly released the door as they passed through and heard a little "Oof" behind him.

Belatedly, he grabbed the door and turned around. His smile and the apology meant to go with it died on his lips. His nemesis, doubly escorted once more, stood there, her own smile fixed and scornful.

"Don't look so surprised," Gina said sweetly. "Even the peasants can become members if they pay." Then she pushed rudely past, the blue-jean twins lumbering after her to stand in line.

Like Myles, Dr. Strager had stepped back so as not to get crushed in their stampede.

"Friend of yours, Myles?" he asked doubtfully.

"More like a newly met enemy."

Before there could be any more questions, the line moved up. In another few minutes they were all directed into the small waiting room. The three sat down on a group of chairs opposite Myles and Dr. Strager, a whispered discussion going on among them.

Suddenly a worn but well-stuffed man's wallet appeared in her hands. She carelessly pulled a twenty from among many bills. Dr. Strager stopped speaking just then, and Myles distinctly heard her say, "Here. This should take care of us."

As a scientist, Myles dealt in facts. But facts went by the wayside now. Every instinct in him clamored that the guys spelled trouble for her, and that flaunting her money was asking for it in full measure. "You damned little idiot!" he wanted to shout, but she was pretending to ignore his very existence. Since he intended to go along with that pretense, he had no choice but to keep his mouth shut.

Dr. Strager, whom he had worked under at the Smithsonian for two years before going to Williamsburg, was an extremely observant man. Ten minutes into their lunch, which had been arranged as a favor to the younger man to discuss some valuable research sources, Strager cocked an indulgent eyebrow at Myles. "Shall we shelve this for now?" he proposed. "Your mind doesn't seem to be very receptive." He smiled meaningfully at Myles's note pad, lying on the table.

For the first time Myles became aware of having doodled over and over in the margins the figure of a skinny little girl atop a fat dinosaur. A skinny girl with a face full of sunglasses.

Even as Myles slid the doodles under a clean page, Dr. Strager's eyes wandered a few tables down to the original. "She has great beauty," he said quietly.

"Beauty!" Myles exploded. Bitterly he repeated his earlier critique. "Why, she's nothing but a rag and a bone and a hank of hair in the ill-dressed uniform of her kind!"

His mentor looked mildly surprised. "And you're an archaeologist! Shame on you, Myles. When have we not had to dig deep and carefully for our most valued finds, washing away the dirt and the dross and the accumulation of years to reach what is rare and precious?" As Myles flushed darkly and looked down at his plate, Dr. Strager continued pensively. "She had a great need to hurt you, so I assumed that *you* had hurt *her*. But she blushed at her own bad manners when she noticed me, so rudeness does not come naturally to her, only hot blood. She walks with grace, her voice is a poem and her figure a delight. The clothes are unimportant, the bones are good and her hair is silken. Yes, young man, I see beauty in her."

Myles pushed back his chair. "Would you like seconds of anything?" he asked abruptly.

"Another piece of chicken, please. While you're gone, shall I order tea, coffee or beer for you? And some cake to go with it or just for myself? You know my lamentable sweet tooth."

His smile as he spoke was gentle. Myles could see that as far as Strager was concerned, the subject was closed. Myles nodded agreement and headed toward the buffet table.

They were moving backward from opposite directions, carrying full trays, when he and Gina had their final collision of the day. It was a grand and glorious crash. Her dishes and his tray went flying. She collapsed onto her knees; he got knocked on his keister. The buzzing room was instantly hushed. A trail of vegetables dripped down his shirt front, and he began to pick chicken parts carefully out of his lap.

Necks were craning; faces were curious and expectant.

Myles drew a deep breath as Gina swiveled around on her knees to face him. He was prepared to annihilate her with words, since nothing else worked.

She rose in the same fluid way she had risen at the Hirshorn fountain. Only a brief moment elapsed before she flung a loud, clear stage whisper all the way to the balcony. "We've got to stop meeting like this, you know. My husband is getting suspicious."

The people in the nearby section of the Court dissolved into roars of near-hysterical laughter. Wave after wave of the sound swept across the room.

Head high, disdainful, like a prideful cat, Gina stepped lightly, daintily, across a puddle of salad and strode away. Myles was left among the bits and the bones and the crockery with murder and desolation in his heart.

Two waitresses merged on him simultaneously, towels and napkins at the ready. He was scrubbed and dabbed at with cold water, cooed over and commiserated with.

Another tray of seconds was supplied. When he carried it back to Dr. Strager, unchecked laughter still followed him, but he was beyond caring. His eyes darted around the room.

"She's gone," Dr. Strager said quietly. "They left almost immediately. But it's not too late, Myles, if—"

"It is too late," Myles replied tightly. "It was always too late. Forgive me, sir, for not having been the ideal eating companion. If we could just get back to those notes . . ."

Chapter 3

Less than two hours later, Myles was alone in the hotel room with Danny-Sue. Her velvety arms clutched him close while she murmured into his ear, "Why, darling, you really *did* miss me, didn't you?"

Her face was only inches away from his, but even as he looked down into the slumberous gray-green eyes, he was seeing the angry sparkle of amethyst and the somber stare of navy blue. Danny-Sue's Mona Lisa smirk turned into someone else's mocking, challenging smile, a smile of pity and disdain.

From far off he heard Danny-Sue repeating, "You really did, didn't you?"

He pulled himself together to play the game out. "Haven't I proved it?" Inwardly, he smiled, reflecting that Danny-Sue, a dear girl, if a simple one, thought that he had and was eager to have it proved again.

Myles was happy to satisfy her so easily. Even as his thumb pressed into velvet softness, he cursed himself for remembering the resistant twitch of another person's shoulders, the pathos of slender, goose-flesh-covered arms.

Much later they dressed and went downstairs to the Apple of Eve for a late supper. Danny-Sue wore a red chiffon cocktail gown collared with puritanical demureness in front and slashed nearly to her sacroiliac in back.

"Gorgeous," he had granted when she twirled around upstairs for his inspection, "but I hope you paid for only half a dress, since that's all you seem to have gotten."

"Do you mind being seen with me like this?"

The question, like the gown, had been meant to be provocative, but he had discovered, a bit sadly, that neither had achieved its intent.

Like an actor on cue, he had said, "I'll be the envy of every man who sees you." Once again he had found her painfully easy to please.

The couple of hours that they spent over supper were a pleasant surprise. Danny-Sue's talents weren't confined to the boudoir. Her training as a stewardess had made her adept at coaxing adult males out of bad moods and restoring harmony to an overcharged atmosphere. She was a fund of choice anecdotes, jokes and good humor. She really cared if the wine was good, the meal was right, the guest was happy . . .

After they returned to their room, a single zip sent red chiffon swirling around her feet. She stood there in bright scarlet bikini briefs, and reaching for the hanger that held her uniform, said softly, "We have more than an hour and a half."

He took the hanger out of her hands and hooked it over the closet bar. "That's all the time in the world," he murmured, and pulled her willingly to him.

Myles tore off his tie and shirt and remained quite still while she rotated her breasts teasingly over his bare chest. When she thrust them harder against him, he pulled her to him, rotating in his turn. Danny-Sue drew slightly away to unbuckle his belt. He promptly brought her closer again, his hands slipping inside the elastic at the back of her panties and sliding sensuously across the ample curve of her buttocks.

With his hands full of Danny-Sue, Myles was struck almost violently by a sudden flash of remembrance . . . a neat little button behind bumping gently over Uncle Beazley's left eye . . .

He growled deep in his throat from rage and frustration. "The devil with her!" he ground out between his teeth. No raggy ghost in jeans was going to run interference this time!

His pants and Danny-Sue's came off together. He flung her onto the bed with such speed and fervor, the springs reacted nearly as loudly as she did.

"Hey, Cave Man, mind the neighbors!" she cried, half in alarm, half in pleasure.

Myles joined her on the bed, wringing cries from her that were filled with delight.

This time it was good, damned good. All the same, after he had driven Danny-Sue to Dulles Airport, he felt a curious reluctance to return to the scene of their late revels. Myles even thought of packing his bag and driving straight back to Williamsburg instead of waiting till morning. Then he reminded himself morosely, speeding across the Memorial Bridge, that it was now well past midnight. Morning was already here.

Common sense told him that, whether he had insomnia or not, he was still too tired for a long drive; and a fever of restlessness warned that he could not go back to the hotel room to read or make sense of his notes. Suddenly he reversed direction and headed down the West Basin Drive.

He knew where he was going.

During the day the Lincoln Memorial could be as much of a tourist nightmare as any other monument in Washington. The constant screech of brakes and the roar of gunned motors mingled with the mood-shattering squeals of visitors. The wonder and the beauty of it were submerged by a potpourri of popcorn eaters and postcard writers. But in the quiet darkness of early morning, while Washington slept and Lincoln sat alone in brooding silence, the statue was a splendid and awesome sight.

Myles had done this before when he lived in Washington, and discovered that the President who had not slept well in the White House was himself a very fine cure for insomnia.

Taking the steep steps two at a time, Myles walked more slowly past the temple columns and came out of the darkness and into the field of light that shed radiance on the great marble statue. On the wall of one of the inner rooms the Gettysburg Address was engraved. He spoke the words aloud, secretly as proud as a strutting fourth grader that he could recite them from memory alone.

"Fourscore and seven years ago our fathers brought forth on this continent a new nation, conceived in liberty, and dedicated to the proposition that all men are created equal. Now we are enga————"

He stopped, his heart hammering. A voice out of nowhere was speaking along with him.

"Oh, for God's sake!" the voice moaned. "Who's there?" he asked sharply.

The voice was plaintive this time, rather than irritated, and there was no mistaking to whom it belonged. "Can't you please save it for the Fourth of July? I'm trying to get some sleep."

Gina had not only given Myles the fright of his life but made him feel the worst kind of fool as well, which was nothing new in their series of encounters. He could cheerfully have taken her by the throat and squeezed until she was incapable of speech, only first he had to find her.

"Where the hell are you?" he demanded savagely.

"Here. Behind Old Abe." She seemed to be strangling on her own laughter, and he marched around the statue, prepared to finish the job for her.

There was a small space between the back of the statue and the wall behind it. To reach it, Myles had to step over the low chain designed to keep visitors from getting any closer. In this space was a sleeping bag, neatly laid out, with the girl's knapsack beside it. She was sitting up, her legs still inside the bag, and as Myles came into view, she yawned hugely.

He forgot his thuglike intentions. "Were you really asleep?" he demanded incredulously.

"What time is it now?"

He looked down at the radium-dial face of his watch. "Ten to one."

"Then"—another cavernous yawn—"yes, I was quite soundly asleep. I've been here since right after dark. I slipped back when no one was around, not even any of the park service people. Of course, I'd cased the possibilities earlier in the day, when I found out . . . when they . . . when I—"

"When they and you what?" Myles prodded disagreeably, sensing she preferred not to answer.

It was too dark to see the play of emotions on her face. That she was struggling with conflicting ones, he had no doubt. The struggle ended with a clearly what-the-hell shrug of her shoulders.

"I needed a free place to sleep," Gina replied. "Those guys I was with ripped off my wallet."

"They did *what?*"

She knew he didn't mean the question literally, but she chose to pretend otherwise.

"They stole all my bread," she explained, in the manner of

a tolerant teacher addressing a dull student. "Well, almost all. I had a couple of dollars and some loose change in my jeans, and I always keep a twenty tucked in my bra for emergencies. Would you call this an emergency?" she asked chattily.

"I would call *you* a basket case," Myles growled, dropping down beside her on the sleeping bag. Gina obligingly moved her legs to give him room. "How well did you know those bastards?"

"Only a couple of days. I met up with them on the road, somewhere in Ohio. I figured it would be safer for me to join forces with them than to go it alone, even though I could get more rides by myself."

"Marvelous judgment on your part," Myles snorted.

Gina shrugged again. "You're being sarcastic, you *think*, but I happen to have been right. They weren't interested in me, not unless I was willing, which I wasn't. They each made their pass, I said no, thanks, and that was that."

"Except for robbing you."

"Mmm, yes, except for robbing me, and that was only money. Anyhow, it was just as much my fault. I shouldn't have let them see I had so much, but you—in the Associates' Court—you made me so mad, I . . . I . . ."

Myles remembered very clearly his own rage at her when she had flaunted that well-stuffed wallet.

"We seem to have the unhappy faculty of making each other mad," he remarked dryly. "How much did you lose?"

"Two hundred, give or take a little."

"Two hun— Good God! Did you report it to the police?"

"What for? The guys were long gone by the time I realized the money was missing. They must have taken it when I was at the lunch buffet, and I ditched them—or maybe they did the ditching—a while later. I went upstairs to see the Hope Diamond, then down to the museum shop. When I wanted to buy a few things there, I discovered my wallet was gone from the outside pocket of my knapsack." She finished cheerfully, "I was a fool to have let them see me put it there."

"You were indeed," Myles agreed cordially, and she made a face at him. "But if you had some loose money in your jeans and a twenty in your bra, why didn't you get yourself a room instead of staying here?"

"Because it's Saturday night."

"That is not what I would call an adequate explanation."

"I bought myself dinner tonight and phoned a service to get

my charges canceled in case Bud and Jerry try to use my credit cards. That left me with nothing except the twenty. I can't charge, and there's no way of getting through to my bank till Monday. So I figured I'd better sleep free tonight and tomorrow and use the cash reserve for food."

"There's always Travelers Aid."

Her shrug was beginning to set his teeth on edge. Why bother? it said this time. "Why bother?" she said out loud.

"Why couldn't you check into a motel and wait there till Monday, when your money would be sent to you?"

Myles couldn't see the mocking grin, but he could hear it in her voice. "Aw, c'mon. One look at me, and it would be, 'Money in advance, please.' Wouldn't you feel the same?" She regarded him slyly.

He declined her bait and stood up. "Come on, I'll help you fold the sleeping bag."

Gina sat where she was. "Come on where?" she asked quietly.

"I have a paid-up hotel room with two beds. I think you'll find one of them more comfortable than the floor here, Mr. Lincoln's presence notwithstanding."

She stayed very still, and he felt himself fairly sizzling with the familiar blaze of anger that he was beginning to associate with any three consecutive minutes spent in her company.

Myles knelt on the sleeping bag and backed her up against the wall. "For your information," he said very slowly, very coldly, very distinctly, "I have spent the better part of this day . . . and night . . . with a tigress from Tennessee. Even if I had the inclination, which I assure you I do not, I haven't the strength to be any kind of threat to you. I am offering you a bed—nothing more. If you want it, get out of that sleeping bag. If you don't, then the hell with you, I'm going back to my hotel."

He rose to his feet and turned to march away.

"Hey, wait," Gina called. "I'm coming with you. It's too late for you to back out. You've made that bed sound too inviting."

She wriggled out of the bag, fully dressed except for shoes, reached for a pair of sneakers tucked into the top of her knapsack, thrust them on and tied the laces. Myles folded up the waterproof bag and tucked it under his arm.

"Thank you. I'm ready," Gina said meekly, hoisting the backpack over one shoulder.

Had she said that too meekly? Myles studied her suspiciously but was diverted by the sound of a guard approaching from the front.

Hastily, they stepped over the chain. Halfway down the marble steps, his hand lightly holding her elbow, they both spun around, without words, without signals, for one last look through the columns.

She gave a queer choking sound, and his hand tightened on her arm as she took a quick step backward, murmuring under her breath, "April?"

"Are you all right?"

"Yes, of course. I thought . . . I just . . . it's so impressive, isn't it?" she finished lamely, moving the rest of the way down the steps with him.

Yes, it is, you shocking little liar, he said to himself, but it wasn't the statue that set you off like that. You look the way you did this morn—yesterday morning, when you ran at me yelling like a banshee for your April, whoever she is. You are one king-sized kook, my girl. Something tells me I should have left you here to sleep with Lincoln instead of at the hotel with me.

Chapter 4

Ten minutes later they rolled into the hotel garage. Gina agreed to leave her sleeping bag in the car and pick it up afterward. Myles carried her knapsack, devoutly grateful he had the room key in his pocket and could bypass lifted eyebrows at the front desk. When they emerged from the garage elevator into the lobby, he walked briskly, hoping to avoid that same reaction and keeping her on his left until they arrived at the floor elevators.

As soon as they reached the room, Myles locked the door behind them and threw the knapsack down on the made-up bed, his face heating up a bit when he saw her give the bed that had been occupied a casual once-over.

"You take the first bath," he offered hastily. "That is, if you want one."

"Do I ever!" she cried. "It's been two days since I've met up with soap and water except in public lavatories. We slept in some kind of hostel last night where there was only a cold-water faucet." She poured the contents of her knapsack onto the bed and pawed among the motley heap of personal effects. "Bath oil, glycerine soap, herbal shampoo!" she squealed in ecstasy, then cast him a doubtful look. "I guess I'd better find something to sleep in."

Myles bowed ironically. "Not for my sake, I hope."

Gina grabbed up some sort of garment. "No, just my own sweet modesty," she chirped, and sashayed toward the bathroom. "Tigress from Tennesee, huh? Looking at that bed"—she turned her head to direct a grin of pure malice at him—"I believe you."

He hefted a pillow and tossed it, catching her square between the shoulders. Gina whirled around and hurled it back at him so fast it caught him full in the face. Giving a delicious giggle, she slammed the bathroom door shut and quickly locked it.

Myles listened to her splash and sing for twenty minutes before he pounded on the door and yelled, "Are you going to be there all night?"

"I'm sorry," she said contritely a few minutes later, "but it was so heavenly I just couldn't bear to get out."

She looked like a well-scrubbed schoolgirl, all red and rosy and natural, her hair turbaned in a towel and her figure disguised in what looked like an oversized T-shirt. The scarlet letters across her chest spelled I AM WOMAN, which was overstating the obvious.

When Myles came out of the bathroom, he was wearing shorts as sleepwear in his own gesture of modesty, Gina had cleared off her bed and was sitting cross-legged on it, toweling her hair. She slanted a quick glance at him, her hands momentarily arrested.

"You look better without your clothes," she told him frankly, "more outdoorsy. You've got broader shoulders than I thought, and a nice, hairy chest. In fact, your body—"

"Those," he interrupted, "are the kind of remarks that little girls shouldn't make to big boys in hotel rooms, not unless they want the consequences."

"I thought big boys were exhausted."

"They've been known to recover."

"Oh, in that case . . ." She resumed her toweling.

"Why the grimace?" Myles asked.

"I'm so tired, my arms are falling off."

"Here, let me."

He pushed her hands away and rubbed her head with the towel until she howled in pain.

"That was marvelous, but no more, please," she begged.

He carried the wet towel to the bathroom, and when he returned she was flat on her stomach, brushing out her hair over the end of the bed. Her raised arms had raised something else—her T-shirt, revealing the curve of her thighs and a few provocative inches of bottom.

Swallowing hard, he yanked the T-shirt back down. The light from the bed lamp shone over her hair, and he made a startling discovery. "I'll be damned—you're a blonde!"

"All my life."

"But yesterday—all those times I saw you—I could have sworn it was—well, forgive me, but a sort of mousy-brown color."

She gave that little giggle again, lifting her face. He studied it reflectively. Not beautiful, except for her eyes, but when the sullen look lifted, piquant—yes, piquant was the word for it.

"That was dirt—road dirt, air pollution dirt, gasoline dirt. I've been hitchhiking, remember, and my last bath was two days ago."

"Where, may I ask, are you hitching to?"

"Oh, I'm making a historic tour of the U.S.A. I've been in Europe for a few years, so I've seen more of other countries than of my own. I thought I'd spend some time in Washington, then a week or two in New York, and maybe get a job in Boston until school starts in September."

"School?"

"Well . . . college."

"I figured you for seventeen."

"Seventeen and a half," she corrected, feeling the same sense of shame she always did when she lied to someone who helped her.

She continued brushing her hair. He watched, fascinated, as the shining strands, electrified by the brush, flew over her shoulders and down her back and even across her face. *Dr. Strager is a better archaeologist than I am, that's for sure,* Myles thought. Strager said that her hank of hair was silken. Myles was conscious of longing to plunge his hands into that pale blonde mass all the way up to his wrists.

He curbed the impulse, of course, but the struggle left him feeling a bit savage. "Is your family as crazy as you are?" he burst out.

"Huh?" The brush stopped in midair.

"Letting you hitchhike around the country and get into all kinds of dangerous situations, letting—"

"*What* kinds of dangerous situations?"

"Those characters you were with today, you don't call—"

"They robbed me, but they weren't dangerous. They didn't mug me, they didn't—"

"And how about right now? You're here with *me*, aren't you? You came without a murmur, like a sheep behind a Judas goat. Okay, it was safe for you to do it, but you didn't know that. I could have been a pervert or a rapist or a murderer—did you ever stop to think of that?"

"But I knew you weren't."

He pounced triumphantly. "How? How did you know? Because of the way my eyes are set? Or because I wear a shirt and tie?"

"I tell you, I knew. April—" She gave a funny whimper and stopped abruptly.

"Yes, we're back to that again," he said. "How exactly did you know, and who the hell is April?"

"None of your business," she replied, the beginnings of tears in her voice. "I was getting along fine until you interfered. You've been criticizing me in your mind since the very first minute you saw me up on Uncle Beazley with all those kids. So it was childish of me. So what? Who did I hurt by it? Anyhow, I wanted to. I always do what I want. And right now I don't want to stay here with you."

She uncrossed her legs and swung them over the side of the bed.

"You may not want to," Myles retorted, "but you're going to. I refuse to have you on my conscience tonight."

She rose and flung the brush at him. He ducked, but the tip of the handle clipped his temple.

With one leap he had crossed over to her and yanked back the covers. "Get in!" He was careful not to shout.

She just stood there, her eyes spitting anger and defiance, so he took her fore and aft by the T-shirt and tossed her onto the sheet.

"If you so much as budge from there . . ." He let an ominous silence say the rest.

Myles heard her begin to cry as he reached over to turn off the light, but he got into his own bed without a word. He was exhausted enough to sleep through a cloud burst, but there wasn't any cloud burst. She cried more like a child than like a young woman, with little sniffles and snorts and funny wuffling sounds.

When he couldn't stand it any more, on went the light again, and he sat down on the side of her bed.

"Have a heart," he begged. She gave a couple of hiccuping sobs. "I'm sorry," he told her softly. "I still think you're crazy to take such risks, but maybe I should have expressed it a bit more . . . more . . ."

"You were m-mean."

"I know, and I'm sorry," Myles said again. Her face was buried in the pillow, the pale blonde strands spread out like a net. He stroked her head gently. Her hair was as silken as it looked; it seemed to come alive under his fingers. "I should have been more—"

"Gentle," she interrupted weepingly.

"More gentle," he acknowledged without a blink. With her face still hidden, she didn't see him rub the spot where her brush had made contact with his head. "Can you go to sleep now?"

She pushed herself up in bed but wouldn't look at him. "I'd like to get a drink of water."

"I'll bring it to you. There are some ice cubes in the refrigerator. Or would you prefer orange juice?" Danny-Sue, thrifty as well as thoughtful, had brought along a container of it with some of her airline's miniature vodkas in order to make their screwdrivers.

"Orange juice would be lovely."

By the time he returned from the bathroom with a full glass for her and half a glass for himself, Gina was sitting up in bed, quiet and composed.

She took a long, thirsty swallow. "Thank you. And . . . and I'm sorry, too." She scratched at the glass with her thumbnail and for the first time raised her eyes to his. "What's your name? It seems funny to be here like this and not know," she told him frankly.

"Myles. Myles Edward."

"I'm Gina. Did you come to Washington just to see the Tennessee tigress?"

He couldn't help grinning at such open curiosity. "No. I also had an appointment with Dr. Strager. He's the man I was with in the Associates' Court when you made a damn fool of me," Myles needled delicately. "Actually, Washington's my home. I work at the Smithsonian, though right now I'm on leave. I have a grant to write a book on colonial craftsmen and their daily lives. During most of my research and writing, I'm staying in Williamsburg, Virginia."

"Colonial craftsmen and their daily lives," she repeated dubiously. "It doesn't have the ring of a best seller."

"It assuredly won't be," he agreed. "On the other hand, it

will pay me for my time, and I'm enjoying the work tremendously. In my field, archaeology and anthropology, it's important to publish. Incidentally, Gina"—he winced as her teeth crunched down on a piece of ice—"I'm surprised you left out Williamsburg in that historic tour of yours. For my money, it's the best of the lot."

Her forehead wrinkled in concentration. "Williamsburg. I've read about it, I think. Isn't that the place they fixed up to look the way it did at the time of the American Revolution?"

"They restored it," he corrected. "Many of the original buildings still exist. Others are reconstructed."

"Is it commercial?"

"Yes, but what isn't? Anyway, the good by far outweighs the bad. In two days there, you can learn more Early American history than you can from several years of high school courses . . . and in a far more pleasant fashion."

She considered his suggestion thoughtfully. The way she considered it was to stare straight ahead with her eyes glued shut, nose wrinkled, the tip of her tongue and her lower lip, sticking out. She looked about twelve years old, and Myles felt a moment's misgiving.

She claimed to be seventeen and a half, but suppose she wasn't? My God, he told himself in sudden panic, there were legal complications about things like this. Somewhat sourly, he pictured himself trying to explain to the law that he wasn't impairing the morals of a minor. It was because he'd had an insane spurt of chivalry that she was sitting there mother-naked under her cotton T-shirt.

He could feel the handcuffs clicking around his wrists at the very moment that she opened her eyes, closed her mouth and said, more to herself than to him, "I might do that. I don't have any set itinerary. Would I—if I—are you seeing anyone tomorrow, or will you be driving back to Williamsburg?"

"The Tennessee tigress is on her way to Dallas right now, if that's what you're trying to find out," he returned bluntly. "If you want a lift, yes, I'm going back right after breakfast."

"Then I'll think about it tonight and let you know in the morning." She handed her glass to him. "Thank you, and good night."

She was snuggled down under the blanket with her back to him by the time he emerged from the bathroom.

"Good night, Gina." Myles turned off the light, hoping it would not have to be turned on again.

There was no answer. Out like the light. He stretched out

on his bed with a groan of relief to be at last in a prone position.

He was just drifting off to sleep when someone, not he, started moaning. It took Myles a minute to orient himself, and by then Gina was doing battle with the bedclothes. He could hear her thrashing around as he groped his way to her in the darkness, not wanting to startle her awake with light.

His exploring hands found her soft shoulders and pressed them back against the pillow, holding on till the tension went out of them. "Shh," he murmured while he held her. "Hush, now, everything's all right."

He kept saying that over and over, and he smoothed the hair back from her forehead and stroked it gently. In about five minutes she was still and silent again, her breathing soft and regular.

Chapter 5

When Gina was a child, she would awaken from occasional nightmares to the sound of her own moans and the terrified slamming of her heart against her ribs. Before her stepmother died, Mimi's smothering plumpness would pillow Gina while a soft cloth blotted the sweat from her face and forehead. Not since then had she come out of a troubled sleep to hear crooning words of comfort.

Gina lay still, eyes tight shut, willing herself to breathe normally, savoring the feathery touch of Myles's fingers on her face and hair and the soft monotony of his voice repeating over and over, "Hush, now, everything's all right."

Who would have thought Mr. Critical could be so kind?

All too soon, deciding she had drifted off, Myles tucked the blanket tightly around her neck and returned to his own bed. She wriggled farther down under the sheet, expecting to fight insomnia the better part of the night, and instead fell instantly and dreamlessly asleep.

Sometime during the night, or perhaps nearer to dawn, just as instantly and suddenly Gina awoke again. No nightmare this time, simply the tension in her neck muscles and the feeling that her brain was swelling up to twice its normal size. It was always the same just before the pain hit.

Gina felt her way to the bathroom, where she had laid her pills out. When she came back into the bedroom, her heart began to gallop in awareness of another presence. Not his. In the gray pre-sunrise he was a shadowy, shifting mound in the next bed.

She turned her head toward the window and saw April. Coppery curls glinting, skin aglow, April was unchanged by the years, as were the blue-flowered sprig muslin and the gold locket nestling just above the lace of her shift.

The shock was as strongly electric now as it had been earlier in the morning when Gina had turned away from Myles's inspection.

It had been several years since April had last appeared. Gina had almost begun to believe she might be gone for good, and there had been a time of grief over the loss.

Then to have April reappear at the same time as the man . . .

Gina supposed she had been silly, playing around like a child on the big dinosaur, but why should it have bothered Myles? He had stood there giving her such a going-over with his eyes, she had had the feeling he could see right through to her bones. If he could, it was apparent he hadn't thought much of them. Funny, because she had liked *his* bones a lot. They supported a medium-height body on a strong-looking frame, and there was strength, too, in the plain lines of his face. Dark hair, brown eyes a bit serious, perhaps, but a full, humorous mouth. She could like that face, she could trust that man, Gina had thought, but she hadn't been given the chance. Something in *her* face had made him turn away very decidedly.

Then Gina had seen April right beside him, and as Gina had run to her, she had melted away behind him. Unable to slow down in time, Gina and Myles had collided and fallen.

The first time, she had thought it was a coincidence. The second time, she had known it couldn't possibly be. April not only had persisted in arranging meetings, she had kept shoving Gina into him.

Gina could have kept quiet at the Lincoln Memorial when Myles had started spouting the Gettysburg Address, and he would never have realized she was there; but by then Gina had known her own mind a bit more. She hadn't really been asleep. That was only the first of the lies she had told him. She had been lying in the dark for what had seemed like hours, seeing that strong, sure face and thinking about April, too.

Gina had wanted so badly for April to stay put and give her a chance to get rid of some of the garbage littering her mind. Almost as badly as Gina had wanted to see *him* again.

In the midst of her wanting, she had heard footsteps and remained very still, thinking it was a guard. Then she had heard *his* voice, and her heart had begun to beat rapidly in excitement and triumph. It had been a while before Gina could steady her voice for the act she meant to put on.

Even as Myles and Gina had parried and thrust at each other, her heart had sung a hymn of praise and thanks to April. Gina should have realized her friend would never let her down. April must have had a reason for bringing them together in the first place. If so, Gina should have counted on her to bring him back.

April undoubtedly had a plan. In her own good time she would share it.

For a moment her image was lost in a blur of Gina's tears. Then it returned, more real, more radiant than ever, and Gina sent her first impulsive thought across to April.

"Why did you leave me . . . and stay away so long?"

The transference of April's thought was clear.

"There was no place in thy life for me."

"That isn't true," Gina disputed hotly. "There has never been a time when I didn't need you."

"Thee forgets the years thou would go thine own stubborn way despite any admonitions that I gave thee."

"Oh, Christmas! When you get angry and Quaker with me, I might as well give up. April"—Gina's hands went out impulsively and then fell to her sides as April smiled and shook her head—"never mind why you left. I'm just so glad you've come back. You'll never know how much I've missed you and how I've wondered . . . there were so many things I never asked about. Who are you, April? *What* are you? And why . . . me?"

April smiled again, gently, tenderly. Her eyes—how extraordinary—filled up with tears. Happy tears, like Gina's. April's words were soft and happy . . . and made no sense. "What an impatient wench you are. 'Tis as true now as when he first said it."

"April, won't you ever let me understand?" Gina asked desperately. "Do you know I went to three shrinks on account of you? One thought I was hallucinating, one thought it was the headaches, and the third . . ."

"The third?"

"He was the worst fool of all," Gina replied. The Quaker woman's silence was more demanding than any question. Gina found herself admitting grudgingly, "He said, 'The hungry heart finds its own nourishment.'" She muttered, "Damn fool." Then, "April, aren't you ever going to explain?"

April retreated a few steps, and as always when she did so, her image dimmed. "Think of me as the bridge between thy old life and thy new one. Soon, now, soon all will be clear."

"How soon?"

"In Williamsburg . . . where we began."

"We?"

But April had faded away into space.

Chapter 6

Gina slept deeply the rest of the night, having ruined all hope that Myles would do the same. He tossed, he turned, he sweated and swore in a half-dozing, half-dreaming state that was a sorry substitute for real sleep.

Not long after dawn, he stumbled into the bathroom, caught a glimpse of his haggard face and red-rimmed eyes in the mirror and swore some more.

He stumbled back into the bedroom and took a look at his roommate's bed. She had kicked off the covers and was lying on her stomach, wrapped in the sheet like a mummy, her head under the pillow instead of on it.

In the clear light of morning, Myles felt not so much a cold qualm of regret as an absolute panic. What the hell had prompted him to bring her here, and why, oh, why had he urged her to visit Williamsburg? From the very first moment of their meeting he had known that the slightest involvement with this teenage girl was something he could do without. Three or four subsequent encounters had only reenforced this judgment. Yet last night, under the spell of the moonlight or the Lincoln Memorial or—be honest, Myles jeered to himself—wasn't it the memory of great amethyst eyes and the impudent sashaying of a little button behind? Whatever his reasons, or lack of them, it was daylight now, and the midnight madness was over.

This nightmare-ridden neurotic juvenile could only spell trouble, and every self-protective instinct in his body clamored for him to be free of her. But how to do it? Well, she had seemed fairly unperturbed at her traveling companions' appropriation of her wallet. No doubt she had the same questionable ethics. If she had a what's-yours-is-mine-if-I-want-it attitude and temptation were put in her way . . . Changing plans seemed to be easy for her.

Myles had left his wallet in his pants pocket, which he now reminded himself had been another mistake. If he had been thinking clearly last night, it would have gone under his pillow. Retrieving the wallet, he extracted a twenty from it, then, after some hesitation, a ten as well. The temptation had to be worthwhile.

He spread the bills apart on the dresser, next to a few of Gina's plastic containers and a lipstick, weighing down their edges with an ashtray. She couldn't miss seeing them when she looked for her personal things.

Afterward, he took the wallet back to bed with him, stuck it under the pillow and this time fell asleep. Sometime later he awoke to the quiet closing of a door.

It could have been the bathroom door, but without knowing how or why, he was quite certain it wasn't. Myles sat up in bed, head clear, fully rested, and with one swift glance at the dresser, saw that the money was gone.

So Gina *did* live by the same casual standards as her pickup friends. So what? It was what he had wanted, what he had expected. He was rid of her. But why the sinking feeling in the pit of his stomach?

Hunger, Myles told himself, stomping over to open the curtains wider, that was why. He let out a howl as he stubbed his toe against . . . against what? He bent down and picked the object up, weighing it in his hands—the hairbrush she had thrown at him last night. Quickly, he had another, less comfortable remembrance. Her rolled-up sleeping bag was still on the back seat of his car. She must have left in a tearing hurry, to forget both items. Afraid he might catch her in the act of stealing?

Myles got his shaving kit and went into the bathroom.

Floating in the sink full of water were three bills. His ten, his twenty and *her* twenty. Her emergency twenty, the only money she had left.

Gina had not left in a tearing hurry, Myles realized, staring at the contents of the sink. If he knew her—and he was beginning to think he did, only too well—it had more likely been in a tearing temper.

So the street-smart girl had read his message clearly, and this was her answer, loud and clear.

As plainly as though she were standing in front of him with that half-sullen, half-insolent smile on her face, Myles could hear her saying, "I don't need your money or your lift or you!"

By the time he had climbed into a pair of slacks and slung on a sport shirt and jacket, he was in a rage to equal any Gina was capable of. Going down in the elevator, Myles sent a smoldering glare in the direction of his fellow passengers, whose glances told him what he already knew—that he was unwashed, uncombed and unshaven.

In return for providing a night's lodging, he had wound up the unwilling recipient of her sleeping bag, her hairbrush and her last twenty dollars.

She was alone, penniless, in a strange city, and he was supposed to have this burden on his conscience! God knew what kind of trouble that girl would get into, let loose on her own, or what kind of kooks she would latch onto next.

By Gina's very recklessness, she had become Myles's responsibility. And when I catch up with her, he thought to himself savagely, so help me, when I catch up with her . . .

He charged through the lobby to the reception desk. Avoiding lifted eyebrows from the desk clerk had been very much on his mind when he had brought her into the hotel. What a difference a few hours could make!

"Did you see a girl about seventeen, long blondish hair, jeans and a knapsack, maybe with oversized sunglasses?"

"Why, yes, she was here around ten, fifteen minutes ago. She wanted to know if I had a map of Virginia and if I knew how far it was to Williamsburg. Then she asked what time the Smithsonian buildings opened." He added apologetically, "I was able to tell her about the time, but I couldn't help her out with a map. I noticed she talked to the bellman a minute or two later." He indicated the man, and Myles marched over to him.

Same questions, it seemed, and not very different answers. The museums all opened at ten; she might be able to buy a map at the gift shop.

Next Gina had approached the doorman. Oh, yes, he

remembered her, pretty little thing. He had been able to give her some pointers about getting out of Washington and on the way to Williamsburg, but she had mentioned she was going over to the Smithsonian first and wondered what time she could get in.

As Myles slammed through the front door and loped along the broad plaza toward the Smithsonian, he realized that one puzzle had been solved. The tantrum that had sent Gina speeding out of his hotel room hadn't prevented her from leaving a number of easy-to-follow signs along the trail. It didn't take a mental genius to figure out the second message she had left for him. She was planning to go to Williamsburg, but first she would be somewhere at the Smithshonian.

The Smithsonian, of course, took in quite a broad territory. Covering the different buildings could take hours, and he still might miss her. The probability was, however, that Gina would retrace the same steps they had taken before. So he would try it that way first.

Myles short-cut through the Associates' parking lot alongside the gay-flowering Victorian Garden and went all around the Hirshorn and its fountain without any luck. No, the guard in the lobby of the art gallery hadn't seen a blonde girl with a backpack.

Myles tried the Castle next. It had just opened and was fairly free of visitors. She was nowhere on the premises.

As he came back down the steps, he glanced frowningly toward the Washington Monument. Neither it nor the distant Capitol provided any inspiration. Should he go back to the Hirshorn and wait there a while, or should he try the Museum of Natural History? Maybe the Court . . . Gina might be having breakfast.

While Myles stood on the sidewalk, hesitating, whoops of joy floated over to him from across the road, where the kindergarten set was enjoying Uncle Beazley.

The kindergarten set . . . Uncle Beazley . . . and a button behind bumping gently backward . . . thin arms covered with goose flesh . . . a waist belted in with a sneaker lace.

It was a positive certainty in his mind even before he had drawn close enough to see her.

Myles approached from the front this time, and Gina saw him coming, though she looked straight ahead through the dark glasses and pretended not to. Today she wore a boy's blue work shirt with the sleeves rolled up to the elbows and the cutoff tail trailing over the tops of her blue jeans. She was balanced casually atop Uncle Beazley's broad back, a leg dangling down against each of its plump thighs. There seemed to be dozens of kids all around her.

Myles came within touching distance. "Get down, Gina."

She took off her glasses with deliberate, unhurried care. The eyes were cold, hard blue this morning, distant and unfathomable. Her words were a bit warmer. "Go to hell," she suggested tersely.

Myles looked at her granitelike face, thrusting chin and sulky mouth, and decided a single action might be worth a few hundred words.

He caught hold of her nearest ankle. There is a point just behind the bone where even the slightest pressure can produce surprising results. His thumb pressure wasn't slight.

Her eyes widened in shock and then contracted with pain. She bore it for half a minute before forcing out the single word "Don't" between gritted teeth.

"Are you getting down?"

Gina nodded dumbly. Myles released her foot and held out his hand. She accepted it gingerly, swung her leg over a three-year-old's head and slid down onto the grass.

"You know, you're a son of a bitch," she said without any particular heat as Myles followed her limping progress over to the tree where she had dumped her knapsack.

"I got your messages."

"What messages?" Haughtily. "I didn't leave you any messages."

"From the desk clerk and the bellman and the doorman. Who knows, maybe there were others I didn't get to interview before I followed your directions."

Her mouth opened to contradict him, closed again. The enormous struggle she was going through showed clearly on her face for about ten seconds. Then she shrugged and burst out laughing.

"I cannot tell a lie," she said, seemingly solemn. "You wouldn't believe me if I did."

"You're right, I wouldn't." He held out a damp twenty-dollar bill, which she made no move to take. "Why did you leave this?"

"To pay for my share of the room."

"I said, *why?*"

"Well, that was why, damn it. I didn't want to be under any obligation to you. You left your own money out for me so I would steal it and get out of your hair. I have many faults, as

I've seen you take note of, but I'm not a thief, even if I consort with them. So I decided to relieve you of my presence."

"*That* message I got, too. Now, take it." When Gina didn't react soon enough, he instructed her softly, "Put this bill in your safety spot, or it will be my pleasure to put it there myself."

She grabbed the bill angrily, folded it into a small square and tucked it down the front of her shirt.

Myles continued to cross-examine. "Why all the trail signs if you wanted to part company?"

She made a prolonged business of brushing the hair away from her forehead and sticking the glasses on, carefully not looking at Myles or letting him get a good look at her.

"Oh, your type has a strong sense of duty," Gina replied in a bored voice. "I figured it would be fun watching you chase around in circles after me."

"And if I didn't and if I hadn't?"

Another shrug. *"Que sera sera."*

"Have you really decided to go to Williamsburg?"

"Yes, I have."

"Okay, let's go back to the hotel, get our things together, have some breakfast and pick up the car."

"I didn't say I was going with you. As far as I'm concerned, you've paid off your debt to society. I meant it when I said I don't want to be obligated to you anymore."

"You're not likely to get a better offer," Myles said teasingly. "There's a strictly enforced state law in Virginia against hitchhiking."

Gina's downturned mouth curved up suddenly in one of the most unpleasantly scornful and cynical smiles he had ever seen on a young girl's face.

"You really think," she asked, and the scorn was in her voice, too, "that on any Virginia highway, law or no law, I can't get some man to stop for me?" She tucked her shirttail down into her jeans. "You *are* naïve. Bye-bye, Myles. Want to bet I get there before you do?"

She turned away with a defiant twitch of the behind, and he never knew what came over him. Tiredness . . . temper . . . or the accumulated exasperation of the last twenty-four hours.

He didn't even remember making a move, though he obviously must have wound up with the force of a discus thrower. The next thing he knew, shock waves of pain were running from his right wrist all the way up his arm. He was staring in stupefaction at the blistered palm which had just delivered such a powerful blow to her blue-jeaned bottom that it probably could be heard on Capitol Hill.

Other heads were swiveling madly around, but not hers. After one strangled yelp, staggering forward, knees buckled, Gina had straightened up and merely stood there very still.

He folded his arms, wrapped in reverent contemplation of the monument, and waited for her to make a move. Myles was braced for flailing arms, flying fists or at the very least a furious tirade.

She turned toward him in slow motion, shaking her head as though to unscramble her brain. If Gina's was by any chance located where he had smacked her, he mused with the first glint of humor he had felt in over a day, it would explain a lot about the way she behaved.

For about thirty seconds they shared an uneasy staring contest. Then, using the same penetrating stage voice which had served to attract everyone's notice after they had collided in the Court, she delivered another public attention-getter. "I *said* you were a son of a bitch."

Heads swiveled around again, but Myles couldn't have cared less. She had whipped off her sunglasses, and he was bemused once more, as he had been the first time. Not only because of her eyes—something new had been added. The tight, pale lips were stretched out in a gamin grin.

"Okay," Gina said, "let's go back to the hotel."

They both reached for her knapsack at the same time, and after a silent tug of war, he got it away from her.

"For God's sake," he snarled, reaction setting in, "can't you do anything without an argument?"

"I've lugged it so far without straining anything, but if you want to play the gentleman, by all means be my guest."

They returned to the L'Enfant Plaza, where he shaved and showered, packed his bag and then checked out. Thirty-five minutes had passed, and not a single cross word had been exchanged between them.

They didn't resume combat again until they had walked across the hotel lobby and into the Greenhouse for breakfast. They were shown to a small corner table. Gina kicked her knapsack under it and sat down with a bounce.

"Ow!" She bounced right up again.

"What's the matter now?"

"My bottom hurts," she announced, massaging it tenderly.

The waitress, waiting to hand out menus, gave them a startled look as she placed the menus on the table and quickly melted away.

Gina sat down a second time, very carefully, favoring her left side. "You certainly pack a wallop," she declared without resentment.

"That was fatherly."

"Not *my* father. He's never laid a hand on me in my life."

Myles muttered under his breath.

"What did you say?"

"I said," he repeated slowly and distinctly, "no wonder he got the results he did."

Myles's lips twitched as he watched Gina's mind working, figuring that one out. First she chewed her lower lip furiously, then she nibbled on her nails. He leaned across the table and gently slapped her hand away. "Big girls don't bite their nails."

Gina shot him a furious glare but lowered her hand. She gave an indignant flounce, which proved to be a mistake. "Ow!" she yelled again.

The waitress, who had been hovering nearby in hope of getting their order, took fright and scuttled away again.

Gina caught Myles's eye, and he saw the gamin grin which completely transformed her face. "Son of a bitch," she mouthed.

He grinned back. "You're getting redundant."

Chapter 7

Breakfast had acutally been cordial. Myles didn't make any further mistakes until he began stowing her knapsack into the car trunk along with his overnight bag. A plastic pharmacy container rolled onto the ground. Gina made a swift grab at it and stuffed it into her jeans.

"What's that?"

"Oh . . . allergy pills."

In a pig's eye, Myles thought. "Before we start," he said aloud, "get rid of anything you have. Sorry if it makes me the stuffed shirt you think I am, but I'm not taking any chances."

"Would you care to translate that into understandable English?"

"Grass, pot, hash. Maybe I'm not up-to-date on all the current names, but if you've got any, get rid of it right now. That's my one stipulation before we drive together."

"Driving together was your idea," she began slowly. "I'm willing—come to think of it, I'm *eager* to split right now. But for the record . . ." She drew the vial out of her pocket and showed it to him. "See? Prescription label." Gina jiggled the cap and twisted it off, pulling out a string of foil-wrapped squares with perforated edges. "Nothing lethal. I know it must come as a shock to you, with a girl of my doubtful habits

40

and morals. Of course, you've only got my word for it, but I neither smoke nor drink nor take drugs."

"Gina, I—"

"It doesn't happen to be a matter of morals, I want you to know. It's the way I feel about *me*. I just don't like any part of me out of control. So, no cigarettes, no booze and no drugs. Now, if you don't mind, I—"

"Gina, I'm sorry."

"I honestly think it would be better if—"

"Deeply, deeply sorry."

"If you'd let me go on by—"

"But I can't. I won't. It's like that old Chinese tradition of being responsible for someone whose life you've saved. I took you away from the comfort of sleeping on the cold ground behind Honest Abe. I caused you to abandon the delights of hitching farther East in favor of going to see Williamsburg. You're my charge now. I'm the one who has to take you there and see that you're safe and settled. It's not for your sake, it's for mine. I want to be able to sleep at night. Please, Gina, say you forgive me and get into the car."

She didn't say anything of the sort, but she got into the car.

In a few short minutes they were across the bridge into Virginia, heading south on 95. Still she was silent. "See, I told you." He pointed out the signs to her. NO HITCHHIKING. And more specifically, UNLAWFUL TO PICK UP OR DISCHARGE RIDERS. No answer. The miles flashed by. Fairfax County. Prince William. Stafford.

"It's nearly two hours more to Williamsburg. Are you going to sulk all the way?"

"I am *not* sulking."

"No? Sorry about that. Your expression was misleading."

The drooping corners of her mouth turned up in a reluctant smile. "You know, you really are a—"

"I know," he helped her out, "a son of a bitch. *You* should enlarge your vocabulary."

Gina leaned back in the seat with a tired sigh. Up till then she had been sitting very straight and tensely. Myles judged that the hostilities were over for a while and ventured into some easy small talk.

"How did you happen to spend so much time in other countries?"

"Traveling with my father and going to school in Edinburgh."

"In Scotland?" he asked, faintly surprised.

"It's got the only Edinburgh I know of," she said lightly.

He had a curious feeling she was annoyed with herself for having mentioned it. Then he decided he must be mistaken, because she went on to explain.

"My father's job takes him to lots of places. He had to be near the American submarine base in Scotland one year. I wasn't too keen about the school—uniforms, curfews, routine, the whole bloody British bit—so whenever the walls seemed to be closing in, I took off to join him, with or without leave."

"How did the school react to a liberated lady?" Myles inquired courteously.

Gina giggled with delight. "After the third time, my father was politely requested not to return me. I was 'creating, err—err—'" Her voice, gently mimicking, took on a soft Scots burr. "'A, err—err—spirit of recklessness, err—err—perhaps a little too American among the other pupils.'"

"I'll bet you were," he agreed appreciatively. "Tell me, Gina, what's the rest of your name?"

"Jacobi," she said, and spelled it for him very softly, very deliberately. "J-A-C-O-B-I, Jacobi."

He had always been proud of his excellent peripheral vision. With his eyes on the road, Myles could still see the strange, cold smile and the purposeful look she was slanting at him.

"You're right in what you're thinking. The name is Jewish as well as Italian," Gina told him in that same soft voice.

He nodded calmly, though he was beginning to steam. "I thought it might be."

They sped through Carolina and Hanover counties in an even more hostile silence than the one that had gone before.

"I'm not going to say it, you know," he declared finally in a voice as soft and deliberate as her own.

"I beg your pardon?"

"Either of those remarks you are waiting for from a reactionary type like me," he explained ever so gently, "That 'My, you don't look it,' or 'Some of my best friends are.'"

Gina gasped, very red-faced. "I didn't . . . I wasn't . . ." And then she paid him the tribute of not going on with the lie. "I beg your pardon," she repeated, but this time there was all the difference in the world in the way she said it. "I'm truly very sorry."

"We're even now," Myles returned briefly. "We've both

made a lot of misjudgments based on the wrong kind of evidence."

"Yes," she admitted miserably, "and we'll keep on doing it. We just don't get along. Why can't you see that?"

"Because I don't agree. Tell me something else. Who or what is April?"

As soon as he saw Gina sit up straight again, legs uncrossed and body rigid, he knew he had jumped this one fence too soon; also, that he wasn't going to get a straight answer. He didn't.

"April?" she said in phony surprise, and for the first time her lovely voice was shrill. "Why, last time I looked at a calendar, it was the fourth month of the year, right after March, just before May." Pause. Then she singsonged, "It's April now. Can spring be far behind?"

His eyes, coldly critical of this performance, slid away from the road for a few seconds to fasten on her. Behind the protection of the oversized glasses, her own eyes blinked, then swerved away. After a while she pulled the lever to lower her seat, curled up and either dozed or pretended to until they reached Williamsburg.

Gina sat up again as they skimmed along a broad, deserted avenue, lined on one side with thick green woods. "This is the Colonial Parkway," Myles told her.

She gave a choked, breathless "Oh!" Then, "Yes, I know."

"The river," he added, "is the James."

"I know," Gina repeated with that same rapturous breathlessness. "I remember. Oh, please, could we stop a moment?"

He slowed down and pulled in at the next historical signpost a quarter of a mile farther on. She slid out of the car almost before he had brought it to a full stop. Ignoring the Tourist Information board, she stepped onto the close-cropped grass and looked out, her glasses dangling from one hand, the other shading her eyes against the sun.

"What do you mean, you remember?" Myles asked, following after her. "I thought you had never been here before."

She tore her intent gaze from the river and glanced up at him, her glorious eyes half scared, half puzzled. Suddenly she gave herself a vigorous shake and began to laugh out loud. "I read about it, silly," she said. "Our river is famous in history."

She put her fingers to either side of her temples; they were beginning to ache. She wondered why he was looking at her so oddly. It seemed absolutely right to be here.

I belong, Gina thought fiercely, and marched toward the riverbank, Myles sticking close behind. The sun was playing hopscotch on the water, skipping along the undulating currents and shooting off sparkling streaks of light. A drooping branch of a weeping willow caught in her ponytail and held her prisoner. Obedient to Myles's command, she stood still while he gently unknotted the lacy, pale green fingers from the strands of her hair.

"I belong," she said out loud, and raced, laughing, to the narrow stretch of sand being nibbled away by the tide. There, she knelt and sat back, Japanese style, against her heels. With her arms crossed over her breast and her head bowed low, she looked, Myles thought, like some ancient priestess in a ritual of worship.

A huge gray cloud blotted out the sun, and the river suddenly became a broad, dull gray expanse. There was something alien and ominous in the shivering, colorless depths to the watching man, but not to the worshiping woman.

Gina stayed motionless for several moments, only to look up, smiling, as the sun returned and poured its radiance on all of them—man, woman, river. She murmured something. Myles was not sure if it was "Our James" or "Our Jamie."

She rose from her knees and suddenly dipped low to him in a curtsy. "Thank you for bringing me back, Myles."

Even as his mind registered that betraying word, *back,* he responded with a mock curtsy. "Miss Gina Jacobi, I welcome you to Williamsburg."

Chapter 8

"Miss Rietta Rind? Welcome to Williamsburg, ma'am."

The girl, who had been the first to stumble tiredly out of the coach, swung around quickly. The hood of her thick traveling cloak fell off tumbled curls that gleamed coppery in the sunlight.

"I'm Mr. Southall, ma'am," he introduced himself, bowing, "the Raleigh innkeeper. Mr. William Rind bade me make his apologies for not being here to greet you, but he is inside the tavern conferring with a group of the burgesses."

"Cousin Cl—Mrs. Rind?" she asked hesitantly.

"Mrs. Clementina Rind is awaiting you at home, just a few yards away. She is, I believe"—he coughed delicately—"close to her lying-in."

"Lying-in!" Rietta stared at him in amazement. "But she had a child in the summer of 1770, less than a year ago."

Southall stared down at his nose at her in evident embarrassment at her forthright remark.

"She is . . . er . . . indeed . . . yes, in a delicate condition."

"What's delicate about it, I should like to know?" Rietta Rind spoke more to herself than to the innkeeper and burst out laughing when she observed the expression on his face.

"Forgive me, sir, perhaps we speak more plainly at home, or else I'm simply too overtired to put a proper guard on my tongue. It's been a weary journey from Philadelphia. If you would direct me . . . and be so kind as to store my trunk for the moment."

"Mr. Rind brought his manservant to attend you." Southall raised his voice to a bellow that could be heard over horse hooves, coach wheels, passing shoppers and loud-voiced vendors. "Dick, Dick, over here! Point out your trunk to him, ma'am, and he'll have you home in a trice."

A moment later Rietta had to crane her neck up at a tall and powerfully built black man. The gentle eyes in his lean, sensitive face smiled kindly down at her.

"It's that one, Dick, but I fear . . . isn't it too heavy for you?"

"Don't you fret, ma'am. From pulling the devil's tail, I be one very strong man." He held out his right arm, pushing up the full white sleeve to show her a bulging bicep. Then he hoisted the trunk onto his broad shoulder in an easy manner that lent truth to the simple boast. "If you please to follow me, ma'am."

Instead of following, she walked alongside him, chatting sociably. "From my cousin's letters I understood you help work at printing her newspaper."

"For nine years now, ma'am."

"Almost the same as me. I started helping my father out in his business before I was ten. Many's the time I've pulled the devil's tail myself. Oh, is this the house?" Rietta asked as he halted. She studied the red brick mansion. "It's very handsome."

"If you'll go up the steps, ma'am, I'll take your trunk through the kitchen way."

"Thank you, Dick. I expect I'll be seeing you often. I hope to help out on the *Gazette*."

"That will be very pleasing, ma'am. Very pleasing indeed."

The louvered doors to the house were flung open as Rietta reached the top stone step. Clementina Rind, her father's cousin by marriage, appeared in the doorway. The loosest of gowns could not conceal that she was, as Mr. Southall had indicated, remarkably close to her lying-in.

"Rietta, my dear," she exclaimed, hugging the younger girl. "How happy I am to see you."

"And I to be here," Rietta replied, returning the embrace with fervor. "But, Cousin Clemmie, what a surprise! I had no notion you were—" She recalled Mr. Southall's face and coughed to cover the intended word, substituting, "in the family way."

"I was afraid to tell you," Clementina confessed merrily. "Four babes were bad enough. I feared if you knew there was to be a fifth, you might not come."

A shadow passed over Rietta's face. "I would have come had there been twice five . . . if you truly wanted me."

"Want you? My dear Rietta, you are the answer to a prayer. Come in, come in." She stood back from the doorway. "Welcome to Williamsburg. Welcome to your new home."

Chapter 9

Gina stood in the dark hallway while Myles unlocked the door to his apartment located in a building a few blocks down from the College of William and Mary. He had sublet it till September from one of the professors, who had left on an expedition in search of Atlantis.

As Myles ushered her in and started flinging open windows to let out the stale air, he said again, "Welcome to Williamsburg. This is home."

The windows looked out over a garden quad alive with colorful flowers. The apartment itself contained a tiny kitchen, a cell of a bedroom, a fair-sized hallway and a spacious living room that had obviously been turned into a study.

Gina parked her knapsack in the entranceway and looked about with an air of unrestrained wonder. Myles realized for the first time that other people saw his place through eyes different from his own. He cast her a look of deep suspicion.

"I hope you don't have a housewifely instinct that forces you to dust and tidy a place so thoroughly, my papers will get all screwed up."

"Hardly a one," she assured him blithely. "You could sink ankle-deep into your research without its bothering me. The only thing is"—off came the glasses, and she stared at him speculatively—"you never run true to type. I would have figured you as compulsively neat."

"That'll teach you to judge in stereotypes," he retorted. "For God's sakes, we're indoors now, so don't put those blasted shades back on. Why do you wear them, anyhow?"

"To cover my eyes."

"To cover your eyes!" he repeated incredulously. "Your eyes are gorgeous. They're glorious. They're your one—"

"My one beauty?" she finished, helpful and unoffended. "You sound like my father. He calls them Elizabeth Taylor eyes. Well, I hate them."

"You're nuts. What have you got against Elizabeth Taylor?"

"I happen to like her. Unfortunately, when I look into a mirror, I see my mother. These are her eyes."

"At seventeen, it's not unusual for a girl to hate her mother. Both my sisters claimed to. It passes, believe me."

"I don't hate my mother; I stopped doing that when I was nine years old. I merely despise her, and I don't like seeing any part of her in me."

There wasn't much that could be said to such a comprehensive statement without a willingness to let the barriers down. Since that condition was absent, Myles thought it more sensible to change the subject.

"Will you be comfortable on the couch?"

"The couch?" Gina appeared startled.

"We're not at the L'Enfant Plaza, dear girl. My monk's cell contains one twin bed, and I wasn't proposing to be gentlemanly and turn it over to you."

"And I wasn't proposing to stay here."

"Why not? It's a sensible idea till you arrange for more money from home or get a job. If you're worried about the proprieties—which would be ludicrous at this point—no one need know. And if it's me . . . well, I should think last night would have told you I'm to be trusted."

"But last night you were exhausted," Gina said, deadpan. "How long does a Tennessee tigress leave her mark on you?"

"Long enough to keep *children* permanently safe from assault."

She burst out laughing. "Touché. All right, thanks. It would be a help. Do you think it would be hard to get a job in this town if I like it?"

"I could get you some references and introductions to take

over to the personnel office of the Colonial Williamsburg Foundation. The only trouble is—do you have a dress or skirt and maybe a pair of shoes instead of sneakers?"

"Not with me. But I can buy some new things tomorrow . . . or Tuesday, if transferring money takes longer. I was planning to, anyhow."

"Fine. Let's postpone the job hunting till you get your new clothes. In the meantime, we'll spend the next day or two seeing Williamsburg. By then you should know whether or not you want a job."

"It sounds great to me, but how about you?" Gina protested, not too urgently. "I don't want to interfere with your work."

"Quite a few of the things we'll do are part of my work. I take notes every time I go through the exhibition buildings. In spite of my own research, the hosts and hostesses occasionally come up with odd bits of information I can use."

She swept him another of those surprisingly graceful curtsies, considering she wore jeans. "In that case, sir, I thank you, and I am yours to command."

"That will be the day."

Faint color tinged her cheeks. "A figure of speech, in keeping with the atmosphere."

"Well, this once I'll take you literally. Do you mind if the sightseeing program starts tomorrow? Frankly, I'm beat right now. What I'd really like is a couple of hours' rest and then an early dinner. Sunday night is the Cascades' buffet supper, which is really something. I'll try to get us a reservation. Afterward we can walk to the Information Center to check about tickets and tours and maybe see the orientation movie. The only thing is . . . can you make do until dinner with whatever scraps I have in the refrigerator? I didn't stock up the last time I shopped, since I knew I'd be away for the weekend."

"No problem. I'm not hungry. Just some juice and a bit of cheese, if you have any, would do me fine. You forced a bigger breakfast on me than I ever eat. I usually have fruit and a piece of toast."

"No wonder you're so skinny. Don't you know breakfast is the most important meal of the day?"

"Bet you learned that at your mother's knee," Gina teased. "For your information, I'm slim, not skinny. I bet the Tennessee tigress is voluptuous. Do you always like your woman padded?" she added sweetly.

"No," Myles lied, "just not skinny like you." She stuck out her tongue at him. "Yes, I learned it at my mother's knee," he conceded smoothly. "Didn't you?"

She laughed with what seemed to be genuine humor. "Lord, no. She wouldn't have noticed if I skipped all three meals."

"That doesn't sound like any Jewish mother I've ever heard of."

"Oh, she—" Gina stopped abruptly, biting her lips, then began again. "I had a stepmother who was a real food-pusher, but she got hold of me too late. Listen," she said hurriedly, "why don't I rummage through the refrigerator and fix something for you? You're the one who seems to be hungry." She sidled quickly toward the kitchen.

Getting away fast was more on her mind than fixing him a meal, Myles realized. All the same, ten minutes after he had made their dinner reservation, she was dishing out a tasty tuna salad with some cherry tomatoes and cold canned asparagus on the side, and a frosty glass of tomato juice to wash it down.

"This is good. There's something different in it."

"Gherkin pickles cut up fine."

"Mmm, really good. You can cook for me any time."

"I aim to please."

She picked up her glass of tomato juice as he lifted his. Over the rims, their eyes met and held. They sat there for a timeless moment, staring, unable to tear their glances away. Something had gone wrong with his breathing, and with hers, too, Myles suspected, watching the faint stirring of her shirt.

A drum somewhere inside his head kept beating out a message he didn't want to hear. *She's seventeen, Myles. Oil and water. Russia and China. That's what her seventeen and your twenty-nine are.*

His temples were bursting. His appetite had disappeared. Myles managed to wrench his glance away and push back his chair. His movements were slow and clumsy. Because his mouth and tongue had gone dry, he said thickly, "I think I'll take that nap now so our evening won't be spoiled."

He had never before closed the door of his minuscule bedroom, reducing it to a claustrophobic cell. He stripped to the buff, lay down on the bed and closed his eyes, but was unable to close out the picture of her sitting at the table, where he had left her. Gina had turned silent and white-faced, her mouth the familiar tight line, her body very upright and displaying that taut stillness he had learned was a sign of inner turmoil.

Myles had hesitated in the doorway and looked back for a single glance. Her head had drooped as she reached out for the sunglasses lying on the table. In the shadowy darkness of the hallway, he had observed the infinitely pathetic care with which Gina had fitted them on again to hide her face.

He slept away the whole afternoon and awoke refreshed. They took turns at the bathroom sink, and he let her use the bedroom to change her clothes.

He had promised himself not to react if she decided her T-shirt was what the well-dressed girl should wear to a Sunday supper, so he was doubly stunned when he saw her emerge from the bedroom.

Gina's full-length silky skirt hugged her hips tightly, and a long slit up to her knees revealed the shapeliest pair of legs Myles had ever seen. Why would she ever wear pants and hide them! he wondered. Her blouse, the exact blue of the skirt, was a soft knit material. It clung to her like a second skin, the long sleeves flattering arms that no longer seemed so thin to him. The low-scooped neckline displayed a part of her that didn't need flattering.

Myles wanted to tell Gina that she looked lovely; that her hair was beautiful, brushed smoothly back from her forehead, free and flowing beneath the wide ribbon tied in a bow at the nape of her neck; that her eyes were blue, blue, blue . . .

Clumsily, all he could come up with was, "I thought you didn't have a blouse and skirt with you."

"Not an afternoon skirt. This thing doesn't wrinkle. I always throw it in for an evening date. And the blouse, too." She cast him a saucy smile. "Relieved, aren't you?"

"Relieved?" Myles opened the door and waved her out.

"You had made up your mind not to say a word if I wore my work shirt, hadn't you?"

"That only shows how wrong a smart girl can be," he told her, locking the door.

"Honest?"

"Cross my heart. It was your I Am Woman T-shirt I was prepared to grit my teeth about."

Gina laughed delightedly, but half an hour later she looked

up from a modest plate of appetizers and interrupted his remarks about the Hirshorn sculptures.

"That was just needling about my clothes, wasn't it? I mean, you do believe in women's rights, don't you? Even you—oops!"

"Right, Miss Tactful, even *I* am not that bad. Yes, apropos of nothing, I believe in women's rights."

"It just shows you shouldn't judge a man by his shirt and tie. I knew you couldn't be that stuffy," she admitted generously.

"Why don't you talk less and eat more?"

"I told you, I have a small appetite."

"Small I don't mind; yours is practically nonexistent. I object to paying for a meal you haven't eaten."

"Nag, nag, nag. *You* should have been the Jewish mother."

But Myles noticed, with some amusement, that she started plying her fork a little more energetically.

It was dark when they left the Cascades, and fairly brisk outside. Nevertheless, Gina insisted on going around to the rear, which looked like a screen backdrop, with carefully placed lights illuminating the wooden hillside and its trickling brook.

"I should have brought my sweater," she said, hopping over the broad steppingstones that lined the brook. "Oh, no," she protested, as Myles took off his jacket and wrapped it around her.

"If you're really concerned about my being cold," he said, "come close and keep me warm." He casually draped an arm around her shoulders. "Let's go home. We'll climb up another time, during the day. It's prettier then, anyhow."

Myles felt her tremble and told himself she was cold, but the drumbeats were sounding in his head again.

Once they were at the Information Center, Gina had a marvelous time collecting brochures and asking questions. Because of Myles's research grant, the Foundation had given him a resident's pass, but Gina let him buy her some admission tickets to the entire restoration site after he solemnly promised to accept repayment when her money arrived.

Then they went to see the half-hour orientation film, *The Story of a Patriot*, which gave such a vivid picture of life in Williamsburg when it had been the capital of Virginia prior to the Revolution.

Myles had seen it at least half a dozen times, but it still gave him the same feeling he got when alone at night at the Lincoln Memorial . . . only a little more so.

But Gina, the would-be hard-boiled *un*sentimentalist, gripped his hand so hard throughout, she practically paralyzed it. During the scene depicting the angry and turbulent night when the British marines had stolen the gunpowder from the magazine and an angry mob had assembled in protest, her remorseless fingers pinched Myles so hard he was moved to protest.

"Gina, have a heart, you're drawing blood."

"Oh, I'm sorry, but I love it," she breathed, and continued to cling until the movie ended and the lights went on.

Myles flexed his hand thankfully, restoring the circulation, as he led her out of the theater.

She walked along with him, filled with the same strange exhilaration about Williamsburg that she had felt about Myles in Washington. Somehow Gina felt inextricably linked with him now.

Later that night Myles stopped by the couch on his way back from the bathroom. Gina was neck-deep in the sleeping bag; her head rested on one of the extra pillows from his bed.

"All set?" he asked.

"Fine, thank you." As his hand went to the wall switch, she added softly, "And thank you for a wonderful evening."

"*De nada.* Good night."

In the bedroom, he remembered that the book he wanted was lying on the corner table near the door of the living room. He groped his way quietly back to get it.

"And thank *you*, too, darling April," Gina murmured in the darkness.

Chapter 10

Gina soon noticed that in Williamsburg, April did not keep popping up in odd places, as she had in Washington. Gina never saw her once, but felt her presence all the time. April was like an aura, and Gina was content to have it so.

Dear God, what was she saying? Content? She had never been so happy in her life.

Monday morning's first chore—aside from convincing Myles that she did not propose to stuff juice, oatmeal with wheat germ, coffee and toast into herself—was to get to a bank.

Myles took Gina to his. While she consulted with the bank manager, Myles went off to do some errands. She met him an hour and a half later.

"All set?" he asked.

"All set," Gina answered. She couldn't help grinning at this easy way of disposing of the complicated series of collect calls and counter calls that had established her credentials, led to the promise of a transfer of funds within twenty-four hours and permitted her to receive the fifty dollars tucked inside the pocket of her striped shirt.

Myles had parked in the business section of town since cars

weren't permitted in the restoration area during the day. He suggested a walk before the actual sightseeing began.

"I want you to get a feel of the town before you go into the buildings," he urged. "You'll enjoy it much more that way."

"Lead on, you're the guide," she agreed.

"No, this is. Here." He handed Gina a small paper-covered book, *Official Guidebook & Map*. "Anything you want to know, this will explain it if I can't."

"Thank you. I—"

"If," he interrupted warningly, "you are about to tell me you'll reimburse me, please don't, not unless you want your head handed to you."

"I was going to say that, but why should you mind?" she admitted a little abashed. "I can't let you keep paying for everything. I know fellowship grants don't go very far. You probably have to keep to a strict budget till your book is done."

He looked a bit embarrassed. "Not so much of a budget that I can't afford fifty cents for a guidebook. I have a bank account in Washington," he added casually. "And you, young lady, must learn to accept gifts graciously."

Gina thought of breakfast at the Greenhouse and dinner at the Cascades and—less charitably—his bill at the L'Enfant Plaza for entertaining the Tennessee tigress. Then Gina reminded herself that she would be able to restock his refrigerator and compensate him in other ways.

"I thank you graciously, Myles," Gina said. She was rewarded with an answering smile as he took her elbow and steered her past a stunted mulberry tree with a broad, gnarled trunk, across the street and out of the way of an open ox cart filled with screeching children.

As they came to a stretch of grass known as the Palace Green, Gina uttered a screech of her own. Scattered over it was a flock of sheep, casually attended by a shepherd in knee breeches, buckled shoes and a white shirt with billowing sleeves. A minute later she was down on her knees fondling a baby lamb.

Myles had to drag her away, and he could do it only with a promise. "You'll see them whenever the weather is good."

They crossed another street. "That's the Wythe House," he told her, pointing. "You remember George Wythe? Signer of the Declaration of Independence. Teacher of Jefferson. You saw him in the film last night."

"Yes, I remember him, but not the house. The house is—"

She stared at it, trying to bring back the passing thought that had slipped so swiftly in and out of her mind, it was gone beyond recall. She frowned in concentration. "I seem to remember something important about him, but it's gotten away from me."

"He was a very famous man of the time. We'll go through the house and you can read up on him, then you'll remember," Myles said matter-of-factly. "It's nothing to bite your nails over," he added. Gina hadn't realized she was doing that. He drew her hand away from her mouth, and before she could prevent him, he looked down at it. "Good Lord!"

Gina flushed to the roots of her hair. She was sensitive about her nails; no one knew better how ugly they looked.

She stood there, braced for one of his caustic remarks or disapproving looks. Instead, he tightened his hold on her hand so she couldn't snatch it away. Then he lifted it up, folded her knuckles over his own finger and placed his lips right on them.

A couple of big tears slid out of her eyes, tears of surprise and a sudden release from pain that she hadn't even known she was feeling. Then Gina felt his kiss against the raw, ripped fingertips.

"We'll have to go to work on these. Your hands are too lovely to spoil," Myles said, as though it were not just her problem, but his, too. In the midst of the comfort these words brought, a moment's panic and helplessness swept over Gina. She had never meant this to happen. . . . What was she going to do about it?

Even as she asked herself the question, the answer came. Walking away from the Wythe House with Myles, Gina began to feel the strong presence of April.

Myles and Gina spent the entire rest of the morning and part of the afternoon going through the Governor's Palace and exploring the formal gardens. Even *she* was hungry enough to allow herself to be led straight over to Chowning's Tavern.

As Myles dragged her off, he promised, "We'll come again, I swear it. And no remarks about budgets," he warned sternly as they took their places on line.

"No, sir," Gina said meekly.

After lunch they went to the Courthouse of 1770, then the silversmith's. The Peyton Randolph House and the Brush-Everard House were last on their list before they wandered down to the music teacher's.

A lesson seemed to be in progress, if the way a small, freckle-faced boy was torturing a horn could be so designated. Gina noticed Myles wince, too, and was about to suggest they leave when her eye was caught by the spinet in the corner. She eased her way through a small circle of tourists to inspect the instrument more closely. While she did, the lesson ended and the music teacher, in his colonial costume, began an informal talk.

Oboe music . . . harpsichords . . . guitars and mandolins . . . Gina let the easy flow of words roll over her and only came out of her comfortable reverie when she heard him say, "In the eighteenth century the violin was the instrument of a gentleman, never a lady. Jefferson was considered the best violinist in Virginia. Patrick Henry could not read music, but he was known as the finest fiddler. He—"

Gina interrupted suddenly, "But sometimes a woman played the violin."

The music teacher looked across at her. "That would be unusual," he said politely.

"She *was* unusual," Gina returned slowly.

A few feet away, Myles was studying her, a frown between his eyes. Gina melted into the group. She was shaking and didn't know why.

She wished she could remember the name of the woman who had played the violin. Where had Gina read about her? It suddenly seemed important.

Gina wrenched her attention back to the present. Someone had asked a question, and the music teacher was in the middle of an answer. ". . . much more difficult to support the violin entirely by hand as the colonials did. Even in Europe only a few highly skilled professionals held the violin under the chin."

Again she heard the sound of her own voice protesting. "But sometimes European virtuosi came to the Colonies and taught their methods."

The music teacher gave her a look that as much as told her, *Honey, please get lost.* "Not very often," he said severely.

"But sometimes," she persisted.

"Time to go, Gina." Myles's hand was on her arm. She was furious about the apologetic glance he sent the music teacher as he steered her out of the shop.

"Did I embarrass you?" she asked coldly when they were standing outside the shop.

"Not me, him," Myles replied, laughing. "Pull your claws

in and don't scratch, my little pussycat. Don't you know the first rule of smart classroom behavior is never to let the teacher realize you know more about something than he does? How *did* you know, by the way? Are you a musical prodigy?"

"Not in the least," Gina answered crossly. "I don't know. Oh, yes, I do. I read about it somewhere."

They had both had enough sightseeing for the day, so they walked back to the car and drove to a market not far from the apartment.

Gina cooked dinner while Myles caught up on some of the work he should have been doing all day. After the dishes were done—he washed, she dried and they both put away— he went back to his typewriter. Gina put on a leotard, spread out a bath towel and did forty minutes of yoga exercises. Then she curled up in the armchair near the best reading lamp and divided her attention between the paperback novel she had picked up in Washington and a bag of peanuts.

She was so damned stupidly happy.

The next day was unexpectedly hot, more like middle summer than early spring. After two exhausting hours of being a tourist, Gina agreed enthusiastically to Myles's suggestion of a drive to Virginia Beach.

"It's too cold to swim, but we can sit on the sand and sun ourselves," he proposed.

They stopped at the apartment for his swimming trunks and her bikini, then drove straight to the beach, passing billboards and neon lights, fast-food stops and beachside motels built in every size and shape to distort nature's own beauty.

Gina drew a breath of relief as they left the miles of buildings behind. Once more she could see the long green hills on the right, and on the left, vivacious gray waves dashing along the beach and foaming over the edges of the sand.

"This is the way it should be," she sighed happily.

Tall wrought-iron gates bordered a curving road that led away from the beach and up to the circular drive in front of the stately Castle Harbour Hotel. Stretching out for nearly a city block, the hotel was a post-Victorian, Gothic monstrosity with turrets, battlements and ivy-colored walls.

Once inside the revolving doors, however, they were abruptly returned to their own era. Walking briskly across a marble lobby hung with modern murals, Myles stopped at the registration desk to speak to a clerk.

Gina, watching from a distance, saw the swift palming of a bill from Myles's hand to the upturned one on the counter. When Myles came back to her, he was tucking a locker key into his jacket pocket. He handed a second key over to her.

"Are you a member here?" she asked as he took her by the elbow and steered her into a cathedral-sized dining room.

"For today I am."

"You mean you bribed that man?"

"I certainly did." He smiled smugly, accepted a menu from the hostess and buried his face in it.

"I'm against bribes," Gina declared severley.

Myles lowered the menu. "The beach here is lovely . . . and very private. Of course, if it offends your principles too much, after lunch we can go back to the nearest public beach. If I'm not mistaken"—he pretended to think about it—"there's one sandwiched in between the nearest fried chicken place and a hamburger joint."

Gina opened her menu. "I have just been corrupted," she said with dignity. "Let's stay here."

After a leisurely lunch, they walked back through the lobby and down a short flight of mosaic steps, separating at the locker rooms and agreeing to meet on the beach.

Myles arrived there first, finding the hotel's beach so unpopulated this April day that less than half a dozen people were scattered around it . . . and only two were in the water, both of them surfers.

While he waited for Gina, Myles arranged for two deck chairs with a canvas awning, more to protect them from the wind than from the sun. He kept an eye on the entrance to the women's dressing room so he could wave Gina over. When she finally came outside, the first sight of her paralyzed his arm, his tongue . . . every part of him except one.

She filled a loose-weave, salmon-pink crocheted bikini that contradicted every theory he had ever advanced about the lack of meat on her bones.

Gina saw him at once and started slithering toward him through the sand with wide, sweeping motions, as though she were ice skating. The accompanying movements of the portions of her anatomy stuffed into the two wisps of cloth she called a bathing suit provoked an intense and instant reaction. Myles felt his trunks getting tighter and tighter, and a film of sweat covered his entire body. He plunked himself down on the sand, his knees drawn up to hide the embarrassing evidence.

"This was a great idea!" Gina greeted him, happily unaware. "I love the feel of warm sand between my toes, don't you, Myles?"

She sank down beside him, balancing on her behind and lifting both legs to allow the sand to trickle between her toes back onto the beach. The surfers emerged from the water and dashed by, screaming joyfully. She flashed them a happy smile, then turned back to Myles.

"Don't you just love it?" she repeated, somewhat surprised at his silence.

The strangled sound that came out of his throat was halfway between a groan and an agreement. She rolled over onto her stomach and started tickling the soles of his feet.

Myles jerked away as though he had received an electric shock. "I'm going for a swim," he announced.

"But you said it was too cold to swim. You said we'd just lie out and sun ourselves and . . ."

Her voice died away as she stared at his taut face and glittering eyes. Gina sat with her arms wrapped about her calves, watching him race toward the water, wade in up to his thighs and, without hesitation, dive into the first big wave.

After a while she followed Myles down to the water's edge and tiptoed into the swirling foam, gasping with shock as it lapped at her ankles. Gritting her teeth, she kept on until she was knee-high in icy water. Then she gave up and watched Myles swim through the waves. They were the only two people in the water now.

Myles, now completely cooled down by his freezing bath, bobbed in the ocean to wave to her. As he did, a surfboard broke through the wave behind him and disappeared below.

Gina waited eagerly for the surfer to reappear; then her mind, numbed like her legs, absorbed the startling message. A surfboard, but not a surfer? When was a board gray and massive and—oh, God!—fin-shaped?

"Myles!" she screamed. "Myles! Come in, quick! There's a shark out there!"

The crashing waves deafened her voice. Myles had turned but could not see her frantic signaling. Without a thought to what she was doing, Gina plunged into the water and swam to him. She didn't even feel the icy cold. All she could think of was that Myles was out there, unknowing, and the shark was behind him.

Yards away, Myles saw her coming toward him, her face panicked, her hands motioning that something was wrong. He stroked swiftly in her direction.

"What's wrong?" he shouted from a distance.

"Shark! I saw a shark near you!"

He stopped swimming, gaping at her incredulously.

"*Will* you come in?" she almost wept. As he hurtled toward her, Gina turned and headed for the shore, looking back once or twice to make sure that he was following her.

Now that he was on the way to safety, for the first time she was gripped with fear for herself, an almost paralyzing terror of whatever lurked in the murky depths about her. A great wad of sea moss floated against her foot, and she pulled up her legs with a scream.

When her feet struck solid bottom, she nearly sobbed with relief. She stood up and staggered through the breakers, Myles only a few feet behind. She waited for him on the shore, throwing herself into his arms when he got close, straining against him.

"I was so scared!"

"It must have been a surfer."

She straightened up indignantly and pointed a finger oceanward. "If it was, he's drowned," she snapped. "Do you see anyone? Anyhow, surfers don't have fins."

He took her hand. "Maybe it was a reflection of the sun on the waves."

"Myles, will you stop talking to me as if I were five years old? I tell you I saw a big gray fin. It was there. I did *not* dream it up."

She tried to pull her hand away, but he held it tight, dragging her along the beach to where an elderly gentleman, wrapped in a plaid blanket, sat in a patio chair, his binoculars trained on the ocean. He smiled as they came up to him.

"Excuse me, sir," Myles began courteously. "My—my girl"—Gina sniffed—"thinks she saw a shark. Have you seen anything through your glasses?"

The gentleman smiled benignly. "Oh, not a shark, my dear," he assured Gina, "just a porpoise. There's a whole school of them out there, blown in by last week's hurricane. They may look like sharks, but that's superficial. The color of the underbelly is quite different, and so is the structure of the jaws and the teeth. You shouldn't have worried. The porpoise is friendly to man."

As they moved on, Gina said, low and sweet, "Next

time I'll dive down to study the underbelly and examine the teeth before I try to warn you."

They had arrived at their own chairs. Myles put his hand on her shoulder and swung her around to face him. "I thought you were imagining things. I apologize," he said humbly.

"Any time," Gina returned brightly. Suddenly her smile wavered and her teeth began to chatter. She started to shiver and shake.

He sat her down on the warm sand and wrapped her in both their towels. When that didn't seem to ease her trembling, he sat down, too, and put his arms around her.

"What's the matter, Gina?"

"I'm sc-sc-scared of sh-sharks."

"Everyone is since that damn movie *Jaws*."

"N-no, al-ways, even b-before."

He regarded her pensively. "You have a thing about sharks and you swam out to warn me there was one in the water?"

She colored as though Myles had accused her of something shameful. "I didn't stop to think."

"That was very brave of you, Gina," he told her quietly.

She shook her head. "No. It wasn't brave. I wouldn't have done it if I had stopped to think. I'm not a very brave person."

"Such an excess of modesty." He tousled her hair. Then he added, his voice indulgent, "I still say it took a lot of courage."

He would never understand her, Myles thought despairingly, never in a hundred years. Gina couldn't have looked more hurt if he had struck her instead of praised her. The gaze she returned him was far stranger than any he had given her. She shifted from the sand up into the deck chair and leaned back, closing her eyes, shutting him out of her world.

"It was not an act of bravery," she murmured.

The other-world expression was on her face again . . . the one that occurred when she spoke to her April. The warning drumbeats echoed and reechoed in Myles's brain, telling him he was getting into too-deep waters.

Chapter 11

The day after Virginia Beach, Gina's third morning in Williamsburg, both Myles and she had chores. After breakfast—to please him, she nibbled a bit of shredded wheat—he dropped her off at the bank and went back to the apartment to work. Before they separated, he penciled a circle around the Williamsburg Lodge on a map inside a brochure entitled *How to Enjoy Colonial Williamsburg*.

"I'll look for you either on the bench outside the front entrance or in the lobby. How much time do you need? Will noon be okay?"

"Make it twelve-thirty. I have a lot of shopping to do."

It was closer to one when Gina shifted her bags and boxes, consulted the map a final time and turned off Francis Street toward the Lodge.

Myles was sitting on the big white bench. He jumped up when he saw her coming and relieved her of the more awkward parcels.

"Good God!" he exclaimed as he got a good look at her. She had been wearing her jeans, T-shirt and sneakers when she had started out in the morning. They were now at the bottom of her shopping bag, and she had on a plaid pleated skirt and a shawl-collared, burgundy velour pullover. Gina was also wearing panty hose and Italian pumps, and was carrying a leather purse comfortably devoid of anything except her new wallet, checkbook and a mess of bills.

"Will I pass muster at the employment office?" she asked cheerfully.

"You look much too elegant to be needing a job," he told her gravely.

"Well, I do," Gina retorted. "I'm in hock for my first three weeks' salary."

"This from the girl who lectures about budgets!"

"Other people's budgets are always easier to keep," she observed. "May I buy you lunch?"

"I'll be damned if you can't."

But when the bill came, Myles wrestled her for it, and he won.

Myles had done some phoning, and they were expected at the personnel office. He received a cordial greeting, Gina a careful appraisal. The job application was handed over with a pleasant smile and an offer of help if it were needed.

She borrowed Myles's Cross pen—reminding herself to buy one of her own—and they sat side by side while she filled out the form.

"Here." Myles handed Gina a slip of paper with two names written on it. "Use these where it says 'Names'—no, on the other side, halfway down—'of Persons Now Employed by Colonial Williamsburg Whom You Know.' I called them yesterday, and they agreed to be used as references when I said you were the daughter of a close family friend." He added lightly, "They are both people whose good opinion I value, so please don't let me down."

Gina had started copying the names. She stopped. "If you're afraid that I might," she said coldly, looking off into the distance, "there's no need for me to use them."

"Gina." He sounded exasperated. "Don't be so sensitive."

She pressed her lips together.

"Gina, write down the names."

Better, but not good enough.

"Please, Gina, write down the names."

She raised her eyes to his and then quickly away, quivering inside at the shock of that look—the laughing tenderness in his eyes, the humorous quirk to his mouth. How Gina loved it when Myles looked at her that way, instead of with righteous disapproval.

She held the pen very tensely as she wrote down the names,

and then, again at Myles's instruction, his own name for a personal reference, after her doctor's and her father's secretary in Los Angeles.

Gina moved a little sideways so Myles couldn't see the rest of what she was putting down. He seemed to be immersed in a roll of papers he had taken from his inside jacket pocket, but one never knew. Too much of what she was writing didn't jibe with what she had told him.

When Gina finally finished filling out the application, she handed it in and heard some careful clichés about their being in touch.

"Don't call us, we'll call you," she said to Myles as they walked out together.

"That's my little optimist."

They wandered away from Merchants Square, walked down two blocks and stepped into Bruton Parish Church to sit in George Washington's pew. Myles led her into the churchyard afterward, and they were near the end of the old vine-covered red brick wall when Gina drew back, unable to account for her overwhelming reluctance to go on.

She pleaded tiredness, and they turned back to the Lodge parking lot while Gina tried to analyze what had just happened to her. It wasn't so much reluctance she had felt as outright terror. In broad daylight, with Myles right beside her and laughing tourists all around, she'd felt a primitive surge of unreasoning fear.

It was all she could do to walk quietly beside Myles. Without him, Gina would have fled in childish panic, though as soon as they got to the car, the spell was lifted.

Myles laughed as she made a quick check—her packages were all there on the back seat. "This is Williamsburg, not Washington," he teased.

Their night was much like the one before, dinner and dishes, then he worked and Gina read. At ten o'clock they put on television for an hour. In the middle of the news they were both seized by a sudden craving for milk shakes. She mixed a concoction of her own recipe in the blender that Myles pronounced as good as any bought in town.

Then bed. And their fourth day together was over.

Myles had an early-morning appointment with an instructor at William and Mary the next day. He was gone when Gina got up, and a scribbled note said he would be back by noon.

She did some yoga exercises, pulled the new velveteen jumper she'd bought over her leotard and departed, breakfastless, for town, leaving a note of her own.

> If you're free at lunchtime, meet me at Chowning's about one. If you're busy, forget it. I don't want to interfere with your work. I'll be back around five.

Gina had no trouble hitching a ride for the few miles to the Information Center, and from there she took one of the free buses that circled the historic area all day. There was something she had to do, and she was glad, in a way, of the chance to do it alone.

Gina went inside the church and felt nothing but peace and the sense of history. Then she turned toward the churchyard, where the graves lay, and experienced not so much yesterday afternoon's fear as a deep sense of sadness. Why should this place she had never been to before, never remembered hearing about, be connected in her heart and mind with personal pain? It baffled . . . yes, and frightened her.

She made herself walk, though quickly, from one end of the cemetery to the other. Gina drew a deep breath of relief when the endurance test ended and she could walk out again on Duke of Gloucester Street.

She strolled along, crossing the road to stop at the weaver's and the bootmaker's. Next, she zigzagged across the wide-open green for a quick look at the brick magazine and guardhouse before doubling back to catch the free bus for a ride to the reconstructed capitol building, site of the original one where Patrick Henry had once called for liberty or death.

When Gina reached Chowning's at ten to one, Myles was standing quite close to the front of the line.

"You're an angel!" she said fervently. "Believe it or not, I'm starving."

He eyed her like a stern parent. "What did you have for breakfast?"

"Oh, I had . . . well, er . . . some juice . . . some—" Under the wilting effect of his skeptically lifted eyebrows, Gina stopped waving her hands and shrugged. "Nothing," she admitted, grinning weakly.

They moved up to first in line.

"And how," asked a voice close to her ear in that same parental tone, "did you get to town this morning?"

"Oh, I . . . I—" she shrugged again. Gina agreed with

whatever great philosopher—she was sure there had been one—who said that white lies were a waste of time; truth-bending should be saved for the real whoppers. "I hitched."

"Well, don't sound so belligerent," Myles responded mildly. "I didn't expect you'd come to harm on a two-mile busy stretch of local road, though next time I would rather drive you."

They were seated before she got around to saying, "You know, you never run true to form. You— Oh, the fruit salad, please, with sparkling cider, and then later the apple pie with black walnut ice cream."

"Now that," he said decidedly, "is the way I like to see you eat. Brunswick stew and cider, please," Myles ordered, smiling at the waitress. Returning to Gina, he asked, "And why should I cater to your love of argument?"

"Well, of all the nerve!" she gasped. "You mean you . . ." And then she gave up, because Myles was laughing at her again, not out loud but with that quirky mouth and softening of his eyes that made her heart turn over.

Gina drew a series of designs with her index finger on the wooden table top. "I hope I'm not keeping you from your work," she said gruffly. "I feel a little guilty about it."

"I'm a big boy," he reminded her. "I know when I can and can't take off. But, as a matter of fact, I met you today because you received a call from the employment office. I think there's an opening for you."

She was half out of her chair before he had finished speaking. "For heaven's sake, why didn't you tell me right away? I should have gone there first!"

"Calm down, your appointment is for two-thirty. You have plenty of time to eat."

Gina had the time, but no longer the inclination. Why, she really couldn't figure out. After all, she didn't need an excuse to stay in Williamsburg.

If she *had* needed one, it was hers two hours later when she walked out of Personnel, officially an employee of Colonial Williamsburg.

Gina danced downstairs to Myles, waiting in the car around the corner. Within moments she poked her head through the window. "I'm starting tomorrow. That's why I lucked out. They needed someone in a hurry because the girl I'm replacing got sick.

"Get in. Where will you work?"

"The Prentis Store. I'll sell things from the crafts program." Gina remained on the sidewalk. "But I have to go over to the costumer's for a dress and things. It may take a little while, and I want to give the store a once-over, too. Why don't you go home, and I'll come back when I'm finished? I'll take a cab, I promise."

"I'll go with you," Myles offered. "If you start tomorrow, you won't be around to distract me any more, so I can afford a few extra hours."

She was a little shook up but tried not to show it. His words could be taken in more ways than one. Myles probably meant that she wouldn't be around the apartment during the day if she was working. Of course, the other, more obvious meaning . . .

"Now that I have some money from home and a job," Gina said tentatively when he joined her on the pavement, "I can look around for a place of my own."

"But you're in hock for all those clothes," he reminded her easily. "Better not be in too much of a hurry."

The lump in her chest melted away and the tightness around her ribs eased up, but the pain at the back of her head became worse.

April. Gina telegraphed a frantic message to her. April, I'm scared. I'm lost. I never wanted to feel like this.

Somehow April was there, for the pain eased up. A voice that only Gina could hear said, "There is nothing to fear, girl."

"That's better," Myles remarked quietly as Gina sighed with relief. "A minute ago you looked as though you had gone to another planet."

Her colonial outfit turned out to be somewhat of a disappointment. She was given six blouses, three skirts and four aprons to mix and match, and one butterfly cap with blue ribbons. Gina could tell that the combined effort, although authentically colonial, would not compare with the elegant cut of some of the more elaborate panniered gowns she had seen worn by the hostesses at the handsome red brick Georgian style palace, reconstructed exactly as it had appeared in the eighteenth century, when it had served as the White House for the governors of Virginia.

"Yours is more practical, especially when summer comes," Myles said comfortably as they strolled along Duke of Gloucester Street so she could inspect her place of work.

A man with a camera around his neck and a small boy

attached to either hand almost ran into them as they stopped in front of the Prentis Store. "Sorry," the man apologized. "It's been a long day. I don't know which way I'm going any more. Could you by any chance tell me where the printer's is? I promised the kids . . ."

Gina smiled in sympathy as the boys tugged at his hands and stepped on his toes, yelling, "Don't stop, Daddy, don't stop."

"You've arrived," she told him kindly. "That's it, the red brick building right over there, the Ludwell home."

"Thanks," he said.

Gina turned from him to find Myles regarding her with narrowed eyes and the righteously disapproving look she hated.

"Why did you do that?" he demanded, and without waiting for a response, he lunged after the man.

They talked together for half a minute, and the man came back, dragging the children along.

Myles returned to her side.

"Do what?" she insisted.

"Purposely misdirect him."

"Misdirect him? Are you crazy?"

"That was the Ludwell-Paradise House you pointed out to him. You called it by name, so you must know it isn't the printer's. His shop is farther down the street."

"The shop is kept in the front of the house," Gina said hotly.

"The Ludwell-Paradise House is privately occupied. It is *not*, and never has been, on exhibition."

Myles seemed to be having trouble holding onto his temper, but no more than she.

Without a word, Gina walked away from him toward the handsome home, up the side stone steps and directly to the louvered black front door. Sure enough it bore a modest little white plaque with a discreet notice: PRIVATE RESIDENCE. NOT OPEN TO THE PUBLIC.

Gina descended the steps and joined Myles where he stood watchful and waiting, his hand on the iron rail.

"I—I must have read the map wrong," she murmured, taking the folder, *How to Enjoy Colonial Williamsburg*, out of her bag.

He unfolded it to show her. "There's the printer's shop, then the Prentis Store. And here we are, at the Ludwell-

Paradise House. Only, as you can see, it's not even listed on the map."

Gina walked over to the garden gate, looking past it to a geometric shrub arrangement. She felt sick and was trembling. She swung the gate open, and it pulled slowly back, constrained by the heaviness of the ball weight. She leaned against it and closed her eyes. Oddly, for the month of April, the scent of holly seemed to be everywhere. Gina heard a woman down the street calling fretfully, "Dickie, you come back here this minute. Dick, Dick Johnson, do you hear me?"

Someone had said that once . . . here . . . a long time ago. . . . Oh, God . . . oh, April . . . I don't understand any of this at all.

Someone was shaking Gina, shaking her hard.

"Gina, damn it—Gina, come back, stop looking at me like that. You're not going to faint, do you hear me? I'm not going to let you."

"Of course I'm not going to faint!" she cried indignantly, opening her eyes. "I've never fainted in my life!"

"Well, you could have fooled me." Myles's voice was dry, but there was relief in his face. "Come on, let's get back to the apartment."

"Yes, let's." She didn't care about seeing the store any more. She'd see it when she reported for work in the morning.

They didn't talk in the car going home, but Gina knew Myles was studying her even while he drove. And that expression was back on his face, the one she dreaded. It was the same look he'd given her when she was sitting on the dinosaur, as though he could see through to her bones and didn't care for their structure.

Sometimes he could read her mind uncannily. It didn't take any great psychic ability right now for Gina to read *his*: *Nutty and neurotic and only seventeen. What have I gotten myself into?*

The closeness that slowly, surely, sweetly, had been building up between them in the last few days was coming apart all at once. She could feel it happening, but didn't know how to go about putting the bricks together again.

Once in the apartment, she combined the leftovers to make a cold meal. Myles carried a tray to his desk, muttering a lame excuse about making up for lost reading. This time he didn't trouble to reassure her that the neglect wasn't her fault.

With his back to her, Gina didn't even have to make a pretense of eating.

The phone rang. With a smothered curse, Myles yanked it off the cradle. "For you," he said. "The airport."

She spoke her name into the phone, listened, uttered brief thanks and hung up. "My luggage has come. I can pick it up tomorrow."

Gina waited for him to say, "I'll take you over." Or, "We'll bring it here." She waited for some indication that this was where she would be and where the bags would come.

"Nice for you," Myles grunted, and buried his nose in a sheaf of notes.

Gina did the dishes, tidied the kitchen and read steadily till ten o'clock, not seeing a single word on the printed pages she turned every so often.

The moment she moved out of her chair, Myles was ready. "Listen," he said as if the thought had just occurred to him. She was certain he'd been planning for hours to say it. "I have to work late tonight. Why don't you take the bedroom and I'll sleep on the couch?"

It was supposed to sound like a choice, but it didn't. It sounded more like a dismissal.

"All right." Gina went to the small hallway closet, half of which had been alloted to her after her grand shopping spree—had it been only yesterday?

When she came out of the bathroom, Myles still had his back to her. "There are clean sheets in the bottom dresser drawer," he said, then turned around to add, "Good night," and came slowly to his feet.

Gina's new, blue cotton challis nightgown halted modestly at mid-calf but dipped low from the V-neck to the tie waist.

They stood there, staring at each other, and he looked as white-faced and miserable as she felt.

"Oh, Gina!"

It was difficult to know which of them moved first or if they came together at the same time. Gina held on to him as though she had been cast adrift at sea and had suddenly latched on to a life preserver; Myles held her so hard she had faint blue marks all over her shoulders for a few days afterward.

When he bent his head and lowered his lips to hers, she turned up her mouth to receive the sweetness of his kiss as though it were the most natural thing in the world.

Several moments later, when their mouths unglued and

Myles said huskily, hesitatingly, "Gina?" she swayed toward him, her hands flat against his chest.

"Yes." she whispered. "Yes, oh, yes."

One of his arms was under her knees, the other around her shoulders as he lifted her. Gina gave herself utterly to the strength of those arms, snuggling as close to him as she could while she drew her lips down from his jaw and along the side of his neck in one prolonged kiss.

Myles kicked the door of the tiny bedroom shut and deposited her on the bed. When he dropped down beside her, she wriggled next to him and lifted her face to his again.

Instead of kissing her face, he kissed her hands, holding both of them between his as if they were rare and precious gems.

Gina started to shake, and when Myles raised his head and she saw the intense burning in his eyes, she trembled even more. Oh, God, this was not going to be a light fling.

"J-just like a movie." She found herself stammering instead of speaking flippantly.

"A movie?"

"The hero always kicks the door shut."

Myles pushed her back down on the bed. "You talk too much." He started untying the bow at the neck of her gown. "And you say the wrong things." She opened her mouth. "Hush," Myles urged, releasing the gathered top and freeing her breasts to his touch. "Just hush."

Fearful, fascinated, Gina lay staring up at him while his eyes held hers and his fingers left a tender burning trail in their wake. Then, suddenly, he was lying across her, his mouth groping, seeking, exploring along the path his hands had just blazed. Gina bore it as long as she could, trying to remain rigid. But she couldn't restrain herself any longer . . . her body arched, her legs pulled up in a desperate convulsion and she heaved away from him.

"Gina! Darling!" He turned her over frantically. "Did I go too fast? Did I hurt you? Did I—"

She knew the second when Myles realized the truth.

His voice faded away. The hands that were holding her tightened like plumbers' clamps. The worry on his face converted to cold, hard fury.

"You goddamn contrary creature," he growled between his teeth, "are you *laughing?*"

It wasn't a question, but a statement.

"I can't help it," she wailed plaintively. "You tickled me."

"Tickled!" he roared, with such outraged male pride in the single word that even as she winced, she cast about in her mind for some way to assuage his ego. She never got the chance.

"What I just did," Myles stated with dangerous calm, "has been known to drive some girls wild with passion."

"I-I c-can't h-help it," Gina hiccuped nervously. "I've got ticklish b-breasts. B-but my spinal column's very sexy," she added, trying to placate him.

She didn't succeed.

Myles stood up and stared down at her with a poker-faced dispassion that, in contrast with what had gone before, was frightening. "Seventeen and a half." He said it half to himself, half to her. "I might have known."

Gina sat up eagerly, more than glad of this chance to be honest. "Myles, would it help if—"

He interrupted her, ruthlessly honest in his turn. "Gina, nothing would help except your getting the hell out of my bed and into your own."

She was wondering if the white, staring intensity of his face was mirrored in her own, when he turned his back abruptly.

"Ever since Washington," he began, addressing the wall, "I've known this wasn't a good idea. Now you've really convinced me." After a minute's frozen silence, he said, "I think you'd better go to bed."

Gina took courage from the unsteadiness of his voice and moved off the bed toward him, reaching out in more ways than one as she murmured tremulously, "Myles, oh, Myles."

"Go to bed, Gina!" he demanded harshly.

She stopped in her tracks, unable to convince herself that his tone held a loverlike uncertainty. She read it all in his face when he turned—desire compounded by dismay that he should feel such an emotion.

Myles wanted her, all right, but not the complications that would come with the package. He was a decent enough man to feel responsible for her, but he damn well didn't want the responsibility.

Gina could have made it easier for Myles. She could have told him some things that would have helped, including an admission that she was twenty-three. Maybe it was her own weakness that prevented her from doing it.

She had her own needs, and bribing a man to sleep with her wouldn't have fulfilled any of them. Gina's personal standards precluded giving more than just her body to a man who wasn't prepared to accept everything about her with all his heart.

Feeling a headache coming on, she went over to the chair and placed her purse closer to where she could reach it later. "Good night, Myles." She closed the bedroom door very quietly behind him.

Gina lay awake, tensly waiting, and soon the pain came. She groped for her bag in the dark, found the container of pills, unscrewed it, tore the tinfoil open with her teeth and put the pill under her tongue. It tasted awful, as always. She wished she had remembered to get some juice from the kitchen to wash away the taste, but it was too late now. Gina would rather endure it than go past Myles in the living room.

He stayed up half the night also, but Gina only saw that he was deeply asleep when she dressed and left the apartment in the morning. There was nothing humorous about his mouth when he slept. He looked very serious with his eyes closed, and she noticed for the first time that he had lashes as long as a girl's, longer than hers.

Maybe this was the true Myles after all, a very serious fellow. Serious, self-righteous, stuffed-shirt Myles. What had made him take her back to his hotel room that night in Washington, and why couldn't he have forgotten to find her when she'd left the next day?

Perhaps, Gina thought, it would have been better if neither of those things had happened.

Chapter 12

Gina hitched a ride to the road in back of Merchants Square and found a place where she could have two cups of coffee. She was going to need them to get through the day at work.

Of course, Gina told herself, lifting her long petticoat skirt to cross onto Duke of Gloucester Street, she could forget about the job and get out of town. It was easier, and it had always been her way before. Myles would probably be overjoyed at this solution to the problem her presence posed.

Then her chin went up, and she said aloud between her teeth, startling a passerby, "The hell with him. I'm staying."

There was a purpose to Gina's being in Williamsburg, and she'd be damned if she would leave before clearly understanding what it was. For a short, happy while Gina had thought the reason was Myles. . . . Well, she was wrong. Myles had only been the instrument. When she knew April's plan . . . then, and only then, Gina would go away.

Surprisingly, the day passed quickly. There was plenty to learn and a fairly constant flow of traffic, and she had little time to brood.

After mentioning casually to one of her co-workers,

Wanda, that she was looking for a place to stay, the girl promptly got on the phone. Wanda spoke to a friend who was living in the York House wing of the Lodge while visiting her college boyfriend. The York House rooms were small nonluxurious and cheap. Except for the summer months, they were usually reserved for student groups. Occasionally a spare room could be latched onto, which was what Susan Langley, Wanda's friend, had done. She was staying on in Williamsburg for another two weeks and would be glad of a roommate to split the nightly charge.

Susan dropped by at Prentis's during the afternoon, and she and Gina immediately took to one another. They agreed to meet at the Lodge after work so Gina could see the room.

It was at the very end of the second floor, which gave a certain amount of privacy. One big window looked out over a grassy quad. The outswept arms of a huge, graceful willow tree provided a mural for the window.

There was only a sink in the room, Susan pointed out with painful honesty. "The bathroom's all the way down the hall, near the stairway. I know that's a drawback," she added, "but not as much as you might think. I usually have two showers and two cubicles all to myself. Frankly, I don't think those kids have any natural functions."

Gina laughed and said she could live with a public bathroom. Traveling on the road, she'd put up with a lot worse.

"I know it's crowded for two people, but I won't get in your hair very much. I'm with Bill most of the time . . . and you'll probably be out a lot yourself. You can have whichever bed you want," Susan offered.

"I'm not worried about the crowding. I just have to— there's someone else. Could I tell you definitely tomorrow morning?"

Suddenly Gina realized she was more furious at herself than she'd ever been at Myles. All along, deep down, she had been hoping for a miracle. Gina still thought that when she went back to the apartment, Myles would say or do something that would wipe out last night.

She hated herself for thinking it, but nothing could keep her from hoping.

"I guess no other roommate will turn up before then," Susan said, disappointed but game.

"Tomorrow," Gina told her firmly. "First thing tomorrow, I'll let you know for sure."

The door of the apartment was locked. Myles answered the bell dressed in a suit, shirt and tie instead of the old slacks and jersey he usually wore for working at his desk. It was the same suit he'd worn in Washington, a tweedy affair with little flecks of rust that seemed to reflect the deep brown of his eyes. Those same eyes now regarded Gina with an expression of careful restraint. No miracle had happened; they were back to last night's game.

"How nice you look," she said lightly. "Going somewhere?"

He seemed almost grateful for her lead. "I have a dinner appointment," he explained. "Some colleagues at the college," he added vaguely.

"Have a good time."

Queen Liz couldn't have inclined her head in a more gracious dismissal, but he lingered on. "I shopped today. The refrigerator's full."

"I'm sure I won't have any trouble finding something." For God's sake, go, and let me cry in peace, she begged silently.

"I may be late, so you might as well take the bedroom again," he suggested awkwardly, "especially since I— You'll have the place to yourself tomorrow night. I have to drive to Washington in the morning to—"

"To see a colleague?" Gina supplied.

He mumbled something about catching up, and she thought with some dispassion that he wasn't doing very well in this exchange. Unfortunately, the observation didn't ease her pain.

He was turning her down in favor of the Tennessee tigress. No doubt she was old enough to relieve him of all guilts. She could supply the simple, elemental, no-strings-attached sex he seemed to want. It was a safer kind of relationship.

Men were such cowards when they sensed the danger of serious involvement, Gina decided. Perhaps if she told him how old she really was, he wouldn't be so scared. But she couldn't tell Myles the truth because she was too scared herself. Once the safety of the lie was removed, her other secrets would tumble out. It was Gina's own weakness that she needed to feel he truly wanted her. She needed the security of knowing her love would be returned. For she loved Myles.

And he was acting like an idiot. She would not let Myles see that his running away hurt her deeply.

"I think I'll take a bath." Gina gave an exaggerated yawn. "It's been a long day."

"Oh, yes. How was the job?" Myles asked politely.

"Fun. I think I'm going to like it. I'll definitely stay on in Williamsburg for the summer." She derived a peculiar sort of pain from the uneasiness her answer aroused in him. Let him wonder *where* in Williamsburg, Gina thought viciously, wishing desperately that he would care enough to ask.

"Well, I guess I'd better be going."

"Yes, do run along." She beamed at him with false bravado. "And have a good time."

Sensing the irony of the conversation, Gina couldn't help laughing. She was acting the hostess in *his* apartment, sending him away from where he belonged and she did not.

Myles didn't appear to notice the hysterical note or the fear in her voice.

"Good night," he said abruptly. "There's an extra key on my desk."

"Good-bye, Myles," she replied softly.

He wheeled about and took an impulsive step toward her, but Gina turned counterclockwise and headed for the bathroom as though he had already gone.

She heard the hall door bang shut as she locked the bathroom door.

"Good-bye, Myles," Gina said again, and smiled wryly into the mirror of the medicine cabinet, trying to ignore the welling tears. "Short and sweet, Gina," she told her reflection. "'Tis better to have loved and lost than never to have loved at all.'" Then she kicked the door so hard the hinges shook. "Who says?"

The number was in her purse. Gina left the bathroom and went to the phone. Why wait till morning? Nothing would change by then.

A woman answered. "Yes, may I help you?"

"Would you please call Susan Langley to the phone? She's in Room Twelve."

After a few minutes, Susan's voice said, "Bill?"

"No, it's Gina. Susan, if you're still interested, you have yourself a new roommate."

When Myles had phoned Danny-Sue the night before, after his disastrous nonencounter with Gina, she had joyfully told him that both her roommates were away on flights and he could come to the apartment.

Myles's second disaster began in Washington the moment he found himself accepting Danny-Sue's enthusiastic hello kiss. Releasing his lips, she waved a bottle of champagne at him. "Courtesy of my airline," she chirped.

Danny-Sue was wearing a sheer peignoir and nightgown, both of white nylon and lace, and both alarmingly bridal.

Myles knew it wasn't going to work within a painfully quick interval. Heart sinking, he realized that, more than anything in the world, he wanted out—not Danny-Sue out of her clothes, as would have been the case a few weeks earlier, but himself out of her apartment.

How do you tell an eager, willing girl who is removing your jacket, unbuttoning your shirt and rubbing her breasts against your chest that you're not interested? he asked himself in desperation. You don't.

He had made the date willingly. Initiated it, in fact. For months Myles had been mad for the broad-hipped, full-breasted, slim-waisted body being offered to him so generously. Now he no longer was. It was simple as that.

How to deal with the situation was a lot more complex, he had to acknowledge miserably, and it didn't include walking out in the middle of Danny-Sue's practiced lovemaking. She didn't deserve that kind of slap in the face.

Maybe some other time, when he regained his sense of humor, he'd be wryly amused at the nobility of his going to bed with a beautiful woman out of kindness and compassion. Now Myles had to concentrate on not looking foolish because of his inability to please her.

It was no use telling himself that the voluptuous body at hand would appeal to the average eye a lot more than the less provocative body he coveted.

"I guess I'm really not average," Myles groaned against Danny-Sue's mouth.

"Huh? What did you say?" she asked, breaking away from a long, deep, smothering kiss.

"Nothing. Nothing important. I like your new perfume," he said to divert her. "You smell absolutely gorgeous."

It was a lie. The perfume was too heavy. Myles felt choked by it.

"I'm so glad. I got it just for you," Danny-Sue cooed, and molded herself against his body. The movement did so little for him, where once it had done so much, that he began to panic.

My God, that witch has made a eunuch of me!

Pleased by his mild tribute to her perfume, Danny-Sue sashayed a few steps away from him. Slowly, provocatively, she shed her peignoir and tossed it over the back of the chair. Then, still more slowly, she pulled down the spaghetti straps of her nightgown. As it tumbled to the floor, she thrust her ripe, full breasts against him with such a startling effect, Myles tumbled over backward onto the bed.

Straddling his legs, Danny-Sue was quick and deft in unbuckling, unzipping and releasing him from the confinement of his slacks and underpants. She would have flung herself on him again, but he fended her off and removed the rest of his clothes himself.

Once in bed, both naked, both eager—she to have him, he to prove himself—nature took over. His mind might be in Williamsburg with Gina, but his body was with Danny-Sue in Washington.

And Danny-Sue was adept at playing that body like a violin. Her hands were everywhere on him, and she used her mouth like a bow to prolong the performance and draw out the sweet torment.

"No more," he told her tersely, moving away from her octopuslike grasp. Myles knew he was deliberately concentrating on his own performance rather than on enjoying himself.

She laughed out loud, sensuously, head thrown back, and he kissed the throbbing pulse in her arched neck and pulled her across his lap, one hand under her head, the other moving down her belly . . . then between . . . then behind. . . . His lips closed first over one hardened nipple, then over the other.

"Now," whimpered Danny-Sue. "Please, Myles, now."

He threw himself on top of her, trying to erase all thought from his mind. Gina receded into the dim shadows for a full five minutes, and he would up putting his hand over Danny-Sue's mouth to smother her shrieks.

"Sorry," he apologized a moment later, removing his hand. "I didn't want your neighbors calling the police."

Danny-Sue flung both arms around him and pulled him back down to her. "That was wonderful," she breathed. *"You* were wonderful, Myles."

He rolled over thankfully onto his back.

"Myles?" Her hand reached out and stroked his arm, forward, back, forward, back, like a sensuous cat.

"Mmm?"

"We're kind of wonderful together, don't you think?"

"Mmm," he said again, a shade less eagerly.

She rolled over, too, looking down at him, her long hair tickling his bare chest. "Have you ever thought about getting married?"

"No, I haven't."

"Then do," she urged. "Think about it for you and me. You seem to find *this* pretty wonderful, too."

"Danny-Sue," he said gently, *"this* isn't all there is to marriage."

She gave a purring little laugh, continuing to stroke him. "I know that, silly, but you must admit it's an important part, and that we—"

"Danny-Sue, I like you very much. I enjoy making love to you very much, but it's not enough. I never dreamed you were serious. I just thought you wanted a . . . a good time."

She sat up and reached for a cigarette. "Until quite recently, that's all I did want. But I'm twenty-seven. It's time I settled down. I want a husband, kids. I *will* make a good wife and mother, you know."

"I do know," Myles told her even more gently, realizing with great relief that what she felt for him wasn't an overwhelming love. She was ready to get married, and there, like Mount Everest, he was. When he faded away, which he certainly would, someone else would take his place. "You deserve the best, Danny-sue, not just a good bed partner but someone who loves you madly."

She smiled wryly. "Why does a guy always tell you how great you are just as he's brushing you off?"

Myles felt a small pang as he thought of Gina, whom he'd brushed off several times and never told how great she was. "A guy doesn't always," he replied soberly.

Danny-Sue gave him a shrewd look from under her lashes. "You're different," she announced. "I noticed it last time, too. I haven't gotten under your skin, Myles, but I would say that some other girl has."

"Yes . . ." He admitted it aloud for the first time, to himself as well as to her. "Some girl has."

Being Danny-Sue, she fed Myles before she sent him home to Gina.

Chapter 13

That morning Gina had lain awake listening to Myles leave the apartment. She got up and went to the window, to watch him exit the building and take the path to the parking area. He hesitated once and looked back, and she drew the curtain in front of her. Then she returned to bed.

After another hour Gina got up again and gathered her things in a heap on the couch. She rolled up the sleeping bag separately. Whatever else couldn't be crammed inside the knapsack, she stuffed into shopping bags and boxes. She'd accumulated a surprising amount for such a short time.

Once everything was ready, she made a quick phone call to Susan, then went for a walk across the William and Mary campus. Gina sat on the grass with her head against an oak tree and watched the students come and go . . . reminded of her own undergraduate days. The hours came and went, too, till it was time to go back to the apartment to meet her new friends.

They arrived early in the evening as agreed during Gina's phone call. Besides Susan and Bill, there was his college roommate, Gary. Gary's chief virute was that he owned a car.

The group was noisy, eager, helpful. Susan took the sleeping bag and one small box; Bill took the knapsack and a large box. Gary picked up a shopping bag in either hand, leaving only a few odd parcels for Gina. He advanced toward her, his arms held out.

He was a big, bumbling guy with short, curly blond hair and a cheerful but homely face. "Don't you feel like taking advantage of me?" he asked, rolling his eyes.

Gina liked him instantly. He was the type everyone liked and no one would take seriously, at least not for another ten years or so until he grew up.

"No," she said, "I don't." As she put her hand on his chest to give him a friendly shove backward, Myles walked through the open door, calling her name.

He looked pale and unhappy and out of breath. When he registered the unexpected scene, his expression turned hostile as well.

This from the man who'd gone off to cavort with the Tennessee tigress!

Gary was staring curiously from Gina to Myles. Gina made no attempt at introductions.

"I came back," Myles announced huskily.

That much was apparent. He must have realized it, too, because a few moments later he pulled himself together with an effort and repeated, "I came back . . . to you," he added very softly at the end.

"Gary," she said, not looking around but still staring straight at Myles, "would you wait for me by the car, please? I'll be right with you."

"Sure thing." He shambled past them, shopping bags swinging.

Gina waited to hear his footsteps thunder down the stairs before she opened her mouth. "You look tired," she told Myles mockingly. "It must have been exhausting, even if you didn't enjoy yourself."

He winced but didn't bother to deny it, for which small courtesy she granted him a measure of grudging respect.

"No, I didn't," he said.

"Your key is still on the desk. I was going to put it in the mailbox."

"No farewell note?"

"I thought my leaving would say it all."

He took a step forward, and she took one back. "I don't want you to go, Gina," he protested.

"I know you don't, and as late as yesterday your saying so would have meant something to me. I wanted so much to hear those words twenty-four hours ago."

"Washington meant nothing. It's over. I told her that. I've come back to you. Doesn't that count for something?"

"Do you think it should? Am I supposed to be flattered because you won the struggle against succumbing to my charms and went off to Washington to get laid? Have you come back here to crawl into the sack with me, too?"

"Don't talk like that!"

"No, I shouldn't *talk* like that, should I?" Gina returned. "Not even if it's the truth. You don't want the truth straight out, do you? You want it all dressed up in pretty language."

"You're distorting the way it really was. I had my reasons for—"

"I know you had your reasons," she interrupted bitterly. "Do you think I haven't seen you agonizing over them this past week? And do you know something? I understood more than you dreamed. I could see it from your point of view. Even if the chemistry is right, a nutty, neurotic, nail-biting juvenile isn't who the mature man dreams of setting up an apartment with."

Gina stopped to take a deep breath. She didn't go on until she was sure her voice wouldn't tremble. "I could have sympathized or forgiven if, in all that emotional ping-pong going on in your mind, you had spared a single thought for me or my needs, but you never did. It was always whether *you* wanted to get involved, or whatever the hell it was you considered sleeping with me would be. You didn't think I had anything to worry about or lose."

"Gina, you're so wrong. If some of that was true in the beginning, it was only because I thought—"

"Thought!" she broke in again with energy. "You actually thought you could walk out on me and that I'd be waiting patiently whenever you chose to come back? Well, I didn't wait, and"—she picked up the last of her parcels—"I'm not staying."

She turned in the doorway for a few last words. "You're a cautious man. In your work, I suppose that's an important quality. In your life—well, it depends on what you want. I admire a man who can follow his heart occasionally." Gina hesitated a minute. Her voice shook in spite of herself. "I suppose I should thank you for all you did for me in Washington and here in Williamsburg."

She ran down the stairs and along the flowered walk toward the parking lot. If he watched from the window, she did not know.

There was no time to settle in at York House after the group returned from the airport with the rest of Gina's luggage. She had to start the noon-to-eight shift at the store.

Even in the evening, when she got around to unpacking, it had to be a halfway affair, since there wasn't enough closet or drawer space. It didn't bother her; she'd lived out of suitcases before.

Gina's work hours varied. Sometimes she was on during the day, sometimes at night. Through Susan, Bill, Gary and the girls she worked with—Mona, Wanda, Lily—she developed a circle of friends. Gina was busy and . . . no, not happy, but nearly content. April was still with her, not as much, but enough for Gina to find it comforting.

In her free time, as the gardens of Williamsburg bloomed with May flowers, she prowled the streets, preferably in the early hours when they weren't flooded with tourists. That was when she most often felt April's presence.

The one place that held her interest above all others was still the handsome brick house next to the Prentis Store, the one she had mistaken for the printer's shop. How she wished it weren't privately occupied. Gina would have given anything to get inside the Ludwell-Paradise House.

The gardens were open to the public, even if the house was not. So, on the way to work every day, she would stroll along the boxed hedges, enclosing neat little rows of herbs, and the garden paths bordered by tulips. If there was no one about, she would stand by the gate, smelling lilacs, and whisper the words that had produced such a powerful reaction the first time. "Dick, Dick Johnson, do you hear me?"

One evening Gina walked through the gate around dusk. The air was nippy, and she stopped near the garden well to wrap a woolen stole closer about herself. Not too far away a door slammed, and a voice called out, "Do you have the letter to mail, ducky?"

"Dick, Dick, do you hear me?"

Gina had closed her eyes. When she opened them again, she gave a cry of fright. A man was standing directly in front of her. When she saw the familiar dark knee breeches and high-throated white shirt with stock, her heartbeats returned to normal.

He was peering down at Gina, his leathery black face kindly and concerned. "Sorry, miss, I thought you called me."

"I didn't hear you coming." Then she couldn't help herself from asking, "Is your name Dick?"

"No, it isn't." He drew back uneasily.

"I'm sorry." Gina tried to say it brightly. "I guess I mistook you for someone else."

He turned to leave and then, a bit reluctantly, turned back. "Are you going to be all right?"

"I'm fine, thank you. Good night." She walked a little unsteadily along the path and came to such a sudden stop at the kitchen door, she felt the jar all the way along her spine. The pain crept insidiously up the back of her neck, striking sharp hammer blows at her head. Sick and dizzy, Gina swayed against a sycamore tree, pressing her face against its bumpy trunk.

When she straightened up, still in a fog of pain, another man was standing at the door, his back to her. He was slight and much more finely dressed than the craftsmen in the shops or the hosts around town. His mulberry jacket blended with his breeches. His tricorn hat of the same color was not the cheap imitation all the children wore about town.

Gina approached, and the man swung around. She reached dizzily for something to hang onto. Suddenly she smelled sweet myrtle in the air and saw April dressed in men's clothes, not in her usual flowered muslin . . .

Somewhere a voice—it wasn't Gina's this time—called out softly, "Dick, Dick, do you hear me?"

Her voice was the barest thread of sound. Impatient nails scratched lightly at the barred door. "Dick, Dick, do you hear me?"

The bolt slid back and the door swung slightly open. A single narrow shaft of light sliced the thick black night, revealing the small, slim figure darting inside. Swiftly the door closed again.

"Lord of mercy, Miss Rietta, you've had me in a powerful sweat! Ten o'clock, you promised me. How come you so long overdue?"

"I know I'm dreadfully late. I'm sorry, Dick, truly I am. I didn't mean to make you anxious, but I went to the Raleigh Tavern, and it was so fascinating I couldn't make myself leave sooner. Half the burgesses were there—Mr. Wythe, Colonel

Washington and Mr. Patrick Henry." She snatched off the tricorn and a brown club wig and shook out a mane of tangled hair. "Why, oh, *why* do men have all the fun and freedom? It's not fair!"

"Not all men, Miss Rietta."

The slave's quiet dignity carried its own reproof. The stormy face under the mass of hair gentled as Rietta's hands clasped Dick's muscled arm in a fit of remorse.

"I'm so sorry. Forgive me. I know it's worse, far worse for you, Dick, but in so many ways women are enslaved, too. Do you know that in the Commons Room tonight I saw public notices for *three* runaway slaves and *two* runaway wives? I honestly think—"

"Miss Rietta, I'll listen to what you think tomorrow. If you don't want to get me skinned alive right now, just you nip on down to the printing room and get to looking like a lady again. I ain't too worried about fooling Mr. William, but Miz Clementina, she's a mite sharper. She's going to start suspicioning soon at these headaches of yours always coming so convenient the same time of night."

"Miss, hold onto me and you'll be all right in a minute."

Gina opened her eyes and looked up in surprise at the man whose name wasn't Dick. She had been standing by the kitchen door in a half-dreaming state and hadn't heard him return.

"Thank you, but I'm fine," she said politely. Why should that make him look at her in such a queer way? Maybe she'd better leave. She smiled and nodded, pulled the wool stole tighter around herself and hurried past him toward the street.

The following day Gina had gone downstairs for supplies, and when she came back, Wanda was busy with some customers who wanted soap balls and sealing wax. A man stood alone near the front of the store, bending forward to read the titles of several leather-bound books.

Gina went around the counter and walked toward him. "May I help . . ."

"Good morning, Gina," Myles said quietly.

"Good morning, Mr. Edward."

"Don't be childish, dear one."

Gina stood there helplessly, flushing with shame because he was right—she *had* been childish, which put her in the wrong—and because those two words, *dear one*, had never been said to her, not in that combination, not in that tone. Gina was fighting the desire to throw herself against his chest and burst into tears.

There were other alien emotions—treacherous ones. She stiffened her spine and reminded herself how badly he'd let her down. She recalled that she was there in the shop to sell.

"May I help you, sir?"

Myles looked amused. "You've really gone Williamsburg in a big way. How eighteenth century you sound for a most twentieth-century girl. Very well, then, little one, you may help me. I should like to buy one of these books. Do you suggest the leather edition or the paper-bound?"

Gina looked down and saw that he was pointing to *On the Choice of a Mistress* by the well-known womanizer Benjamin Franklin.

"It's a matter of personal preference," she said coolly, though she was burning inside.

"I happen to be asking yours."

"I . . . I . . ." And then Gina saw that she was playing into his hands. "The leather, of course; it's fifteen dollars. The paperback is three twenty-five."

"I'll take the leather. Do you accept checks?"

"If you have proper identification, sir." She stabbed him with a smile.

Myles wrote out a check and handed it across the counter to her, and then, poker-faced, added his driver's license. Gina's hand moved slowly to accept them. For some reason she was terrified of touching those bits of paper. . . .

The bell on the door jangled gently as he walked in, but there seemed to be no one about. Suddenly a girl bobbed up from behind the counter and was illuminated in the golden bar of sunlight drifting in through the window at the far end of the room. Her dark auburn curls, surprisingly uncapped, and clubbed in a man's fashion at the back of her neck with a bow, took on a coppery glow.

Clothed in a simple flowered gown, her figure was light and pleasing, but by no means extraordinary. She had large, glowing black eyes and skin that was unfashionably tanned. Her nose was too long and straight, her mouth too wide and laughing for the popular mode.

No insipid miss, this, Jeremy thought, intrigued, as she greeted him courteously but with a manner of quiet assurance. "May I serve you, sir?"

He held two folded papers in his hand. "I was asked to give these to Mr. William Rind, the printer."

"Mr. Rind is unwell, sir. He keeps to his bed today."

She held out her hand—a bit imperiously, he thought. The gesture tempted him to tease her. "Is there no gentleman I can deal with?"

He was surprised at the quick anger that narrowed her eyes into two dark slits. He might as well have committed some great offense.

"Mr. John Pinkney, who assists Mr. Rind, has gone to the next county on private business," she told Jeremy. "If thee insists on dealing with a male, I can go to the printing room and fetch Isaac Collins, who is twelve and lacking in wisdom. Or there is Mr. Rind's servant, Dick, who does not lack for wisdom but is somewhat less educated than I. Which of them would you wish to see, sir?"

"Neither, ma'am. I throw myself on your mercy. I did not mean to offend." Jeremy handed his papers across to her. "I was asked if Mr. Rind would be so kind as to insert these advertisements in the next issue of his *Gazette*."

"He will be pleased, sir."

Rietta unfolded the first paper and smoothed it out on the counter. Her quill made small marks in the margin as she read aloud. "The noted horse, Piccadilly, stands at my plantation in York Town and will cover mares at five pounds the season each mare, thirty shillings the leap."

She looked up. The dark eyes were laughing now. "We will be pleased to accommodate Piccadilly for the horse-loving gentlemen of Virginia."

Jeremy opened his mouth and then shut it again. He'd be damned if he'd explain himself to her, pert miss that she was.

She smoothed out the other paper, lifted her quill again and began to read aloud once more. "Runaways from the subscriber this week past, two Negro men . . ."

Her voice faltered and was still. One dagger's look was cast at him before Rietta lowered her eyes, put down her pen and resumed her reading in silence.

> . . . two Negro men, one an outlandish fellow of middle size, broad-chested, with a bold, impertinent countenance and haughty manner; the other a slight youth with a star-shaped scar on his left cheek who is fond of liquor and apt to sing indecent songs when he indulges. They have both been whipped for hog-stealing a few days ago,

and their backs must still be sore. A reward of one pound
for the older man, thirty shillings for the youth.

>   Samuel Buffington

When Rietta looked up at Jeremy, he was stunned to see the glitter of tears in her eyes.

"Will you pay in cash for these advertisements, Mr. Buffington?"

"I am not Mr. Buffington," he told her slowly. "He bade me ask that you put the money owed on his account. But if I may so presume, ma'am, I would greatly desire to know in what way I have offended you."

Her words came out with such soft scorn, he had to strain to catch them. "I doubt that thee would understand, sir, even if thee were told."

"Pray try me, ma'am."

She spoke more calmly. "Perhaps I should not blame you, since you are not Mr. Buffington. Still, you were willing to be his messenger for this notice." Rietta tapped it with a slim tanned hand. "I have not yet been in Virginia long enough to accept that men may be owned by other men and treated as lesser animals."

Jeremy twitched the paper around and read it slowly. Then brown eyes looked squarely into black. He crossed his arms on his chest and surveyed her at his leisure. When he spoke, his voice was firm and censorious. "You judge me harshly, ma'am; also, too hastily. Mr. Buffington is an acquaintance of my father's who chanced by our home yesterday in regard to the sale of a horse. On learning that I was returning to Williamsburg, he asked that I save him the ride into town to deliver these messages. I did not know their content until now."

Rietta's cheeks were bright red, but her chin came up sturdily and her glance was direct. "I must ask thy pardon, sir."

He had watched her silent struggle in amused sympathy. The leap of emotions on her face was far easier to read than his lawbooks.

"I am ashamed," Rietta added presently. "I despise self-righteousness in others, and I have been guilty of it myself. Cousin William—Mr. Rind, that is—accepts these advertisements. They appear in almost every issue. I feel they are wrong, yet I continue to work for the *Gazette*, so by what right may I condemn others?"

"A most handsome apology, if"—Jeremy grew cautious again—"it was so intended."

A dimple showed in one corner of her mouth when she smiled. It made the smile slightly lopsided . . . and enchanting.

"Your views are hardly surprising, coming from a Quaker," he remarked encouragingly.

"I am not a Quaker."

"But you speak in the Quaker way. Not always, but just—"

"Just when I become angry or excited, did you not observe it? I regret, sir"—the lopsided smile flashed briefly again—"that my Quaker speech is a sign of my temper, not of my beliefs. My mother was a Quaker till she married, but they read her out of meeting for wedding my father, who is cousin to Mr. William Rind and professes no faith at all. My mother continued to speak in the Quaker style, and though I studied not to, when I lose control of my feelings, I often lose control of my tongue, too."

"In fact, you are that curious contradiction—a Quaker spitfire?"

"I fear so."

Jeremy laughed out loud. "I doubt it. I would guess, Miss Rind, there is very little that you fear."

The glow went out of her face. "Very few men are fortunate enough to live entirely without fear."

"Or women?"

"Or women."

They stood staring at each other in dawning wonder. Then she looked away, biting nervously at her lower lip. "I will give Mr. Buffington's advertisements to Mr. Rind and write the money owed on his account." She spoke rather breathlessly for someone who was standing still. "I give you good day, sir," she added formally, and waited for Jeremy to take his leave.

Her hands reached out for the notices, and so did his. His fingers moved firmly to clasp hers, grew firmer when she strove to draw away. The bell on the door jangled twice, but neither heard it.

"Young lady," a rough voice broke in, "please to tell Mr. Rind that Mr. Gibbs begs a moment of his time."

"Miss, do you carry these here tricorn hats for children?"

The question seemed to be coming from very far off. It was Myles who answered for Gina. "Over in that corner."

Myles was leaning across the counter, holding her by the elbows. His fingers were hard and piercing.

"What on earth are you doing?" She tried to wriggle free.

"Keeping you on your feet," he replied somewhat grimly. "You looked like you were about to faint."

"Don't be ridiculous!" Gina retorted. "Why does everyone keep thinking I'm going to faint?" He had let go, though she could still feel the pressure.

Myles pounced immediately on her careless remark. "So I'm not the only one?"

"Damn it, I've told you before, I never faint."

"Then where do you go, Gina, standing on your feet and traveling off to some never-never land of your own?"

"Where I go and what I do are not your business."

"You should have said that in Washington when you jumped off Uncle Beazley and came running at me. *Then* I might have listened."

"Go away, Myles. Please, *please*, let me be."

"May I have my book?" he asked calmly. "After all, you did accept my check for it."

With angry speed Gina slipped the slim volume into a paper bag and handed it across to him. She looked up only when Myles said, quietly and seriously, "I'm going, Gina."

She would have said good-bye if he hadn't grinned at her over his shoulder, assuring her as he stolled toward the door, "But I'll be back."

That night, on her way to the coffee shop, Gina stopped at the Lodge desk to check for mail. Three letters and a paper bag with the insignia of the Williamsburg craft shop. She stuffed the letters into her purse while looking helplessly down at the bag, which she herself had handed to Myles. Only now there was a gift envelope attached to it bearing Gina's name. She drew out the card.

> Leather is tough and, like the printed word, endures.
> A most symbolic gift.

No name, of course. Why should there be? Any more than she needed to look inside the bag. Gina tossed it into the bottom of her purse, and later that night hid it away in the farthest corner of the bottommost drawer of her dresser.

"Let me be, Myles," she whispered, trying to remember the eyes that had once looked at her and found her wanting. Instead, Gina heard a faraway echo, *Dear one . . . dear one . . . dear one . . .* and she ran out of the room and through the hall, plunging dangerously down the stairs and into the night.

Gina walked the still streets for more than an hour. When she came out of the blackness, back to the lights of the Lodge, she had almost made up her mind to get out of Williamsburg.

Gina climbed the wide wooden stairs, feeling the arteries in her head expand. With this grim warning of the prelude to pain, she was unsurprised to find April drifting just ahead, the hem of her gown gently dusting the steps. When April reached the top, she turned to smile at Gina and shake her head.

"It would be easier to go," Gina said aloud, pleadingly.

April shook her head again, dark auburn curls dancing. Her words formed in Gina's mind: "Don't be childish, dear one."

Numb with shock, she watched April slip away.

Chapter 14

Myles would not have believed he could miss anyone as much as he missed Gina. The sullen mouth that, when it turned to laughter, could light up the world. The voice like a siren's song. The mercurial changes of mood. Dirty hair tied with a sneaker lace; clean, brushed blonde hair flying about her face. How much she had to say when they were talking, and how still she could sit when he was working. Her quick wit and even quicker temper. Her glorious eyes daring him, provoking him, inviting him. The feel of slender shoulders beneath his hands; the breathtaking body in a leotard, bending over or upside down or twisted like a pretzel to do one of her exercises. The daily argument about whether breakfast was or was not an important meal. And that one time when she had spread out her lovely hands with their chewed-off nails and told him shyly, "I didn't bite them today."

Her presence was still in the apartment through little signs after a week had gone by. Her tortoise-shell comb left on the bathroom shelf, small bags of mint leaves she had hung in the front hall closet. The big towel with the lion's face that she used when she did her yoga. Three paperbacks on the night table next to the bed. And in the kitchen, in the middle of the sink counter, the smashed remains of her sunglasses under a can of grapefruit juice.

The last had been a message, clear and simple. She had broken the glasses deliberately and left them to let him know she wasn't hiding behind them any more.

Gina had said a hell of a lot of other things . . . bitter and hurt moments she had stored up and was able to tell him about before she had moved out.

Myles remembered all of it.

It had been like having a hot shower unexpectedly become ice-cold the instant he had walked through the apartment door and seen that great oaf with the athlete's body and cherub face standing so damned close to her . . . and the calm, scornful words and look Gina had cast at him.

Myles had kept telling himself at first that he was better off without her. When he had admitted to himself she had spoken only the unpleasant truth, he had felt a wrench of pain.

Finally he had realized it didn't matter who was right or wrong. His love was hot-tempered. His love could give lessons in obstinacy to a mule. His love was moody and impossible. But still his love.

Whatever she was, just as she was, he wanted her. He loved her. Myles had said it to himself experimentally: I love her. And then, triumphantly aloud, "I love her."

The next day he had gone to the Prentis Store, but not to tell her. He knew Gina would be neither ready nor receptive. No, he just had to see her again, his stubborn darling, and at the same time issue his challenge. To let her know in clear and simple English that she wasn't going to have it all her own way.

The book was only the beginning.

Keeping track of her wasn't too difficult. Myles knew where she lived; he knew where she worked. He was able to enlist a few spies to get hold of her schedule. Susan Langley was particularly susceptible to his sad tale of blighted romance.

They began to giggle, Mona and Lily and Wanda, the moment Myles entered the shop. After a few days, no one ever made the mistake of trying to wait on him, even if Gina were busy with a customer and someone else were not.

He would lean against the counter, looking off into space, like a man with all the time in the world, till Gina was free.

He tasted the small triumph of standing still as he eyed her, forcing her to come to him.

Myles dragged out the buying of a quill pen for twenty minutes and a mob cap for about fifteen. They spent almost half an hour on the merits of lavender soap balls as opposed to bayberry. The day he bought an expensive handmade basket, Myles felt the cost justified an hour of her time, despite the crowded store.

Gina knew that everything he bought would wind up in her mailbox with a casually affectionate note. She didn't acknowledge this by so much as the bat of an eyelash when he bought rock candy or a slate and charcoal or half a dozen marble-sized cannonballs. Initially, when it came to the more expensive items, she had whispered fiercely, "I don't want you to buy this."

"Are you refusing to sell it to me?"

"You've been spending too much money."

"Are you refusing to sell it to me?" he had repeated. Myles had seemed outwardly grave but had enjoyed himself tremendously.

Gina had snatched the sheepskin rug off the counter, rolled it up grimly and tied it with string. While he had counted off the rather staggering total, Myles had thought with satisfaction that every cent he spent put him deeper and deeper into her thoughts. He was in so deep now that, like it or not, she would never have him out of her mind.

The day he bought her a lovely Delft inkwell, she demanded in a gloomy undertone, "Why do you have to be so pigheaded?"

"It takes one to know one," he returned cheerfully. Then, a little louder, "You will wrap it nicely, won't you, please? It's a present for my girl."

"You damn fool! I hope you don't have enough money to eat this week. And I'm *not* your girl!"

He had come a long way since Washington, when Gina's lack of inhibition had had him crawling around in his skin. Now, the more she blushed, the more Myles laughed, while at least eighteen of the twenty-odd people in the store swiveled, mouths agape, to stare at them both.

Two days later Gina turned the tables. A handmade basket twice the size of the one he had bought for her was delivered to his apartment. Its contents came from the gourmet shop in town. Two three-pound smoked bacons. Little tins of smoked oysters and sardines, even one of octopus. Packages of rice crackers and English biscuits. Jars of pickled onions, baby corn and mushrooms. Exotic teas and spices. Bottled water and two packs of Japanese beer.

Gina's card, unsigned as all of his had been, inquired simply, "War or Peace?"

Myles drove the long way around town to park behind the Lodge, then walked over to the Prentis Store.

"You're not very consistent for a girl who hoped I'd be starving this week."

"I was just trying to show you that two can play your game."

"That's what I've been trying to show *you*, Gina," he said gently, "only it's not a game. Will you have dinner at the apartment and help me eat some of what you sent?"

"Certainly not."

"Another time, then."

"No, damn you, not another time."

Though most of their meetings were forced by Myles, not all of them were. One day he came upon her in the middle of the morning as he crossed the green near the magazine. The flock of sheep were drifting over the grass, and near the big oak in front of the guardhouse sat Gina with one of the baby lambs, its face nuzzling her knees. From her fiercely maternal expression, she might have been holding a baby in her lap.

Myles sat down beside her, his back to the tree trunk, and for once she granted him a faint smile as she cuddled the lamb closer. The tender, adoring expression in her eyes, Myles decided ruefully, might better have been saved for him.

The shepherd recovered his lamb, and wonder of wonders, Gina remained with Myles beneath the tree for another ten minutes, listening to him talk and occasionally even troubling herself to respond.

She was wearing one of the colonial-type gowns required in the store. As she stood up and brushed the grass off her dress, he noticed that it was new. Made of a soft cotton almost the color of her eyes, its underskirt patterned with small blue and violet flowers, the dress stood out from her sides, properly panniered and stiffened by layers of petticoats. The neck, cut low and square, showed edges of the same creamy lace as her long, flowing sleeves.

"I see they gave you a new gown. It's very attractive."

Gina shook herself a little and fluttered her petticoats. "No, this is mine. I had it made by a dressmaker here. I wanted to be more authentic . . . and I don't like wearing other people's clothes."

"Obviously an only child." He grinned, recalling his sisters' many battles on that same subject.

A strange, distant expression settled over her face, what Myles thought of as her staring-into-space look.

"Yes," she said, "I was an only child."

She spoke to him, though looking out across the green, the tip of one leather buckled shoe digging up the turf about her. "Myles, why don't you give up? I was planning to stay here for the summer. You're liable to drive me out sooner."

Such a long pause followed that Gina finally glanced down at him.

"What I do, I must," he said, meeting her eyes squarely. "What you do is up to you."

"If you make me go—"

"If you go, go, but don't blame your cowardice on me," Myles interrupted harshly.

She gave a hollow little laugh. "At Virginia Beach, you kept extolling my bravery."

"And you denied it."

"Yes."

There was a strange expression on her face again. He heard the echo of her murmured words. "It was not an act of bravery." Damn! Why were they so familiar?

Suddenly, as vividly as if it were yesterday, it came back to Myles. The day so many years ago. The hot, dusty railroad station. The dirty, desperate boy in coveralls, running between the rows of benches, gun in hand, turning to fire at the two policemen chasing after him . . . return fire, people scattering, screaming, scrambling out of the way.

In minutes it had been over, the boy led off in handcuffs, and, right near Myles, the young mother lifted by her husband off the child she had protected with her own body. "My brave darling," the father had said, wiping her tear-stained face even as she had shaken her head in denial.

"It wasn't courage! It was love," she had told him.

"It wasn't an act of bravery," Gina had said to Myles, shaken by her terror of the supposed shark. The last half of her sentence had been left off . . . not what it *wasn't*, but what it *was*—an act of love.

Dear God, she had as good as confessed it then, and he had missed his cue. Myles had let her down then, as he had let her down both before and after.

But never again, Gina, my love, he vowed fiercely to himself, watching her drift away as casually as the sheep without bothering to say good-bye.

"Someday, love," he added under his breath to her retreating back, "you're going to get a lesson in manners."

He leaned against the tree and studied the gentle swing of her wide skirts as she walked, the graceful way she gathered up a handful of skirt and petticoats to clear them of some obstacle. It was a constant marvel to Myles that a girl who seemed wedded to her jeans could handle a colonial dress with such un-self-consciousness.

Unexpectedly, before Gina whisked out of sight, she half turned to smile at him, a smile so tantalizing, so filled with sudden warmth and the promise of intimacy, that it brought Myles straight to his feet, hot blood racing to his head. By the time the heat had receded and the throbbing in his temples had eased, Gina was out of sight.

"My God!" he muttered, not profanely, and slid down the tree trunk to the ground.

Chapter 15

Jeremy paced restlessly about the upstairs chamber long after the rest of the household was abed. He could not sleep himself because of the notion that something momentous had occurred in his life. He had had no concept of it earlier in the day when he received an invitation from Mr. Wythe to go to the Apollo Room.

Mr. Wythe, unlike other great gentlemen of Virginia, seldom frequented the Raleigh Tavern. He and Madame Elizabeth greatly preferred the comfort and elegance of their own fireside. Hardly an evening passed without good friends gathering in their home for food and drink and lively discussion. There was no more stimulating talk in any home in Williamsburg, as Jeremy would ruefully remind himself on the long afternoons when he yearned to be fishing on the James or riding his father's acres instead of being cooped up with his lawbooks.

Mr. Wythe did not say so, but it was for his pupil's pleasure that Jeremy was being taken to sup at the Raleigh. Half the burgesses seemed to be gathered there for the evening meal and nearly the other half appeared afterward to drink and gamble.

The first person to greet Mr. Wythe was Tom Jefferson,

whom all knew to have been Wythe's favorite pupil. Jeremy was astonished when he was made known to Mr. Jefferson in rather flattering terms. This was more than Jeremy expected, considering some of his mentor's remarks the last time Mr. Wythe examined him on the laws of contract.

Mr. Jefferson was a tall man with a high-bridged nose, but less than well-looking. Jeremy could not but be disarmed to receive his compliments, and Jefferson was kind enough to add that Mr. Wythe's regard was never undeserved.

The younger man listened eagerly, expecting an exchange of views on topics of the day—the troubles with Britain, the ruined state of the East India Company or, at the very least, the great cockfight to be held at the Gloucester Court House. Instead, the two lawyers fell into talk about the difficulties of obtaining just payments for their legal services in this year of 1773 and the steps by which debtors might be forced to disburse the monies owed to lawyers.

At this point, Jeremy deemed it tactful to excuse himself and wandered over to observe the card play. While he watched a lively game of loo, he suddenly sensed that he himself was being observed. He looked around and became aware of the fixed regard of a slight youth in a suit of fine mulberry with a brocade waistcoat. He was inspecting Jeremy with a faint air of hostility that could not but perplex the law student, as he would swear they had never met.

The moment the youth became conscious of Jeremy's regard, however, he turned away so abruptly, it was plainly evident he was wishful to avoid a confrontation.

This piqued Jeremy's curiosity as nothing else could have done. He soon made it his business to shift his position and then to saunter slowly about the room and come upon the odd youth from another direction.

Unnoticed, Jeremy regarded him carefully. As the youth sipped in a rather finicky way from a pewter tankard, Jeremy was more positive than before that they were not acquainted. And yet there was something . . . a certain familiarity . . . he knew not what . . .

He approached the stranger directly to solve the riddle. "I beg your pardon, sir," he began easily. "I think we were introduced at Mrs. Campbell's Tavern this Sunday past, but there were so many present in the party, your name escapes me, as I am sure mine does you. I am Jeremy Stuart, a law student, living with Mr. George Wythe."

The proper course would have been for the youth to deny

the meeting but reveal his name. He did neither, and his behavior was more strange than formerly, for his face turned a bright red. "You m-must be m-mistaken, s-sir. I—I have just arrived in W-Williamsburg this evening," he lied. Before Jeremy could reply, he stuttered on even more incoherently. "I have as yet n-no ac-acquaintance on the t-town." Something in his air, if not his very words, indicated he would be well pleased to continue without Jeremy's.

It was not Jeremy's general custom to force his company on others, but his curiosity had reached a fever pitch.

"I am happy to be your first acquaintance, sir," he persisted, ignoring the desperate look the other was casting about the room, as though begging someone to relieve him of this pestilential fellow. "Will you join me in a glass of beer or perhaps some punch?"

"You are too kind, sir," the young man squeaked in the voice of a boy seesawing on the brink of manhood, "but I am drinking cider." He put the tankard to his lips and took a long swallow. "I give you good even, sir," he said, then took a hasty leave. "My friends are without. I must not keep them waiting." He set his mug on the nearest table with a loud thump, bowed awkwardly and walked quickly from the room.

To acquire friends in the space of a few sentences must surely argue a high degree of skill. With a quick glance toward Mr. Wythe, most happily settled with a group of burgesses, Jeremy followed his new acquaintance from the Apollo Room into the Commons.

The youth was standing near the bar, gazing earnestly at a list of notices posted on the wall. He was reading carefully and apparently with displeasure, for a fearful scowl now marred his face. That, too, struck a chord of memory in Jeremy. One thing, however, was certain. The stranger did not appear to be someone hurrying to meet his friends.

Jeremy came up so close behind him that when the boy turned around, they collided.

"Oh, I beg thy pardon!" he gasped, straightening his wig.

"Not at all. I believe the fault was mine," Jeremy said politely, noting the bright red color that again spread over the young man's face. "I believe I disturbed your reading. The notices must be of particular interest tonight."

"Only the usual reports of runaway slaves and equally enslaved runaway servants and wives."

"You consider women enslaved?"

"Thee, of course, does not?" he demanded so heatedly

they began to attract general attention. Either he observed the interest they were exciting or else he suddenly remembered his waiting friends. "Good night, sir." He clapped his tricorn on his head and almost bolted from the room.

Jeremy started to rejoin Mr. Wythe but stopped short with such abruptness that once again he collided with a guest, half the contents of whose tankard were spilled.

Several precious moments were lost in an exchange of apologies and courtesies that included the buying of another small tankard of beer.

When Jeremy reached the street to check on the incredible notion that had come to him—and surely it must be the wildest impossibility—he could see a slight, cloaked figure hurrying west a few hundred yards away on Duke of Gloucester Street.

That would be the direction she would take, if the figure were a she, as he was now almost certain it was. Surely the situation stretched beyond the realm of coincidence, that twice in the same week he should encounter a young woman and a young man who both lapsed into the Quaker way of speech when their passions were aroused.

Jeremy followed at a safe distance till the cloaked figure stopped at the Ludwell home, rented by Mr. William Rind, the public printer. When she turned in at the gate, he was in time to hear a soft voice whisper, "Dick, it's me," and a faint scratching at the door. Jeremy crept through the gate himself, careful not to let it swing free. He advanced to the well and concealed himself to one side, under a myrtle tree. The kitchen door opened, and in the revealing light that shone over the garden for about ten seconds, the cloaked figure slipped through, pulling off her tricorn and her man's wig. As she did so, the tumbled copper-brown curls of the Quaker spitfire fell down her back.

Jeremy made his way out of Mr. Rind's garden as silently as he had entered it. He was overwhelmed by the evening's events, and so absorbed in trying to make sense of them that he unconsciously headed for home.

In the front bedroom of the Wythe house, he had already started to remove his clothing before recollecting he had abandoned his preceptor at the Raleigh.

Hastily Jeremy rebuttoned his waistcoat, retied his stock and seized his tricorn from the blockhead that Madame Elizabeth had not removed even after she discovered that he never wore a wig.

Fortunately, Mr. Wythe was still so engaged in conversation, Jeremy's absence had gone unnoted. He formally excused himself for the evening but did not go straight back to his room. Instead, he walked along the streets toward the Rind house, which was now in darkness.

Later, Jeremy sat down at his desk with his journal spread before him, aware that he was introducing a new and baffling element into its pages. He had thought, when he first came to read under Mr. Wythe, that his pen would deal solely with the great men and rousing deeds of these troublesome times. Save for the northern ports of Boston and Philadelphia, nowhere was so much politicking taking place as in Virginia.

There must have been a score or more of men at the Raleigh this one night whose names figured in the secret reports which everyone knew that the governor, Lord Dunmore, sent off to the king. Events discussed at the tavern occupied the thoughts and plans of their enemies, such as Lord North, and their friends like Charles Fox and Mr. Burke.

Jeremy found it strangely humiliating that, instead of on great men and great deeds, this night his thoughts were completely concentrated on one peculiar, headstrong girl. More even than he yearned to be at the center of action at the Raleigh, he longed to know what *she* could be about! Why did she don men's garb and frequent the public rooms forbidden to her sex?

He suspected that he was the first person to stumble onto her secret, which carried with it a burdensome responsibility. On the one hand, Jeremy felt obliged to keep her unsought confidence. On the other, it might be that her own well-being demanded an end of this hazardous masquerade.

Jeremy slept badly, his mind riveted on the hostile youth in mulberry brocade and the glowing girl in the flowered gown. How surprising, and how inevitable, that these two intriguing persons should be one!

The following day, he rose at six in the morning and reread his latest journal entry. In it was a further source of embarrassment. He had to confess he sounded not only priggish but less than honest. Truly, he must contrive to see her again, but there was no obligation involved.

Chapter 16

Myles had spent the evening with some friends who lived near the William and Mary campus. When he left their apartment close to midnight, the air was wonderfully warm for May, quiet and still, sweet with the scent of the first spring flowers.

Like the most lovelorn of fools, instead of getting into his car and heading straight to his lonely bed, he meandered down Duke of Gloucester Street, turned onto Francis and wound up in the garden on which Gina's York House window fronted. The night was beautiful, and he longed for a glimpse of his lady love at her window.

In any properly conducted love affair, Myles reflected ruefully, she would sense his presence, fling open the casement and toss out a rose.

So much for romance. Gina's window remained uncompromisingly dark. After a while, feeling remarkably foolish, he started back the way he had come.

The quick tap, tap of feet—the only sound evident except for his own footsteps—made Myles turn his head as he walked out onto Francis Street again. He could barely make out a solitary figure moving toward the main entrance to the Lodge. The figure passed under a street light for about two seconds. "Gina!" he yelled, and raced toward her.

She wore jeans, the I Am Woman T-shirt and her hair bound back with the sneaker lace. She looked like the unkempt, exasperating creature he had found behind the Lincoln Memorial. The sight of her took him back in more ways than one, and he reacted accordingly.

"Where the hell have you been, and what the hell are you doing walking the streets alone at this hour?"

"What the hell right do you have to ask?" she retorted.

"Gina," he began warningly, and to his surprise, she did an about-face.

"Oh, for heaven's sake! I was restless. I went for a walk."

"Girls," Myles gritted between his teeth, "do not walk the streets alone at midnight, not if they have any brains."

"This is Williamsburg, not the big bad city."

"There are kooks everywhere. You don't have to make it easy for them."

"Oh, Myles!" She made an impatient gesture that said it all. *Oh, Myles, you pompous, conservative, fuddy-duddy!* Suddenly a smile of unholy glee lifted the corners of Gina's mouth. "And what were you doing here at midnight, Myles?" she asked demurely.

"Looking up at your window," he said, and that simple truth, which she had guessed but never expected to hear him admit, made her step back from him almost fearfully.

He pressed his advantage. "Gina, would you like to hear a theory about why you were so restless?"

"Not in the least," she snapped.

Myles would have expounded on it anyhow, despite her claimed lack of interest, if he hadn't noticed with something of a pang that she looked both tired and tight-strung; her mouth was more than usually downturned, and her eyes were feverish.

"Come on." He took her arm and urged her around. "You don't have to go through the lobby. I'll see you to your room."

She went with him, docile as one of her adored baby lambs. "Dear me," she said, "that was a very short lecture . . . for you."

"Someday, and I wish the day were now, I'm going to lay you out and spank you silly."

"Not if you value your family jewels," she told him gently.

He noticed with relief the rejuvenating effects of this exchange. The tense lines had eased out of her face, and the sparkle had returned to her beautiful eyes.

"That's what I like," he commented as they climbed the wide stairway, "a delicate, old-fashioned girl."

"That's what you should have, Myles, and it isn't me."

She was serious for once, but he pretended not to realize it.

"I know. Ain't life hell?" As they walked along the flagstone flooring, he added idly, "Have you been doing anything exciting lately?"

"You bet." She grinned maliciously at him. "I've attended a series of lectures at William and Mary on an interesting subject—Women Making It Professionally in Men's Domains."

"Such as?"

"Medicine, law, art, architecture, religion—all the jobs your sex likes to hog," she noted sweetly.

"Which professional barricade are you planning to storm at your advanced age?" Myles asked, eyebrows lifted.

"It's important to all women, no matter what their age, to fight against discrimination!" she exploded.

"You're right," he agreed mildly.

"Sorry. I didn't mean to blow up at you."

"You never do."

Gina blushed and seemed glad to reach her door. "I'd ask you in for a drink of warm soda, but I don't want to disturb Susan," she whispered.

"Gina," he admonished, "how you continue to underrate me. Susan left for home the day before yesterday. You have the room to yourself now."

As she stood there, a bit pink and embarrassed, Myles took the key out of her hand, unlocked the door and returned the key.

"How about dinner at the Lodge tomorrow night?"

"I'm having dinner there tomorrow night . . . but not with you."

Myles whistled all the way back to his car. He rather thought he'd had the best of this particular encounter and that the last helpful piece of information would permit him some prior planning.

He arranged to have dinner the next night with the wife of a friend who was attending a convention in California. He had asked if Myles would look in on Cecily now and then. This dinner obliged his friend and benefited Myles.

He spotted Gina the moment he and Cecily walked into the restaurant. She was one of a party of six, which included Mona and Wanda. Not surprisingly, her escort was the cherub-faced student who had carried her shopping bags out of Myles's apartment.

About five minutes after he and Cecily were seated—he chose the chair facing Gina—Gina spotted him. He saw her eyes widen. Then she seemed to be having trouble deciding whether to smile or frown.

One searching glance at Cecily, a tall and extremely pretty brunette, and Gina evidently cast her vote for displeasure. Her attention was withdrawn, and she immediately became overly vocal and vivacious. From time to time Myles looked in her direction and noted that, if she continued at her present rate, she wouldn't have a fingernail left by the time the evening was over.

He came up behind her at the buffet table about twenty minutes later. "Having a good time, Gina?"

"Lovely," she said, pointing her nose toward the ceiling.

"Liar." He helped himself to a heaping portion of shrimp. Her own plate was half empty. He eyed it disapprovingly. "If I were paying for your meal, I would certainly feel cheated."

"Fortunately," she pointed out before stalking off, "you are not."

Half an hour later he saw her at the dessert table and hastily offered to get Cecily the fruit tart she was struggling to resist.

Gina, with strawberry shortcake in her hand, backed around the table in the way that was peculiarly her own. Myles was in her path by design, not by accident.

The crash was not as glorious as the one they had had at the Associates' Court in the Museum of Natural History. They collided without falling, and only one piece of cake went flying.

They both sank to their knees simultaneously to retrieve it, looking a bit like two revivalists at a prayer meeting. The situation did not attract everyone's notice, but there were enough people nearby to make the effort worthwhile.

"We've really got to stop meeting like this," Myles bawled at her lustily. "My wife is getting suspicious."

In the midst of the laughter, Gina scrambled to her feet and, being Gina, reacted in a totally original fashion. Her smile was positively Cheshire-like, and in her eyes was the dawning of a new respect.

"I didn't think you would dare," she told Myles almost admiringly.

"You have a lot to learn," he answered calmly. "Where

you're concerned, I would dare anything." He saw the chill come back to her eyes, and before he could hear it in her voice, he quickly said the rest of his piece. "I let you down once, Gina. Are you going to hold that against me the rest of our lives? I never will again."

"I know you won't, because you're not going to get the chance."

"Who are you fighting, Gina—me or yourself?"

She started to speak, then changed her mind, grasping her lower lip between her teeth and trying to get her face under control. She was about to leave when Myles said softly, persuasively, "It's a losing battle, darling, and the ending's inevitable."

He watched her, smiling, as she swung fiercely away.

Chapter 17

"Cousin Clemmie! Cousin Clemmie!"

A whirlwind in blue skirts and lace-edged petticoats came sailing into the parlor, her face hidden behind the pages of a newspaper.

Clementina Rind set down her silver teapot. "Rietta, dear," she began, but the whirlwind buried her face deeper and interrupted her.

"Cousin Clemmie, listen to this essay on women from Purdie and Dixon's *Gazette*. You haven't read it yet, have— Oh, of course not, John Pinkney has just returned from fetching it. Hear this . . . 'Those who consider Women only as pretty figures, placed here for ornament, have but a very Improper Idea of the Sex—'"

"Well, child?"

"Oh, that is but the start. There's nothing to disagree with yet, but wait, it's how they go on. 'Men destined to great action have a certain fierceness, which only Women can correct.' No great action for women, you observe?"

"My dear, it's no more than they have said before, and I never saw you quite so heated. We'll discuss it later. Just now I—"

"Dear ma'am, I have only begun. I could forgive them

111

much that went before, but listen now." In a voice choked with fury, she read on. "'If Men require the tender application of Women to render them more tractable, those, on the other hand, equally want the Conversation of Men to awaken their Vivacity . . . besides female Minds'— Good God! Pay heed to this part—'Female minds, overwhelmed with Trifles, would languish in ignorance if Men, recalling them to more elevated objects, did not communicate Dignity and Vigor.'" She dashed angry tears from her eyes. "It's not the education men deny us that makes us insipid, you understand, only our own pitiful brains."

"Rietta, calm yourself. Why not—"

"Please, Cousin Clemmie, let me finish. 'If men are of stronger Frame, it is the more effectually to contribute to the Happiness of those who are more delicate.' More delicate, indeed! I wonder if either of those gentlemen has ever seen a woman brought to childbed. The long, tormented hours of labor for the delicate ones, while he of the so-called stronger frame drinks himself into a stupor till the business is done."

"Rietta, enough!"

"'One sex was not designed to be the Oppressor of the other . . .' Of course not, it simply turned out that way—"

"Rietta, be silent!"

"'We are born Women's Friends . . .' Ha! I'll believe that when they give as much consideration to covering their wives as they do their mares . . . 'and that strength—'"

"Rietta Rind, will you cease your clack? I have been trying to tell you these last five minutes that we have a guest."

"We do? Good gracious!" She pulled the paper down from her face and burst out laughing. "I'm so sorry, Cousin Clemmie, I didn't mean to shock one of your friends. I—I—"

A figure moved in the shadows, and instead of the expected matron in cap and cape, a young man in a sober and elegant suiting of brown came forward to take her reluctant hand and smile into her scarlet face.

"This is Mr. Stuart, who is reading law with Mr. Wythe. Mr. Stuart, may I make you known to my husband's cousin, Miss Rietta Rind of Philadelphia, who has lately made her home with us."

"I am honored, madam," he said easily, addressing Mrs. Rind rather than Rietta, "but I believe that Miss Rietta and I have met before."

At these words, Jeremy felt rather than saw the girl at his side stiffen up as though a paralysis had affected her tongue.

"Yes, I am quite certain it was Miss Rind who attended me," he went on casually, "when I brought in some advertisements on behalf of Mr. Buffington."

There was a pause while the older woman glanced with puzzlement at the younger, and the gentleman studied Rietta serenely, something akin to tender amusement on his face.

It was that look which made up Mrs. Clementina Rind's mind. "If you will excuse me, Mr. Stuart, I will take Mr. Wythe's message to my husband. There is no one whose good wishes he will value more. Rietta, do give Mr. Stuart another cup of tea, if he can bear the patriot's brew we so misname. Good afternoon, Mr. Stuart. I hope to have the pleasure of seeing you another time."

"Your servant, ma'am." He bowed. "I will certainly call again, if I may."

There was another short pause after she rustled out of the room. "Have you lost the permanent use of your tongue?" Jeremy inquired of Rietta civilly. "I certainly did not intend the sight of me to be quite such a shock as that. I would as certainly regret the loss of your conversation. It has such . . . such spice of originality."

"Why did you come here?"

He raised his eyebrows. "Why, I believe Mrs. Rind told you. I came to deliver a note from Mr. Wythe to Mr. Rind."

"Mr. Wythe sends his notes by servants."

"Exactly. In this case, I am his humble and obedient servant. Come, now," Jeremy continued persuasively, "after I spent so much thought contriving how we should meet again, should I not take advantage of a heaven-sent situation when I heard Mr. Wythe instructing Nathaniel to deliver his message?"

"I would expect you, sir, to take advantage of any opportunity," Rietta remarked with a barbed smile. This provocation drawing from him only a shout of laughter, she added, shrugging, "Oh, do sit down. I am instructed to give you tea, remember." As Rietta handed him a cup, her manner softened. "Indeed, we are all grateful for any message from Mr. Wythe. Cousin William is always so pleased to hear from him. He brought Cousin William to Williamsburg originally, did you know that?"

"No, I did not. When was this?"

"Some seven or eight years ago. Cousin William had a prosperous newspaper in Annapolis then, and here in Williamsburg there was only one, with nothing disagreeable to the Crown's view ever appearing in its pages. So Mr. Jefferson and Mr. Wythe and other men of more liberal views approached Cousin William to move his *Gazette* here."

"The idea appears to have been mutually agreeable."

"Yes." A faint sadness shadowed her face. "Which is another reason I am glad that Mr. Wythe still concerns himself with Cousin William."

"Something is amiss?"

"He is dying," Rietta answered curtly.

Jeremy put down his cup. "I am very sorry, Miss Rietta," he said gently.

"I do not think he knows," she responded, half to herself, "and Cousin Clemmie fears but will not face it. . . . Pray, sir," she rallied herself to say with an air of self-mockery, "I beg you not to look at me with quite so much sympathy, lest I burst into self-pitying tears."

He took his tone from hers and matched it. "I can't believe you would be guilty of acting so like a 'delicate woman.' I am persuaded that any tears of yours, like your Quaker speech, would be a sign of temper."

"You deduce a great deal from one short meeting, Mr. Stuart," she observed demurely.

"I have never been proficient in mathematics, but even I can count that our meetings, previous to this one, add up to two."

She sat very straight and stared at him in consternation. "I think thee m-must be m-mistaken, sir," she faltered.

"And I think," Jeremy told her deliberately, "though you make a dashing boy, I prefer you in your laces and your lutestring." He added casually, "I like your custom of going without a cap. Your hair is much too pretty to hide."

Rietta seemed to be having trouble with her breathing. "H-how d-did you kn-know?" she finally managed to ask.

"You give yourself away." He grinned. "Quaker spitfires do not abound in Williamsburg."

With great effort she forced herself to say, "I . . . I . . . you have my thanks for not speaking of it before Cousin Clemmie."

"Then she doesn't know?"

"Of course not. You don't suppose—" Rietta broke off, eying him with displeasure at having been trapped so neatly. "You have lawyers' ways already," she declared resentfully.

"For God's sake, why do you do it?"

"There were only three occasions," she defended herself.

"I have been helping with the writing of the *Gazette* since Cousin William took ill. I was used to it from my earliest years. My father is a printer, too, in Philadelphia. It was such a tame, bloodless way of writing, merely to copy from government reports and attend the public sessions of the burgesses and the General Court. My cousin always mingled with both men of affairs and ordinary men in their more private and social moments. He considered them his best source of news, and so do I."

"You must surely know how unwise it is of you."

"What harm if no one knows? Well, yes, *you* do, but I am persuaded you won't betray me."

"For the present, no, but I make no promises for the future." Jeremy's eyes were twinkling. "Before you lose *thy* temper," he teased, "pray remember that it is hardly politic to antagonize a creditor, even if the debt be silence rather than money."

She considered him a moment in frowning silence; then, before he could guess at her intent, she had risen and sunk into a deep curtsy before him. "It seems I have no alternative, Mr. Stuart, but to throw myself on the mercy of the court."

Rietta's palms were gracefully upright alongside her billowing skirts. The bowed head caused chestnut curls to tumble from the back of her neck over the front of her shoulders. Looking down, Jeremy could see not only the lace edging of her chemise above the rounded bodice but much else that an upright position would have concealed.

He set his teeth so hard his jaw ached from the effort of restraint required to keep his hands off the slender neck and chestnut head, and his eyes from the swelling whiteness below her shift.

"Acquitted," he said huskily, and immediately she bounded up with the coltish grace of the boy she pretended to be, kicking free of her skirts and sweeping back the coppery curls.

"Conditionally," he added. "Only if you will allow me to escort you to the Apollo Room at the Raleigh for the next ball there, dressed, I must insist, in a gown."

Her eyes grew round with surprise, then narrowed in concentration. "Why?" Rietta asked baldly.

"Because, Quaker spitfire, your company would please me," he said gently.

"Your father is a burgess?"

"Not any longer."

"A planter?"

"Yes."

"And you read law with Mr. Wythe, one of the most outstanding men in Virginia, and his friends are your friends, while I am a printer's daughter as well as a printer's cousin. I sometimes work in the shop below and get ink on my hands. See, it does not remove easily. Sometimes I work in the shop out front and sell. . . . We have Mr. Fielding's *Tom Jones,* leather-bound in four volumes, if you are in need of an expensive gift for your father. What I am trying to say, Mr. Stuart—"

"What you are trying to say need not be said, Miss Rind. I wish you to come to the ball with me. I wish to walk with you and have further conversation with you, and I very much wish to dance with you. I assure you my father need not concern you any more than yours concerns me."

"I will . . . I will ask Cousin Clemmie."

"Why not *tell* Cousin Clemmie instead?" Jeremy suggested easily, bowing over her hand. "I shall call again, Miss Rietta, to discuss our plans."

"Thank you," she whispered.

"Thank *you,*" he returned politely.

Then they were smiling at each other—warm, secret smiles—and her hand was in his, and the new, dazed knowledge was on both their faces . . .

The Virginia Gazette, published by Alexander Purdie and John Dixon at Williamsburg

On Thursday, the 19th instant, after a lingering illness, died Mr. William Rind, publick printer to the Colony, who supported the Character of affectionate Husband, kind Parent and benevolent Man.

His remains were interred last Saturday afternoon in the Church of the Parish of Bruton.

"Miss Rietta, I would have come sooner had I known. I was on a visit to my home, and only on my return this morning was I informed by Mr. Wythe. I offer you my most profound condolences. How do you and Mrs. Rind go on?"

"Fortunately, we have not had much time for grieving. There is a newspaper to be run."

"You intend to continue the *Gazette?*"

"Why so astonished, Mr. Stuart?" Rietta asked lightly. "Have you been reading Purdie and Dixon on the abilities of women? Yes, Cousin Clem intends to continue the *Gazette*. It is a matter of necessity, not only inclination, or did you not know that there are five fatherless infants to be supported?"

"Good God, no, I did not."

"John and I will stay on and help."

"John?"

"John Pinkney. He is Cousin Clemmie's closest kin and has lived with my cousins even longer than I. The truth is that all of this last year, while Cousin William was failing, the three of us have been managing most of his affairs. So circumstances are not much different from before . . . if the public can but be brought to believe that a woman can run a newspaper."

"*You* can make anyone believe anything," Jeremy declared boldly.

"Thank you, Mr. Stuart." A brief smile flitted across her face as she stood up. "In that case, I had best get started, had I not? You do understand we are greatly occupied now?"

"Of course." He followed her to the door, and when Rietta would have sketched a small curtsy, he took her hand instead. "I have not forgotten your promise. I know I will have to wait for our ball, but there are other means of meeting."

She tried to retrieve her hand. "I—I do not see how. We—we— Oh, yes, Dick." She turned thankfully as footsteps stomped behind them. "Do you need me?"

The sleeves of the servant's shirt were rolled up above the elbows of brawny brown arms; he rolled them down as he spoke. "Mr. Pinkney's needing you in the print room, Miss Rietta."

"Thank you, Dick. Pray excuse me, Mr. Stuart. Dick, please show Mr. Stuart out."

With a fleeting glance that mingled faint apology with a measure of relief, she turned and fled.

Chapter 18

As May drew to an end, Myles became strongly aware that he was not getting much further with Gina. True, she battled royally with him on almost every offered occasion, but he began to feel it was becoming more of a Pavlovian response rather than the expression of a strong need. He would rather have her enmity than her indifference.

He tried staying away from her for a longer period, but when Myles would reappear, he could hardly flatter himself that his absence had made any change. During the bad moments that came on him in the night, he would wonder if she had even noticed.

Mornings, hope revived, he would march out again to do battle. It was, if nothing else, a unique method of going after a girl. As a boy, Myles had mooned over King Arthur's knights and dreamed of slaying dragons for his lady. He had never dreamed his lady would turn out to *be* the dragon.

On a clear June day he awoke to the brilliant notion that a definite time limitation should be set for patience to remain a virtue.

Myles leaped out of bed to study the rough worksheet he had drawn up of Gina's schedule. A full day at Prentis, but an hour for lunch. She was going to have lunch with him, by

God, if he had to drag her out of the store, across the road and into a restaurant by the silken hank of her hair!

His caveman fervor was properly damped when he turned up at the shop only to discover that Gina hadn't. "She's not working today," Lily explained. "She traded her day off with me."

"I think Gina mentioned she was going to lunch with Wanda and her aunt," Mona offered.

Unfortunately, since he didn't know Wanda's aunt or where she lived, this kindly bestowed tidbit failed to help him. Disconsolately, Myles wandered down Duke of Gloucester, across the Palace Green, and then doubled back along Nicholson Street.

He saw her on the other side of the street, headed in his direction and tearing along as though a pack of rodents were snapping at her ankles. She went flying by as Myles crossed over to her, and he flew after her, seized one arm and spun her around. He saw great, terrified eyes in a white, staring face; then she flung herself into his arms, her whole body shuddering.

"Gina, what is it, dear heart?"

"April!" she gasped. "April! April!" Her hands trembled against his shirt front. "It was April," she sobbed. "I saw April."

Myles put his arm around Gina and drew her away from the curious, up North England Street and around to the garden behind the windmill. He lifted her easily over a collapsed section of the snake fence, his heart stirring with pity because she was so light and pliant between his hands, so unlike Gina.

She stood there, shivering and shaking, until he followed her over the fence and led her past the pumpkin patch, the squash and the sunflowers to a tremendous log lying on its side. When the tourist season was over, it would be cut to make a new support for the windmill. At present it served as a perfect screen for the pair.

He sat with his back against the log, and Gina twisted sideways beside him, her head burrowing into one of his shoulders and her hand clutching the other.

Myles held her hard, patting every inch of her anatomy his hands could reach. Unashamedly, he uttered whatever words of love and reassurance came to his lips, while part of his mind wrestled, dazedly, with the fact that he could feel and say so much so freely.

Eventually Gina's sobs subsided to occasional whimpering

sounds as her body became still against him. When he felt her first faint effort to strain away, he knew that *her* mind was at work again, too.

Myles would not let her go. He stroked her hair and tense shoulders, kissed her exposed temple and one ear, then whispered, "Gina, who is April?"

She jerked away from him and sat up, rocking back on her heels. "No one," she said. "I mean . . . it's just some silliness of mine."

"Then tell me about the silliness."

"I . . . I can't."

"Can't or won't?"

She looked down, not answering.

"You've been wailing that name like a banshee from the very first moment I met you. I have a notion *she* was why I met you in the first place. Silly or not, I want to know." He studied the shuttered eyes and watched the drooping mouth turn sullen and willful again, and the most godawful fury came over him. "You might as well talk, because you're not leaving here until you do." He shook Gina with angry purpose. "Who the bloody hell is April?"

After Gina's first instinctive resistance, she wanted to talk about April. Gina *had* to tell someone, and in spite of everything that had happened between them—maybe because of it—Myles was the one she trusted most to keep his mind open and his mouth shut. She would tell him what he wanted to know, a carefully edited version, of course.

"The first time I saw April," Gina began conscientiously, now sitting with her back against the log instead of against Myles, "I think I was about eight and a half."

She began to laugh at herself a little because she had spoken only one sentence and already the protective phoniness had set in. What did she mean, *think?* Gina had studied the newspaper clippings often enough, God knew. She had been eight years, five months and seven days old.

The custody battle between her mother, Naomi, and her father had raged for several weeks. Gina had sat through her part of it, squirming with discomfort. She relived it all now, talking to Myles.

"It was warm for April and the courtroom felt damp and airless. I remember my dress was made of some nylon mixture. It stuck to me, and I kept thinking longingly of the jeans and knit tops that I had lived in when I was with Mimi, my father's first wife."

Gina was quiet for so long that finally Myles prompted, "Go on."

She hugged her knees and turned her neck to stare at the windmill. They seemed a world away from the stuffy courtroom and the judge making the incredible pronouncement . . .

"Naomi got custody of me," Gina told Myles dully. "Daddy got visitation rights. It made no sense, no sense at all. We all knew that *he* wanted me and *she* didn't."

Gina swallowed hard. "I was sitting between Mimi and Daddy. He was half frantic himself and at the same time trying to make *me* understand. Mimi was crying her eyes out. I kept telling her, 'Don't cry, Mimi. I'll come see you all the time, I promise I will.'

"Which didn't prevent me, when the police matron came to take me, from kicking her in the shins and butting my head in her stomach."

She smiled wryly up at Myles. "Daddy said the same thing to me that I had said to Mimi. 'I'll come see you all the time.' Then he went one promise better. 'I'll have you back for keeps someday. Just be patient, sweetheart.'"

Gina leaned back against the log. "I was nothing if not a realist, and even at that age I could figure out that a man about to go off on a six-month job in Africa wouldn't be able to drop in very often at a New York apartment."

"Did he?" Myles asked.

She shrugged. "Naomi was much too smart to stick around and find out how much visiting he could manage. She took me home to England. At least," Gina amended bitterly, "it was home to her, never to me. It wasn't until years later, when I went there with Daddy, that I thought of England as anything but a fish-cold country with fish-cold people like my mother's family. Their aristocratic noses had a way of wrinkling up at the sound of my Italian-Jewish name, the only one of that mixture introduced into their clan in the last six hundred years."

"Weren't you perhaps just a little oversensitive?" Myles asked gently.

"No way." Gina grimaced. "Believe me, they let me know how they felt, plain and clear. I took it then, but long afterward I used to wonder what made them so proud of such inbred purity. They were so damn blue-blooded, most of them didn't have anything left in their veins, red *or* blue. Cousins had married cousins with fantastic regularity, all except my grandmother. She gambled on an Irish title, but after having produced my mother, Grandad bit the dust, and the title went to a younger brother. So, no wealthier and with only a redheaded daughter to show for it, Grandmother came back to England and married her cousin George."

"Did Cousin George and Grandmother have any progeny?" Myles asked.

She grinned. "Three sons, each one more pale and wan and washed-out-looking than the other. George and Grandmother looked exactly alike, and their children—my uncles James, John and Henry—looked like their parents. My mother certainly bewildered them—all that vitality, to say nothing of her beauty."

"Was she so beautiful?"

Gina closed her eyes, seeing Naomi as she used to be, trying to make Myles see her, too. "She had a gorgeous head of red-gold hair, creamy satin skin, a sexy mouth, eyes like mine . . . , I suppose I should say mine are like hers. She was quite fashionably tall and slim, with a slinky walk and a sensational body. Oh, I admit she must have had a hard time growing up among them, suspiciously reared as a changeling-in-reverse. Years later, figuring it all out, I could even have found it in my heart to pity her if I hadn't known Naomi was a prime example of beauty being only skin-deep. In every other way that counted," Gina finished coldly, "she was a true member of that fish-cold clan and really just as ashamed as they were of my father's background."

"Why did she marry him?"

"At the time they met, it must have seemed expedient. Her career as an actress was foundering, and there was all of Daddy's lovely money and the byproducts of travel and fame.

"It must have been a brutal shock to her when his career came to a stunning standstill and, financially, he began to run downhill. Poor bitch," Gina added with chilling dispassion. "Naomi never once realized it was because of their arid marriage. She couldn't begin to understand that he thrived on love and warmth and a different kind of beauty from hers."

"Was it lack of money that ended the marriage?"

Gina gave that irritating shrug again. "Eventually, I suppose. She could have tolerated the drying up of his talent, but never of his bank accounts. Their debts got bigger and their quarrels got nastier, and it was very much a two-bedroom marriage. The best times were when Naomi landed an occasional out-of-town acting job and Cissie, our five-day-a-week maid, lived in temporarily."

Gina smiled reminiscently. "Cissie was six feet tall and skinny as a telephone pole, with an easygoing nature. She made the best lemon meringue pie I've ever eaten, and I adored her. I was never as happy as when Naomi took off on one of her jobs—which I now suspect had been arranged sub rosa by Daddy—and Cissie became part of our household.

"It was sometime during one of those halcyon periods that Daddy first took me to Mimi's. Much later, I learned that Mimi was his first wife. Naomi had broken up their marriage."

"Mimi lived out in Southampton, Long Island, on a triangular point of beach where the Atlantic and the Shinnecock Bay met in roaring, foaming splendor. The view from the front windows was of scrub brush; from the rear, of the sky and the ocean. The backyard was sand and seashells, to crunch underfoot or to collect. Mimi's house was an oversized saltbox of weathered shingles, more like a Cape Cod cottage than a Southampton summer home. Nothing inside it was valuable, just pleasant and comfortable and a bit shabby, like Mimi herself.

She was the unfussiest woman Gina had ever met. Half an hour with her, and the most nervous person would begin to unwind. That included Gina, and it certainly included her father. She never saw him look so peaceful or content, or laugh so boyishly, as when they were with Mimi.

"Going home from our third visit with Mimi," Gina continued to a patiently waiting Myles, "Daddy told me, in the usual oblique way he communicated anything concerning Naomi, that Mimi wasn't a friend of my mother's. Naomi was expected back from California the next day, and I understood quite clearly that he meant I shouldn't mention Mimi to my mother or she'd spoil it for us. I told him it'd be our secret, which was my way of saying he shouldn't worry, I wouldn't let the cat out of the bag."

"Did you ever?" Myles asked.

"No, I didn't." Gina smiled ruefully. "Someone else did . . . but that was later on. For a while, things were okay. When there were no acting jobs and Naomi got restless, Daddy scraped up enough money to send her to one of the places she loved—Palm Springs, West Palm Beach, Bermuda, Jamaica, the Virgin Islands. She always acted as though

Castro kept Americans out of Cuba just to spite her personally. We would take her to the airport, wave her off with flowers and candy and magazines, then turn east at the exit and keep going till we got to Mimi's."

One day in late May—how her father managed it, Gina never knew; more debts, she supposed—Naomi went off to Europe for the entire summer. Before her departure, Gina overheard her father suggest that Naomi take their daughter along, since he'd be going back and forth to California quite a lot and she might be lonesome.

Gina didn't worry that he meant it. She knew if he seemed *too* willing to let Naomi go without their child, she might get suspicious. This way she backed off fast, saying she couldn't drag an eight-year-old around England and France and Monte Carlo. It would tie her down too much, and Gina would be bored with the places she was going to. As long as Cissie was there, even if Gina's father wasn't, Gina would be happy and well taken care of.

"And were you?" Myles wanted to know.

"You bet. The day after Naomi left, Daddy arranged for an answering service to monitor calls to the apartment, and then he packed Cissie and me off to Mimi's to spend the summer." Gina laughed almost happily. "Mimi took one look at the clothes in my suitcase and consigned almost everything I owned, except underwear, to the attic for the next few months. Then she hauled me off to town to buy shorts and cotton blouses and jeans, sweat shirts, a windbreaker with a hooded jacket and a couple of pairs of sneakers.

"That summer with Mimi was the happiest of my life," Gina reflected. "Unfortunately, it didn't remain a secret. Too many people my parents knew weekended in the Hamptons. They went to the same restaurants and antique shops and summer theaters. Months later, in January, someone must have gotten a tremendous amount of pleasure from telling Naomi about Mimi."

"I take it," said Myles, looking at Gina's face, "that it was bad."

"It was very bad," Gina agreed. "The quarrels got bigger and uglier as the weeks went by. In the end, Naomi turned so nasty toward me for what she called my 'disloyalty' that Daddy secretly packed me up again and returned me to Mimi."

Gina studied a patch of tobacco plants with their large, kite-shaped leaves. "I didn't know until afterward that he had done it without her knowledge or consent. It took investigators and lawyers to track me down. Then came the lawsuit to restore me to my mother, and Daddy's countersuit to leave me where I was.

"After the decision, when I kicked the police matron, the judge took me to his private chambers for a few minutes to reason with me. It was a mistake on his part, since I wasn't feeling reasonable. He sent a guard to bring Daddy. They talked outside the door together, leaving me alone for a few minutes."

Gina had stood at the window and stared sullenly out at the traffic below. Her rage turned inward now. She wasn't prepared to believe anything that the judge *or* her father said. Her father could have gotten away from Naomi if he had really wanted to; he had done it before, hadn't he? He was smart enough and strong enough to do anything. A treacherous thought invaded her mind and wouldn't be pushed away. Maybe he didn't really want to. She had pressed an aching head against the pane.

"I didn't hear anyone come through the door," Gina continued, eyes closed, remembering, "but I felt a presence and turned around. There was April, in a long, blue-flowered dress that was prettier to my eyes than anything I had ever seen Naomi wear to an evening party."

April stood on the other side of the judge's desk, smiling at her so kindly, so . . . so *lovingly*, that Gina felt a sudden release of the tight little lump in her stomach that was half anger, half despair.

"Hello," Gina had said. "Who're you?"

"April. Call me April."

"Silly, April is a month. It's April now."

"The month of growth and new life," April had said in her whispery way, which wasn't really in a speaking voice but more like a sound inside Gina's throbbing head. "Yours is just beginning. If you are patient, it will be the one you want."

"I want to live with Daddy and Mimi."

"I promise you, one day you will."

"How do you know?"

April's smile was serene and beautiful. Gina felt the warmth that seemed to wrap her in its arms even as they stood there, a room apart. She battled with insecurity and the remembrance of Naomi and promises broken. As though April knew this, her message came through loud and clear at the very moment she herself was fading away. *Trust me, I won't fail you.*

When her father came into the room, Gina flung herself into his arms and begged him to promise he'd try to get her for keeps. He swore he would on his mother's memory, and Gina knew that was the most sacred promise he could make.

"He kept his promise, didn't he?" Myles reminded her.

She hesitated. "Yes, I suppose, but it took a hell of a while. What I didn't know till long afterward was the reason why. It took a hell of a lot of money, too.

"Over in England, April kept drifting in on me from time to time, reassuring me that all would be well.

"When summer came, Daddy demanded his visitation rights in one lump period and came and got me. I knew he had gone back to Mimi. Mimi, not Naomi, was his wife now, and to my simple way of thinking, nothing could be better. It meant that when he got me back, Mimi would be my mother.

"The second summer on Long Island wasn't quite the joyful one of the year before, not with Naomi's home in England waiting for me at the end of the rainbow."

Gina ran her fingers lightly across the log. "When I pestered Daddy about having me for keeps," she said, low-voiced, "he repeated his promise. 'I'm working on it all the time, Gina *mia*.' He was, too. He did everything he could in those days to pile up money. He had always been a dynamo for work, but now he usually had two or three projects going at once, the sooner to buy off Naomi. Mimi told me all about it later, when we lived together."

Gina hesitated. "Once, only once, I tried to tell Mimi about April. She reacted with a half-amused alarm, saying I was seeing and hearing things because of all the hot apple pie and ice cream I'd eaten before bed.

"I loved Mimi dearly, but I should have realized that she could never accept anything unless she could touch or taste it, reach out and get a grip on it. She was too much of the real world." Gina smiled ruefully. "I tried with my father, too. On my Christmas visit later that year, when they were living in California, Daddy took me to Disney-land. While we were wandering through Fantasyland, I tried to tell him. He gave my hair a tug and said, 'Such imagination. I think I'll make a writer out of you when you grow up. Then we can work together.'

"I gave up on telling anyone after that. In a way, I wasn't sorry to have it be a secret. That made April even more special. No one else I knew had a lovely dream lady like her. She was mine, all mine."

Myles brought Gina back to the main discussion. "What happened next?"

Gina shifted onto her back and gazed up at a flowering branch. "The next year, when I was almost eleven," she continued obediently, "Daddy paid for me to go to school in Switzerland. Of course, Naomi didn't know that, two days before I went to Geneva, my father and Mimi had arrived there for a six-month stay.

"I saw April very seldom when I was in Switzerland," she murmured dreamily. "Gradually, I realized she mostly came around when I seemed to have a special need for her. Like the time not too long after Naomi had caught on to our trickery and yanked me out of my Swiss school. She was living in a small suite in one of the older London hotels, and she didn't want me with her any more than I wanted to be there. I had to sleep on the couch in her pokey living room, which most certainly must have cramped her style when her escorts brought her home. She always had a man in tow, because she was still what in England they called a smasher." Biting contempt crept into Gina's voice. "Soon she would start seeking consolation for lost opportunities in a martini glass."

After Gina arrived from Geneva, Naomi took to coming home much later at night than she had before. So Gina was alone when the pain struck. God, but it was awful; she had thought she was going to die. Gina was cold and shivering and hot and sweating and shaking all at the same time. She managed to turn on the table lamp near the couch, but when she tried to get up, she fell over onto the floor.

It seemed easier to stay there, and no one outside the door heard her thin little screams.

Except April . . .

One moment Gina was on the floor, doubled up with pain, and the next moment April was beside her. Though there was never any touch between them, it was as though Gina could feel cool hands on her head and then on her body, soothing away the terrible pain.

April told her to get to the phone. Gina grit her teeth and really made an effort, but she couldn't. April insisted that she push the chair ahead of her and crawl.

And that was how Gina did it, inch by painful inch, until she could tug at the dangling telephone wires and pull the instrument down to the floor.

"I'm awful sick," she had moaned into the receiver. After that the front desk took over, but April stayed with her till the ambulance arrived.

"The pain will be gone soon, but the happiness is just beginning," April had told her while she was being bundled onto a stretcher.

"What happiness?"

"You're going home, little Gina."

"Forever?"

"Forever is a long time. Be content for now."

They got Gina into surgery before her appendix burst. When she came out of the anesthetic, her father was there. By the time she left the hospital, he and Naomi had worked out their new agreement. Gina belonged to him now, and Naomi was the one with visitation rights.

"Life got very good for me then," Gina assured Myles. "We lived mostly in California during the next three to four years. Our home was in Beverly Hills and had a swimming pool, though secretly I still preferred Mimi's beach house.

"I missed April, but I think she knew I no longer had such a desperate need for her." Her expression softened. "What I remember most vividly is that the first time I called Mimi 'Mother,' she cried and cried. As far as I was concerned, she *was* my mother. She still is. I never forgave my father for marrying again after Mimi died, even though he claimed to be doing it for my sake."

"What happened to Mimi?" Myles asked gently after a long silence.

"She was killed in a car accident, on the way back from taking Daddy to the airport. I was fifteen at the time. After that, Daddy and I lived and traveled all over Europe, and April went with me all the time. She continued to stay by me when we came home and he married again, and then one day she up and disappeared."

"Why do you suppose that happened?"

"I don't know," Gina answered dully. "I was miserable and uncertain, but she wasn't there. I was bitter and reckless and willful, but she didn't seem to care."

The years passed. Gina thought April was gone for good, but her absence was more of a dull ache at the back of Gina's mind than actual pain. If she didn't probe, it didn't hurt too much, so she took care not to probe.

Gina could still feel the double shock of twisting around on the gigantic model dinosaur and seeing Myles give her an impersonal once-over, and then, just as he decided to move on, April was beside him.

April, her April. Gina couldn't believe it.

When she knocked Myles down and found April gone, it was all Gina could do not to make a spectacle of herself and burst into tears. But she needn't have worried; April kept coming back. Wherever Myles was, *she* was.

At first Gina had thought Myles was the reason. That hope died suddenly the day he left to go to Washington, but she was still convinced that April had used him to bring her to Williamsburg.

Williamsburg. Gina had been all over the world but had never found a place she immediately felt she belonged to. And yet it was crazy, too.

Queer things kept happening, not only the sense of déjà vu. Gina had directed the man to the Ludwell-Paradise House because she was so *sure* the printer had worked there. In the music shop, she had spoken about the girl violinist during the eighteenth century. Gina told Myles afterward that she had read of her somewhere. That wasn't true. Gina simply *knew*. She seemed to know and feel so much in Williamsburg, but that awareness had not frightened her until today.

Myles remained attentive while she talked of April. Gina's story didn't take long because she carefully pruned out certain people and places that would clue him in on whatever information she would rather not give him.

Myles had come a long way from the Washington Samaritan who didn't want to get involved with a neurotic hippie. It was unbelievable that he should be sitting so quietly, taking the supernatural calmly in his stride.

He pounced on the weak spot immediately. "What I don't understand is why you've suddenly become frightened. Look, I've been with you a number of times when your dream lady turned up. You were always overjoyed, behaving as though she were your best buddy. Why is today's appearance different from all those others?"

Gina shivered slightly, reliving the moment. "Because today I saw her, and she wasn't there. I mean, it wasn't April, it was a picture."

Myles took her by the shoulders again, very, very gently this time. "I'm sure *you* know what you mean," he said in the kindest of voices, "but it's a bit too convoluted for me. Now, take a nice, deep breath and try again."

Gina took several good, deep breaths. "It was a portrait of her that I saw. A *real* portrait."

"Where?"

"Wanda took me to her aunt's house for lunch. The aunt is descended from the people of Colonial Williamsburg, and she lives in their original house. It's one of those privately occupied homes that hasn't been deeded to the Foundation. After we ate, Wanda showed me around the whole house. Then, coming down the back stairs, I saw a group of miniatures hanging on the wall. Wanda told me they'd all been done in the seventeen hundreds. One of them was of April."

"Miniatures aren't always too clear. Are you sure it wasn't a chance resemblance?"

"Resemblance!" Gina repeated excitedly. "Myles, I know that face as well as I know my own! I tell you, it was she, down to the last detail, even to her blue-flowered dress. And her hair, a dark brown shade with reddish glints in the sunlight, falls in curls from the back of her neck, where it's tied in a big bow. She has dark, laughing eyes, and the special smile she gives me is the same as the one in her picture."

Gina laughed shakily. "Wanda must think I'm crazy. I gasped out some ridiculous excuse and ran out of the house like a loon."

After a while she looked up at Myles uncertainly. "Why do you think I was so frightened?" Before he could answer, Gina started to explain herself. "I guess it's because the whole situation has changed for me. When I was young, I never questioned the miracle of her being. When I grew up . . . well, I read as much as I could about such things and decided that perhaps I was a bit of a psychic. I talked to a psychiatrist once, and he said that the answer might be much simpler. I needed her, so I had made her up. Whichever it was, I accepted her as a marvelous gift—up until today. Even when the neurologist—" Gina broke off, biting her lips. "But, of course, he was wrong," she went on quickly. "The tests showed I didn't have a brain tumor." She shivered. "But now I'm scared, Myles. Don't you see? If April was a real person *two hundred years ago*, it's a *ghost* I've been seeing since I was a child!"

"I doubt it, Gina. But if it's true, then you were correct in one of your conclusions—you're a bit of a psychic. Let's not dismiss the psychiatrist altogether. There could be something in his diagnosis. In other words"—Myles moved his hands over Gina's shoulders and down her arms—"it's a combination of a lot of factors that produced her. I should think that finding out she was once a real person would make you feel better, not worse."

"Maybe it will when I've had time to think about it." Gina wished she weren't so conscious of those caressing hands along her arms. "My first reaction was instinctive," she admitted. "Pure panic."

"That was only natural."

Now his fingers were as light as feathers, smoothing away the damp strands of hair sticking to her forehead. She found herself trembling, but not with fear. They were talking about April, and thinking about each other.

"How long had it been before you saw her again in Washington?"

"She went away when I moved out," Gina whispered, "after my father—" She caught herself just in time and pushed his hands away very decidedly. Standing up, Gina brushed the dirt and grass off her skirt. "It was quite a while." She added casually, "I don't think April approved of my living on my own. And . . ."

"And?"

Gina wiped off Myles's indulgent smile with the reddest herring she could think of. "I don't think she much liked my sleeping around."

"No," he agreed in the clipped tone of voice that indicated a carefully controlled anger, "I don't think she would like that very much at all."

Checkmate, Gina thought dully, walking ahead of him toward the opening in the fence. If that didn't stop him, nothing would. Or would it just make him more determined to—

"Gina," he said behind her.

"Yes?" She kept right on going.

"It's not going to work." There was laughter in his voice. He swung her around to face his amused eyes. When she opened her mouth to protest, Myles only laughed again and gave her a shove that sat Gina down hard on the ground near the sunflower patch. "You know we're not going back to the cold war," he said, dropping down beside her. "Not after today."

"We're not going back to the way it was before," she flashed. "I can promise you that."

"I know it." Myles took her hand and planted a quick,

warm kiss on its palm. "I know I have to earn my spurs. All I'm asking is the chance to do it. Have dinner with me tonight."

"I have a date." He gave her a sharp, questioning look, and Gina answered it. "Truly I do. With Gary."

"Tomorrow, then?"

"Yes."

"How about making it early, followed by a concert?" Gina nodded, and he grinned. "I hear there's a girl violinist."

She was glad of an excuse to extricate herself from such an emotion-charged atmosphere. "I *told* you there were girl violinists," she said, wrinkling her nose at him.

"So you did, wise little Gina. How many odd things you know."

When he helped her back over the fence, they were laughing together as though he had said something exquisitely funny.

Chapter 19

"John said you wanted to see me, Cousin Clemmie. Did you know the new shipment of books from England has arrived? He's unpacking them. Oh, and I just ran upstairs to see to Maria. Sarey says she is feeling much improved and does not need poulticing any longer."

Jeremy, rising politely from the winged chair in the front parlor, smiled at the familiar, impetuous way in which she spoke, then frowned a little because her walk was less light, her air less untroubled. She looked both thin and tired.

All these things he noted as he murmured conventionally, "I am happy to see you, Miss Rietta."

"Mr. Stuart." She gave him the slightest of curtsies and remained standing in the doorway, poised for instant departure.

"Sit down, do, Rietta," Clementina Rind said. "Mr. Stuart has a most pleasing invitation for you. If you will excuse me, Mr. Stuart, I will see to the child before I answer the demands of my business."

He smiled gravely at Rietta once they were alone, and attacked without warning. "It has seemed a very long winter with your avoiding me, Miss Rietta."

"I did not." She colored, avoiding his eyes. I—perhaps I did," she acknowledged faintly. "It seemed wiser."

"May I ask why you thought it wiser, or should I perhaps ask, for whom?"

"For both of us. For obvious reasons. We live in different worlds, Mr. Stuart. Before Cousin William died, it was dif— Oh, you are too intelligent not to understand me!" she declared impatiently.

"Then I must be less intelligent than either of us had supposed. I cannot comprehend why Mr. Rind's death affects my wish to pursue your—" She looked up quickly. "Your friendship," Jeremy finished smoothly.

"I have not the time for friends," she replied in a tight voice. "The *Gazette* occupies us almost constantly, and when it does not, there are the children. Two of the others are sickening now, just as Maria is on the mend."

"Do you propose to give your life to Mrs. Rind?"

"No, sir, I do not. Cousin Clemmie will not always need me. If she does, then whatever I have to give her, I will give gladly. There was a time when I was needful, and she—who is kin to me only by marriage, I would remind you—offered me a home." Rietta's voice shook. "More than a home."

Jeremy came to stand over her. "Forgive me," he said quietly. "I did not mean to criticize Mrs. Rind. My remarks were prompted by my concern for you. I have missed you most abominably. You refuse all my invitations, and you disappear when I come to call. If Mr. Wythe had not kept my nose so firmly glued to my lawbooks, I would have been in flat despair."

In one of the lightning changes of mood that were so much a part of Rietta, she smiled up at him—the charming, lopsided smile that had enchanted him from the first.

"You to succumb to flat despair! *That* I will never believe," she claimed gaily. "First and last, you are a fighter, Mr. Stuart."

"I am glad you recognize it, Rietta."

The meaning in his voice was so unmistakable, she was, for once, at a loss for words. Rietta sat with her head lowered, the clasping and unclasping of her hands in her lap speaking more eloquently.

Presently she looked up and reverted to the former subject. "I would not wish you to think that I am overworked or— You must believe that I am happy, very happy, in what I do. There is no responsibility greater than the reporting of public events in a newspaper. Cousin Clemmie entrusts much more serious writing to me now, such as the foreign dispatches. I attend the sessions and—"

"I trust you still aren't going abroad in mens' clothes in search of your . . ." Studying her once-more reddened cheeks, Jeremy said, "I see that you have been." He walked over to the fireplace and stared into the flames, his fingers beating a forceful tattoo on the mantel. "I wish that you would not."

She sought to placate him. "It was only once or twice."

Jeremy turned back to her. "I wish I had the right to say that you might not do it at all, since once or twice is too often for my peace of mind."

Rietta jumped to her feet. "There is nothing on this earth that could ever give you or anyone else such a right!" she declared with angry passion.

"Not even a husband?"

"Especially not a husband. I'll not take a man to order my conduct, you may be sure of that. Do you wonder that I am so filled with gratitude for the *Gazette* and Cousin Clemmie? They permit me to be a free woman."

"Yes, I had forgotten." He was now as angry as she. "You told me as much at the Raleigh. To you, marriage is enslavement."

"Not marriage in itself, sir," Rietta said with contempt. "It is men who have made it so."

"And what kind of marriage would a woman make who felt free to go her own way, indifferent to a husband's wishes?"

"Are we speaking generally or specifically, sir? I would know before I answer."

"I am speaking of you, Rietta Rind," Jeremy replied softly and furiously.

"Then I can speak of what I know," she responded with deliberate calm. "My husband—if I took one, and if he gave me what I want of marriage—could make great claims on me. If he asked, for his peace of mind, that I give up my occupation, why, then, since I would never heedlessly seek his discomfort, I would." She inclined her head. This time her smile was not agreeable. "Does that answer your question, Mr. Stuart?"

He studied her, frowning, but no longer angry. "To understand the workings of your mind is a marvelously intricate process. Two minutes ago you said you would not give any man the right to—"

"Not the right to *tell* me," she interrupted excitedly. "Why should it be a man's right to tell a woman what she may or may not do? But to *ask* me, as one human being to another, and for me to consent so as not to give him pain. Dear God, why can you not see the difference?"

Jeremy suddenly came and knelt beside her feet. "Perhaps because thinking of your night excursions gives me so much anxiety as well as pain. And now I begin to see that the pain is partly jealousy. You mingle with other men in a way I do not like. Would you give up going abroad at night if I asked you to? I am prepared to *ask* most humbly."

"Oh, don't. Do get up, please. Cousin Clemmie—someone might come in."

He dusted off his knees and returned to the fireplace. "You have not given me an answer."

"But we were speaking of requests between partners in a marriage," Rietta objected.

He approached her once again. "Are you ready, then, to speak of marriage, ma'am?" Jeremy asked bluntly, and saw his answer in the rapid flutter of the laces at her bodice and in her movement of quick withdrawal.

"I thought so." His hand reached out, and with his thumb under her chin, he tipped her head back. She had no choice but to meet his eyes. "Don't look like that. I shan't eat you," he said reassuringly, then set her body in a quake again by adding, less reassuringly, "Not yet."

She still seemed unable to speak, and he laughed lightly. "I had almost forgotten my purpose for this visit." He extracted an envelope from a small pocketbook inside his jacket. "Mrs. Wythe begs your company for a musical evening this Friday next. Are you fond of music, Miss Rietta?"

"Exceedingly fond, sir."

"Do you play an instrument, ma'am, or is that a tactless question? All the young ladies in Williamsburg tease the spinet a little or can play enough on a harpsichord to look entrancing as they entertain."

Rietta's one-dimple smile appeared again. "I can do both of those."

"You will have the opportunity come Friday. May I *ask* you please to be ready when I arrive at eight o'clock to escort you?" When she hesitated, Jeremy reached for her hand again. "I asked you very humbly."

"I will be ready at eight o'clock, Mr. Stuart."

"I will count the hours till then, Miss Rietta."

"You sound like one of the more poetical effusions our readers send in to the *Gazette*."

"Perhaps you render me poetical."

"I prefer my compliments in plain, sincere prose."

"In that case, Rietta, allow me to say sincerely that I love you, plainly that I want you, and in prose that you were right. I am first and last a fighter, and I shall fight anyone I must to get you, yourself included. I give you good day, ma'am."

He left her feeling torn between anger at his highhandedness and breathlessly bemused by his frankness.

"I have a good mind not to go," she said aloud, knowing her words to be hypocritical. Even as she said them, she was planning her wardrobe.

Rietta was dressed and waiting in her best on Friday at eight. Her gown was of apricot satin with an embroidered bodice and underskirt. From a slender chain around her neck dangled a gold locket. Her curls were piled higher on her head than usual.

"I never realized before." Jeremy Stuart turned toward Clementina Rind. "She is beautiful, isn't she, ma'am?"

"I am surprised you have only just noticed, Mr. Stuart."

"I was diverted by other, more noticeable things about her."

A small foot in its buckled shoe set up a busy tapping.

"I have a tongue of my own, if anyone cares to address me directly."

"If there is one thing I have never had any doubt about, Miss Rietta," Jeremy assured her with cheerful impudence, "it is your ownership of a tongue."

Her hooded cape lay folded on a chair. He placed it carefully about her shoulders and handed her the brocade muff and lace fan that had been lying beside it. "Shall we fight it out as we walk to Mr. Wythe's?" he suggested agreeably.

There was no quarreling, however.

As Jeremy took her arm and led her down the outside steps, she asked, "How did Mrs. Wythe come to invite me?"

"Madame Elizabeth—Mrs. Wythe—is my dear, good friend. I have spoken much of you to her. Her invitation obliges me, it is true, but I think she and Mr. Wythe have a great curiosity to become acquainted with you."

"Mr. Wythe, too? You will have me doubly nervous."

He let go of her arm to take her hand. "No need. There is not a kinder or gentler man in all of Williamsburg."

Rietta gave Jeremy a teasing smile. "Nor a cleaner one. I did not bring my pomander tonight."

"It's true, but how do you know?"

"Why, Mr. Stuart, those daily baths of Mr. Wythe's are a matter of public record and comment. When first I came to Williamsburg, I would often slip out at six of a morning and walk across the Palace Green, close to his residence, solely for the pleasure of hearing him roar. The sounds, I was told, harmonized with his sprint to the well, naked to the waist, and his dousing with pails of cold water by a servant." Her smile was bright with mischief. "For so gentle a man, he makes a prodigious noise."

"Have you walked near his gardens recently?"

"After the first year I grew weary of the concert."

"You must listen again. There are two performers now," Jeremy told her. "He and I sprint and are doused daily together. Indeed, I think he would have tossed me out as hopeless in my first months of study if I had not partnered him in this other pleasure."

"So that is why I have not needed to perfume the air about you either," she said slyly. "I am indeed grateful to Mr. Wythe."

He tightened his hold on her hand to punish this impertinence. "You and he have much in common otherwise," Jeremy remarked. "He, too, had a Quaker mother, and he holds what are considered most advanced ideas on the education of women."

Rietta pulled her hand free and swung around eagerly to face Jeremy. "Oh, now I really long to meet him!"

"Come along, then. If I know Mr. Jefferson, the music will have begun."

It had. Three black servants were entertaining, one on the oboe, one on the guitar, while the third sang.

Mrs. Wythe, gracefully acknowledging the introduction and welcoming Rietta at the door of the small parlor, whispered, "Such a disappointment. We are short one violin. Rather, I should say, one violinist. Thomas sent his instrument by a servant earlier, but later there was a message that he was too unwell to attend. We will miss his performance unless we can prevail on you, Jeremy . . ."

"To take the place of Thomas Jefferson? I beg you will

excuse me, Madame Elizabeth. I do not wish to be laughed out of Williamsburg. You know—none better—what an indifferent performer I am. Whenever I commence to play, Mr. Wythe discovers urgent business in his wine cellar."

"Madame," Rietta began, and then stopped, as though sorry she had spoken.

"My dear?" Mrs. Wythe prodded gently.

"I was going to say," Rietta continued somewhat diffidently, "that if you do not think Mr. Jefferson would object to a stranger's using his instrument, then perhaps I . . ."

They were both looking at her in astonishment.

"My dear Miss Rind, Jeremy told me you were a girl of many unusual talents. Do you really tell me you play the violin?"

"Yes, ma'am, I do."

"Then I can assure you Thomas would be delighted to give you the use of his violin. I will inform my husband."

She bustled off, leaving them alone.

"Mr. Jefferson is a skilled performer," Jeremy noted quietly.

"I heard Mr. Henry play at the Raleigh one evening. He—" Rietta broke off, her scarlet cheeks and sudden confusion telling Jeremy under what circumstances she had heard Patrick Henry play. Then she tossed her head defiantly and asked, "Do you admire *his* playing?"

"He is considered the best natural fiddler in Virginia."

"You must judge for yourself, of course, but I would not be apprehensive of his opinion on my ability."

Though still doubtful, he nodded. In a short time, Mrs. Wythe returned to them. There was a little stir when Rietta was presented to the company and Thomas Jefferson's cherished violin was produced. Rietta set aside her fan and made a pad of her handkerchief, laying it against her shoulder as a rest for the violin while she studied the music.

One gentleman stood ready with his violin; two others gripped their horns. Rietta placed herself beside Mrs. Nicholson, who sat at the spinet.

When the group finished, there was strenuous applause, and urgent requests for a solo from Rietta. Without demur she complied with a popular song from *The Beggar's Opera*.

The demand for an encore brought the impish sparkle to her eye that Jeremy was well acquainted with. He was not unduly surprised when she sang as well as played her next selection.

> "I married a wife of late;
> The more's my unhappy fate.
> I took her for love
> As fancy did me move,
> And not for her wordly state.
>
> For qualities rare
> Few with her compare.
> Let me do her no wrong.
> I must confess
> Her chief amiss is only this:
> She cannot rule her tongue."

Rietta cast a saucy look across at Jeremy as she repeated her last chorus in different variations.

> "She cannot rule her tongue.
> She cannot rule her tongue."

Mr. Wythe voiced the curiosity of all when he questioned her about the unusual posture she used to hold her violin, resting it against her shoulder and under her chin instead of balancing it on her arm.

"My mother taught me this method, and she in turn was taught by a master from Europe."

There was no doubt that, among all the distinguished company gathered, the printer's cousin was the belle of the evening.

"Your mother must have been a rare woman," Jeremy observed as they walked home from her evening of triumph.

Rietta could only nod.

"Has she been long dead?"

"Fourteen months before I came to Williamsburg."

"And mine the year before that."

"It is the common fate of women to die young, used up."

He turned to stare at her, perplexed by the bitter despair in her voice. "I think perhaps you exaggerate," he said gently. "My mother was one of the happiest persons I ever knew."

"And mine . . . much good it did her."

There was a short pause. "Are you like her?"

"In looks, no. Her hair was much more red and her eyes

were blue. I favor my father's family. She was—how shall I put it?—not of the common mold. She came from a strong line of independent women. Her mother made a runaway marriage with a Quaker, and my mother was read out of meeting by the Quakers for her marriage to my father. My grandmother, too, was musical, and what the rest of the world considers overeducated."

"You are musical and educated as well, so your father must have concurred in her beliefs," Jeremy said thoughtfully.

Rietta shrugged. "At one time, perhaps. Some of his ideas originated with Mr. Franklin, for whom my father worked in Philadelphia when he was a young man. As long as it suited his convenience, he was pleased to have me that way. Later on . . ."

"Later on?" Jeremy prompted when she showed no signs of completing the thought.

"Later on I came to Williamsburg."

He knew this was not what she had started to say, but it seemed better to leave matters be. Instinct advised against his pressing onward.

"I was very proud of you all this evening," he told her. "Whenever someone praised you, I swelled up like a bullfrog. It was the same as being praised in my own right. They are speaking, I would say to myself, of my—"

"Of your what?" Rietta challenged, pausing before the entrance to the Rind residence.

"Why, of my *un*promised bride," he answered lightly.

"*Un*promised, yes. Be pleased to remember that."

"Until I change your ideas on the subject."

"I shall enjoy the spectacle of seeing you try, Jeremy."

The irony of her curtsy and her expression was not lost on him. "Why, ma'am, I appear to have progressed in just this one evening," he declared, following behind her as she mounted the stone steps.

"I beg your pardon." She turned to face him.

"I have been hoping for an end to your 'Mr. Stuarting' me, and behold, it is done."

"A very good night to you, and I thank you for an exceedingly pleasant evening, *Mr.* Stuart." With that, Rietta whisked herself into the house.

Chapter 20

Proceedings of the House of Burgesses
Tues. the 24th of May, Geo. III, 1774

This house, being duly impressed with apprehension of the great dangers to be derived to British America from the hostile invasion of the city of Boston, in our fifth colony of Mass. Bay, whose commerce and harbor are on the first day of June next to be stopped by an armed force, deem it highly necessary that the said first day of June be set apart by the members of this house as a day of fasting, humiliation and prayer.

Geo. Wythe, C.H.B.

"Good morning, Mr. Stuart."
"Good morning, Mistress Rind."
"Oh, very well, good morning, *Jeremy*."
"Very well indeed, *Rietta*."
"Have you come merely to trade names? I truly have not the time to—"
"Mistress, I am a customer with cash to make a purchase.

Your cousin, Mrs. Rind, assures us in every issue of the *Gazette* that as such we are highly valued."

"If you propose to pay cash, you are not only valued, you are unique. What can I do for you?"

"My father is coming to town next week, and our family will celebrate his birthday here. I wish to buy him a book. Have you any suggestions?"

"Come to the other side of the counter. Books are displayed on the end shelves. What are his interests?"

"He enjoys history or a good novel."

"We have Goldsmith's *Roman History* or Stockdale's *Antiquities of Greece*. . . . not too exciting. Has he ever read *Tom Jones?* I believe I recommended it to you last year."

Jeremy came behind the counter to argue playfully with her about each book's merits. They finally decided on *Joseph Andrews: His History and Adventures;* a handsome, marble-paged edition in two volumes, elegantly bound in leather by Baumgarten.

He counted out the cash from his pocketbook, studying her carefully, her thanks were so fervent.

"Are things going poorly with the paper?" he asked bluntly.

"Not the paper." Rietta made a small gesture of resignation. "The paper should be doing well. We have more subscribers and a goodly number of advertisers to profit us, but it is difficult, nigh impossible at times, to get the gentlemen of Virginia to discharge their just debts. Even the fees Cousin Clemmie earns as public printer for the town are not always forthcoming. She must hint to the burgesses very broadly before we can obtain our monies."

"It's only one month since our evening party at the Wythes', and you look worn and unwell," Jeremy observed brusquely.

"Not I. It's Cousin Clemmie I worry about. She grows weary and discouraged. She has too many burdens . . . Pray don't look at me like that."

"Pray how am I looking?"

"As though you would gladly take on all *my* burdens."

"Is that so terrible?"

"Yes, because in some of my weaker moments, I feel inclined to allow you to."

"Rietta, my darl—"

"No, no, Jeremy, the moment has already passed." She

smiled brilliantly. "See, you have made me strong again. Tell me, when does your family arrive?"

"On Thursday, the second of June. They were to arrive on the first, but my father wrote to postpone it by one day." Jeremy grinned. "He says that he prefers to pray for Boston in the privacy of his own home and without fasting."

He fished a letter out of the pocketbook still lying on the counter. "Listen to this. 'I will fight for the civil rights of Bostonians as I would for Virginians, and I will work to avoid civil war. I do not perceive, however, that the sacrifice of my morning eggs and bacon and of my evening beef and ale will in any way contribute to this struggle, which I therefore decline to make.'"

Rietta laughed aloud in delight. "He sounds an original and charming man."

"I am in high hopes you will think so when you meet him."

She looked up at Jeremy quickly, questioningly, as he folded the letter and replaced it.

"He asked me to arrange for the rental of the Daphne Room at the Raleigh for a private family dinner on the first day available, which proved to be Sunday, the fifth. After I did that, I was told to engage your attendance."

"Your father knows about . . . that I . . . that you—"

"That I love you and wish to marry you? Indeed he does."

"And he . . . how does he . . . ."

"He is most anxious to meet with you, and for me has nothing but the sympathy of a fellow sufferer."

"I don't understand."

"My father has wished for a long time to marry Sally Custis of Richmond, whom you will meet at the Raleigh, too. Cousin Sally has shown herself even more hardhearted in the matter than you, for at least you have never refused me."

"I cannot refuse what I have not been asked," Rietta retorted, then colored from her bodice to her hairline.

"I have carefully refrained from giving you the opportunity," Jeremy returned cheerfully. "My father is more importunate. He has asked Cousin Sally and has had his hopes dashed at least three times that I know of in the two years since her husband died."

"You . . . you don't mind that he wishes to replace your mother?" Rietta asked faintly.

"No one could ever do that. But Sally would make a place of her own, and I think she would give my father as well as herself a happier life. She has two small daughters I would welcome as sisters. My family has always known and loved her. She is not really kin, only a close friend. She and my father grew up together. After his marriage, she became my mother's closest friend. In every way, it would be desirable."

Jeremy saw that Rietta was still looking dubious. "Wait till you meet Cousin Sally. You will love her," he promised. "I have yet to meet anyone who did not."

"That remains to be seen."

"You will come, then?"

"I will come as long as it is understood . . ." She looked at him a bit helplessly, at a loss as to how to proceed.

"As long," he finished for her gravely, "as my family's inspection does not bind you to an engagement?"

Rietta's lips quivered slightly, but all she answered was, "Precisely."

"I promise that this dinner will not alter your *un*promised status." He turned in the doorway, the two volumes of *Joseph Andrews* tucked under his arm. "Will you wear your apricot gown?"

"Perhaps."

"Pray do."

"Why?"

"Because, my little hypocrite, you look beautiful in it, as well you know. One more thing. Did you bring your own violin from Philadelphia?"

"I have my grandmother's, inherited from my mother. It was made by a famous Italian violin maker."

"Will you allow me to fetch it to the Raleigh before our party? My father wishes to hear you play."

"Oh, Jeremy!"

"Do I ask too much? Would you rather not?"

"No, it isn't that. I never tire of playing. It's you. You have obviously made it impossible for me to fulfill all your glowing descriptions. You view me— You are blinded sometimes."

"My dear girl, so are you if you think I love you for anything but what you are. You are lovely to look at, intelligent to speak to, exciting to be with. You are skilled in music and writing, loyal and generous in friendship and possessed of other qualities I need not mention, only that they cause me restless days and sleepless nights." Jeremy continued amiably, "You are also hot-tempered, overly impetuous, stubborn, frequently silly and fanciful, sometimes exasperating beyond measure, and I have wanted to shake you as often as I have wanted to kiss you. But I think we had best discuss this in more detail at some future date," he added, his voice rising to prevent her attempt to break in. "I will send a servant for your violin on Sunday and will arrive myself at four to fetch you . . . in your apricot gown."

Jeremy Stuart could never be quite certain of his Quaker spitfire, who was inclined to turn skittish when he pressed her. Therefore, it seemed he had won one small skirmish in their private war when he arrived at Mrs. Rind's residence just before four and found Rietta wearing the apricot satin.

It was incredible that he had once observed every individual allurement of her face and figure and had computed their sum total to be anything less than the peak of beauty. Laughing and lovely, she took his breath away.

He could not say as much for Mrs. Clementina Rind. She looked very unwell indeed. Rietta's concern for her was not as unreasonable as he had feared. Yet, to his shame, Jeremy resented it. He wanted the deepest of his darling's concern as firmly centered on him as his was fixed on her.

When they arrived at the Raleigh, Rietta unthinkingly started toward the front steps.

"Pray allow me, ma'am." He steered her in the direction of the side door. "You would not know this, of course," he said, grave as a judge giving sentence at the General Court, "but there is a separate entrance for ladies so that their delicate sensibilities need not be offended by the slightest contact with the male ruffians who frequent a tavern."

Rietta choked up in a fit of giggles like a little girl and had not finished with this chortling by the time he brought her into the Daphne Room. So it was that his family saw her for the first time, half adorable child, half beautiful woman. She captivated them completely.

Jeremy had asked Mr. Southall to lay on a bountiful feast for them, and he had done so to the absolute satisfaction of all. A fine roast, a fat turkey and two huge bowls of fresh oysters, as well as the usual vegetables and hot breads, adorned the table. After the second course there were apple and pecan and custard pies. When the linen was removed, the servants brought in wine, nuts and fruit, including a basket of special nectarines sent by Mrs. Wythe.

When the meal was over, Rietta played on her violin. Even

Jeremy's young brothers, Tom and Billy, who tended to grow restive upon hearing music, listened silently, and Sally's eyes filled with tears.

Mr. Stuart kissed Rietta's hand with the greatest gallantry after she was done. He assured her that her playing was as much a birthday treat to him as the volumes of *Joseph Andrews* he had received from Jeremy.

Then, to his son's everlasting gratitude, he gave her a pressing invitation to come to Scot's Haven in the months of August and September, when Jeremy would be at home and Sally would bring her daughters for their annual summer visit.

Rietta displayed none of her usual nervousness about wishing to accept this invitation, only making the proviso that Mrs. Rind must be in good health and able to spare her.

Jeremy had never seen Rietta so soft, so gentle or so sparkling as she was this night, and he himself had never been so happy. That he would win her he had never dared let himself doubt but this night, for the first time, he was able to believe that the prize was within his grasp.

My Quaker spitfire, he thought, how much, how very much I love you.

The Virginia Gazette
Published by Clementina Rind
Aug. 25, 1774

The printer of this paper can with infinite satisfaction assure her customers that she will shortly, should Providence be pleased to restore her health, be enabled to conduct her business. But we now drop a hint to every customer that he is served at very great expense, which cannot be defrayed without punctual remittance; nor would the cash due for advertisements . . . be unacceptable.

Though Jeremy was partially prepared by other intelligence from Williamsburg concerning Mrs. Rind, the arrival of Rietta's note at Scots's Haven containing a second put-off brought such disappointment that he decided to ride into the capital and judge the situation for himself. Immediately after this determination, Jeremy dispatched a message to Madame Elizabeth so his early arrival would in no wise inconvenience her.

There was no spot on earth he loved as well as Scot's

Haven, yet his heart beat faster at the prospect of leaving, because soon he would be with her who occupied his thoughts to the exclusion of all else.

The last six weeks away from Rietta had seemed endless. Even in the midst of the gay company his father gathered around him, there was only loneliness. Jeremy had known for some time that love might be a fever, or even more than that, a veritable conflagration in the blood. Before me met her, he had not dreamed that neither peace nor joy nor heart's ease would be his while he was separated from his heart's desire.

"Rietta, my Rietta," he murmured aloud.

In Williamsburg the following day, he took the steps of Mrs. Rind's house two at a time as Rietta was coming down them. They collided, and the papers in her hand went flying.

He thought Rietta's face lit up at the sight of him, but if she was in truth overjoyed to see him, she was equally anxious that he not know it.

"Oh, thee clumsy oaf!" she scolded, bending to retrieve the scattered sheets. He had stooped to do the same, so their heads had a second sharp encounter. This caused the straw hat tied with ribbons beneath her chin to fall back from her head. The sun kissed her hair with streaks of red, and bending over her, he could not resist from performing the same office.

"Jeremy, contain thyself!" she gasped.

"How can I when you are near enough to tempt me?"

She straightened up, very bright of eye, very red of cheek, and held onto the stair rail. He gathered up her papers, and she busied herself setting them in order.

Over her shoulder Jeremy read aloud, "*A Summary of the Rights of British America.* What is this?"

"A draft of resolutions written by your friend Mr. Jefferson to the delegates of the Virginia Convention. His friends commissioned Cousin Clemmie to print it, and this first copy is promised to Colonel Washington," she added proudly. "I am taking it to him now."

"I know where his lodgings are. Shall I be your messenger?"

"Thank you, Jeremy, but it will be good to take the air. I have been indoors so much lately." She continued diffidently, "I was instructed to deliver the pamphlet to Mrs. Campbell's Tavern, where he is to sup tonight. If you wish to walk along with me, I would be pleased to have your company."

"I would be honored, my dear Miss Rind," Jeremy said with mock formality as he tucked the pamphlet inside his waistcoat and offered her his arm.

"My father received your letter yesterday," he told her as they strolled east toward Mrs. Campbell's Tavern on Waller Street. "We were all grievously disappointed."

"I, too, I assure you." Rietta was unaware that her fingers were pinching his arm through its broadcloth sleeve as a measure of her distress. "I *promise* you, Jeremy, I would have kept my word were it not that Cousin Clemmie is so ill."

"I know, dear heart. Mr. Wythe has kept me informed of matters here in Williamsburg."

Her color rose high when he so styled her, but she let it pass without comment.

"I have all manner of messages for you. My father regrets your absence and bids me inform you that you are to come to Scot's Haven any time in the future that you are able to. My brothers send a reminder that you are to bring your violin. Anne and Molly, Cousin Sally's girls, are greatly desirous of making your acquaintance. And Sally would have you remember that, though she looks forward to seeing you at Scot's Haven, you are promised to her at her home in Richmond as well."

"How dear of them all." Jeremy noticed that her eyes grew luminous with tears. "How I hope that I am able to . . ." Rietta did not finish. There was no need to. They both knew what she would have said.

He was torn again by conflicting emotions. Those very qualities he so loved in her, her loyalty and her ardent, generous spirit, contributed to his own unease. His heart was full of jealousy because she gave so much of herself to others. There seemed scarcely anything left over for him. He felt strongly that she loved him, despite his never having been able to wring the admission from her. He was weighted down by the dread doubt that love alone would never be enough to win Rietta for him.

The Virginia Gazette
Sept. 29, 1774
John Pinkney for the Estate of Clementina Rind

On Sunday last died Mrs. CLEMENTINA RIND. It ill becomes the printer to pretend to characterize her. It shall, however, be his most ardent study to protect her children.

The servant, Dick, took Jeremy up the back steps from the print shop to the parlor. Rietta was alone there. He had no words to offer, only both his hands in comfort.

"I saw you in the funeral procession at Bruton, Jeremy," she said quietly, "and we received the beautiful flowers from Scot's Haven. I thank you all so much."

"My poor darling," he said tenderly. "You have had more than your share of grief this last year."

Her face contorted in pain, and seeing her bite down hard on her lower lip, determined not to weep, he cast about in his mind for a conversational diversion.

"What are your plans, Rietta? Will you—" He braced himself even as he asked, "Will you go home?"

"Home? Home!" she repeated, her eyes catching fire. "This *is* my home."

"I thought you might be contemplating a return to your family in Philadelphia."

"I have no family in Philadelphia," Rietta stated in a hostile voice. "Only my father, and he has married again."

Before Jeremy could get any further than "But did not—" she interrupted him in that same cold way.

"His home ceased to be mine when his second wife came into it. Cousin William had invited me often for a visit. My father wrote to him, urging that the invitation be extended again. I came here, and Cousin Clemmie opened not only her home to me but her heart."

Rietta's hands, lying in her lap, were balled into two tight fists. "I know you have often wondered why she always came first with me. Now you have the reason. I was wounded when I arrived. She made me whole again. Employing her kind heart and her practical common sense, she made me feel useful and needed. There was nothing I would not do for her and hers."

Tears glimmered in Rietta's eyes once more, causing her voice to grow husky, and Jeremy quickly set about soothing her.

"Then let it be a comfort in your sorrow that you did exactly that. In her affliction after Mr. Rind died, and during her long illness, you were able to repay in some measure all her kindness."

Jeremy took her hands in his. "As for me, whatever the

cause, I am selfishly glad that you are not going away. Wooing you in Williamsburg is difficult enough, but even my stout heart fails at the thought of courting you the distance between here and Philadelphia."

He smiled teasingly as he spoke, inviting her to smile with him. She did not oblige him, but tried to free her hands.

"Jeremy, you must not—"

"Don't say it," he warned, keeping a tight hold on her. "I will not listen. Nor will I say any more just now. I know it is neither the time nor the place. All I ask, when you work out your plans, is that you keep in *your* mind the sole plan I have in *my* mind for you. I desire nothing so much in this life as to bring you to Scot's Haven as my wife. My family is waiting to welcome you—"

"I am needed here more than ever," Rietta burst out. "As Cousin Clemmie's nearest kin, John Pinkney is guardian to the children. But he cannot care for them without me. And he needs my help as well to run the paper. We have worked together all this while. We must continue to. I cannot plan a future apart from here yet."

"I know all that, Rietta," Jeremy said, although inwardly he consigned John Pinkney to perdition. "All I ask is that when you make those future plans, they include me."

Chapter 21

"Gina, my parents are driving through Williamsburg on their way to visit my sister in Sarasota. They'll spend a few days with me around the weekend on the twenty-fourth. I want you to come to dinner with us on Saturday night."

They were strolling through the Folk Art Collection. Gina's spine stiffened and her face became so deliberately blank, Myles thought she would have made a good model for one of the poker-faced primitives.

"It's no big deal," he told her in a rather gruff voice as she still hesitated. "A meal and a few hours in the company of my parents. You might even like them," he added sardonically. "I rather do myself."

"It's not that." Gina kept her gaze on a plump little cherub asleep in a red rocking chair. "It's just that I've always made it my . . . my policy not to get involved in these family things."

"One dinner does not constitute involvement. Your only commitment is to appear, and your only obligation is to behave."

"Your need to say what you did shows that you have some reservations," Gina pointed out sulkily, chewing on her thumbnail.

He pulled her hand down and held it firmly in his own. "Dear Gina, darling Gina, why must you be such a pain in the ass?" he asked her wearily.

"I don't know," she admitted candidly. "Won't you be sorry if I am with them?"

"I'll have to take my chances, won't I?"

"As long as you understand that's what you're doing," she retorted. "Okay, one dinner with Mama and Papa coming up. Where are they from, by the way?"

"New Haven, Connecticut, same as me."

"Establishment types?"

"Let us rather say established."

"Conservative?"

"So-so."

"They're beginning to wish you would marry some nice, solid girl and raise a family?"

"They carefully refrain from saying so, but yes."

"Have you told them anything about me—anything at all?"

"Only that there's a girl here I want them to meet."

"Will they consider that significant?"

"They might."

"Myles, I owe you an apology," Gina said in awe. "I think I've underestimated your guts. Do you have any idea what basic incompatibilities you'll be trying to blend?"

"I realize you like to think so."

She turned sulky again. "Well, being presented to parents makes me feel like a slab of meat in a supermarket—inspected on both sides, poked at for bad spots and pried into for my packaging."

"Have you, at your august age, been presented to the parents of many men?" he asked overpolitely, wondering, not for the first time, how she had crammed so much living into so few years. Sometimes Myles found it hard to believe she was only seventeen.

"Enough for me to put an end to it," she answered a shade too nonchalantly.

"God almighty, Gina, it's no big deal," Myles repeated.

Surprisingly, she backed down. "Okay, okay, cool it. I said I'd come."

Having won his point, Myles was content to drop the subject. They finished their tour of the Folk Art Collection and strolled over to Waller Street to have lunch at Christiana Campbell's Tavern.

Afterward they walked some more, without paying much

attention to direction. Almost without their knowing it, they arrived at the public gaol.

"Do you have your admissions ticket with you?" he asked.

Gina opened her shoulder bag and fished around inside for awhile. Her hand, when it finally emerged, was holding up a somewhat dog-eared ticket.

They joined the waiting line and crowded with the rest of the group into the gaoler's private quarters for the first part of the lecture. Gina seemed no different from the average tourist. She shuddered over the small cells and the wall fetters. She smiled at the throne, which represented advanced plumbing, and was surprised to hear that Blackbeard, the pirate, and his men had been jailed and later hanged here.

In the outer gaolyard, Myles noticed a sudden change in her. Others on the tour rushed, shrieking joyfully, to the stocks and pillory to try them out and have their photographs taken. Gina watched the first man climb into the stocks, and Myles saw her bite down hard so on her lower lip that the tissue she dabbed it with became specked with blood.

Then a woman mounted the steps to the pillory and allowed her husband to fit her into it, an awkward position requiring her to bend her knees and hunch her shoulders in order to permit her head to pass through the opening, then to raise her arms so that she could thrust them into the wrist holes.

The woman laughed as her head was confined, but Gina's light tan seemed to fade to a ghostly whiteness. The summer crop of tiny freckles under her eyes stood out darkly against her unearthly paleness.

"Gina, for the love of God, what's wrong?"

"It's not funny." She beat her knuckles together. Her voice was so low and hoarse Myles had to strain to hear it. "Oh, God, it was never funny. It can be agony to stand like that. It wasn't only the discomfort. There was also the shame and abuse. People watched and pelted fruits, decaying vegetables and rotten eggs. They were cruel and pitiless, and the punishment was often in excess of the crime."

No use to question or cajole. No time now even to try to fit this additional piece into the puzzle of the girl Myles loved so dearly but seldom understood.

"Gina," he said, putting one arm around her to turn her about, "what you say is true, but it happened two hundred years ago."

He led her out of the fenced yard and fairly propelled her

down Nicholson Street. He wanted to get Gina as far away and as fast away as he could from this painful spectacle.

She had read a great deal of American history, Myles reminded himself, lying sleepless that night, staring up at the ceiling with his arms under his head. She had told him so herself. Especially since coming to Williamsburg, she had read up on colonial history. Gina didn't have to tell him that she had a dramatic turn of mind and a too-vivid imagination. These were things he knew full well for himself.

And yet . . . having seen her suddenly pale face and suffering eyes, Myles could have sworn that she had spoken from the agony of personal knowledge. Which was ridiculous. The girl was simply a superb actress. Either that or a witch.

Considering how she had turned his well-ordered life upside down, he was sometimes more inclined to the second theory.

"Jeremy, oh, Jeremy, please wait!"

He was about to turn his horse toward the Jamestown Road, bound on an errand for Mr. Wythe a few miles out of the city, when he heard Rietta's voice. He turned his mount back as she approached, panting.

"I saw you in the distance. I was praying you would hear me. Are you hurried, or could you carry me a short distance?"

He had dismounted and was holding the reins loosely. "You know I am always at your service. Is something amiss?"

Her face was pale, her manner distraught, but she attempted to laugh.

"Only that I must find Isaac—Isaac Collins, our apprentice. There is a most important errand he neglected."

"Boys are frequently feckless. I'm sure he'll soon return," Jeremy said soothingly. "You should not be too hard on him."

"You don't understand. Dick saw him." Rietta looked about to weep. "He had a basket of eggs and rotting produce. A—there is a woman b-being p-unished today at the gaol. I fear he was bound for there. Please," she begged, "will you take me?"

He put his hands around her waist and lifted her sideways onto the saddle bow. Then he led the horse down the street until he came to a mounting block and was able to seat himself behind her on the animal.

It was not far to the yard of the public gaol. As they drew

up to it, Jeremy tied the reins of his horse to a huge oak tree, which others had already done. Such a large number had gathered to see the spectacle that even as he accompanied Rietta through the crowd, he had strong doubts of her ability to pick out one small boy among so many.

"There he is!" she cried. Jeremy followed her closely as she pounced. "Isaac Collins, how dare you come here? Thou knowest thee were to go to the post office and return directly. Dick has need of thee."

"Aw, Miss Rietta," the child whined, "I delivered the papers right off. I just took a few extra minutes to have some sport."

"Sport!" She seized the basket from him and dashed the egg he was holding out of his hand. It broke over Isaac's breeches as she delivered a stinging box first to one of his ears and then to the other.

Jeremy followed, grinning, as she ruthlessly shepherded her young charge to the edge of the crowd. "Dost thou call it sport to throw rotten fruit at the defenseless creature in the pillory? Is it not enough torture that the woman must stand there and will afterward be lashed?"

"Aw, Miss Rietta," the boy sniveled, rubbing his ears, "everyone does it."

"Everyone!" she all but shrieked. "Does that make it right?"

"Rietta," Jeremy interposed quietly.

"Go home! Go home this instant!" She stamped her foot at Isaac. "And thee hast better be there by the time I am!"

As Isaac scampered off, Rietta began to weep unrestrainedly. Jeremy took the basket from her and set it on the ground in order to put his arms around her. She accepted the embrace, sobbing quietly against him.

"What is it, dear heart?"

Rietta raised her head and wiped her eyes with her fingers, like a little girl. "Her husband abused her constantly, but no one interfered," she murmured, trembling. "Only when *she* finally turned on *him* was the majesty of the law invoked."

"I seem to remember hearing the case discussed," Jeremy said slowly. "Yes, now I recall the circumstances. But, Rietta, she assaulted him so badly with a rock, she may have addled his wits permanently. He is still in the hospital for lunatics. While he—"

Jeremy stopped himself, and Rietta waited a full minute before prompting in a dangerously calm voice, "Go on, say it.

He beat her within the limits proscribed by law—is that what you were going to tell me?"

"Well—"

"To be sure, he did, and the fact that he did it almost daily doesn't count. The law is so just, so explicit, a man can always stay well within it. He knows the exact size of the weapon he may use and precisely how many blows he may strike while still enjoying the full approval of the law."

"Not approval, he—"

"This town, this noble capital of Virginia, and all the other towns like it, including my own Philadelphia, all of them so concerned with British tyranny and the rights of Englishmen. Not one word do I hear that their great and glorious cause of American freedom will improve life by so much as a hair's breath for any Englishwoman. American justice—"

People were turning around, suddenly aware and frowning. Jeremy grasped her by the arm in genuine alarm. "Rietta!" He shook her. "Be still at once!"

Startled and pained by his grip, she fell silent and unresisting as Jeremy almost dragged her to the oak where his horse was tied. He led Rietta by one hand and the horse by the other until they were a safe distance away. Then he turned to scold her.

"Have you no sense, girl, talking like that in a crowd? It could have quickly become a dangerous mob."

"I said naught but what was true."

"Rietta Rind!" His exasperation was evident. "Sometimes common sense must prevail over speaking the truth. Patriots are sensitive on the subject of the American cause. In New England they tar and feather those who disparage it. Here they have not gone that far, but we have already had mock trials in which the too-outspoken have been humiliated and made to beg pardon. For you to commit the folly of such talk in a place like the gaolyard . . . don't you understand that in the hands of a mob a woman might be severely used? Do you think I could have saved you single-handedly?" Jeremy demanded savagely.

Rietta stood before him, head bowed, not answering. But if he thought her position denoted penitence, he was disabused of the notion when she finally lifted her defiant face.

"Rietta," he said, then softly again, "Rietta. You are impossible, my love." His fingers trembled slightly as they took hold of her chin to keep her looking at him. His laugh was a bit unsteady. "I would like to use you severely myself."

She pulled free of Jeremy. "I don't doubt it. Why should you be different from any other man?" She tossed her head and walked away from him.

He sprinted forward, spun her around and backed her up against the horse's flank.

"What did that mean?"

"It meant that you have just stated for me one of the reasons I do not wish to marry you."

"Then please explain it more clearly." Now *his* voice was the cold and threatening one, but she appeared unaware.

"I don't wish to give you the rights over me the law so generously allows."

There was a dreadful pause during which Jeremy struggled for command of himself. "We have been acquainted—friends, I thought—for these many months. I would have said we had come to know each other well. And after such a length of time, this is your opinion of me? That I am cut of the same cloth as the wretch responsible for putting that poor creature in the pillory? That I am some kind of monster you could not entrust yourself with? That you might go in daily peril of receiving physical abuse?"

Rietta winced slightly at the scorn in his voice.

"Believe me, Mistress Rind," he ground out between his teeth, "your peril as my wife would not be as great as it is right now!"

Much to Jeremy's astonishment, she put a hand to her lips but could not hide the smile forming there. Then she began to laugh. "Oh, Jeremy," she gurgled, "thy face! I don't think I have ever before seen thee truly in a temper. And to threaten me, thee who are so kind and gentle, as though I do not know thou wouldst never lay a hand on me."

"Then *thee*," he returned a bit grimly, "are much surer of it at this moment than I."

They walked till there was no one else about. He tied the horse to another tree and suggested, "Let us sit on the grass and talk a moment. There is something I must know."

"John will be wondering where I have got to," Rietta said uneasily.

"Then John may wonder a little longer. Sit down," he directed curtly. She sat obediently, and Jeremy stood over her. "If you are so sure that I am a gentleman, what was that all about a few minutes ago?"

"I was in a passion. I said more than I should have. It has nothing to do with you. . . . Oh, Jeremy, what I cannot bear is not the fear that you would mishandle me, but that the law *gives* you the right to. The day a man puts his ring on her finger, a woman becomes his property. He owns her as he does his house, his horse, his hunting dog. He owns the clothes on her back, any money or property that was hers, even the children that she bears. He possesses her."

"She possesses him, too. If they love one another, could that not be wonderful?"

"To be possessed in love . . . yes, that might be splendid, but to be a possession is demeaning. Would *you* promise to obey *me* in the marriage ceremony?"

"Would you take me if I said yes?"

Rietta jumped to her feet. "This is ridiculous. I must get back to the shop. Will you help me onto the horse, or must I walk?"

He delayed her again with a hand on her arm. "I don't wish you to obey me, Rietta, only to love me."

"You don't understand."

"No, I must confess I do not understand why you raise all these impediments in the way of our happiness."

She took his hand from her arm and lifted it to her cheek, rubbing the palm gently against her face. "I would not be restful to live with, Jeremy," she whispered. "I think thee deservest better."

"Let me be the judge of what my desserts should be," he whispered back. "I will get all the rest I need in my grave. While still here on earth, I ask much more."

A tear fell slowly from each of her eyes, and, very tenderly, he put his lips to her cheeks and kissed each droplet away. Then he swung her onto the horse.

They did not speak on the short ride home. Only at her door, lifting her down, did he ask, "Will you join me on Sunday? There is something I wish to show you."

"On Sunday?" She hesitated.

"All day," Jeremy said firmly. "We will sup with the Wythes. You have not had a holiday in many months. The servants can take care of the children, and Mr. Pinkney will have to spare you."

Rietta's face lit up. "It sounds delightful. Very well, then, yes, I will manage it somehow."

"Why all the mystery, Myles? Where are we going?"

"To Jamestown, not for all the usual stuff, but to show you one special thing that should make your little women's lib heart proud and prove to you that there's nothing new under the sun."

Forty minutes later they had climbed the embankment that overlooked the diamond-sparkling river. Gina was staring through the railings that protected the spreading tree whose split halves separated the crumbling gravestones.

"This is going to make me proud and show me what?" she scoffed.

He looked around. "Well, I was going to let the tour guide do it, but he seems to be down at the statue of Pocahontas, so here goes. These are the graves of Dr. James Blair, the founder of the College of William and Mary, and his wife, Sarah Harrison Blair, who broke her engagement to another man—she had signed a written contract to bind her, and it cost her father a packet to get her released—so she could marry Dr. Blair. The wedding ceremony in 1687 rocked all Virginia. In fact, it even brought shocked comment from as far away as England. The bride refused to answer properly when the minister asked her if she would love, honor and obey her husband. 'No obey,' she said, shaking her head. He tried again. 'No obey,' she repeated. The poor, baffled minister looked at the bridegroom, also a minister, who signified his consent, and the third time around she was only required to love and honor him."

"I like the sound of her."

"Naturally."

"What does that mean?" Gina bristled.

"Why, only that a girl of such spirit would naturally appeal to you," he replied innocently.

"Huh!" She turned her suspicious eyes toward the gravestones again. "Did it work out?"

"He was twenty years older and known as a contentious Scotsman. She was pigheaded and took to drink. They had no children. Who's to say?"

"Why did you want me to see this so badly?" she asked as they moved in the direction of Pocahontas's statue.

"It was close to three hundred years ago, Gina. She was just as gutsy as any modern girl."

"And the moral of that is?"

"Figure it out for yourself, Miss Independence. Come on." Myles took her arm. "We might as well join the tour as long as we're here."

"In a minute. Tell me, are there any more graves?"

"Yes. Quite a few of the original and early settlers are buried over there. You want to see them first?"

"If you don't mind. I . . . I was reading something about them the other day that interested me."

"Don't belabor it, Gina. No explanation needed."

"I beg your pardon."

"So you should. You tell an extraordinary number of white lies." He led her around a large rock. "That is, I hope they're white." And then, almost with detachment, he said, "My, this is a colorful conversation. Your face is quite red and your eyes have gone navy blue. I notice they do when you get emotional."

"Myles . . ."

"What?"

"Nothing. Just Myles."

"In your own good time, Gina. When you're ready to talk, I'll be around."

"Patience on a monument?" she mocked him.

He shook his head slowly, smiling. "Not on your life, sweetheart. I'm just giving you a bit more rope." He added cheerfully, "I decided a month or two ago that where you're concerned, patience isn't a virtue." Then, without any change of expression, he said, "Come along. It's this path here."

Inside Mr. Wythe's closed carriage, with a fur rug wrapped around her legs and Jeremy's shoulder touching hers, Rietta relaxed deliciously.

When they first departed the city, she had been absorbed in the country scene, but after a few miles she turned her head into Jeremy's shoulder and closed her eyes.

"Are you asleep?" he asked presently. "I can find no other possible reason for the silence that prevails."

"Mmmm."

"A most comprehensive reply."

The shoulder on which her head lay was shaken slightly by his laughter, and she murmured a protest.

"Your pardon, my love. If that be the way of it, then let us both be more comfortable."

His arm went around her. He pulled a second rug over them. Rietta's eyes opened wide for a moment, then, accepting, closed again. Soon she slept in earnest.

"Rietta. Rietta. Wake up, love."

The hood was pulled back from her cloak, sending cold

drafts whistling about her neck. Hands smoothed her hair into place. Yawning, she opened her eyes and found Jeremy's smiling into them.

"We are arrived," he informed her. "Pray why are you so exhausted?"

"Charley, the youngest, had a toothache last night. John Pinkney and I took turns holding him." She hid another yawn behind her fingers and accepted Jeremy's help down the carriage steps.

"We won't be long, Aaron," he told the liveried servant.

"But where are we?" Rietta asked plaintively. "You've made it such a mystery."

"Jamestown."

"Where the first Virginia settlement was?"

"Yes. We were ahead of your Pilgrims by more than ten years."

"I warrant it's of interest," she said doubtfully, "but you might have chosen a finer day."

"We are not here to see the ruins of the settlement. If you wish to, I will bring you again come spring. There is only one special place here I want to show you." Jeremy took her arm and turned her about. "It is here, this way."

A few moments later Rietta was standing near a grave site. There were two stones, separated by the trunk and spreading roots of a sycamore tree.

"Dr. James Blair, the minister who founded the College of William and Mary, and his wife, Sarah. The graves were once side by side, but that tree grew up between them and cracked the stones. Wags took to calling it the mother-in-law tree because Mrs. Harrison opposed the marriage for her daughter."

"There is a special reason why you wanted to bring me here?" Rietta asked in puzzlement.

"Sarah Harrison Blair is the reason. I wanted you to see the resting place of a Virginia girl who, nearly ninety years ago, refused to say *obey* in the marriage ceremony."

"Truly?" Rietta gave Jeremy her lopsided smile, eyes dancing in delight. "Did she truly?"

"Not only most truly but most publicly. It was not argued out until the wedding guests were all assembled and the marriage was in progress. Whereas I, Miss Rind of Philadelphia, stand ready to make agreement beforehand that the so-objectionable word *obey* will be excluded from the service."

"You would be a laughingstock."

"I doubt it. If so, I care not."

"Oh, Jeremy, what am I going to do about you?"

"I told you. Marry me."

"Oh, Jeremy, you are—"

"Hush. Don't speak." He yanked Rietta hard against him, his lips on hers giving her no choice but to be silent. "I don't want to hear from you what I am or what I deserve," he whispered into her ear as he held her breathless in his arms after their kiss. "You have exaggerated ideas of my virtues. I can be as small-minded as anyone else. I am feeling particularly small-minded at the moment."

"Why, Jeremy?"

"Because if you are going to be exhausted from caring for a sick child, I would prefer that it be one of ours. And I would myself prefer to be responsible for your sleepless nights."

"I'm chilled." She whirled around. "We had best return to the carriage."

He followed close behind her. His voice sounded amused. "I do believe you are blushing, Mistress Rind, you who talk so blithely of pregnancy and childbed and compare the covering of mares and women."

In the carriage headed toward Williamsburg, Jeremy reminded her, "You did not answer me, Rietta. You once said you could not because I had never asked you. That no longer holds true. You have just been asked."

"I can't say yes, Jeremy."

"Then don't say anything. I refuse to accept your nay. Do you still feel bound by your obligations to Mrs. Rind?"

"Not as much . . . there are . . . circumstances. I can't tell you about them now. But I would be less than honest with you if I made my obligations the reason. I appreciate the concessions you are willing to make. I probably could not find in all of Williamsburg—or in Philadelphia, either, if it comes to that—another man willing to take *obey* out of the marriage service. I know there will never be anyone as good and kind, as enjoyable to be with, but I am not yet ready to bind myself. And marriage, even of the best, is a bind for women. Something in me won't let me do that to myself, no matter how much I care for you, and I do. I care greatly. This doesn't make any sense to you at all, does it? I keep hurting you, which is the last thing in the world I want to do."

"You have great power to hurt me and also to make me supremely happy. You have never before admitted that you care for me. Could you bear to express your feelings a bit more strongly, and then I will plague you no more today?"

She did not pretend to misunderstand.

"I do love you, Jeremy."

"And I love *thee*, my Quaker spitfire."

Chapter 22

There was nothing the least bit loving about Jeremy five days later, however, when he was shown into Mrs. Sarah Hallam's private parlor.

As Mrs. Hallam, with a pleasant word of excuse, went out and closed the door, Rietta rose from the couch and greeted him quietly.

"Good afternoon, Jeremy."

"Is it?" he asked bitingly. "I am afraid I had not noticed. Tell me, or do I ask too much—am I being unreasonable to consider that you owed me the courtesy of informing me of your change of residence?"

"I moved into my room here only this morning, and I have been busy settling in ever since. I intended at the first opportunity to send word to you."

"Indeed? And if I had not called on you, when might that have been? The summer of '75, perhaps?"

"Tonight, or, I promise you, tomorrow morning at the very latest. Please don't be angry with me, Jeremy." Her mouth trembled, and so did her voice. "Pray don't scold me any more. I am miserable enough without that."

Jeremy came quickly to her, his anger melted at once. "My

poor darling, what is it?" He put his hands on either side of her face, lifting it for his close scrutiny. "You have been weeping, love. I have never known you to do that. Tell me what troubles you."

She smiled tremulously. "I am not so different from most women as that. I weep aplenty, but I prefer to do it in private."

"What happened? Why are you now living here?"

"John Pinkney decided that I must. It is so altogether foolish, but it appears that there was— Oh, it's all so stupid, as though the servants and Dick and the children were not chaperones enough. But my being a spinster and he a bachelor—well, it seems he heard talk about the two of us living in the house alone. Alone! Did you ever hear of anything more ridiculous—alone in that full house!" She winked back angry tears. "No one gossiped all the time Cousin Clemmie was sick, as though if we had it in mind to do so then, we could not have misbehaved with the greatest possible ease."

Rietta accepted Jeremy's proffered handkerchief and blew her nose vigorously. "I told John I did not regard the gossiping of evil minds, but he was adamant. He arranged for my lodging here, and he—or rather, the paper—will pay the cost. I shall still receive a small sum in cash for my own expenses, as I have in the past. I will go to the house every day, of course. *That* appears to be eminently respectable. It is only after candlelight that the danger of misbehavior exists."

"Rietta, your feelings are understandable," Jeremy said cautiously. "On the other hand, Mr. Pinkney acted in the best interests of your reputation. Since it burdens him even more as far as the children are concerned, he has my admiration."

"The children should have been the first consideration," she returned fiercely, "not the gossips!"

A sudden change of expression altered Jeremy's face. "Is this what you meant at Jamestown when you said your obligations to the children were less . . . that circumstances had changed . . . ?" His eyes narrowed. "Good God, did you know about this?"

"I knew, yes, that I must leave my cousin's home, but it was not yet determined where I was to go."

"Why did you not speak of it to me?"

His voice was calm, but Rietta was not deceived. She recognized that a great deal of anger lay behind his indirect reproach.

"Because you might have used your knowledge as a weapon."

"To do what?"

"Push me into wedding you."

"You infer, I collect, that I might take advantage of your unhappy state and your homeless condition to press my suit when you were too weakened to resist?"

She came close to him and rested her hands against his chest. "No, Jeremy, I do not, so you need not look at me so intensely. I meant I was so miserable that, at a word from you, I might easily have tumbled into your arms and said yes to marriage, which would be as bad for you as it would be for me."

"How so?"

"Because then we would neither of us ever have known whether I would do the same at a happier time. I think, my dear love, you have too much respect for yourself to want me in such a way. Or do I judge you wrongly?" she asked softly.

His hands covered hers. Jeremy studied her uplifted face, and presently she felt his deep, shuddering sigh against her fingertips. "No, damn you, you do not."

"I thought you would be happy about this," she said after a while.

"To see you unhappy?"

"Not that, but now I feel free to please myself. Did you know your father had asked me to come to Scot's Haven for the holiday festivities in December, when Sally will be there, too?" Rietta watched, smiling a little, as a look of incredulous joy spread across Jeremy's face.

"You will go?"

"I have already writ my acceptance. Your father will send a carriage for me as soon as I tell him the day and the time I wish to leave."

"The day and the time *we* wish to leave, Miss Rietta Rind. We will journey home to Scot's Haven together."

They set off on the morning of the fifth of December, the carriage stopping first at the Wythe House for Jeremy and then going on to Mrs. Hallam's for Rietta.

Early as it was, John Pinkney left the printing office to bid her good-bye. The two men greeted each other stiffly. Pinkney was an upright, intelligent man, but Jeremy had always sensed an antagonism in him which he reciprocated. He resented Pinkney's proprietary air toward Rietta, even the touch of John's fingers on hers as she was handed into the carriage. It was not the first time Jeremy had felt this way, but he was honest enough to admit to himself that Mr. Pinkney had never said or done anything to deserve his antipathy. Jeremy's reaction was prompted more by jealousy. Because of their work together on the *Gazette* and their mutual care of the Rind orphans, the publisher and Rietta shared much of their lives in areas Jeremy could never hope to touch.

"A safe journey to you, Mr. Stuart," Pinkney called through the carriage window. Then his voice changed subtly, becoming at once lower and more intimate. "Rietta, my dear, I shall be awaiting your answer most eagerly."

Jeremy thought she colored slightly as she replied, "I will write within the week, I promise you."

Rietta seemed wrapped in thought as the horses set off at a steady trot. Uneasy thoughts, for her eyes were cast down and she was chewing at her underlip in the way Jeremy had long ago noticed was her tendency when the balance of her mind was disturbed.

Presently, he reached for her hand and held it lightly. "Love, I suggest you stop savaging your mouth. I doubt it has done anything to merit such punishment."

She turned in her seat and gave him an all-embracing smile. "Oh, Jeremy, I am going to enjoy this holiday. I am determined to be happy!"

"Will it take such determination for you to be happy in my company?" he teased. "Or have you some new problem to overcome?"

"You are the easiest person I know to be happy with," Rietta answered extravagantly. "And, in addition, I will have your family and Cousin Sally. I will be at Scot's Haven, which I have been longing to see. Did you know your voice changes when you speak of it? It becomes almost like a lover's. And Sally wrote that there will be feasting and dancing and merrymaking, all the things I have missed for so long."

He was diverted into talk of Scot's Haven and his father's holiday plans, but one small corner of Jeremy's mind noted that she had avoided answering his question.

Near their journey's end, he could not restrain himself from asking, "You have a problem with regard to Mr. Pinkney, do you not?"

Rietta looked quickly out the window, but not quickly enough to avoid his seeing that her cheeks went crimson.

"About what must you give him an answer?" he pursued. "Is he asking you to return home?"

Even as Jeremy spoke, he realized with sharp clarity that he very much preferred her to stay on at Mrs. Hallam's. He would by no means be pleased to have Rietta living under the same roof as John Pinkney.

"Yes," Rietta said after a slight pause. "He wants me to come home."

Jeremy tried without success to keep a note of sarcasm out of his voice. "He no longer fears the gossips?"

"I thought we were not going to discuss problems, but simply be gay and happy," she protested.

"Your face wasn't fashioned for deception, Rietta," he told her slowly. "You give yourself away too readily. It is evident he *does* still fear the gossips. Why, then, does he now think it practicable, when he did not before, for you to live in the same house with him?"

She was not quick to reply. "Look at me." Jeremy pulled her around to face him. Suddenly the answer struck him with stunning force. "By God, it isn't possible! The fellow wants you for his wife!"

"Why is it so impossible?" Rietta retorted, stung. "*You* do."

"It's not his wanting you that concerns me, but you. . . . Let me think. Pinkney said he would await your answer, and you—" She cried out as he seized her shoulders. "You said you would write within the week, which means—" He gave her a violent shake. "Why, you little bitch—it means you didn't refuse him at once!"

"Jeremy!" she gasped.

"Don't 'Jeremy' me! Just tell me this instant what the hell made you delay turning him down!"

Rietta opened her mouth, but not soon enough for him, and another shake preceded her low-voiced answer.

"The children. I felt I should consider them . . . and what Cousin Clemmie would have . . ." Her voice faded away completely under Jeremy's look of scorn and fury. She lowered her eyes, and when she had the courage to raise them again, she could only echo faintly, "The children."

"Damn the children!" he shouted. "And be damned to you as well! I believed you were serious and sincere in your objections to being bound by marriage. Now it appears you do not object to having a family of children supplied for you. To save you the trouble of begetting your own, perhaps? And Mr. Pinkney. Pray tell me, is he malleable? I would warrant so. I wager that he will dance to any tune you choose to fiddle. In truth, he appears the kind of husband you might not find so objectionable after all."

Rietta clasped her chilled hands underneath the fur rug. "You are unfair, Jeremy, as well as uncivil," she declared quietly, unaware that the carriage had passed through a high arched gate and was turning up a broad driveway lined with towering elms.

"And you are ripe for the lunatic hospital if you think I will permit you to wed anyone but me!"

Jeremy heard the hiss of her indrawn breath, then she leaned forward to look him squarely in the eye. Rietta spoke with apparent calmness, but her pronouns gave her away.

"Permit me!" she repeated. "Permit me. If thee thinkest that anything I do, sir, requires thy permission, then thee, not I, art the mad one."

Neither one noticed that the carriage had come to a halt.

"Nevertheless, Miss Rietta Rind, on the morrow we will repair to the library and compose a letter to Mr. Pinkney that will settle his pretensions for good and all."

"Will we indeed?"

"Never doubt it," Jeremy confirmed, and clasped her in his arms.

When the carriage door was opened, Rietta was still held by his kiss, and her own arms, seemingly without any will at all, helped secure him to her. It took the coachman's discreet cough, as he lowered the carriage steps, to sever their embrace.

Jeremy leaped from the carriage first and handed Rietta out. As they approached the graceful red brick house with its walls of climbing ivy, Sally Custis, throwing a warm shawl over her green silk gown, came rushing down the stone steps to greet them, followed in a more leisurely fashion by Mr. Stuart.

Just before the two couples met, Jeremy's hand, lightly holding Rietta's elbow, tightened punishingly about her arm.

"Remember," he said, distinct menace in his voice. "Tomorrow morning in the library."

He received the full blast of a brilliant but derisive smile before Rietta turned to answer his father's welcome.

They sat twenty-four to supper, which caused Rietta to smile to herself as she admired the Chinese-figured wall covering.

Jeremy, seated next to her, urged softly, "Share your jest with me."

"Your father told me this was only a *small*, informal family gathering to celebrate the holidays." A wave of her hand seemed to indicate the entire company as well as the Wedgwood ware, the crystal, the silver and the elaborate, carved epergne with its cluster of dried flowers.

"My father, like most Virginians, is never happier than when playing the host. He would double the numbers and still consider this gathering modest." After a moment's silence, Jeremy added, "He is especially happy, as I am, that we finally have you beneath our roof."

She inclined her head the merest fraction of an inch by way of an answer, and he interpreted her continued silence correctly.

"I see I am still unforgiven," he said.

"What did you expect when you have not even troubled to apologize for your barbaric behavior?"

"Barbaric behavior?" His brows knitted. "Isn't that slightly exaggerated, Rietta?" He studied her profile with its reddened cheek and barely managed, as enlightenment dawned, not to laugh aloud. "I collect you refer to the kiss I gave you, ma'am, and the ungentlemanlike, if apt, designation I bestowed upon you. I would never dream, however, of apologizing for the kiss, love," he whispered into her ear. He smiled gently as Rietta's startled eyes met his and then quickly looked away. "It gave me far too much pleasure, particularly your return, and gives me much to look forward to. What a passionate wench you are, to be sure!"

Her hand trembled so, the spoon she was holding clattered against the soup bowl. "Jeremy, don't. Pray stop this," she entreated.

He shook his head. "No. I will not stop telling you, in all the ways there are, that I love you. Now, drink your peanut soup—Aunt Hannah makes the best in Virginia—and then I will allow you to give a little of your attention to the handsome gentleman on your left who has been trying so hard to catch your eye. He is Harry Sinclair from the

Carolinas and is by way of being my third cousin. You need not fear, though. I have already informed him that you are spoken for."

Most of the gentlemen and half the ladies retired to the card tables after the meal, but Rietta excused herself on the score of fatigue.

As Jeremy saw her pass out of the room, he, too, excused himself and caught up with her in the hallway. "Are you really going so early to your bed?"

"I was up at five this morning," she reminded him a bit nervously. "You must remember I am unaccustomed to late hours."

He waved away a hovering servant and himself fetched a pewter candlestick. "I will light your way upstairs."

"There is no need for you to leave your other guests," she urged hastily, holding out her hand for the candle.

Rietta's waiting hand was seized and given the same treatment that her lips had met with earlier.

"I will light your way upstairs," Jeremy repeated firmly, and drew her hand beneath his arm.

She had perforce to go along with him, which she did in silence, her head and her color both high.

He gave her a sidelong look and spoke with gentle malice. "You can stop trembling. I was not planning to kiss you again . . . not yet, that is."

"How kind of you to reassure me."

"You don't deserve to be kissed," Jeremy continued imperturbably. "Perhaps after you write to Mr. Pinkney . . . if I am satisfied with the contents of your letter—"

"Then you might favor me?" she queried sweetly.

"I make no promises, but it is possible."

"May I have the candle, Jeremy?"

Rietta took it from his outstretched hand, then asked him softly, "Will you wait a moment? There is something I wish to give you."

She went into her room and set the candlestick upon the bedside table, then swiftly returned to him, casting a quick look up and down the hallway. As Jeremy stood in silent astonishment, her hands reached to the back of his neck and drew his face down to hers. Even as earlier he had kissed her, she now kissed him.

But when Jeremy's eager acceptance changed and he would have grasped her waist to pull her against him, Rietta stepped back over the threshold to her chamber.

"Good night to you, Jeremy," she said rather breathlessly, her eyes alight with triumph and something more. "Perhaps tomorrow in the library, if I am better pleased with *your* behavior, I may think you more deserving of *my* kisses."

She closed the door in his still-startled face.

"Mind you"—she raised her voice to make sure he could hear her through the thickness of solid pine—"mind you, I make no promises. I can only say 'tis possible."

Chapter 23

For all her boldness in the candlelit hallway the previous night, Rietta could not meet Jeremy's eyes across the sun-filled breakfast room the next morning. At all times when her attention was not centered on the Custis girls, Anne and Molly, who sat on either side of her, she firmly fixed her gaze on a heaping plate of eggs and griddle cakes.

Only once did she lift her eyes, vaguely searching the table for the syrup pitcher. Encountering Jeremy's amused glance, she immediately veiled them again.

"Molly," he said, "I think Miss Rind would like the syrup." He passed it across to Molly, who shoved it over to Rietta.

"Thank you," Rietta murmured, to either or both of them, careful not to look up.

Jeremy was seemingly absorbed in conversation with his cousin Harry when the girls started making plans for their morning's play, all of which included Rietta's presence. That Jeremy's attention was divided became evident as he leaned across the table and interrupted in a loud, firm voice, "After dinner, perhaps, young ones. This morning Rietta and I have business in the library. There is an important letter she must write."

Both girls began eager objections, only to be interrupted

again, this time by their mother from the far end of the table. "Anne, Molly, don't be rude to Jamie," she reproved mildly. "You must not monopolize Rietta's time when she has business affairs to attend to."

"We will walk this afternoon," Rietta promised, squeezing Molly's hand while smiling reassuringly at Anne. "My business will not take long, not"—she cast a look of challenging defiance across the table—"not more than an hour."

"It need not take more than ten minutes," Jeremy muttered close to her ear moments later as he steered her toward the library. "Not if you are as quick with your pen as you are with your tongue."

He closed the library door behind them and led her to the slant-top mahogany desk standing between two floor-length windows. Rietta glanced out at the wide expanse of lawn, spread out like an emerald carpet, then at the distant fields sloping down to the James River.

"Oh, how beautiful," she breathed.

"Yes, it is, and I will take you over the grounds later so that you may admire the view from all sides. But now, sit here at my father's desk. I have paper and ink all ready." Jeremy pushed back a Delft vase filled with boxwood leaves and dried larkspur and picked up the quill, regarding it critically. "This needs mending, I think." He rummaged in a side drawer and produced a small penknife. "While I sharpen the pen, pray you sharpen your wits so you will know precisely what you have to say."

Rietta had seated herself obediently, but as he went to work on the pen, she pushed back the chair a few inches and leaned against it, staring up at him mockingly. "I have nothing to say to John Pinkney that has not already been said," she told Jeremy, her lips quivering in a barely concealed smile.

He threw down pen and knife to free his hands for grasping her shoulders. "Rietta," he warned, "do not try me too far."

"You are unreasonable," she complained meekly. "Poor John only asked me once. I see no reason to refuse him twice."

His hold slackened, and she sank back into the chair.

"Refuse him!" Jeremy echoed quickly, then frowned. "You said naught of refusal when he handed you into the carriage."

"But, Jeremy, how could I? He had asked me only the night before, when he came to see me at Mrs. Hallam's. He had not pressed me for an answer. Indeed, he made it plain that he thought I should consider his offer long and carefully before I made my final decision. It was to be a match entered into for the benefit of Cousin Clemmie's children, this being the only way we could continue to care for them together. John 'esteems, respects and admires' me," she went on glibly, hands folded primly in her lap like a schoolgirl reciting her lessons. "He believes 'these are sentiments capable of providing a strong foundation for an enduring marriage,' especially when my impulsive spirits are properly tempered by the great responsibilities of that estate."

"You are jesting. He could not have said all that."

"Oh, but he did. I assure you he said all that and a good deal more."

Rietta stood up, eyes sparkling wickedly. "Jer–emy."

"I mistrust that voice. What now?"

"Would *you* promise not to make the duties of my marriage bed too onerous?"

"Good God, he didn't!"

She shook her head in disagreement. "On the contrary, he did. I suspect, Jeremy, he's much more of a gentleman than you."

"I'll spare your blushes by not telling you what *I* suspect." He put his arms around Rietta and pulled her to him. "The duties of your marriage bed, my love, will be as onerous as my strength allows—only they won't be duties. Now"—he put her from him—"have done with this. When was there the opportunity for you to refuse him? You were promising to consider his offer when he bade you good-bye yesterday. You told me as much in the carriage drive."

"He asked me to consider, so I did. I thought about what Cousin Clemmie would have wanted. I thought about it for all the rest of that evening. Long before I blew out my bed candle, I knew that not even for the children, not even for Cousin Clemmie, could I wed with anyone but—could possibly let myself be wed to John," she amended hastily. "So I rose at dawn yesterday and wrote him a letter, saying all the proper things."

"But when was it delivered to him?"

"I have not sent it yet. Oh, Jeremy!" Rietta cried, exasperated. "How can thee be so stupid? He asked me to consider for a while. I am fond of John. I did not wish to humiliate him by informing him so promptly that I could not even stomach the notion of having him. I brought the letter with me, thinking to send it in several days." She opened the reticule dangling from her wrist. "It is here with me now."

She produced and held out to him a small, folded piece of parchment, sealed with red wax and addressed in bold writing to John Pinkney, Esq., at the printing office of Clementina Rind on Duke of Gloucester Street in Williamsburg.

Instead of expressing pleasure, Jeremy deepened his frown. "Henrietta Rind!" he exploded. "Did you have that letter with you in the carriage yesterday?"

"Yes, Jeremy."

"Then all the while we were arguing, you—"

"Yes, Jeremy."

"Do you know," he remarked thoughtfully, "that I feel a strong inclination to throttle you?"

"Yes, Jamie," she replied with great and loving tenderness, "I know you do."

His arms reached out and she went into them gladly.

"Why didn't you tell me?" he murmured against her hair.

"I meant to, but you were so busy telling me that for a few minutes I lacked the opportunity. By the time I had it, I was angry, so I . . . I—"

"So you decided to torment me a little by way of punishment?" Jeremy suggested, and saw the answer in her laughing face. His hands moved up and around Rietta's neck. "Definitely, I shall throttle you," he promised, even as his fingers caressed.

"Yes, Jeremy."

"I will spare you if you call me Jamie again. It was my mother's name for me. Only she and Sally have ever used it, but neither made it sound quite the way you do."

Rietta rubbed her cheek softly against his. "Did they not, Jamie?"

"They did not. Rietta, will you marry me?"

"I don't know. I want to, but I can't yet. Oh, Jeremy, be patient a little longer. I—"

"Say Jamie."

"Yes, Jamie. Jamie, will it help if I promise I will marry none but you?"

"It will help just a little for just a while."

"Then I promise you this much, Jamie. I will marry no one but you. I do love you, Jamie. I love you so much."

He gathered Rietta to him once more, feeling her wildly beating heart against his, and regarded her almost pityingly.

"My poor Quaker spitfire," his voice teased, but his eyes were compassionate and loving. *"Thee* knowest *thee* art fighting a losing battle. Very well, fight on a little longer. I will have you in the end."

Molly and Anne were waiting outside the library. They pounced on Rietta as soon as she and Jeremy entered the hall.

"Miss Rietta," they chorused, "will you come walking with us now?"

"Would you like to see the horses?" Molly offered.

"Wouldn't you rather go down to the river?" Anne coaxed.

"I'll show you my own darling sheep," Molly wheedled, slipping a warm hand into Rietta's. "Uncle John gave him to me. I call him Baby Johnny."

Anne tossed her head. "Oh, she's so silly about that sheep. There's a real baby we could show you. Amos's wife had a darling little boy last week."

"I am not silly. You're silly yourself," Molly accused. "Babies are always getting born."

"No, they're not, you stupid!" Anne shouted. "I've never seen a baby be born before."

"You didn't see this one be born either. It was hours old when you saw it. You're always lying." Molly turned to Rietta with a scornful expression. "She's always making up stories. You can't believe a word she says."

Anne grimaced and made fists of her hands, the better to pummel her sister. "Liar yourself!" she screeched. "Mean, horrid liar!"

Jeremy, aghast, pulled them apart at the same moment Cousin Sally and his father came hurrying from the small parlor to investigate the sounds of strife.

Mr. Stuart tried to hide a smile behind his hand while Cousin Sally spoke severely. "Anne, Molly, I'm deeply ashamed of you both. I warned you before we left home that I would not tolerate such bickering at Scot's Haven. If you cannot behave like young ladies, then perhaps we had better return to Richmond."

"Now, Sally, they didn't mean—"

She whirled on Jeremy's father in a fury. "Stop interfering, John. You spoil them shamelessly when they come here, and *I* have to cope with the results."

"They need a father."

"A father who gives in to them on every occasion?"

"A father wouldn't do that . . . only a part-time cousin."

Jeremy grinned at Rietta as he relaxed a hand on the girls' shoulders. "Do you think," he whispered, "I had better pull the new combatants apart before they, too, come to blows?"

Rietta left him to decide for himself and continued talking earnestly to the Custis girls, who studied the carpet with downcast eyes, sniffling slightly. When Rietta stood aside from them, Molly was the first sister to speak.

"Cousin John, we apologize for behaving so badly in your house."

She dipped a little curtsy to him as Anne addressed their mother. "We're sorry we shamed you by our manners, Mama. We won't do it again, honestly, we won't, if you'll please let us stay here."

"We're sorry, everyone." Molly cast a beaming smile at Rietta. "There, did we say it right?"

"Beautifully," Rietta approved. "Now, if you'll go off by yourselves for the next two hours and play quietly without disturbing anyone or quarreling, the three of us will take a long, long walk after lunch and you will show me everything. The horses, the river, the sheep *and* the baby."

They scampered off happily, and the others were left staring at Rietta.

"Whew!" Jeremy whistled, then smiled apologetically. "Sorry, Sally, but I've never seen your terrors come out of a tantrum so fast."

"Nor I," agreed Cousin Sally. "You have a magic touch with children, I think, Rietta. You'll make a wonderful mother."

Rietta turned scarlet as Jeremy's mocking eyes met hers. "Won't she, though, Sally," he said cheerfully, "once she gets over the strange notion that it's other people's children she must mother."

More quickly even than Anne and Molly, Rietta whirled and fled upstairs. But all the running away in the world couldn't hold back the memory of that look in Jeremy's eyes.

For the entire week, wherever Rietta went and whatever she did—with the Custis girls or without them—Jeremy was there, his eyes always on her with that look of loving amusement. It was a week of constant gaiety, punctuated periodically by prolonged meals abundant in food, laughter and convivial conversation.

There was gaming every day, with the men betting hugely and the ladies more modestly at whist and loo and old maid.

They played cribbage and backgammon as well, and the gentlemen spent hours apart in the billiards room. The card games continued for some after dining, while others in the party read aloud from popular novels and poets or acted out plays by Jonson and Shakespeare.

There were horses for all who wanted to ride, and the men organized quarter races for their own entertainment. Hunting took place when the weather permitted, but Jeremy chose instead to give Rietta riding lessons; this to the amazed delight of Anne and Molly, who could not at first believe any adult would be in need of lessons. They regarded riding as the next step after walking.

There were musical evenings at which Rietta played her violin. And, to accommodate those wild for dancing, impromptu little balls often occurred, as well as more elegant, planned affairs.

All these activities extended into the next week and those following it. Rietta gladly allowed herself to be swept up in the prevailing spirit of merriment, only occasionally becoming trapped with several sluggish ladies who would sit over their embroidery or their gossip and tear to shreds the characters of those who did not.

Jeremy came upon her during one such encounter. From the salon doorway he studied her flushed cheeks, set mouth and darkling eyes, then moved quickly to stand beside her, one firm hand planted on her shoulder so that she could not rise from her seat.

"Your servant, ladies." His easy smile and bow addressed them all. "You look quite blooming."

A buxom matron, wearing an overly elaborate gown of a disastrous shade of purple, looked up at him with the sharp eyes of a ferret and responded coarsely. "Ha! Save the pretty speeches for your printing wench. She's the one you meant."

Jeremy colored angrily, opened his mouth to retort and instead yelped, "Ouch!" He cast a reproachful glance at Rietta, who had just given a hearty nip to the arm pressed against hers.

She rose from her chair with fluid grace. "How kind of you to say so," she told the matron before presenting her back. "Do let us stroll, Jeremy. I feel a strong need for some *interesting* conversation."

They walked in stately silence from a roomful of women suddenly struck dumb. Jeremy gave way to his laughter only when they were safely down the hall.

"Cousin-by-courtesy Tasmin Fairchild has met her match in you, I would say."

"I mind her less than some of the others," Rietta returned coolly. "She merely says aloud what the others think."

"This would not be your life. My brother George . . . you've heard me mention him?"

"He's studying medicine in Edinburgh. You expect him home in the spring. The sewing circle says he's exceedingly handsome," Rietta recited, holding up a finger for each fact.

"George is my *older* brother. I am a second son. By the law of primogeniture, my love"—he smiled—"the eldest son inherits all, or almost all. I have some money from my mother and even more from my father's uncle, who died childless. Still, I will have to make my way as a lawyer." Jeremy's smile grew tender. "Have you been thinking all this while that I studied under Mr. Wythe to fill my idle days?"

"Jamie, oh, Jamie." She flung her arms about him, her tears wetting his neck.

He managed to free himself of this damp embrace and pull Rietta into the billiards room, shutting the door.

"You must be the only girl in Virginia," he marveled, his eyes teasing, "to weep for joy at discovering a rich property has just slipped out of her fingers."

Embarrassed, she wiped the tears from her cheeks and said, "It has naught to do with me. I only—I just—I thought—"

"Hypocrite," he reproached.

She turned and seized hold of the nearest French cue hanging on the rack. "Will you give me a game," she asked to divert him, "or would it shame you to be beaten by a female?"

"You are not going to tell me you play at billiards?"

"I was going to tell you precisely that, but I won't if it shocks you too greatly. Yet the truth is, I play well. My father taught me. The printer he bought our business from had set up a table in a room he built onto the back of the shop. My father turned it into a political club, which was at once entertaining and good for business. The gentlemen came to play billiards and damn King George, and they bought the political tracts we had strung up on lines hanging from wall to wall."

Forty minutes later they emerged from the billiards room, flushed and laughing, and Jeremy straightaway amused the company with the story of their hard-fought game.

"I won," he finished, chuckling, "but, by God, it was a close-run victory."

The men looked at Rietta with admiration, which was perhaps what prompted one young lady to remark spitefully, "You seem to shine at all things masculine, Miss Rind—working at a newspaper, playing the violin, and now billiards as well."

Jeremy would have spoken up, but Rietta's fingers pressing on his elbow stayed his defense of her.

"Why, Miss Nelson," she said in a voice of quiet meekness that deceived no one, "nowhere in the Commandments have I found the abilities mentioned to be thou-shalt-nots for women. Perhaps you should study the Commandments yourself, my dear, paying particular heed to the last."

She smiled into the scarlet face of the girl opposite, and dipping a curtsy to Sally, murmured, "If you will excuse me, ma'am, I promised to furnish your daughters with another chapter in the stirring adventures of Lady Robina Hood. I must get to it immediately if I am not to be late to the dinner table."

Rietta walked out of the suddenly hushed room with dowager stateliness, and Jeremy, offering a courtly bow to the assembled company, followed her.

"The Tenth Commandment," they heard Cousin Sally muse quite clearly. "Let me see . . . ah, yes, 'Thou shalt not covet thy neighbor's house'—nor, I believe, anything else that is his, including a son."

Chapter 24

Jeremy ranged himself alongside Rietta as they went up the graceful stairway. His voice was husky with suppressed laughter. "And I thought, poor, foolish male that I am, I must be your protector against the tabbies, both young and old."

She cast him a sidelong glance. "I have told you before, I can look after myself."

"But I never saw you prove it quite so devastatingly, my love. Tell me, who is Lady Robina Hood?"

"Oh, the most daring creature, I assure you. Actually, a royal princess whose true love was killed by the wicked king, her father, so that she would marry the ugly prince of his choice. Instead of which, she escapes to the Colonies in the name and clothes of her lover. There she travels about the land, having a grand time and helping poor people everywhere."

Rietta paused a moment for breath and then showed him a face of laughing delight. "She particularly helps women who are forced by their fathers into distasteful marriages or are mistreated by disagreeable husbands. They leave their homes and band with her in Shirley Forest. Molly and Anne are completely enchanted by her. They receive only a chapter before bedtime," she added righteously, "on the days their own conduct has been quite praiseworthy."

"Oh, my God!" he groaned. "Lady Robina Hood indeed! Was she the best model you could imagine for those little demons? Praiseworthy, ha! Wait until they break out in their usual conduct. They'll do it with a vengeance, you may be sure."

Rietta turned up her nose. "Stuff and nonsense," she said airily.

Some five hours later, she was saying miserably, "Oh, Sally, I'm so sorry."

Sally had tapped at her door after finding the girls' beds empty when she had gone in to take a look at them before retiring.

"They put bolsters under the bed coverings so that anyone looking in from the doorway would be deceived." Sally shook her head ruefully. "But I had thought Anne seemed a bit feverish earlier tonight, so I pulled down the covers to feel her brow."

John Stuart sent servants to search the house and grounds, but Jeremy went immediately to his brothers' room.

He returned to the upper hallway, where the women were waiting.

"Gone," he announced cheerfully. "Same thing. Bolsters under the blanket. Sally, love"—he took her hand—"don't look so worried. It's plain they're off together on some prank. What's more, I think I know what it is. There's going to be some cock-fighting down at the quarters tonight. I heard Big Mose speaking of it to Billy . . . and I think Molly was present." Jeremy frowned in concentration. "Yes, I'm sure it was Molly. Later I heard her and Anne quarreling with Tom and Billy. It was something about girls having the right to see the same sporting events as boys. I didn't pay much heed at the time, but I seem to recall"—he shot a glance at Rietta—"Anne's saying there was a way girls could get to do the same things as boys."

"Oh, dear Lord," Rietta moaned. "Lady Robina Hood."

"I wouldn't be surprised," Jeremy returned.

Lady Robina Hood had to be explained as speedily as possible, and Rietta was relieved to find Cousin Sally more amused than angry.

"So that's how you've kept them behaving so angelically." She turned to Jeremy. "Jamie, do you think . . . the cockfight . . .?"

"I suspect Tom and Billy will be down there, accompanied by two younger friends who wear very ill-fitting clothes, pull their tricorns forward to hide their faces and, incidentally, need their bottoms tanned."

"It will be my pleasure," Sally declared fervently. "Just find them for me, Jamie, dear."

"I shall." He pressed her hand. "Leave it to me. Why don't you get my father and wait for me in the library, Rietta? I think Sally should have some brandy."

He ran down the stairs, and though Rietta felt herself in the way, she could not forbear seeking Mr. Stuart and following him and Cousin Sally into the library. It was impossible to sleep or stay alone in her room until all four children had returned.

Sally began to pace nervously. "I know they're safe and Jeremy will bring them back," she said almost apologetically, "but until they're here, I won't be able to rest."

"Of course not," John Stuart agreed. "Wait till I get hold of those rapscallions of mine for enticing the girls into such a piece of mischief!"

Sally laughed a bit hysterically. "In all fairness, John, it is highly probable that Anne and Molly did the enticing."

She was answered only by a grunt, but a moment later he gave a sudden shout that caused Sally to stop in her tracks and Rietta to jump in her seat. "Damn it, Sally, it's you I blame, not them! I keep telling you your girls lack the schooling only a father can give, just as my boys are in need of a mother's gentling influence!"

A servant entered with the brandy that had been rung for and was waved away after he had set down the tray. Mr. Stuart poured out a generous amount for Sally and brought the glass across the room to her.

"No, I don't need it," she murmured distractedly.

"Woman!" he roared. "Drink it down and no more nonsense!"

To Rietta's surprise, Sally smiled slightly and acquiesced. Mr. Stuart returned to the decanter and helped himself liberally, staring moodily into the fire as he drank.

At this point, Rietta decided that she, too, stood in need of a stimulant. She rose, walked over to the tray and proceeded to serve herself.

John Stuart stirred slightly. "Sorry, m'dear. Was rather forgetting your presence."

Rietta sipped tentatively, remaining as thoughtful as the

other two. Jeremy entered this scene of silent drinking a quarter of an hour later, pushing ahead of him a rather sheepish and shamed-looking Tom and Billy, and Anne and Molly, as predicted, in their ill-fitting boys' attire.

Rietta, having received one long, ironic look from Jeremy, kept her eyes cast down and never ventured a word.

Mr. Stuart began to shout impartial censure on all four. Tom, after a quick exchange of eye signals with Billy, stepped forward manfully and put the entire blame on himself and his brother.

A sniffling Molly contradicted him. "No, we made them," she insisted. "They didn't really want to take us, but we sneaked into their room and borrowed their clothes, and then we made them take us."

A quick quarrel sprang up among the children as each strove to take the blame. Rietta began laughing hysterically, Sally burst into tears and Mr. Stuart swore aloud in vexation.

Jeremy judged it prudent to step into the fray. "Off to bed, the four of you. This is no time for discussion."

They scuttled off gladly but were stopped at the door by an ominous edict from Mr. Stuart. "Thomas. William."

"Sir?" they chorused.

"I will see you both here half an hour before breakfast."

"Yes, sir," they agreed.

The door closed quietly behind them.

Sally had stopped crying. Her foot tapped the floor and her eyes sparkled angrily. "Not my girls, too?" she inquired, falsely sweet. "You will punish the boys, while my girls, who were the instigators, will go scot-free?"

"If they go scot-free, as I make no doubt they will, it is because you fail in your duty," he answered her harshly. "I do not have the right to switch your girls. You have not given it to me. If you had, I would, and I think"—he strode toward her and stared down into her angry face—"I think I would start with you, Sally Custis."

The anger died out of Sally's face. She began to laugh, and could not stop. The more she laughed, the more furious John Stuart became. He half raised his hand—

Jeremy leaped forward. "Sir!"

With a glare evincing positive dislike for all of them, John Stuart marched out of the library.

Sally said quietly, "You had best go after him and try to calm him down, Jamie."

"Yes, I will. You must excuse him, Cousin Sally. He was quite upset, he didn't mean—"

"Yes, he did, but never feel you need excuse your father to me, Jamie. Go now, dear boy, and thank you."

The door closed a third time, leaving Rietta and Sally alone.

Sally picked up her half-full brandy glass from the table and eyed it critically. "I have often wondered why men turn to drink as a way out of their troubles. I've a mind this night to find out." She finished the liquid in several swallows and refilled the glass. "Will you join me, Rietta?"

"I think . . . I would like that very much."

Rietta accepted the full glass of brandy Sally held out to her and sank down on the couch. Sally joined her. "I thought . . . for a moment he looked as though—was he really going to hit you?"

"My poor, darling John. I think he actually might have. A pity."

"Pity?"

"That Jamie stepped in. Now we'll never know."

Rietta stared. "You *wanted* him to hit you?"

Sally absently swirled the contents of her glass. "Why, yes, I think I did, if it meant that for a moment, just one single moment in our lives, he would lose control. He's such a good man . . . kind, gentle, courteous and always"—her voice turned suddenly sardonic—"always so damnably controlled."

Seeing Rietta still looking bewildered, she smiled a little sadly. "No one would be more horrified than John if he *had* hit me. It might have brought him out of himself for once. I would have seen Johnny, my darling harum-scarum Johnny, whom I grew up with, not John Stuart, widower, who thinks me a fitting chatelaine for Scot's Haven and the proper stepmother for his sons."

"Why, you love him!"

"All my life," Sally admitted softly. "All my life." She drank deep of her brandy.

"But why have you not accepted him, then? Jam—Jeremy told me that Mr. Stuart has asked you several times to be his wife."

"Because I love him," Cousin Sally replied, staring as somberly into the fire as John Stuart had earlier. "Because I love him." Her voice pitched higher each time she repeated the words. "Because I love him."

She gave Rietta another sad smile. "You don't understand, do you? How could you, when you have had all of Jamie's heart since the first day you met. He told me so himself. John and I were children together, then boy and girl, and I loved him always. When I was sixteen and ready to have him turn to me as a man, my mother's goddaughter, Eleanor Harwood, came here on a visit from England. It was the same for John as with Jamie. From the first day he saw her, I never had a chance.

"After they were wed, I accepted Francis Custis. He was rich and handsome, enough older than I for him to spoil me royally as well as love me. I was grateful, and because of my gratitude I tried hard to make him happy, but Francis was no fool. Despite that we were reasonably content together, he always knew something was missing. I wanted to love him as he deserved, but he felt the difference. It was impossible for me to give my heart's deepest passion where I felt only warm affection. All our years together Francis thirsted and hungered for what it was not in me to give. He died never having had it. And fifteen months after Eleanor died, more than twenty years after I first waited for him to do so, John asked me to wed him. It was a very *sensible* proposal. I needed a husband, he needed a wife. My girls needed a father, his younger sons needed a mother. A house and servants both need a mistress. We were old friends, and though our hearts were buried in the graves of our loved ones, for the sake of the living we should strive to make a life together. He would do his best to see that I never regretted it."

Sally paused, casting Rietta a rueful glance. "I had been sitting at my desk when he arrived, and Francis's old penknife lay before me. I wanted to take it and jab it into John's heart. I wanted to scream at him and curse him for my lost years of love. I wanted his arms bending my ribs, his kisses burning on my lips. I wanted him to feel sick with desire for me, and he spoke so reasonably of everyone's needs but mine."

Rietta absentmindedly finished the last of her brandy and made no protest when Sally immediately refilled the glass.

"It seems to me," Rietta began, then hesitated. "I've sometimes thought . . . you see, I've watched the two of you . . ."

"And drawn some shattering conclusion?" Sally mocked.

"I think in spite of what you say, Mr. Stuart does love you."

"Oh, yes," came the careless response, "I know he does."

"But . . . but . . ."

"He's asked me to marry him many times over the last two years, the same businesslike proposals. Between the first and the last one, he's been so set on doing things properly, he never took time out to discover that he wanted me for himself."

"You couldn't let him—show him . . .?" Rietta hinted delicately.

"I watched a man suffer because I couldn't love him enough," Sally said in a hard voice. "I'll not visit that fate on myself. I've waited twenty-four damnable years for John to tell me he loves me, and unless—until—he does, *he'll* wait for me the next twenty-four. I'll get what I want or he'll wait forever."

"Men don't wait forever," Rietta observed. "They usually marry elsewhere."

"If it must be, it will be," Sally intoned drearily. "I didn't die of it once. I won't again. Have some more brandy."

"Thank you. Really, it's quite delicious when one gets used to it, isn't it? I think I'll have Lady Robina Hood try some brandy with her warm milk and butter. Oh, dear, I suppose you'd rather I didn't write about Lady Robina any more."

"No, no, you keep on writing, she sounds a delightful heroine. I'll simply have to make sure those imps of mine understand the difference between what they're allowed to read and what they're allowed to do."

"Oh, good. I *do* like Lady Robina. I like her very much. . . . Cousin Sally, I feel quite . . . queer . . . I think I must be sleepy." As Rietta said this, she slid very gently off the couch and onto the floor, still in a sitting position.

Arms lifted her. Jeremy's voice, distressingly loud, sounded in her ears. She winced at the cracking thunder of his laughter.

"Sleepy, you say? My dear Sally, that's a new word for her condition. The two of you have disposed of the better part of a full decanter of French brandy."

Rietta made an effort to open her eyes, hoping to correct his injustice. "Your father had a full glass," she reproved, and closed her eyes again.

She felt herself being shaken and wondered irritably why he was so amused. In blessed silence she was borne upstairs— the sensation was one of floating. Jeremy laid her gently on the bed, Sally standing nearby, and Rietta sighed with disappointment to feel his hold slip away.

"Jeremy," she murmured.

"Yes, love."

With an effort Rietta remembered what she was trying to say. "Sally said . . . she said . . . I want to know, it's t-true. Your arms b-bend my ribs and your kisses b-burn. Tell me, are you sick with desire for me?"

"She doesn't know what she's saying, Jamie," said Sally, faintly embarrassed.

"I do so know."

"Yes, Rietta, I am indeed sick with desire for you."

"Good . . . oh, good." She rolled over onto her side, curling up her legs in a childlike manner. "I wouldn't . . . want to be sick . . . all alone."

Rietta woke to blinding sunlight and a head that seemed much too large and heavy to belong to her body.

"Oh, God!" she groaned, closing her eyes and trying to turn over.

"Good morning, Miss Rietta."

"Ugh." She peeked up out of one bleary eye at Anne and Molly's small, stout mammy, who stood at her bedside, tray in hand.

"Daniel, he mixed you this potion, and Mr. Jeremy said I is to see you drink it down every drop, same as Miss Sally did."

"Don't mention drinking." Rietta shuddered. "Please go away."

"If I do, Mr. Jeremy, he'll come back and pour it down your throat. He says to tell you he promises he'll do just that."

"You're torturing me. Go away."

A brief peace descended over the bedroom, broken by Jeremy's voice, crisp and uncompromising. "If you choose to drink like a man, you'll have to reap the consequences. Come on, Lady Robina Hood, sit up and drink your medicine."

"I can't. It's probably nasty-tasting."

"It's exceedingly nasty-tasting, but once you get it down, it will bring you back to life." He eased her up on the pillows. "Give me the glass, Mammy. I'll tip it down your throat for you," he offered Rietta, "if you want to hold your nose."

She gritted her teeth, grabbed the glass and swallowed as fast as she could. When it was half empty, she stopped, turning pale.

"You're doing fine. Finish the rest," Jeremy encouraged her, and she managed to choke it all down.

She shuddered again. "What was that?"

"I had better not tell you. At least not right now."

"Mr. Jeremy," Mammy interrupted severely, "now she's got her medicine down, you clear out of here. You got no business in a young lady's bedroom."

"I can't think of a pleasanter place to be."

"*Mr.* Jeremy, shame on you."

Rietta turned her head around cautiously when he had gone. "I can move. The pain's going. Ooh, that was awful, Mammy, but I really do feel better."

"Sure you do. Now I better get back to my babies, unless you need some help dressing, honey."

"Thank you, Mammy, but where I come from, big girls dress themselves."

Later, getting into her clothes, Rietta regretted her statement of independence. Her body was still slightly numb and her fingers seemed all thumbs.

Scattered memories of the night before didn't help her stumbling progress. Did I say those things, or was it Sally, or did I just dream them? she wondered.

"Oh, please, God," she moaned, struggling into her shift, "let me only have dreamed it."

When she came out of her room, she saw Anne and Molly sitting on the top step of the stairs, looking unusually solemn.

"What's troubling you, poppets?" Rietta asked brightly.

"Tom and Billy just went down to the library to see Uncle John," Anne said mournfully. "It truly was our fault."

"They're probably going to be punished because they wouldn't tell on us." Molly's lips quivered.

Rietta peered over the stair rail. "Tom! Billy! Wait for me." She sped downstairs. "I'm going to see your father first," she told the boys. "You wait ten minutes after I go in—remember, a full ten minutes—and then you knock on the door." She smiled encouragingly. "Don't worry it's going to be all right."

"Come in."

John Stuart looked up forbiddingly as Rietta answered his invitation. His face softened when he saw who it was.

"Mr. Stuart, I've just been with Anne and Molly. The boys are not to blame for last night's escapade. The only way they could have prevented it would have been to carry tales to you or Cousin Sally." She smiled persuasively. "Now, you know that would violate the code of any proper boy, would it not? Besides," she rushed on eagerly before he could form a response, "it was as much my fault as the girls', maybe more. I gave them the idea."

"*You* did?"

"Well, Lady Robina Hood did, and I'm to blame for her."

"Lady Robina Hood?" he repeated in astonishment. "I think you had better explain, because I'm dam—I don't know what in thunder you're talking about, my dear."

Quickly and breathlessly, Rietta explained. When her voice finally trailed off, John Stuart was eyeing her somewhat grimly.

"You are right, the boys should be let off. As for you . . . I wonder," he mused, "if Jeremy fully realizes what he's letting himself in for."

He laughed, seeing her color rise high, but even as she blushed, Rietta seized her advantage.

"Cousin Sally will be so relieved," she lied unblinkingly. "When I spoke to her this morning, she was terribly distressed that you would punish Tom and Billy unjustly."

"Since when is Sally afraid to speak her mind to me?" he inquired sardonically.

"Oh, I shouldn't think she would ever be afraid of that . . . but . . . but—"

"But what?" he demanded sharply, seeing she made no effort to continue.

"Haven't you ever noticed, sir, that people of even the highest intellect can be just as foolish as anyone else when it comes to being in love?"

He gave a short, unhappy bark of laughter. "Sally's not in love."

Rietta seemed to hesitate. "Well, of course, you should know, sir, but—"

A knock sounded on the door, and Tom and Billy, looking quite chastened, appeared in the doorway.

"Yes, what is it?" Stuart asked testily.

"You told us to be here, Father," Tom said.

"I did?"

"Last night," Billy offered helpfully. "Remember?"

Their father waved them away. "Well, run along now. And next time don't let those two minxes lead you around by the nose."

Before the boys bolted out, Billy bestowed a wink on Rietta, and Tom beamed so happily that her heart melted with tenderness. They both reminded her so much of Jeremy.

When the door closed, John Stuart cleared his throat. "You were saying something," he remarked, pretending to rifle casually through the papers on his desk, "about Sally."

"About Sally, sir?" she repeated innocently.

"That she was . . . is . . . does . . ."

"Love you, sir? I think so."

"Did she tell you that?"

Rietta reacted as if shocked. "Goodness me, no! She wouldn't want to give herself away. It's merely that I—well, I can't help noticing . . . things."

"I think you're imagining things, not noticing them," he answered shortly. "I've lost count of all the times I've asked Sally to be my wife."

"Yes, I know."

"Oh, she mentioned that, did she?" he growled. "Then if she feels as you say, why hasn't she snapped me up?"

"Perhaps you haven't asked her properly, sir."

"Asked her properly!" He glared at Rietta, almost strangling on his own words. "I've all but begged the wench. I've practically been on my knees to her this whole last year. Time and time again I've given her all the reasons that make marriage the only sensible choice for both of us."

"Oh, I see," Rietta mused, as though to herself. "So that's the way it was."

John Stuart was staring at her with growing suspicion. After some moments of silence, during which Rietta managed with some difficulty to preserve a serious expression, he urged her, "If you know something that I do not, pray enlighten me."

"I cannot speak for Sally," she said with that same air of hesitancy, "only how I might feel in her circumstances. And in many ways I feel we are alike, except that—"

"Yes, yes, go on."

"I was merely going to express my belief, Mr. Stuart, that a woman of character wants to be asked, of course, but certainly not begged. And she prefers a man, a real man, standing on his feet, not kneeling at hers. On the other hand, a woman of any sensibility, even at Sally's advanced age . . ."

She bit back a smile at the outraged protest that rose to his lips. "Sally's advanced age! Why, Sally is only—" Stuart interrupted himself. "You were speaking of a woman of sensibility," he reminded Rietta more calmly.

"Such a woman doesn't want to hear all the *sensible*

reasons for being wed. Why, if Jeremy had done that to me, I could have torn the love out of my own heart and dismissed him long ago."

She was not pretending now; her voice shook with the passion of her sincerity.

His father was looking at her with such incredulous wonder that Rietta could not forbear smiling openly as she rose from her chair. She took a deep breath for the final difficult thing she had to say.

"I am sorry if you think me unladylike, Mr. Stuart." Rietta blushed even as she went on doggedly. "But the plain truth is that I think you would have done better long ago if, instead of telling Sally how much you desired her to be mistress of Scot's Haven, you had informed her how greatly you desired her as mistress in your bedroom."

By the time Rietta had finished, his complexion was also a vivid red. She almost ran out of the library, and they did not meet again until breakfast.

All through the meal she was conscious of his eyes darting back and forth between Sally, at the foot of the table, and herself, seated halfway between them. Speculative eyes, smoldering eyes. She avoided them, head bent, so much quieter than usual that Jeremy began to study her in wonder and speculation.

Midway through the meal John Stuart pushed back his chair and leaned forward, calling out Sally's name. She did not appear to hear him.

"Sally!" he repeated so compellingly that conversation ceased and everyone's eyes, not only Sally's, became riveted upon him.

"Yes, John?"

Having her full attention, he proceeded more quietly. "When the postrider came, my letters included an invitation from the palace. The governor is giving a ball this day a week to honor the queen's birthday and the birth of a child to Lady Dunmore."

"Yes John. Will you attend?"

"That is for you to decide."

"Me?"

For all Sally's apparent serenity, Rietta, watching closely, saw the tension in her face and that she hid her trembling hands in her lap.

"It is four years since there was a woman in my house," Stuart continued with aplomb, "and I am determined there shall be one again. My boys need one, and so do I, just as your girls need a father. In case I never made it clear to you before, I want you for my wife, Sally, but not only for the children's benefit. I want you for myself because I love you, but I am out of patience with your excuses and delays."

His fist came down on the table, rattling dishes and overturning a glass. "It is you I love and you I want, but if you say me nay again, then I swear I will go to the governor's ball and offer for the first spinster or widow I dance with. And I'll keep on offering until one of them tells me aye. Now I ask you again, for the last time, Sally, will you or will you not have me?"

They stared at each other across the length of the table for a long, breathless moment.

"I'll have you, John," Sally said.

She tore her eyes away from Stuart's ardent gaze and turned to the gentleman on her right as calmly as though she had not just settled her life's happiness.

"Samuel," she chided, "you have hardly eaten a morsel, and the omelets are so delicious. Anne, dear, please pass the spoon bread to Cousin Samuel."

Anne passed the spoon bread to Cousin Samuel as John Stuart rose determinedly and strode past everyone until he had reached Sally's chair.

"*Our* guests will excuse you," he said in a low but firm voice. Sally stood up at once, her face rosy and radiant. Without offering excuses, she preceded him out of the room.

Daniel, the butler, closed the door behind them, but not before the entire breakfast party saw Mr. Stuart stop in the hallway and take Sally into his arms.

Excited conversation and congratulations filled the already charged atmosphere, under cover of which Jeremy leaned across Molly to address Rietta. "Now, how the hell did you bring that about? The boys said you were shut up with him for a considerable time before breakfast, and I'd swear it was you who did it."

Rietta laughed and shook her head. "I merely gave him some hints on the proper way to propose marriage to a willing woman."

At this, Jeremy flung back his head and roared with delight.

Chapter 25

The moment breakfast was over, Jeremy hooked his arm through Rietta's and led her to the library.

Closing the door behind them, he faced her, eyes twinkling, and taxed her again with having united Sally and his father.

"What arts did you use, my little witch, I should like to know?" he demanded.

"If it was witchery," Rietta replied demurely, "you can hardly expect me to confess it."

He started chuckling again. "Oh, Lord!" he choked. "The expression on some of their faces when he said he would ask the first woman he danced with at the governor's ball. Speaking of which, a letter for you from Williamsburg came in the same post as his invitation."

He moved toward the desk and handed the letter to her. Rietta accepted it hesitantly, then stiffened her spine and broke the seal.

"From John Pinkney in answer to mine," she murmured.

Jeremy nodded. "I thought as much."

An uneasy quiet settled over them as she scanned the single page. It became obvious to Jeremy, watching sympathetically, that she was giving the letter a second reading.

Presently, she walked over to the grate and tossed Pinkney's reply into the blazing fire. When Jeremy gently turned her around to face him, she looked up and could not see him for her tears.

"Rietta?"

"I am not to come back to the *Gazette*. I expected him to say so." She smiled forlornly. "I don't know why the actual words came as such a shock. I knew we couldn't live under the same roof or work together after this. John will take over the ownership of the paper, with Dick to help him and the children's share will go into the estate. The Masons—Cousin William was an active Mason—are making themselves responsible for the children."

Jeremy took out a large handkerchief and carefully wiped her face.

Rietta tugged at her lower lip with her teeth, then shrugged and smiled again. "So another phase of my life is over and you, I can see, do not regret it a bit."

"No, I don't," Jeremy admitted. "Would you want me to play the hypocrite?"

She pulled free of him, suddenly impatient and angry.

"Rietta, you are unreasonable. Why are you blaming me?"

"Because you are glad. You think I have nowhere to turn and that therefore I may turn to you."

"I have been waiting all this time for you to turn to me out of love, so I think I might be spared your accusations now." His exasperation was barely controlled. "There was always the possibility you might decide to go home to your family in Philadelphia, which would hardly be a happy choice for me."

"I have told you before, I have no home or family in Philadelphia. My father has a second wife, who I assure you is no Sally, and a new son, which leaves no room in his heart for a daughter."

"Strange."

"What is strange?"

"I wrote to your father quite some months ago. His answering letter showed no lack of love or concern in his heart for you."

Rietta stared at him incredulously. "You wrote to my father? What about?"

"Don't be a simpleton. About you, of course. Would you care to see his reply?"

"I *insist* on seeing it."

Jeremy's brows went up, but he said only, "Wait here while I fetch the letter from upstairs."

Within five minutes he had returned.

"I asked his permission to make you my wife," he told Rietta calmly. "I have been waiting a long time for what seemed a propitious moment to show his reply to you. Judging by your face, this doesn't seem exactly the right moment, but here it is."

Rietta almost snatched the close-written pages from his hand. "Why would you have thought you had to write to him?" she asked scornfully.

"Yes, he seemed to think you would react this way. I suspect now, Rietta, that he understands you better than you understand yourself."

Disdaining to respond, she walked over to the window and stood there, reading mostly to herself but occasionally muttering snatches and phrases aloud.

Dear Sir:

I am in receipt of yours of the 15th instant regarding your intention to make your addresses to my daughter, Rietta. You are not unknown to me by reputation, as the widow of my kinsman William Rind had previously writ to me on the subject of your interest in Rietta and given me her assurance that you are a young man of sound judgment and good character. I held Mrs. Clementina Rind in such high esteem that her assurances sufficed me, and I would be happy to see you succeed with my daughter.

At the same time I must inform you that Rietta's knowledge of my approbation may help to prevent rather than to promote your union. It may not be amiss for me to warn you that the intelligence of such an alliance being agreeable to me could be the very cause of her refusing you. Since the occasion of my own second marriage, to please me has never been an object with her, and by way of disapproving my married state, she has herself been most determined in maintaining her celibate condition.

Mrs. Rind considered that your appearance of complaisance and outward good humor may alike be deceptive and that, if such a condition be possible, you are of even more determined mind than my daughter. I hope

Mrs. Rind to have been right, as the gentlemen here in Philadelphia who addressed my girl were more easily cast down. To speak bluntly, sir, no female of my daughter's nature ever was intended for celibacy, so it would gratify me if you can persuade her in her own interest, though all I can do in the matter is refer you directly to her.

In the event of a marriage between you, the unsettled condition of our country has so affected my affairs as not to permit me to state now what I can do for her, but she will have all her mother's furnishings together with a valued collection of books and musical instruments, including a fine harpsichord imported from England. By her maternal grandfather's will, which is unknown to her, she will have made over to her on her wedding day the five hundred pounds with accrued interest that should have been her mother's dowry, had my wife pleased her own father in the choice of a husband.

I would be exceedingly grateful if you would keep me informed of what progress you make with my daughter.

*I am, sir, your obedient servant,
Charles Rind*

P.S. Withal she is stubborn and headstrong, as we both know, and your courtship thorny, I firmly believe that once she is won, my Rietta's husband will be the most fortunate of men.

Rietta raised a mutinous face when she had done reading. "*His* Rietta indeed!" she cried stormily. "You are both right to believe that I would never marry to please *him*."

She sped across the room, and her father's letter would have followed John Pinkney's into the fire if Jeremy had not been equally fast. He stayed her hand with fingers fastened painfully around her wrist.

"The letter is mine," he said. "Return it to me, if you please."

He carefully refolded the letter into the same well-worn creases and placed it in his pocketbook while Rietta rubbed at her wrist.

"I am sorry if I hurt you, but you are a bit casual about other people's property."

"Which property do you mean?" she taunted. "My father's

letter or my father's daughter? They are one and the same to you, are they not?"

Jeremy ignored this. "Rietta, why did you leave home?" he asked abruptly.

She walked slowly back to the window, and for a while he thought she intended not to answer. Then she spoke dully, her back to him.

"My mother was a rare woman in these colonies," Rietta told him. "Beautiful, highly intelligent, educated. She worked with my father on our newspaper, as Cousin Clemmie did. She played the violin far better than I, the pianoforte and harpsichord, too. She sang like an angel and she spoke four languages. Like her mother before her, she was independent enough to have married my father in the teeth of her family's opposition. She never regretted it either, even though her Quaker brethren no longer accepted her. My father and she, and I with them, were so happy together, there wasn't any room in our home for regrets. The only sorrow in our house was the death of my brother at his birth, when I was about six. Otherwise, we—"Rietta turned with a tiny, helpless gesture that stabbed Jeremy's heart. "Otherwise, we were so happy," she whispered. "So happy."

After a few minutes Rietta announced in a hard voice, "She died when I was fifteen. We never did know the reason. It was quite sudden. The doctors gave all sorts of mysterious explanations, but the truth was, they didn't know.

"I thought my father would go out of his mind with grief. I thought he would never get over it. He . . . he was so wild, I had to be the strong one. But after a while he regained his senses and said we must manage somehow and be a comfort to each other. So *I* became the mistress of the house and played the violin to him of an evening. He talked over his business affairs with *me* then, and I helped him more and more in the shop. And six months and eleven days after my mother died, after he had raved to me that his life was no longer worth living, he brought home another wife."

"I can see that would have been difficult for you to accept." Jeremy said gently, "but cannot you see it was no reflection on your mother? With so much love as he had, he must have needed someone else to give it to. Besides, Rietta, what is your father's age?"

"I don't know. I'm not sure. About five and forty, I suppose. What has that to do with anything?"

"Everything, I should imagine. When your mother died, he was not much above forty. More than a business, a home, music and exchanges of the mind were in question. He is a man, Rietta, with a man's body and a man's needs. Those did not die with your mother. For the love of God, you who have been so often open and honest about the relations between men and women, can't you see it was a *wife* he needed, not to take your mother's place, but simply to be a woman to him?"

"A woman!" Rietta jeered. "She was only ten years older than I, a plain, awkward, skinny, stuttering old maid. Did I tell you my mother was beautiful? Her hair was thicker and more auburn than mine. She had bright, glowing eyes and clear, soft skin. Her step was light. There was a radiance about her. It was an affront to my mother's memory that he should have chosen such a one in her place. Someone no other man ever wanted. Why, her own brothers called her Homely Hannah. She stumbled around the house, falling over the furniture, breaking my mother's precious china. As for brains . . . *Yes, Charles . . . Whatever you say, Charles . . . You're so wise, Charles, so brilliant, you explain things so clearly . . .*"

The mimicry of Rietta's voice turned once again to cold anger. "And he, my wise, clever father, like a cat at its milk bowl, he lapped it up. All the butter and honey and fulsome flattery and fawning. He swallowed it so easily, his folly made me ill."

"I see," said Jeremy.

"What do you see?" She paused in her nervous pacing up and down the room. "Why are you looking at me like that?"

Jeremy ignored her questions. "When did you leave home?"

"When I was seventeen," she returned sullenly, "and their son was born. I heard my father say to her, 'You have given me the one thing I have hungered for all my life.' He who had always told me he felt no need of a son when he had me!"

She shrugged. "I knew I had no home any more. *They* were the threesome now, and I the outsider. Soon afterward the invitation arrived from Cousin Clemmie. She had often asked me to come to them before, but this time I suspect my father had solicited her to invite me. I didn't care, just so that I could leave Philadelphia. I did leave within the month, and I have never been back."

"I see."

"You keep saying that with a schoolteacher expression on your face. Exactly what is it that you see?"

"That you were jealous."

"I? Jealous of that bag of bones?" Rietta shrilled.

"Very jealous, Rietta. Not because she usurped your mother's place, but because—in your mind—she usurped yours. If she lacked brains and looks, it is obvious that *you* used yours as an added advantage of cruelty toward the poor thing. They must have immeasurably increased your ability to be unkind. If she is all that you say, have you not realized it is possible, out of gratitude for your father's affection, she may have believed all those things she said to him? And he, without feeling great passion, may have found great comfort in her love?"

Jeremy gave Rietta a studied look that was like a cold hand placed against her heart. Never before had she seen his mouth so set, his eyes so contemptuous when they dwelled on her.

"No wonder they were glad to see you go," he said, as much to himself as to her, "if during those first two years of their marriage they had to endure your playing Lucifer in their poor pitiful paradise."

She would not allow the spasm of pain that knotted her insides to show anywhere on her face.

"Pray, sir, have you any further criticisms to offer to my conduct? You have said so much, I would not want to deprive you of the pleasure of condemning me utterly."

"Even at those times I was most angry with and exasperated by you," Jeremy continued slowly, "my love and admiration have always been boundless. I never thought I would ever feel ashamed of you. Deeply, deeply ashamed of your lack of understanding and compassion and of your own loss of dignity in being so mercilessly uncharitable."

She had paled noticeably under this barrage of words but stood silent till he was done, stricken by a scorn that might signify the ending of love, aghast with the awareness of truths she had never before faced.

Rietta met his eyes, unflinching, seemingly uncaring, her trembling hands hidden in the folds of her overskirt. And Jeremy, for once misreading the proud look on her face, made a fierce gesture of impatience and left her.

It was Sally who found her sitting on a footstool by the fire, weeping over *A Midsummer Night's Dream,* and would not be satisfied or turned away before Rietta had told her the full tale.

The house party began to break up the following day—more than a month after it had begun in December—as the first guests took their reluctant departure.

Jeremy turned from saying his farewells to see Rietta slowly creeping away from the group of guests who were to remain. He confronted her squarely. "Rietta, will you walk with me?"

"N-no, I . . . I . . . I c-can't." She pulled herself together with an effort and stopped babbling. "I . . . I promised Molly and Anne that I would give them a billiards lesson."

"Tell them we both will give them one in exactly one hour from now. I want to talk to you away from this house."

"I think you—we have said all there is to be said."

"I disagree. Get your cloak."

Jeremy's mouth was set in the mulish way that, Rietta had come to learn meant she had tried him as much as she dared. With a curious flutter of pleasure that this was so, she ran to get her cloak.

They took the path leading to the stables.

"Sally tells me you are going to Richmond with her."

"Yes. I am to be companion and governess to the girls and general helper. I thought she was merely being kind at first by making the offer, but she convinced me she really needs me if she is to accomplish all she must, including the selling of her house before her return to Scot's Haven for the wedding in May. They are waiting till May, you know, to be sure your brother George will have arrived from Scotland."

"I am glad, very glad, you are going with her."

"Yes," Rietta said valiantly, determined not to show the wild desolation in her heart, "I thought you might be."

"Even though it means I may not see you for nearly four months," he blundered on in complete unawareness of her misery, "I would rather know you are safe and snug with Sally than alone in lodgings in Williamsburg or far out of my reach in Philadelphia. By the time of the wedding, my studies with Mr. Wythe will be over, and then—"

"You change your mind quickly, sir!" Rietta cried, stung. "Only yesterday you were chastising me with your tongue because I would not return to be a dutiful daughter and kindly stepchild."

Jeremy regarded her with amusement. "Did I do that?" he asked.

"That . . . and much more. I do not understand your present concern for my future plans. You made it quite clear my inhuman conduct had destroyed your respect for me."

"I did nothing of the sort," Jeremy denied sharply. "I deplored your conduct, which was abominable, but I said nothing about—"

"You said you were ashamed of me. You said—"

"So I was, and so I shall be until you make your peace with them. What has that to do with my loving you?"

"Everything, I thought."

"Rietta." His icy hands clasped together beneath the curls at the back of her neck and made her shiver even as warmth returned to her heart. "My adorable, idiotic Rietta. I think you behaved very badly. I think your father, when all other reasoning failed, was at fault not to have slapped you soundly. But I could not stop loving you for that or for any other reason. I could not— Why, Rietta, are your tears because you thought . . ."

But she was sobbing much too hard to listen, and presently Jeremy stopped talking and was content to hold her tightly against him, his arms under the cloak drawing her ever closer.

After a while she quieted, and he lifted her face and kissed away the last stray tears on her cold and wind-red cheeks.

"We must return to the house or you will be frozen. But there is just one thing more that I must say. The spring will mark a new beginning for many of us, more so than in any other year. My father and Sally will begin their new life together. George will be coming home to take up his life here. I will be leaving the Wythe's to start my own career. And you . . . you, most of all, will have to reach a decision. I learned something from my father when he spoke to Sally yesterday. There is a time to ask and a time to stop asking. You know I love you, Rietta Rind. You know I have waited these many long months for you to consent to be my wife. Now the decision is in your hands. In May, when you come back for the wedding, *you* will have to tell *me* whether you will take me for your husband. If you say nothing, then neither will I. Your silence will be answer enough."

Rietta stared at him with such large solemn eyes, he could not help laughing a bit.

"You look like Anne or Molly caught in an act of mischief."

"I do love you so much, Jamie," she said in a little-girl voice.

"The question will be whether you love me enough to put away childish doubts and give me your trust as well. Say nothing now. Think well these next four months, and I will have your answer in the spring."

"In the spring, Jamie."

Chapter 26

Myles and his parents arrived early at Christiana Campbell's Tavern. Gina had told Myles she was expecting a long-distance call from Spain and would meet them at the restaurant.

In spite of the long waiting line, it was not long before a hostess clad in a powder-blue, colonial-style gown with cream lace sleeves, escorted the Edwards to a square wooden table in one of the first-floor rooms.

Mrs. Edward looked about with interest, first at the corner dresser with its display of pewter and ceramics, then at their own table with its tin candlesticks and dolphin-patterned tableware.

"It's all so quaint and charming!" she exclaimed.

"Well, George Washington is supposed to have supped here," her husband said dryly. "If it was good enough for him, I suppose it's good enough for us. I hope the food lives up to the decor."

"Can't you think of beauty instead of your stomach?" she reproached him.

"I certainly can," he retorted promptly. "Right now there's a beautiful girl standing out in the hallway."

Myles followed his father's gaze, and his heart swelled with pride and a loving tenderness. Even if Gina had chosen to be outrageous and worn jeans and her work shirt, she would still have been his love, his girl, but she had done him proud.

Her chiffon dress was a riot of wild flowers in soft pastel shades on a white background. A cummerbund reduced her waist to incredible smallness, and layer upon layer of material swirled down to the tips of silver sandals. A lacy white stole was draped carelessly about her, trailing halfway down the back of her dress.

"The girl is Gina," Myles told his parents, and felt rather than saw some of the tension go out of his mother. He found himself wondering, not altogether humorously, what she had been expecting.

He pushed back his chair and stood up. "Excuse me. She may not have seen us."

He went out to the hallway and came up behind her. She was standing in front of a mirror, patting a loose strand of hair.

"You look lovely, Gina."

She turned quickly, and as the stole slipped back, he saw that her dress was fashioned with a halter top, no bra, no sleeves, only a simple tie around her neck and a neckline dipping low enough to be provocative without being indecent.

Her hair was a little different tonight, the sides combed into waves and held in place by jeweled clips before falling in a beautifully straight and neat cascade. Her eyes were bright and her color was high, but Myles thought he detected some of the same tension he felt in his mother.

He spoke soothingly, holding out his hand. "My parents are seated. Shall we go?"

"In a minute." Gina opened her beaded bag and took out a small white leather box. "I want to put on my necklace. Do you think an opal will suit this dress?" she asked gaily, lifting the top of the box.

It was an opal, all right. Minerology was not his field, but Myles had studied enough, as an archaeologist must, to know that the opal on the chain dangling loosely from her hand was the real thing, and so was the circle of diamonds around it.

Gina put the jewelry around her neck. "Would you fasten it, please?" She swept up her hair with her hands, and he clasped the necklace behind her neck. She dropped her hands and whirled around to him. "How does it look?"

The opal hung just above the V of her neckline, catching fire from the colors in her dress.

"It looks perfect," Myles said briefly. Which it did, but he was also bitterly aware that more than an opal pendant hung around her neck. There was the price of six months' income from his mill shares; and where in hell had the jewel come from?

"Ready?"

"As soon as I put on my earrings." She reached inside her purse for another box and removed two small, star-shaped diamond earrings from it. After she had fastened them on, she faced him demurely. "I'm ready now."

When Gina turned demure, it was time to call out the marines. As she walked beside Myles to the table, he heard a delightfully feminine sound of taffeta petticoats that in no way reassured him. The sparkle in her eyes was decidedly militant.

However, Gina was perfectly courteous, if somewhat cool, during the introduction to his mother, and a shade more cordial to his father, who had ordered a carafe of wine during Myle's absence. Gina declined the offer of a glass, joining Mrs. Edward in a request for tomato juice.

"Don't mind me if you want a drink, my dear," the older woman said.

Myles's spirit groaned within him.

And rightly so.

"Thank you," Gina returned sweetly. "I never drink, but don't mind *me* if *you* want one."

Myles broke in with some questions about the family, which kept them busy for the next several minutes. Gina sat and sipped her juice, looking like Little Miss Muffet. Myles could cheerfully have crowned her.

The foursome were somewhat more relaxed when the clam chowder was served. Conversation became more general.

At one point, Mr. Edward leaned over to Gina and lifted the opal by its chain. "That's a mighty pretty stone, Gina," he complimented her easily. "I've been admiring it since you sat down."

"Thank you." Gina smiled at him. "My father bought it for me when we were in Australia."

"Your bag is lovely, too," Myles's mother chimed in. "The way those pink and blue and green beads blend in with your dress makes a perfect match. Were they bought together?"

"Thank you," Gina repeated, a trifle more formally, "but the way they match is pure luck. My father bought the bag for me in Paris, and the dress—I think we got the dress in Spain."

"Which country did your earrings come from?" Myles queried politely, and for a moment he saw a flash of the Gina he had wanted his parents to know.

She grinned. "Touché. As it happens, Victor bought them on Forty-eighth Street in New York."

"Victor?" he said quickly.

"Victor. My father." Myles frowned a little, and Gina asked airily, "Are you thinking the name sounds familiar? Victor's the American version. Try Vittorio."

"Vittorio . . . good God, Vittorio Jacobi!" Myles stared at her incredulously. "Your father is Vittorio Jacobi, the movie director?"

One weight had been lifted from his chest when he discovered the source of her jewelry. Now another weight descended.

"It never occurred to you to mention that you were his daughter?"

"The subject never came up, Anyhow, I prefer being known as me, not as my father's daughter."

"Okay, I'll buy that. What I'm not buying are all those lies you laid on me."

"When did I do that?"

"You told me your father was in the service. I distinctly remember your mentioning—it was on the drive from Washington—that he had once been stationed in Scotland."

"You're mistaken. What I said was that my father's job took him to lots of places, and it does. He produces and directs films all over the world. I mentioned that one year Victor had to stay near the submarine base in Scotland. Well, he did. He was making a documentary about the Loch Ness monster, and he had permission to use the facilities of the base."

They both knew that her version was a crock of snow, but also that this wasn't the time or the place to quarrel about it. God, but she was exasperating!

Mrs. Edward quickly looked at her son's forbidding face and broke in with well-intentioned, if heavy, tact. "Goodness, this spoon bread is delicious. How can we be expected to eat a main course?"

As far as he was concerned, Mr. Edward announced stoutly, that would not be a problem; but Myles's mother had struck a sympathetic chord in Gina.

"I always get stuffed too soon myself," she confessed, "which your son cannot get through his head."

The two men became sidetracked with other matters for a while, during which Myles breathed somewhat more easily because the ladies seemed to be doing fine. When he turned to them again, they were discussing Scottish poetry and prose.

"At your age," Mrs. Edward was saying, "I had a favorite heroine called Babbie, from—"

"The Little Minister," Gina interrupted happily, "by James Barrie. I liked Babbie, too. She had spunk."

"Goodness," Mrs. Edward marveled, "I didn't think your generation had even heard of Barrie."

"I haven't read Barrie, Ma," Myles teased her, "But I'll bet I can describe your heroine."

"I don't need you to," his mother said almost dreamily. "She was beautiful, high-spirited, warm-hearted, generous, impulsive—"

"Modern translation, Dad," Myles broke in. "She was sexy, stubborn, hot-tempered, wild and reckless, but she had a good heart."

"I don't know how a son of mine can have so littly poetry in his soul," Mrs. Edward remarked good-naturedly.

"This food is poetry enough for me," his dad contributed, and Gina gave a happy giggle.

"You're a realist, Mr. Edward," she told him gaily.

"How about me?" Myles prodded with a touch of malice. "Would I have fallen for my mother's favorite heroine?"

"Probably," Gina answered, unperturbed, nibbling on a corn stick. "Kicking and fighting against it every minute."

"Do you really think so, Gina?" Mrs. Edward asked, and the two of them looked Myles over as though he were an amoeba on a miscroscope slide.

Suddenly, almost as though she'd felt herself getting too close and was frightened by it, Gina stiffened and withdrew into her shell. They had to start talking around her again.

After their main course was served, an awkward silence descended. Only Mr. Edward, plowing his way through an assortment of seafood, seemed not to sense it.

It was Mrs. Edward who threw herself into the breach. "Speaking of heroines' names, Gina," she said, dipping a large fried shrimp in mustard sauce, "I've always been particularly fond of yours. Were you named after the actress?"

"No, for my grandmother. Actually," Gina added in the

clipped voice Myles was beginning to detest, "it's a nickname. My real name is Pieragina."

Myles deliberately scraped his chair back a few inches the better to stare at her, but she was careful not to look his way.

"Pieragina," his mother repeated. "How charming and unusual. Myles, why did you never tell us?"

"For the simple reason that I never knew," he replied with a depth of bitterness he realized was out of proportion to the problem. Or was it? Gina had worked overtime at hurting him this evening, and she seemed to be succeeding.

His mother's glance flicked over him and returned to Gina. "It's such an unusual name."

"I was named for my grandmother. My Italian grandmother, not my English one—she was Pieragina, too."

"But I thought . . . didn't you say, Myles . . . ?"

Gina sat there with a curling smile on her lips, letting Mrs. Edward get all flustered.

Myles came to his mother's rescue. "You had given me to understand your mother was Jewish," he said without any finesse.

"My stepmother. I called *her* 'Mother'."

"Your real mother couldn't have been that bigoted," Myles remarked flatly. "She married your father."

"You forget," Gina reminded him sweetly, "he was filthy rich. When the money went"—she smiled impartially at all of them—"soon after so did she."

"Your . . . your parents are divorced, then?" asked Myles's mother rather feebly.

"There was no need," Gina assured them sunnily. "It turned out they had never been married." She swung around in her chair to stare straight at Myles. "That's something else I never told you, did I? Do you mind that I'm a bastard, Myles?" she almost purred at him.

His eyes were unflinching. "I couldn't care less that you're a bastard. What I mind is how hard you work at being such a god-damned bitch!"

"Myles!" Mrs. Edward's voice registered three octaves higher in outrage. "You have no—" She stopped quite suddenly, and the rage that had possessed Myles for a moment eased a bit.

He looked with affection at his father, who sat placidly, apparently unperturbed, as he ate his way through the meal with seemingly bovine concentration. There wasn't the slightest doubt in Myles's mind that a well-placed but gentle kick had been responsible for the abrupt little jerk of the body his mother had given when she broke off in midsentence.

"I'm sorry. I'm not . . . this isn't . . . oh, God, I knew this was a terrible idea! I'm behaving horribly, and it would be better if . . ." Gina's voice trailed off miserably, and she was half out of her seat when Myles's arm arrested her movement.

"Sit down." His hand on her shoulder urged her none too kindly.

"Myles, please, I—"

"Sit down." His fingers dug deeper. He added, for her ears only, "Before I belt you."

She thumped back onto her chair.

"And eat your dinner."

She cast a desperate glare at him, and reaching out blindly, latched onto his fork. He quietly exchanged utensils and felt her hand shaking, so he brought it up against his cheek and held it there for a moment.

Gina's head swiveled slowly around, and her eyes, awash with tears, met his. She gave Myles the strangest look, one that would keep him lying awake for hours that night, trying to figure out its subtle nuances.

"Eat your dinner." This time he said it quite gently. "My father hates to pay for food that isn't eaten."

"That's right," Mr. Edward agreed cheerfully. "Can't bear to see a full plate go back to the kitchen."

A brief silence followed before Mrs. Edward threw herself loyally into the breach again. "When I'm doing the cooking at home, I mind, but who cares in a restaurant? It's not my responsibility."

"Say, Myles, did you hear that your old friend Bobby Czarnecki's uncle is running for assemblyman?"

"No, I hadn't heard. I've been out of touch with Bobby for years. Republican or Democrat?"

"Republican," Mr. Edward grunted. "I sent in a contribution."

Gina stopped pushing the crab imperial around on her plate and glanced directly across at Mr. Edward with a sudden, shy halfsmile. "I think I ought to warn you that I'm—I mean my family—we're Democrats."

Mr. Edward's eyes twinkled at her. "Well, little lady," he said genially, preserving what at home was always called his great stone face, "all evening long you've been trying to shock me. You can finally take credit for succeeding."

The waiter came to remove their plates, and Gina, with a nervous sidelong look at Myles, admitted to being finished and allowed the man to take away her scarcely touched food.

As an excuse to leave the table, she murmured something about her hair and fled out to the crowded hallway. Myles excused himself abruptly and went after her.

She was leaning against the stairwell, intensely aware of his presence but refusing to look at him.

"Gina."

"Oh, please, I know I made a fool of myself."

"Gina, look at me."

"I can't. Go away, please."

"Why did you do it, Pieragina?"

That brought her head up sharply. Then she looked away again. "I don't know," she replied, obviously miserable. "Right now I honestly don't know. Maybe away from here, by myself, I'll be able to figure it out." She rubbed her forehead distractedly with the heel of her hand. "I told you it wasn't such a good idea, getting me together with your parents. I warned you that—"

"God almighty, Gina, what's the big deal? What's so unusual about a man bringing his parents to meet the girl he hopes to marry?"

"Marry!" She recoiled as if he had said something obscene. "Who said anything about marriage? Why, you don't even *like* me!"

Myles chose his words carefully, "The fact that all too often—like right now, for example—I feel an overwhelming impulse to kick your tail up one side of Duke of Gloucester Street and down the other does not mean I dislike you. Quite the reverse."

"Wanting to get me into bed is not—"

"I love you, you damn, silly fool. That's why—God help me—I want to marry you."

Gina didn't answer, and neither did she resist when Myles put an arm around her to lead her back inside.

At the table, rum cream pie and coffee were being served. Gina put a hand over her cup, her face the color of new-fallen snow. "Would you get me some tea, please?" she asked the waiter in a low, unsteady voice.

While she waited for the tea, Myles noticed that she kept playing with the beaded bag in her lap, nervously snapping and unsnapping the clasp. Finally, Gina gave a peculiar little shrug and a nod of her head, as though settling a private argument with herself. She opened her bag again, head bent, and began rummaging in it with eager desperation.

"Lose something?" Myles asked in a quiet voice.

"No, I just . . . I just . . ."

Her eyes, which she lifted to him for a few seconds, had a frighteningly feverish look. She continued to paw around inside the purse and then, in a sudden frenzy, pushed her cup aside and dumped the contents of the bag on the table.

Loose change, keys, a comb, a hankie, a used ticket to the Governor's Palace, a bus pass and a few other odd bits of paper lay jumbled together. A quarter and a lipstick rolled over the edge of the table, and Myles bent to retrieve them. When he lifted his head, Gina was staring almost with horror at the motley collection before her.

"Lose something?" he asked again.

"No. Yes." She swept everything back into the purse and dropped it into her lap. "I'm not sure," she added vaguely. "I thought I—" Then she bit her lips, splayed the fingers of both hands and pressed them firmly against her temples.

The waiter set a teapot in front of her. Gina poured the liquid with shaking hands and took a few sips. The Edwards saw her turn quite white. She carefully rose to her feet, somewhat in the manner of a drunkard trying to prove he can walk a straight line.

"I'm sorry." Her voice wasn't much louder than a whisper. "You'll have to excuse me. I'm . . . I'm not feeling very well." Gina let go of the chair back, to which she was clinging. "So sorry," she said again, assuming a rather pathetic attempt at dignity. "Didn't . . . didn't mean to spoil your evening." Unsteadily, she retreated through the crowded tables and past the waiting line.

Myles turned to his parents. "I'm sorry, too, but I have to go after her. I must make sure she's all right."

"Of course you do," his mother agreed. "The poor child."

"The poor child," Myles echoed, grimacing, "needs a good kick in the pants."

Mr. Edward grinned, but his wife surprised him. "The poor child needs taking care of," she corrected. "You go along Myles. Look for us later in the Lodge lobby or maybe on the benches in front. It's a lovely night."

"Bless you, Ma." He gave her cheek a brisk kiss and pushed his way forward until he had reached the outside porch.

He was seconds too late.

By the light of the lanterns he could see Gina mounting the free bus at stop number three, near the restaurant. The vehicle lumbered off, turning right onto Francis Street, and Myles followed after it. The walk would be shorter than waiting for the bus.

Chapter 27

When he reached the Lodge, Myles took the shortcut through the rear entrance, as Gina had done. Hurrying along the brick walk under the covered portico, he could see the flutter of her flowered chiffon skirt disappearing through the entrance to York House.

He took the broad, metal-tipped stairs two at a time and turned right. Gina's room was the last one on the left. He had brought her to it many times but had never been beyond the door.

Now it swung open wide, and Myles could see her clearly. Gina had not heard his steps coming down the hall; she was making too much noise with the opening and slamming of drawers as she searched in panic through her clothes.

"Oh, God, where is it? I know I had it. Let me think . . . let me think . . . " She punctuated her words with occasional, great racking sobs.

Myles entered the room and shut the door quietly. "Gina, what in hell are you looking for?"

"My pills. I can't find my pills."

Myles had a quick vision of a plastic pharmacy container rolling out of her knapsack in Washington, and the flare-up that had followed his first suspicion.

"Your allergy pills?"

"They're not allergy pills," she said, tears rolling down her cheeks.

He looked at her shaking hands and too brilliant eyes, and all his earlier misgivings came flooding back. "I thought you didn't take drugs."

Gina smiled bitterly while her tears continued to fall. "Oh, gallant Myles, trusting Myles, you love me, but you always believe the worst. My pills—they're for migraines. All the stuff I have was given to me by doctors to take care of the symptoms I get with a migraine."

"Then why all the elaborate lies?" he shouted.

Gina winced and put her shaking hands to her temples again. "They're not elaborate," she sighed wearily. "They simplify things. Everyone understands allergies. Migraines call for questions and explanations. People think if you have them you're neurotic."

"Well, you are," he said in a softer tone, knowing that at this point even a normal-sounding voice could stab at her painfully. He went over and gentled her with his hands. "Now, instead of panicking, think. What did you have the pills in, and when do you last remember seeing them?"

"They were in a gold-colored plastic pillbox, not one of those tiny ones that are easily lost. Mine is at least two inches by four, and it's divided into six compartments, so I always have whatever I could possibly need with me." Gina added weepily, "I never go anywhere without it."

"What do you fill it from? How about the vials from the pharmacy? Don't you have anything in those?"

"That's just it. I . . . I . . . I emptied them all yesterday to refill my pillbox. I planned on getting all my prescriptions renewed this week. Oh, Myles, I feel so sick." She dropped down on the end of the bed and put her head against her knees, rocking back and forth. "If I can't find them, I'll have to go back to the hospital for a shot."

He was methodically searching through her drawers, but he still caught the significance of her last words.

Finished with the bureau, Myles checked the desk near the window, then the night table between the twin beds. He ran a hand over the closet shelf, knelt down and searched the floor. As he approached the sink on the inside wall, his foot struck something, and he found himself looking down at Gina's yellow pillbox.

After half filling a glass with water from the sink, he went to the bed. "Gina, here it is."

She wrenched so hard at the cover of the box, half the contents spilled out onto the bed. Sifting through them eagerly, she fairly flung two pills of different colors into her mouth and drank all the water, then let the glass fall carelessly onto the bed while she picked out a square of tinfoil and tore at the edges with her teeth, releasing a tiny round, green tablet.

"I'll get you some more water." Myles reached for the glass.

"No, please. The crackers on the window sill."

Puzzled, he brought back a box of wheat crackers hidden behind the curtain.

"This one I diggolve under my tongue," Gina explained, smiling wanly. "I need something to take away the taste." She took a cracker, but as she began to chew it, Myles noticed that she was turning pale again. Beads of sweat had appeared on her forehead and were mixing with her tears.

"Are you going to be all right now?"

Anxiety made his voice sharp, but Gina misunderstood and drew away from him like a hurt child.

"Of course. I'll be fine." With an effort she swayed to her feet and looked at him with eyes glazed over from pain. "Th-thank you for finding them. Perhaps you had better go back to your family now."

Myles pushed her down on the bed and sat beside her, holding onto her hands. "Gina, darling, please tell me the truth."

"I don't know," she whispered, her face contorted. "I'm supposed to take all my stuff before a headache starts up. Once it does, the medicine may be too late to do much help."

"Is the pain very bad now?"

"Awful."

"Is there anything I can get you that will help? Maybe some tea? You didn't drink any at dinner."

"Not now. Maybe later." She shivered convulsively. "Stomach—not too good. Best . . . rest . . ."

He knelt and took off her silver shoes. Then he stood her up with him and turned her around to undo the dress. His hand had just reached for the bow at the back of the neck when Gina pulled away from him with a strangled cry. She wrenched at the door and was flying down the hall, Myles a few feet after her.

He had to stop short of following her through the door marked "Women." For the next ten minutes all he could do was pace back and forth on the ugly mustard carpeting.

A young couple passed him on the way to their room, and the girl began to giggle. Myles thought wearily that he probably did look peculiar parading up and down before the ladies' room like an anxious father in a maternity ward, but what else could he do?

An elderly women came along next, headed for the stairway. She seemed to be both kindly and competent.

"Ma'am, could you help me, please?" He gave her his most helpless-male smile. "My friend went in there some time ago . . . she was feeling quite ill. I can't go away till I'm sure she's all right. If you'd be so kind . . ."

The woman nodded majestically and pushed through the door like a ship in full sail. In about three minutes she was back.

"I think she's feeling better, young man. She asked me to say thank you and tell you to go home. I offered to stay with her myself, but she refused. She seems a very independent person."

"Too damned independent," Myles groaned. "Ma'am, tell me, do *you* think she's all right?"

"I think she feels better for having vomited," the woman said with great dignity, "but my personal opinion is that she is still in considerable pain and needs someone to look after her." She suddenly tapped his chest with her forefinger. "I'm a schoolteacher. I've always noticed that some of the most independent ones have a great fear of their need to rely on others."

"That's my girl." He nodded. "Thank you, ma'am. I'll see to her. Tell me, is there anyone else inside?"

"No one at all. She's all alone."

When the woman was out of sight, Myles straightened his back, squared his shoulders and made a determined beeline through the sacred portal.

He had to go through another swinging door, and as soon as he did, he saw Gina. She was wearing only the briefest of pink lace briefs; her dress had been slung over the top of one of the two cubicles. She sat on the floor, hunched up against the corner wall, her head slumped over her knees and her hands dangling limply. She might have been posing for a statue of Desolation.

"Gina."

She looked up, astounded, and then immediately hunched over again, this time crossing her arms protectively in front of her. "Go away, you fool!" came a muffled voice from behind her arms.

"Not without you."

"I'll be okay, Myles, honestly. The nausea's gone, but I'm too weak now to get dressed and go back. In a little while I'll be able to."

As he knelt next to her, Gina lifted her head and whispered huskily, "April was here . . . the headaches. They seem to be connected with her coming to me. But now she's gone, and the headache stayed."

He bent over and put his hands on either side of her waist. "Stand up. I'll hold onto you."

"Myles, don't. Will you please stop? This is ridiculous. I don't have anything on—hardly."

"Your modesty is misplaced. I've seen a woman's breasts before," he said mildly, pulling her to her feet.

"I'll bet you have," Gina muttered, hiding her chest against him all the same.

The door behind Myles opened. He was holding Gina, but she was blocked by his body. When he turned his head, he met the astonished green-eyed gaze of a freckle-faced teenager.

"Oh, my goodness, I beg your pardon!" she gasped, astonishment giving way to red-faced mortification. "I thought this was the ladies' room!"

"It is," Myles stated baldly, and swung around, giving the girl a glimpse of the limp proof. "Would you help me, please, and get her dress?" He nodded toward the cubicle.

Still blushing madly, she came forward, and as she reached for the garment he managed to lift Gina up into his arms. It wasn't easy. Gina didn't weigh much, but she was dead weight.

"Would you put it around her, please?" he asked.

Gina's head was on his shoulder; she was still using her hands to cover herself.

The girl draped the dress over Gina's shoulders and tucked it very carefully in front.

"Now, if you'll hold the outside door open," Myles requested.

The teenager darted ahead, and he used his shoulder to push through the swinging door after her. She held the outer door open and peered up and down.

"There's no one around," she said in a conspiratorial whisper.

"Thank you very much. You've been most kind."

"Oh, that's all right," she returned awkwardly, blushing redder than ever. "I hope your friend is feeling better."

His "friend" was feeling better enough to be shaking with laughter, and the resulting movement of her bare skin against his shirt front had Myles sweating profusely.

All thought other than to help Gina ended as soon as he lowered her onto the bed. She rolled over on her stomach, crossed arms pillowing her head, and the much-maltreated chiffon dress dropped to the floor. He picked it up and hung it in the closet, then came back to Gina.

"Head still hurt much?"

"It's pretty ghastly," she admitted.

Myles kneaded the back of her neck, and she gave a little moan of pleasure. "Ahhh, that's good."

After a few minutes she lifted her head cautiously. "Myles, why don't you go back to your family? There's nothing you can do, and I feel guilty keeping you here. I'll try to sleep."

"Will you be able to?"

She didn't answer.

"Listen to me. As it happens, there is plenty I can do. I'm going downstairs so I can phone Mother and Dad without disturbing you. They were anxious about you . . ."

He ignored her murmured, "I'll bet."

"They'll want to hear that you're okay," Myles continued firmly, "and when I come back I'm going to make you a lot more comfortable. Do you have cotton pajamas or a nightgown?"

"Sure. I guess so."

"Put them on while I'm gone. Remember, it has to be cotton, not nylon. Nylon's too slippery."

"Too slippery for what?" Gina called weakly as he went down the hall again.

Myles reached his parents at the restaurant, arranged to meet them for breakfast and used the lobby phone to speak to room service.

In less than fifteen minutes he was back with Gina. She was lying on the bed, curled up on her side. He recognized the nightgown instantly. It was the one that had almost lured him into making love to her that night in his apartment.

"Cotton or not," he said crisply, "this is too much material. Mind if I take it off?"

As he asked, he was doing it, leaving her in only the pink panties again.

While Gina watched, becoming a bit wide-eyed, Myles slung his jacket around the back of the desk chair, threw his tie over it and rolled up the sleeves of his shirt.

"Turn over onto your stomach."

She turned with a great deal of care.

"Put your arms down at your sides. Try to breathe easily and relax."

He sat beside her on the bed and started massaging her neck again. She purred with satisfaction. Then he went to work on her shoulders. When his fingers moved over her head, exerting pressure at certain points, Gina gasped.

"Try to stand it for a while. It'll ease up soon."

"What is this? I've never had a massage like this before."

"It isn't a massage. For want of a better name, it's known as acupressure."

"How did you come to learn it?"

"I dated a Japanese woman years ago when I was living in New York. She got me interested, and I took a number of courses—beginner's right through to advanced. I'm told I have good hands."

"They're bloody marvelous. Myles, do you—"

"Not so much talking, just relax and get the benefit." His hands moved down to her back. "Now take some nice, deep breaths and hold them, exhaling when I press down." After several minutes he told her to lie on her back, and she flopped over obediently.

He worked on her right arm and leg and then went around the bed to start on her left side. She kept her eyes closed, breathing so evenly he thought she might have fallen asleep.

"Gina," he said, barely above a whisper, and her eyes opened instantly. They were clear, darkly blue, almost tranquil. "How are you feeling?"

"Wonderful."

"The pain?"

"Not quite gone, but compared with the way it was before . . ."

His hand was on her forehead. She pulled it down suddenly to her mouth, and he felt her lips moving against his palm.

"Gina," he protested as she rolled onto her stomach again.

"I want to. I didn't know you could be this kind, and I'm so grateful, I—"

"I love you, Gina, and gratitude is the last thing in the world I want from you."

The bed creaked under his weight as he settled himself next to her, one hand on the small of her back, the other stroking her head. She stiffened as she felt his lips on her neck. They lingered a moment and then roved over her spine, the tip of his tongue circling around and down.

"Myles! D-don't d-do that."

"I thought you said you had a sexy spinal column."

"I do," she gasped. "My God, M-Myles!"

"I'll stop if you want me to."

Before Gina could answer, there was a loud knock on the door. She jumped, holding her head again.

"Room service," Myles reassured her. "I asked them to send some things up."

He went to the door, paid and tipped the boy, then took the tray and set it down on the desk. "Would you like some tea now?"

"Love it," Gina sighed. "My mouth is so dry, and I still have a horrible taste from the Ergomar."

She eased herself into a sitting position, and Myles propped the pillows from both beds behind her. Then he brought her a cup of tea, steaming hot, and sat down on the bed facing her while she sipped it thirstily.

"*Sooo* good," she murmured. Over the rim of the cup, Gina's eyes held his. "You're full of surprises, aren't you, Myles? Tennessee tigresses and Japanese acupressurists."

"To say nothing"—he let her have it with both barrels—"of Vittorio Jacobi's bastard daughter." He put out a hand to steady her cup. "You said it, not I," he reminded her.

"I hurt you, Myles. I didn't mean to do that." She put the empty cup and saucer on the night stand. "No, that's not true. I had a great need to hurt you, I can't think why now. But I'm sorry, I'm so sorry that I shamed you in front of your parents."

"We'll talk about it tomorrow," he said gently. "I think you should try to sleep now."

He took a towel from the rack over the sink, knotted it at the top and filled it with ice cubes from the pitcher on the tray. "*Voici,* your ice pack, madame, amateurish but effective. It should deal with the rest of your headache. I seem to remember, from Washington, that you sleep on your stomach."

She nodded.

"Okay. Over on your stomach now. Do you want the ice at the front or the back?"

"On top, please."

He placed the pack against the top of her head, using the extra pillow as a brace to keep it from sliding down.

"Now I'm going to turn out all the lights," Myles continued, doing so, "and give you a final treatment. I'll open the door so we'll have some light from the hall. Relax completely and try to sleep. Sleep as late as you can in the morning, and I'll come by for you."

He opened the door, and a faint thread of light shone in, enough to indicate her outline on the bed. Gently, through the blanket he began to massage her back and shoulders.

"You're floating on a cloud, high up in the sky, where there is no pain . . . floating . . . floating . . . completely at peace . . . You're relaxed and comfortable and at peace. . . . The pain is gone, all of it gone. Your mouth is no longer dry. You're comfortable and at ease." His fingers manipulated the back of her head. "You're tired, pleasantly tired, and you want to sleep. . . . You want more than anything else to sleep."

In the shadowy room two hands reached up and behind and caught hold of his. "I'm comfortable and at ease and completely free of pain. I'm tired, pleasantly tired, and I want more than anything else to sleep. Will you stay and share my bed, Myles?"

Now *his* mouth was dry and his heart was pounding, and he felt a sick churning in the pit of his stomach.

"Because you love me, Gina?" he asked evenly.

She didn't answer.

"Or because I love you, and this is your way of being grateful. Is this how you propose to reward me?"

After a while she asked almost pleadingly, "Must it be either? Can't it be because we do have a feeling for each other? You know we want one another . . . that way. And . . . and for once I'm not embarrassed to admit that I don't want to be alone."

"You're not going to be alone, Gina. You're going to sleep, and to dream of me all night. You're going to have the best night's sleep of your life, I guarantee it. And when you wake up, I'll be with you. You see, Pieragina"—he dropped a light kiss on the top of her head—"I do want you *that* way, but in every other way, too. So make up your mind to it. It's marriage or nothing. Commitment. Responsibility. The whole bit. All or nothing."

"That's"—she yawned hugely—"that's blackmail."

"So it is, and you're in my power. Now shut up and go to sleep."

Myles continued to knead her shoulders and back. Five minutes later, when he whispered her name, she was breathing deeply and evenly, her head turned to one side and her arms flung out. She did not answer.

"Good night, my impossible love," he whispered, kissed a damp strand of Gina's hair and put the improvised ice pack in the sink.

Out in the hallway, he listened for a moment to make sure the sound of the closing door hadn't awakened her. Then he went home.

Chapter 28

Myles met his parents for breakfast in the Lodge's coffee shop at nine the next morning. At about nine-thirty, he excused himself to check up on Gina.

She answered his knock, wearing a pair of ragged khaki shorts and a T-shirt. She glowed with good health and good spirits; last night might never have been.

Last night was very present in her mind, however, as was evidenced by the deep blush that spread over her face. He grinned maliciously as the blush grew deeper and her cheeks hotter.

"Well, well," he needled, "you're remembering your offer." Then, more kindly, "How is your head?"

"It's fine, thank you." She squirmed a little. "I do mean the thank-you," she said, and blushed some more.

He took pity on her and changed the subject. "My parents are having breakfast downstairs. They're leaving for Florida right afterward. Will you come and say good-bye?"

Gina hesitated, then replied without enthusiasm, "I suppose I should apologize to them."

"Yes, I suppose you should," Myles agreed, and she made a face.

"Wait outside. I'll be right out."

Gina closed the door. When she opened it again a few minutes later, she was wearing a paisley skirt and knit shirt, and her hair was tied back neatly.

She was quiet as they walked to the coffee shop. Once or twice Myles saw her lips move soundlessly; rehearsing her apology, he suspected. He was sure of it when she stood at their table, gazing into the distance instead of at his parents. Without once drawing breath, Gina reeled off a remorseful speech.

Her apology over with and accepted, she agreed to a breakfast of soft-boiled eggs, toast and tea while Myles had a second cup of coffee.

"Are you sure you're feeling completely well again?" Mrs. Edward asked solicitously.

"Can't you tell by looking at her?" Mr. Edward answered for Gina. "She's bright-eyed and bushy-tailed this morning."

After breakfast he left to check out, Myles accompanying him. Gina went with Mrs. Edward to the gift shop for some last-minute buying.

In the parking lot, Mr. Edward ignored Gina's outstretched hand and bestowed a hearty kiss on her cheek. She turned hesitantly to Myles's mother, who kissed her in turn.

Then Mrs. Edward embraced her son. "All she needs is security, Myles. You can give it to her."

"I'll try, Ma." He hugged her, and her eyes filled up with tears.

There was another quick round of kisses and hugs, and the Edwards were gone.

Myles turned to Gina as they strolled back from the parking area. "What shall we do with the rest of the day?"

"I'll be busy, Myles."

He frowned. "You're working today?"

"Well, no, not exactly." She plucked a leaf from a bush and chewed on it nervously. "I . . . I have to pack and . . . and—" She choked on the leaf, spit it out and blurted, "I'm moving."

"You're *what?*"

"Moving. Into an apartment. A sublet. Furnished. Just till the end of August. I figured since my room isn't air-conditioned, it would be unbearable in the summer. It's mid-June and boiling already. And I miss having a kitchen." As Gina recited these details, she was looking at him from under her lashes.

"Just how long have you known about this?"

"T-two weeks."

"Another of those inconsequential matters that wouldn't be of any interest to me?"

"No, I . . . I—" She swallowed. "I was going to tell you later. I was planning . . . well, I thought it would be fun to . . . to . . ."

"To . . . to . . . what?" he prompted.

"To make a date with you and not tell you and let you try to pick me up at my room," she confessed miserably.

"And then what?"

"Then you'd go down to the desk and they'd give you my forwarding address and—"

"And?"

"Well, either you'd come or . . . or you wouldn't. I thought you'd probably come, considering . . ."

"Considering what?"

"Where it is," Gina answered quite meekly.

"Which is?"

"Half a block from you."

Myles contemplated her for a long moment. "I'd have come, all right, if for no other purpose than the sheer pleasure of wringing your neck." He studied her again. "What made you change your mind about telling me?"

"Oh, I don't know." She flapped her hands vaguely. "All at once it seemed so stupid and childish and—oh, you know, petty. I don't want to play games with you any more."

"Well, that's progress of a sort. I never wanted to play them in the first place. Are you all packed?"

"Almost."

"How were you planning to move—by cab, or with the chubby collegiate who assisted your last move?"

"By car. My own. I bought one a few days ago."

"If you can afford a car, why the devil were you hitchhiking from California?"

"I wasn't. I was driving an old camper I'd used for—used before. It broke down in Ohio and wasn't worth fixing, so I sold it for what I could get, sorted my stuff and decided to hitch to Washington. I figured I'd buy a car there. Meeting you kind of changed all my plans."

"It changed mine, too, by God!" Myles swore with feeling. "Come on. Finish packing. I'll take everything down to your car and follow you to the new place. If we hurry, we can still have most of the day for ourselves . . . Where would you like to go?"

"Jamestown, please."

"To see Sarah Harrison Blair again?" Myles teased.

"No. As a matter of fact, I'm interested in the graves of the other settlers. I thought maybe one of them would jog my memory."

"Which one?"

"The one I'm descended from. I can't remember the name. It suddenly came to me the last time we were there that my grandmother Waverly once mentioned there was an American branch of the family, beginning with the Jamestown settlement, and that one of them had died in the Great Famine."

"Jamestown it is." He couldn't help adding, "Though I thought you weren't interested in your mother's family."

"Oh, I don't mind the dead ones."

There was something chilling about the matter-of-factness of her words.

"You dislike your mother that much?"

"She's a bitch," Gina replied briefly. "So you see, I come by it naturally. Does my saying that shock you? It shouldn't. I assure you, the dislike is mutual. I haven't seen her in years. Naomi spends most of her time with the flotsam on the Riviera, and between lovers she dries out in her favorite Swiss sanitarium. She refers to Victor publicly and privately as her First Big Mistake—I'm the Second—but she hasn't any compunction about his footing the bills."

"Do you love your father?"

Gina turned her face away. "Yes," she admitted finally.

"That's not something to be embarrassed about, Pieragina," Myles said with gentle irony. "It's no secret to the world that Vittorio Jacobi is quite a guy. I'd only fault him as a father."

She turned back swiftly. "He's a *wonderful* father."

"He has no business letting you run wild."

"Oh, that's what you mean." She shrugged. "He couldn't stop me from doing what I wanted."

"That's what I'm complaining about." Myles's expression was grim. "He should have tried. I told him so."

"You did *what?*"

"I told him that, since he couldn't seem to control you, perhaps he wouldn't object to my taking on the job."

"What are you talking about? You never even heard about Victor till last night. I don't think this is funny at all."

"Last night, after I left you, I called a friend of mine who works in a New York theatrical agency. He came up with a Beverly Hills address. I wrote a letter to your father and mailed it first thing this morning."

"He won't get it. He's in Europe."

"I sent it special delivery, marked 'Personal,' 'Urgent' and 'Please Forward.' I'm sure his secretary will take the hint."

"But why? Why did you write?"

"A girl underage needs parental permission to marry. I pointed out that I couldn't do a much worse job of taking care of you than he has."

"In this age of women's lib, you asked my father's *permission* to marry me?"

"A necessary detail till you're eighteen."

They had nearly reached the entrance of York House, but Gina was laughing so hard she had to sit down. She happened to collapse into one of the big wooden rockers, and rocked so violently between spasms of mirth that she nearly overturned it.

"Oh, Lord," she gasped, wiping her eyes, "if I could only be there when he gets the letter! What I wouldn't give to see his face! Even his worse critics have never denied Victor a sense of humor. He'll probably think it's a riot and forgive any insults that went along with your request. Tell me, Myles, how did you word it? 'May I have your daughter's hand in marriage?' Or were you more formal? 'Honored sir, having the highest esteem for your amiable daughter, I offer you my most earnest desire to take her for my wife.'"

Highly pleased by her own humor, Gina started rocking and giggling again.

Myles looked down at her and said, "I can't remember the exact words, but I believe I was less flowery and more direct. 'As you can see from the above explanation, it is very much against my better judgment that I am in love, quite madly in love, with your quite maddening daughter. I think I can give her the security she needs, the love she's afraid of and the care she pretends not to want. I would greatly appreciate your written consent for me to marry her. If I don't get it, I'll find some way to marry her without it.'"

Gina's eyes started to fill when Myles was halfway through, and by the time he had finished, tears were streaming down her face.

"Do all your proposals make you cry, Pieragina?"

"Why do you keep calling me that now?" she sniffled.

"It's your name."

"I know, but it makes me feel different. It's easier to be Gina."

"'Gina' fits in with those games you play. I prefer 'Pieragina.'"

"She might disappoint you, too."

"How?"

"We're neither of us very reliable. Myles, sooner or later I'd let you down. I can't help it. It's the way I am. And besides, I'd let you down in other ways."

"Such as?"

"I'm not very good at . . . you know . . . at the physical side. I've tried, I really have, not as often as I pretend to you, but . . ."

"I'm delighted to hear that, at least. Have you ever loved anyone before?"

"No, not anyone I—no, no, I haven't."

"Then don't worry."

"With a Tennessee tigress to compete against?"

"I'll match you against her any day in the week." Myles reached out and pulled Gina to her feet. "Technique can be learned," he explained, grinning. "Emotion has to come naturally."

She was still thinking that one over as she finished her packing. She was very quiet, very thoughtful, and he left her to it until they started to lug her stuff downstairs and out the building.

"Pieragina," he said softly, "do you realize that in a slightly roundabout way, inadvertently or not, you admitted you love me?"

"It wasn't inadvertent."

"Come again?"

"Marriage no, but I do love you, Myles." Gina dropped the small but heavy suitcase she was holding, and it landed on his right foot. Myles was so carried away he didn't feel the pain in his toes until hours later. "Shall I follow you or will you follow me to the apartment?" she was asking even as he stumbled over the cases to latch onto her.

"You follow me, after I kiss you."

They stood in the parking lot, with boxes and bundles and suitcases all around them. Myles held her in his arms, where he had always known she belonged, and kissed her with all the passion that was in him. When they broke apart, to the sound of applause from a few interested spectators, he laughed out loud.

"See, even strangers know."

"Know what?"

"You're not simply going to be *good*, my darling Pieragina, you're going to be *great*."

Chapter 29

These last two months and more Jeremy had worked harder at his lawbooks than he had ever before, receiving much praise from Mr. Wythe and incurring the gentle censure of his dear lady. "I did not bring you into my house that you might study yourself to death," she scolded him on more than one occasion.

When not at his books, he was immersed in public affairs with his wise mentor. Mr. Wythe knew full well that what Jeremy most wanted was to be busy. Wythe kept him so by having Jeremy assist with research and draw up the numerous documents of such great necessity to the cause of freedom. Thomas Jefferson's pamphlet *The Rights of British America*, which Mrs. Rind had printed, was their constant guide.

Jeremy had told Rietta he must have her answer in the spring, and she had agreed. Now that April had come, spring might be considered to have arrived. In just three days his time with the Wythes would be over and he would return to Scot's Haven. Rietta was to come from Richmond with Sally for his father's wedding, and Jeremy felt certain that as soon as he saw her, he would know his fate. One look, without her saying a word, and he would have his answer plain.

His dwelling house on Francis Street, part of his inheritance from Uncle Bentley Stuart, had lain empty these last six weeks. Mr. Randolph, who handled all his uncle's affairs and now his, had received several inquiries from genteel persons. But Jeremy had instructed Randolph to delay further.

If Jeremy did not marry, it would be more practical to lease the house again and go into lodgings himself. If Rietta accepted him . . . why, then it might make a very suitable home for them, for a few years at least, until he he was in circumstances to build on the James River land near Scot's Haven that his father had given him.

His uncle's former house was a red brick, somewhat square-shaped and small, but agreeable. The outbuildings were well kept and the garden was flourishing, vivid with tulips from Mrs. Wythe's own bulbs. He thought Rietta would like it very much.

My God, how can I write so calmly and prosaically? Jeremy asked himself, sitting before his journal. His heart pounded violently at the thought of her. When he wrote her name, his hand shook like that of a palsied old man.

It was unthinkable that she would deny her own heart and his for scruples that had naught to do with either of them. Was he to act the trembling, fearful schoolboy brought before his master?

Nay, Jeremy decided. He would instruct that the go-by be given to all who made inquiries about his dwelling and would set in hand improvements to prepare it for his bride.

Dawn was fast approaching. Jeremy continued to write because he could not sleep. He must do as he had done many an April night, he thought—walk the streets of Williamsburg to cool the blood that coursed so hotly through his body.

Almost immediately upon putting down his quill and leaving the house, Jeremy was caught up in strange, disturbed proceedings that made him forget his own affairs.

Scarcely had he walked a half-dozen blocks when he heard pistol shots and signal bells, followed by cries of confusion. Almost before his eyes the men of Williamsburg filled the streets, until in an instant the town looked as it did on market day, the only difference being the nature of the crowd and the darkness that accompanies the breaking of dawn. The men, armed with muskets and other manner of weapons, carrying lanterns and torches, many still in a half-dressed state, were in a rebellious mood that boded trouble. So quickly can a crowd become a mob.

PROMISE ME FOREVER 235

Jeremy joined with others, and the information spread as they marched along that the watchman had given the first alarm. He had espied a party of marines from one of His Majesty's vessels on the James, stealing gunpowder from the public magazine.

The throng had gathered too late to save the powder from being conveyed aboard the armed vessel, which fact so incensed the people that violence seemed imminent. Angry groups formed, each man throwing out his views. Now and again, one would shout louder to gain the attention of all the others.

Jeremy heard more than one man, shaking a fist, roar that the governor, Lord Dunmore, was more interested in the fat fool who sat on the English throne than in the folk of Virginia.

"We are free Englishmen! Is this how they treat their own countrymen—coming under cover of night, while good citizens are in their beds, to rob us of our own property?"

Such were the sentiments of all, and passions were so aroused, for a while there seemed to be little chance that calm and reason would prevail.

Then, in the midst of the storm of fury, something happened that pushed all else from Jeremy's mind. He had been moving from group to group, dropping a calm word here and there, where it might do the most good. As he approached another small cluster of men who were arguing hotly, Jeremy heard a sudden, muffled cry. He might have paid no heed to it had not a member of the group wrapped his cloak more tightly around him and moved away in what appeared to Jeremy as a rather stealthy manner. He had half turned away himself when he was struck by something familiar about the slight figure as it struggled through the crowd.

Then enlightenment dawned, and with a mighty oath Jeremy followed after. It was no easy feat to keep track of one small, fleeing figure in such a shifting, struggling mob, especially when the person in question was bent on escape.

Rage as well as strength of purpose gave vigor to Jeremy's use of elbows, knees and legs in carrying on the chase. Scarcely six or seven minutes after he had heard the gasp of dismay, he was laying bold hands from behind on the cloaked shoulders.

"Pray, sir," a woman began, speaking deep in her throat, still thinking to deceive him. "I must—"

"You must indeed!" he cried, whirling her about to face

him. "You must be mad, Rietta Rind, to be out at such a time, among such as these, in your men's garb! God, if you had been detected! Do you think only patriots are abroad tonight? Pull your hat farther forward and hold your lantern lower. No, rather give it to me so your face will be better shielded. We must hurry, for soon it will be fully light."

At one and the same time, he stretched out a hand for the lantern and took her arm to head her away from the crowd. Rietta held stubbornly onto the lantern and tried to jerk free of his hold.

"Oh, Jeremy, no one here will recognize me. Please let us stay a while. I want to see what they decide to do."

"Are you staying at Mrs. Hallam's?" he asked, as though she hadn't spoken. His face tightened at a suddenly unpleasant thought. "You're not back at the Rind house, are you? You're not working on the newspaper for Pinkney again? Is that why you came out here?"

Jeremy hurried her along, protesting, while pelting her with questions. Rietta had no choice but to accompany him, however reluctantly and rebelliously.

They were both breathless and disarranged by the time he had led her far from the greater mass of people, and his temper had in no wise cooled. For every question he had thrown at her, there were more than two in his mind. He framed the answers silently to himself, and none of them pleased him.

"Where are you staying?"

She answered him as stiffly as he had asked. "At Mrs. Hallam's." She hung back a little as he turned her in the proper direction. "Why must you be so highhanded, Jeremy?"

"Highhanded!" He strove to control his temper. "You are not without brains, though you seem so often oddly disinclined to use them. This was no minor escapade. Mobs are dangerous. You could have been hurt. There were elements involved. If they had discovered you were a woman . . ."

"Why should they be any faster to discover it than you?"

"What?" he gasped stupidly.

"We have not seen each other for twelve weeks. I did not think we would meet again only to quarrel."

Even as he held onto her, Rietta slued around, lifted her tricorn and sent it flying through the air.

He gaped at her. "Why did you do that?"

"I will have no use for it, will I?" she replied tenderly. "My proper Jeremy, thee wouldst not wish thy wife to parade abroad in men's clothes, wouldst thee?"

"Almighty God," he said, though not profanely. He lifted the lantern to light up her face even as she raised it to his.

He had written in his journal only short hours before that he would know with one look. The look of love, naked and unashamed was on her face; a look of longing that echoed the urgent hunger of his own heart and body.

Jeremy carefully set the lantern on the ground. His arms went under the cloak; his hands slipped beneath the brocade waistcoat to draw her close and seek out her warm, tender flesh. They said wild and foolish and wonderful things, one to the other, and when they had said enough, he silenced her with his lips.

He kissed her flushed face, her half-closed eyes and, lastly, her mouth, which moved against his with equal eagerness. He held her against him, rocking Rietta to and fro. Presently, it was her arms that sought him out, her hands that brought his face down again, her mouth demanding its due.

He recalled with great thankfulness in his heart those lines from her father's letter: *To speak bluntly, sir, no female of my daughter's nature was ever intended for celibacy.* Jeremy would have not only this girl whom he loved so to be his wife but also a responsive, not passive, body lying in his bed.

"I love you, Jamie. Sometimes I thought I would die of missing you. I fell asleep to thoughts of you, and in the morning when I woke, they were all still with me. It took every measure of my strength not to run back to you from Richmond and say—"

"Say what, my most beloved?"

"I want to be your wife, Jamie. I want you for my own. I want never to be free of you again. Or let you be free of me."

"No more doubts?" he asked huskily. "No more fears?"

She placed her face into his hands and spoke against his palms.

"Away from you, with time to think, time to know the loneliness of being without you, everything became so simple. If I—if we give ourselves freely, as a gift of love . . . if it is mutual and of our own free will, then we are neither of us owned or possessed."

"I am yours, my Quaker spitfire. I have been yours from the very first."

"You are not alone, then, Jamie, and you will never be alone again. I am yours now, too, yours forevermore."

Jeremy yearned to hold Rietta in his arms again, but some of the voices in the distance seemed to be drawing closer, and it would be wiser to get her safely home to Mrs. Hallam's.

As they walked along more quickly, he repeated all his questions and she answered them in order.

"I still have many of my things at Cousin Clemmie's, and some of my summer clothing is stored at Mrs. Hallam's. I wanted to see the children, too, and say good-bye to Dick, who has been my good friend since I came here. I would feel happier if I could be certain that they also were contented." Her fingers on his arm gripped tighter. "Then, too, I wanted to make my peace with John, restore our friendship. We have been through too much together to break our ties. I did not want to start a new life feeling I had left things undone from the old. Mostly, I . . . I . . ."

Jeremy waited, one hand caressing her cheek. Rietta said in a Delilah-like voice, but with an honesty that was hers alone, "I did not want to wait another three days to see you, so your father sent me here in the carriage."

Jeremy willed his own voice to emerge steady and natural. "Why did you go out tonight?"

Her hand fell away from his arm. "For adventure," Rietta confessed meekly. "I couldn't sleep for thinking about seeing you in the morning. So I got on with my packing. I was just folding the breeches, wondering whether to leave them or pack them, when the noise and confusion broke out. It seemed like fate. I thought one last, rousing adventure could not do any harm . . . and I was curious."

He both hugged and shook her gently. "You are always curious," he stated with a rueful smile. "Pray why do you consider our marriage will be the end of your adventuring? Rather, it will be the beginning of new ones we will share together."

"Oh, Jamie." Her eyes in the light of the upheld lantern were more brilliant than the stars. "Oh, Jamie, I hope it will always be like this for us."

They reached Mrs. Hallam's just then. Most reluctantly, he bade her good night, corrected it to good morning and watched her slip through the side door.

Back at the Wythes', Jeremy sat before his journal again,

afraid to believe such happiness was real. Could he have won her at last?

Yet even as he dreamed of their future, he knew he would never experience a greater joy than that of the supreme moment when she had told him, *You are not alone, then, Jamie, you will never be alone again. I am yours now, too, yours forevermore.*

Chapter 30

They had been wandering for nearly an hour among the grave sites and ruins, bickering amiably and laughing about the possibilities of which one might have been her ancestor.

"Not one of them rings a bell. Maybe I'll write and ask my grandmother Waverly." Gina laughed again, this time not as pleasantly. "Though it might give the old girl a heart attack to hear from me."

"Don't, Pieragina."

"Don't what?"

"Hate so much."

"Oh, poor Myles, the family man. If you're worried about my grandmother's tender sensibilities, I promise you she has none."

"I don't give a damn about your grandmother, only about you. It's you your hatred hurts, Pieragina."

"Pieragina again." Her expression softened. "You really meant it, didn't you? That's my name now."

"Unless you don't want it to be."

"Don't want it to be," she echoed faintly, sinking down on the grass near a worn tombstone. "It was my name the first eight and a half years of my life. I loved it."

"I don't understand." He sat down beside her a bit

awkwardly; there was a lack of leg space. "What do you mean, it *was* your name?"

One of her hands flew to her mouth, but before she could start chewing on her nails, he drew the hand away and held it on the grass.

"Come on," he coaxed. "Your nails are doing fine. You don't want to ruin all that good work."

Myles put an arm around her, and at first she resisted him with braced shoulders and a tense spine. Then suddenly her body was fluid against him, her head nuzzling his arm and her hair tickling his neck.

"I told you about the custody suit, didn't I?" she murmured. "And how Naomi won? It turned out that she and Da—Victor had never been married at all, so I *was* a bastard. The first thing she told me when we were alone in the apartment was that Victor wasn't legally my father and that his wasn't my name at all."

"Is that all there was to it?" Myles prompted after a long silence.

"By no means." Gina grinned. "I called her a liar."

"And your mother?"

"She raked my face with her nails. Unlike mine"—Gina's grin was in no way diminished—"Naomi's were impressively long and well shaped. They left a nice, bloody track down my cheek. The argument for accepting the Waverly name was indisputable. Unfortunately from her point of view, when she took me home to England, her family didn't accept me at all. The first thing my grandmother objected to was my outlandish foreign name. She told Naomi that since my birth papers had to be changed anyhow, they might as well get rid of the 'Pieragina,' too.

"'The child,' she said—boy, you should have heard the way she kept calling me 'the child'; it would have frozen Vesuvius in eruption—'the child should have a decent Christian name. Call her Jean.'" Gina lifted her head from Myles's shoulder. "I didn't know she meant a *given* name. I jumped up and shouted at both of them. 'I'm not Christian. I'm Jewish!' Wow! What a scene. Needless to say, I became Jean Waverly, and how I hated it. When Naomi gave me up, the first thing Victor did was to change my name back."

She stared off into the distance, at the back of the statue of Captain John Smith, high on its stone pedestal, looking out in seemingly endless contemplation of the broad river the captain had first explored.

"Is it to spite your grandmother that you insist on being Jewish?" Myles asked matter-of-factly.

Gina's head swiveled slowly around and her eyes met his, bright and hard and suspicious, as they had been on the drive to Williamsburg from Washington. "What do you mean?"

"Not what you think," he responded quietly, "so stop thinking it or I'll swat you. As a scientist, I deal in facts. And the facts are that by blood, heredity, whatever you want to call it, you're only one-quarter Jewish, three-quarters Gentile."

She stopped bristling and answered him just as softly. "But I'm not a scientist. I don't deal in facts. I deal in feelings. My father is not the least bit religious, but culturally, historically—yes, and *ethically*—he considers himself a Jew. As a matter of fact, probably the most important part of it for him is the ethics. You see, both his father and his Catholic mother died in a Nazi concentration camp as Jews, so he thinks that to deny his identity would be a betrayal of them." Gina made a curious grimace. *"He* identified with them, and *I* identified with him and with Mimi, my stepmother. There was never any question in my mind what I was."

"A Jewish *shiksa*," Myles said, straight-faced.

"Well, well, well." She looked him up and she looked him down. "Tennessee tigresses, Japanese acupressurists, and now it seems you've done a little romancing among my *lantsmen*, too. You're a creature of contradictions, Myles."

"Now, that's the pot calling the kettle black with a vengeance. It so happens I worked for a year as an exchange student on a dig in Israel, and there's one fact I learned there that might be important to your feelings. Under Jewish law, the child of a mixed marriage takes the religion of the mother."

"So?"

"So by strict application of the law of your own people, your father was never Jewish, and neither are you."

Gina smiled challengingly, a Cheshire smile peculiarly her own. "I know all about it. I first heard that when I was in high school. It got me so aggravated, my father took me to the movie set the next morning to talk to a priest who was working with him as an adviser. The priest was very young, very kind. He suggested that if it was important to me, I could convert. So Victor made an appointment for me with a rabbi, and I marched right into his study and demanded instant conversion. The rabbi wasn't so young, but he was very kind, quite a psychologist in his way. We talked for hours. . . . Actually, under his careful manipulation, I did all the talking while he sat and listened. Then he explained that hating my mother and wanting to spite my grandmother were not really adequate reasons for becoming a Jew. Even if I had better ones, he said, I was too young to decide something so important in my life. I would have to think about it, study and reason and talk it over for months, even years. Strangely"— her voice softened in remembrance; her eyes became dreamy—"I wasn't disappointed when I left him. I felt almost uplifted, like a knight sent out to search for the Holy Grail."

She put out her hand and lightly tapped Myles's cheek with one finger. "I found it, too. Years later, when I went back, I was able to convince him that my heart was pure, my motives ditto. I did convert. So you see, Myles, I am a Jew. And because I am, as you so rightly pointed out, any children of mine will be Jewish by birth."

"Then it appears that mine will be, too," Myles stated.

For just a moment her bright smile wavered. Almost angrily, she dashed away a sudden rush of tears. "Damn you, Myles, you . . . you . . . somehow you always disarm me."

"Somehow you always distrust me."

She turned her back on him. "I don't mean to. Honestly, I don't."

"Don't you? Don't you really? Over the months you've fed me bits and pieces. Do you think I'm such a fool I don't know when you're holding back? I love you, and you've admitted that you love me. I wish you would prove it with an act of faith."

"What kind?" Her voice was muffled.

"The truth, Pieragina. The whole truth."

"Would you marry me the way things are between us right now?"

He put his arms around her from behind. "Is that a proposal?" Myles kissed her neck and shoulder and whispered close to her ear, "If it is, the answer's yes. I would marry you any time, any way, anywhere."

Gina turned swiftly to face him, still confined by his arms. "Myles. Oh, damn you, double damn you. Don't you know I wish I could? You make it sound so simple and straightforward and once-upon-a-time. Do you really think *you* and *I* could live happily ever after?"

"If you're looking for guarantees, I'm all out of them today." He let got of her somewhat impatiently. "I keep thinking you're older, forgetting what a kid you are in actual years."

She paled a little, biting at her lip.

"Pieragina, I don't know about ever after, but this I believe with all my heart. If we both want it and we both work at it, we can create an oasis of love and security for ourselves." He took hold of her again, gently, lovingly, willing her to feel, to share his faith. "If we do that, then I'm positive we can achieve as much happiness as any two people are able to in this crazy world."

Myles could see she wanted to believe him. Her face was a two-way mirror which clearly revealed her struggle with both her new desires and all her old doubts and fears.

"Enough for today. We'll talk of it again when you're more ready."

Gina smiled gratefully, and her color returned a little. When he stretched out his hand across the mossy grave, she placed hers in it acceptingly; and as they walked along the sea wall, her grip tightened.

"How beautiful the river is today," she said softly, stopping to watch the play of sunlight on the water. "How it reduces our small problems." Her eyes closed and she half whispered, "When the fish are fled and the James dries up, why, then I might cease to love you."

She stood there, swaying slightly, eyes still closed. Myles remained beside her, afraid to move, almost afraid to breathe, reluctant to break the magic of the moment.

Slumberously, Gina opened her eyes to him, and the sun turned their blue to purple before a glaze of tears quenched their glow. As she had done the night she kissed his palm, she spoke against his fingers. "I'll never forget your saying that to me, Myles, dear, dear Myles. No matter what happens between us, I hope you will always remember I feel the same about you, too."

When the fish are fled and the James dries up, why, then I might cease to love you.

Yes, that said it all for him, too . . . except Myles had never in his life spoken such words aloud.

Chapter 31

On a late August day in 1775, the postrider stopped at Scot's Haven. A servant brought the mail to Jeremy, and as he deposited a letter from Philadelphia into Rietta's lap, he was breaking the seal on one of his own from Sally.

He looked up from the first paragraph to announce with satisfaction, "They will be home in a se'ennight."

"Only a week?" Billy moaned.

"That means," Tom muttered, "we'll be back at our books in a se'ennight and a day."

"I can't wait to see my present," Molly declared ecstatically.

"It's Mama and Uncle John you're supposed to be anxious to see," Anne instructed in a superior voice. "Do you suppose it will be new wax babies?" she added in her more usual manner.

Jeremy came to the end of his letter and looked up, laughing. "I think Sally is planning to invite half of Virginia to our wedding, Rietta, no doubt to placate all the people she did not ask to hers and Pa's. Does your father say when he and your stepmother and brother will arrive?"

Receiving no answer, he regarded Rietta carefully and saw

245

that she was staring down at her letter as tears coursed along her cheeks.

"They're not coming," she announced flatly. Then, on a sob, "My father's ill, Jamie, very ill."

George caught Jeremy's eye, rose tactfully and shepherded the girls and his young brothers out of the room, hushing all their protests.

"Ah, Jamie," Rietta said, "if you only knew how much I wanted to have them here. I wanted them to see my happiness and to—What you told me long ago was true. I was jealous and spiteful, and I behaved badly to my father and was cruel to Hannah. I wanted this chance to make amends, and now . . . and now—" She covered her face with her hands and wept.

"May I see the letter?" He read it through, prepared for her next remark.

"Jamie, I must go home. Forgive me, but our marriage will have to wait. I would never be able to forgive myself if I didn't see him again and ask him . . . beg him—What kind of life could we have together with this on my conscience?"

He shook his head. "No, my love."

"Jamie," she entreated, "I know I have used you shamefully in the past, too. I know it must seem to you only another put-off . . . but cannot you understand? You have read Hannah's letter. It is like what afflicted Cousin William, and you know such consumptions are seldom recovered from."

Jeremy took her into his arms, gentling her with his hands. "Rietta love," he bade her softly, "calm yourself. I understand completely. But rather than delay the wedding, we will push it forward. My father and Sally return in a week's time. We will hold our marriage the evening they arrive or the following morning. The county will have to accept another private wedding in the Stuart family," he added in a teasing way, and won a faint smile from her.

She heaved a deep sigh of relief and remained quiet in his arms. Presently she raised her head to ask, "But afterward?"

"Afterward," he told her promptly, "we will have four days to spend alone together, either in our house in Williamsburg or here at Scot's Haven. Then we will go to Philadelphia with the Wythes."

"With the Wythes!" she echoed, round-eyed.

So then he told Rietta of the offer Mr. Wythe had made a month before. Jeremy was asked to attend him in the capacity of secretary when he went to the Continental Congress in Philadelphia as a Virginia delegate.

"He pretended at the time to have much need of my services," Jeremy explained, "but in truth, he well knows what a great learning experience this would be for any young man starting a career in the law."

"You never told me you gave up such an opportunity," his love reproached him.

Rietta blushed hotly and becomingly when he assured her gravely, "Our marriage had just been arranged. I promise you I would rather make love to you than draw up documents, even for Mr. Wythe. Now it appears I shall be able to do both."

She still had some doubts and objections, which Jeremy succeeded in soothing away. Then he dispatched a note to Williamsburg to acquaint Mr. Wythe with his change in plans.

His ever-kindly teacher was most prompt and flattering in repeating his pleasure at acquiring Jeremy's services, and mentioned Madame Elizabeth's delight at having Rietta's company on what would doubtless be a tedious journey, even though they would travel comfortably in the Wythes' fine-sprung carriage and stop over at the best inns.

Chapter 32

It was just past eleven in the morning when Myles received the call at his apartment. He was still in a state of shock when he walked into the Williamsburg Inn's dining room an hour later.

His letter had been forwarded to Vittorio Jacobi in Spain, where he was working on a picture. The most Myles had hoped for was a reply as soon as possible. He had never dreamed Gina's father would practically be camping on his doorstep within two weeks.

In response to Myles's questions, the maitre d' said, "Mr. Jacobi? Yes, sir, he's expecting you, if you'll come this way."

The film director rose to shake hands as Myles approached the window table at which he sat.

"Mr. Jacobi? I'm Myles Edward."

Vittorio looked Myles over as calmly and critically as Myles was appraising him. They both smiled. Marriage certificates or not, Myles thought, Gina couldn't disclaim her father. There was no mistaking from where she got her dark, straight smudge of eyebrows.

However, this was the only point of resemblance between them. Vittorio Jacobi was a tall man, somewhat stocky, with red-blond hair retreating from a high forehead. He had a narrow, bony nose, and his broad, high cheekbones gave a rather Oriental cast to his face. His eyes were gray, very sharp, very alert.

Myles sat down opposite him, and both having agreed on Bloody Marys, Myles decided to do away with polite preliminaries.

"It's quite a surprise to see you here, Mr. Jacobi."

Vittorio elevated his eyebrows rather exaggeratedly. "After your most unusual letter?" There was very little accent in his voice; it was more Richard Burton than Sergio Franchi. "You didn't expect me to answer it immediately?"

Myles said awkwardly, "I had hoped you would write or phone, of course. I thought you might . . ."

"Only hoped or thought." Jacobi nodded as though to himself. "I see my girl has you well brainwashed. You think I'm a typical Hollywood egotist in love with his career and more concerned with his publicity than his family?"

"Gi—Pieragina has said only good things about you," Myles corrected carefully. "It's plain that she loves you and was very happy living and traveling with you at one time. What happened to change it, I don't know. I only know that when I first met her in Washington, she was hitchhiking with a couple of bastards who later in the day stole her wallet. The same night I found her sleeping on the floor in back of the Lincoln Memorial. When I offered her the extra bed in my hotel room, she accepted it without questioning my motives. I know that, aside from being somewhat psychic, she is frightened, insecure and neurotic. She has nightmares and migraines and visions. She is mortally afraid to admit that underneath the veneer of cynicism, she is warm and loving and passionate. She is so desperately in need of human contact, she behaves like a bad-tempered schoolgirl when anyone appears to get too close to her."

Jacobi had listened poker-faced to a summation any average father could easily resent. Obviously, Vittorio wasn't average.

"I would say you've described my girl accurately."

"Then, with all due respect, sir, I cannot see why you have allowed a girl of seventeen such self-destructive license. It seems to me you shouldn't object to our marriage. I don't believe it will harm her any more than some of the other things she has done or will go on doing."

"You state your case well, Myles. You permit, as my possible son-in-law, that I call you Myles? After lunch, when we are private again, I will state mine, but here comes my Gina now."

His Gina, in her colonial dress, was fast bearing down on them, her face shiny with excitement, her blonde hair tumbling down her back in disarray. She stared at her father, winking back tears.

"Daddy! Victor! When I got the message to meet you here, I couldn't believe my ears. I thought it was some kind of joke. Aren't you supposed to be in Spain, Da—Victor?"

He had gotten up and hugged her hard. Myles thought she stiffened in resistance for a moment, but then she embraced her father also.

"I still prefer 'Daddy.' Sit down, Gina *mia,* and say hello to your young man."

"My—oh, my God!" She seemed to notice Myles for the first time, and her horrified glance swept from one man to the other with anything but pleasure. A violent blush crept slowly up toward her hairline and down her neck, disappearing into the lace of her shift.

She flopped ungracefully into the chair a waiter had pulled out. Myles stared at her, perplexed, but he detected a lurking twinkle in her father's eyes and couldn't account for either her embarrassment or Vittorrio Jacobi's amusement. Both seemed excessive.

She waved away the offer of a drink. "Have you two been together long?"

"Only a few minutes," her father said. "Not long enough for any profound conversation." He still seemed to be enjoying some private joke at her expense. Nevertheless, she appeared reassured at his words; her shoulders relaxed visibly.

They studied their menus for a while, and as soon as the waiter left, Gina challenged her father. Myles might not have been there.

"Are you here because of Myles's letter?"

"But naturally."

Her shrug held a touch of scorn. "I never thought you would take it so seriously."

"I would hardly travel five thousand miles if I thought it wasn't."

"Are you going to try to convince me you came all that way just because of me?"

"My dear child, it is many years since I have tried to convince you of truths you prefer not to believe."

For all that he spoke quite mildly, there was no mistaking the rebuke in his voice. The abrupt casting down of Gina's eyes showed he had struck a nerve.

"Is this a private quarrel," Myles asked lightly, "or can an interested party join in?"

Vittorio replied easily. "My daughter and I will delay our quarrel—if she insists on one—until we have dinner alone tonight. You and I, Myles, will continue our talk when she returns to work after lunch."

"No, Daddy, please," she said in alarm.

"Gina *mia*, this young man sent me a straightforward, honest letter, which impressed me so much I have come to answer it in person."

"This is the most ridiculous thing I've ever heard of!" she snapped. "Asking permission to marry me!"

"Under the circumstances—*as he appears to see them*"— Jacobi seemed to be stressing this last phrase—"I consider it a very sensible approach."

Gina gave an angry little laugh. "And how much did you think I would be influenced by your opinion?"

"Not at all," Vittorio answered rather sadly.

They remained silent as their lunches were served, and Gina's father's next remarks concerned only Williamsburg. First they discussed the Foundation, and then Myles was subjected to a short but extremely penetrating examination of his work. While this was going on, Gina picked sullenly at her salad.

Myles observed, without any particular pleasure, that her bad manners weren't reserved for his parents alone. When he couldn't stand it any more, he spoke abruptly to the bowed head across the table.

"Your father has come a considerable distance to be with you. You haven't seen him in a long time. Must you behave like an obnoxious brat?"

She fluttered her eyelashes as she said scathingly, "Oh, poor Myles, I've embarrassed you. You don't love me any more."

"On the contrary, I love you very much, which is why I mind having to be ashamed of you."

The downward sweep of her lashes was genuine this time; her hands and lips both trembled.

Myles turned his attention back to Mr. Jacobi. "You must

understand," he continued where he had left off, "that digging is just the beginning of an archaeologist's work. He—"

"I have to get back to the shop," Gina broke in. "I'm sorry," she said to her father as she stood up. "I apologize to you both." Then she looked at Myles. "Don't you think you might get tired of hearing me say I'm sorry all the time?"

Myles grinned at her. "Don't you think the time might come when you wouldn't give me so much cause?"

Her answering grin was a bit wry. "I wouldn't take any bets on it if I were you. She addressed her father again. "Vi— Daddy, I'll be able to go home, get dressed and be back here by seven. Will that be all right? When do you leave?"

"First thing in the morning. Seven will be fine."

She walked away quickly, then stopped two tables away and suddenly returned, standing with her back to her father.

"You're not going to understand," she told Myles, "but it won't be the way you think it will be. I really wasn't trying to—Oh, what's the use?"

She left again and this time did not come back.

"That was an inspired piece of direction. It must be at least five years since I've heard my daughter apologize to anyone for anything." Jacobi's hand shot across the table. "For what it's worth, you have my consent. Of course," he added as they shook hands solemnly, "she goes out of her way to do the opposite of what would please me, so perhaps it would be just as well if neither of us advertised my approval."

He must have noticed Myles's gesture of impatience, because his smile broadened. "You think I do not control my daughter enough?"

"You said it, Mr. Jacobi," Myles answered frankly. "I certainly don't."

"But you see she is not easily reasoned with and yet too old to spank."

"Not in my book," Myles muttered.

"You think I have spoiled her on the one hand and neglected her on the other?" Jacobi suggested matter-of-factly.

Somewhat chagrined, but not enough to keep him from telling the truth, Myles acknowledged, "I guess I do."

"Will you bear with me if I explain both myself and Gina?" Then, without waiting for an answer, he continued thoughtfully. "There was spoiling, I agree, in the beginning. Partly, it seemed a miracle to have her at all. Partly, there were my own guilts to assuage. First, then I gave her such a mother, and second, that I allowed her to be taken away from me."

"But I understand there was a custody suit."

"There was, and the law decided, not I. But guilt is not always rational, and much of what happened stemmed from my own . . ." Vittorio paused briefly. "It began just before the war, the Second World War. I came to England as a refugee, though not a penniless one. My father had managed earlier to get some money sent out by way of Switzerland. Still, England is not the easiest place to be a foreigner. After the war ended, I was glad to go to America. I even volunteered for duty in Korea so that I might get my citizenship sooner. In Korea"—he gazed off into the distance—"I fell in love for the first time in my life, and also the last. The Army in those days did not look too kindly on interracial marriages, and they wrapped up such applications in enough red tape to discourage and delay. I was still filling out forms when she was killed."

Jacobi shrugged. "Life goes on. I came home to good work in films. As sometimes happens when it matters least, I achieved almost instant success. There were many women available. In my profession there always are." He smiled deprecatingly. "Nothing personal, nothing to be proud of. They're all on the make. But in my culture, family is all. I wanted something more solid and secure in my life. So I looked around for a candidate, someone who would understand that I had already had my great romance, and I found Mimi."

His look softened. "I met her on a visit to a friend in the hospital. She was his private nurse. She had soft blonde hair curling all about a pretty face. Mimi was short and a bit plump, and I had known some of the most beautiful women in the world. I could hear the shock waves reverberating throughout the industry. . . . *What does he see in her?*

"What I saw was a warm heart, a gentle manner, peace and serenity to come home to, a wealth of love and devotion to pour out. Unfortunately, she was unable to have children. This, and the fact that she was afraid of planes and would not travel with me at a time when I had to travel constantly, was what finally came between us."

He signaled the waiter to refill their coffee cups.

"Perhaps I am not being completely honest," he mused. "Perhaps everything would have been fine if I hadn't met Naomi on one of my trips to England. Naomi Waverly," he explained, "was—if we are to speak biologically—Pieragina's mother. She was also quite the most stunning woman I had ever seen. Men's tongues hung out when she walked into a room, and mine was no exception. She had one other fatal attraction—her upper-crust English voice. In many ways I was still the bloody little foreigner, overwhelmed because an exquisite specimen of the English aristocracy was climbing into bed with me.

"Agh!" he grunted. "With all my knowledge, all my experience, it disgusts me even now to have been so stupid, such an easy prey for a cold-hearted bitch who did not hesitate to use a bevy of clever, whore's tricks. We were married months before I realized there wasn't an ounce of honest passion in her entire body."

Myles was puzzled. "You married her? I don't understand. If you married her, how can Gina be—"

"A bastard? Quite easily," Jacobi answered bitterly. "Naomi got me in the oldest way known to trap a man, one that many a London shopgirl would be too proud to use. Six weeks after we met, she came to me weeping that she was pregnant. I had thought she was protecting herself. Oh so innocently did she protest that she thought *I* was doing the protecting. I didn't stop to think. I was still infatuated. But even more than that, I suddenly realized I wanted the child. How I wanted my son."

He smiled ironically. "It was, of course, to be a son. How could a man of my background believe otherwise? So I flew home and threw myself on Mimi's mercy, and much to my surprise she refused me a divorce. She knew all about Naomi. The usual good friends had informed Mimi of our affair, and she had made it her business to find out as much as she could. 'She's a no-good bitch who will make you miserable,' Mimi told me. 'But what about the baby?' I asked her, and she answered, 'I'll take the baby.' Final verdict. No divorce."

Vittorio drained his coffee cup and requested more. "I thought it was my own idea. Much later, I realized how Naomi had maneuvered, or perhaps I should say *out*maneuvered, me. I arranged for her tickets and she flew to Mexico, where I joined her. I got a Mexican divorce, which, since Mimi had not agreed to it, was hardly legal. But it permitted me to go through a marriage ceremony with Naomi the next day. Most of all, it permitted my name to appear on a birth certificate as Pieragina's father when she was born in New York some six months later.

"The marriage, legal or not, was a terrible mistake. But my daughter . . . she was another story. The first time the nurse dumped her into my arms, I knew I was crazy to have wanted a son. I gave her my mother's name." Jacobi lifted his eyebrows. "Naomi used to say terrible things about that name later on, but at the time of the baby's birth, we were living in a Park Avenue co-op and her Fifth Avenue charge accounts were unlimited, so she played at being the devoted wife and mother.

"Money quickly became the bone of contention. I had sold our Beverly Hills home, and Naomi resented that half the proceeds went to buy Mimi a house on Long Island. She begrudged the monthly income I gave Mimi; she begrudged every cent that wasn't spent on her alone."

Almost to himself, he mused, "The artistic temperament is a peculiar thing. I have always thought it was an exaggeration. But the truth is, during the years I lived with Mimi all my work seemed to be touched with magic. Not much caring for it, I made money hand over fist. When I lived with Naomi, my ability seemed to dry up. Nothing I did came out right. Within a few years I had spent everything I had made in the good years, and I was deeply in debt. Naomi and I had stopped sharing a bedroom a year after Gina was born. She had her insurance policy in the baby, and *I* didn't want to go near her. Naomi was beautiful and a bitch, and she bored me to death."

He shrugged. "I stayed with her because of my Gina, but I lined up out-of-town acting jobs for my wife whenever I could. She had barely enough talent to cover the bottom of a shot glass, but she was convinced she could be another Vivian Leigh. I encouraged her so I would have more time alone with Gina or with both Gina and Mimi."

Jacobi must have seen some doubt on Myles's face, because he said, "Oh, yes, I began to see Mimi again very soon, and I took Gina with me whenever I could. Pieragina had the wardrobe of a princess, bought at the best specialty shops, and all her toys came from F. A. O. Schwartz, but it was Mimi who gave her the first mothering she had ever known.

"In the end, Naomi found out. We had one last, sickening quarrel, and I took the child and moved back with Mimi. Naomi sued for custody, and when the case came up, she made a very moving plea to the judge about her concern for her daughter's soul if Gina stayed with me. The judge was not unduly impressed, especially when it was brought out under questioning that Naomi did not attend church and had only started making arrangements to get Gina baptized three weeks before. It looked very much as though we were going to have our time with Gina split down the middle, when Naomi pulled an unexpected rabbit out of the hat."

Vittorio gave a short, bitter laugh. "She had her own daughter declared a bastard in open court by proving my divorce from Mimi was not legal. Therefore, her own marriage to me was invalid, and any child of that marriage was illegitimate.

"An illegitimate child, I discovered, is the complete property of the mother. Naomi got full custody. Afterward, she met me on the court steps, blasted me with her Madonna-like smile while the newspaper photographers snapped pictures, and whispered, 'You want her? Buy her back.'

"I was willing, God knows I was willing. The only trouble was that I was also dead broke and in debt. Mimi said we would do it, do it together. But it was almost impossible to get Naomi to agree on a reasonable price.

"In the end, Mimi told me I had to realize it would take several years and I should concentrate on my work. When I did that, somehow it all came back. Within two years I had my first Academy nomination, and the money began pouring in. When Gina was ten or eleven—I've lost track now—she had an emergency appendectomy, and I flew over to England and made Naomi a final but substantial offer. The money was too tempting, and a growing daughter was getting to be a nuisance. Except for her eyes, Pieragina can't match her mother for looks, but there was a promise of loveliness to come. There still is, I think. Anyhow, the papers were signed, Gina was finally mine and I took her home to Mimi. Home to Mother, Gina said."

Jacobi seemed to have drifted away in thought from Myles, who remained tactfully silent for a while, then made an effort to recall him. "Is that when the spoiling began?"

"I suppose so. With me maybe, not with Mimi. She was far more sensible than I. Loving, you understand, but firm. Gina thrived on it. We were a family . . . for a few short years. Mimi was killed by a drunken driver, and Gina and I became everything to each other. I gave her everything. But she was never a brat, never whining or demanding or uncaring of other people. Everyone I worked with loved her, and I took her with me all over the world and put her into various schools. If there wasn't an adequate school where we were, I would hire a tutor. She was a bright, quick girl. She did very well. And she mothered me, too, trying to make up to me for Mimi.

"You understand that there were women in my life?" Jacobi asked Myles almost anxiously. "Nothing important. I had no desire to marry again. Also, I tried for Gina's sake to be discreet. She must have known, but she was discreet, too. It was never mentioned.

"I suppose," he said slowly, "I tried to fool myself that she didn't really know . . . until one weekend when we were home in California, and I thought she was staying at UCLA. There was this little actress I was dating who slept over. Sunday morning around eleven, there was a knock on the bedroom door, and before I could say anything, Gina waltzed in, loaded down with a big tray. 'Breakfast for one coming up,' she sang out. Then she saw the two of us. I don't think I'll ever forget that moment as long as I live. If she had cried, or been angry, embarrassed, anything but what she was."

"Which was?"

"She didn't turn a hair, but behaved as though finding us in bed together was the most natural thing in the world. That's what got to me the most, her not being surprised, upset, *anything*, just taking it for granted. I knew I was doing something wrong, and I made up my mind to change it.

"I can tell you, Myles, the crazy way a man's mind works is not the same as a woman's. I figured if I was going to give up my women, what I needed was a wife. And it would be good for my girl to have a mother. I had thought it out once before in precisely that practical way, and the plan had worked fantastically. I didn't see why it shouldn't work again."

Vittorio looked at Myles ruefully. "Some of my kinder critics have called me a genius. They should only know. In my private life I can be as dumb as any other dumb male. Helen had been my secretary for years. Gina knew and liked her. She had a bit of Mimi's quality of peacefulness and was a sensible, comfortable woman. So I asked her to marry me, and when she agreed, we flew to Las Vegas for the ceremony. The next day we went straight to the college to tell Pieragina."

"Who was naturally not at all delighted?" Myles deduced.

"That is expressing it mildly. As it happens, I have found unexpected happiness and contentment with my wife. But from the point of view of my relationship with my daughter, that has been a disaster. She has despised me ever since."

"Or perhaps has been humanly jealous?"

"Of course, but God help anyone who tries to tell her so. Particularly when I compounded my error by presenting her with a brother."

"I'll be damned. And she said she was an only child."

"Gina prefers to think she is and rationalizes it by saying that she is Mimi's only child. In this way she can refuse to acknowledge both Naomi and Helen, as well as the boy. I understand her feelings, in part. In the beginning it was a shock to us, too. Helen was forty and I was nearly fifty when we got married . . . I remember Gina's telling me, when she heard Helen was pregnant, that it was indecent."

"I hope you smacked her."

Vittorio smiled a bit sheepishly. "No, I was somewhat handicapped at the time. I almost felt it was indecent myself. In time, of course, I was inordinately proud, which, again, Gina chose to misinterpret. Davey has never, as she insists on believing, taken her place. My daughter is dearer to me than anyone in my life, though my son is a fine little boy."

"How many months old is he?"

Jacobi stared at Myles. "Davey is almost four years old."

Myles stared back. "F-four y-years?" he stammered foolishly. "But that's impossible!"

Facts, bits of information, impressions out of the past, all whirled madly around in Myles's head, rather like the colors in a kaleidoscope, until a final pattern emerged.

"This is what you've been leading up to all along," he said slowly. "This is what you've been trying to tell me."

"Gina is not seventeen, Myles. She is twenty-three. She has her B.A. degree in political sceience, though she attended five—no, six; I forgot her summer at the Sorbonne—colleges to get it. She has been accepted into three top law schools. I believe the main purpose of her trip East was to look the schools over and decide which one she would attend." He regarded the younger man sympathetically. "I see you are shocked."

"I am shocked, yes. But I am also feeling extremely murderous." Myles stood up. "I think, Mr. Jacobi," he said very distinctly, "I have a few choice things to say to your daughter."

"Sit down, Myles." Vittorio sounded very much in command of this show. Myles stood there, undecided, and Gina's father repeated, "Please sit down, Myles. There are some other points to be discussed."

Myle acquiesced, and waved away the immediate reappearance of a silver coffee pot. "No. Give me a whiskey, please."

"Make that two," said Jacobi, a twinkle in his eye. "An excellent remedy for shock."

"Do you blame me?" Myles demanded, bitter. "That unconscionable little liar has made a damned fool of me from the start!"

"Do you think that was her intent?" Vittorio asked. "It seems to me that before she left she was assuring you very strongly that she had *not* meant to do that."

Myles gulped his drink and continued to feel rather sorry for himself. "I don't know what to think any more," he half groaned.

"She has not had an easy time, you understand. Always she has lost what she most loves. Disliked by her own mother, despised by her family in England, deserted by me—as she must have believed herself to be when the court gave her to Naomi. Also, please remember that at the time she was labeled a bastard, the epithet was neither popular nor chic, which it has since become in our circles. Gina was ridiculed and whispered about and ostracized when she was much too young to understand why. Tell me, have you ever seen the papers she carries in her wallet? The ones referring to the custody suit?"

"Her wallet was stolen in Washington," Myles reminded him.

"If I know my Gina, she has sent for other copies. It is an obsession with her. The newspapers dealt very leniently with Naomi, the beautiful, innocent aristrocrat seduced by the Don Juan movie director. I remember one of the headlines said, 'She Loved Not Wisely But Too Well.' Most articles gave the impression that I left her alone to bear our unwanted child in disgrace. I always found that ironic, remembering her suite—a single room wouldn't do—at a hospital in New York usually known as the Hotel. Flowers enough for a state wedding. A refrigerator full of French champagne. Jewelry brought up by a bonded messenger so she could choose my gift to her. And two nurses for the baby the first month after she came home so Naomi would never have to lift a finger for her. I never saw Naomi play with our child or hold her or kiss her. Gina was simply an insurance policy, which in the end did pay her handsome dividends.

"You think I've spoiled my daughter. If I have, I thought I had cause. But as to her behavior these last years, I have been helpless. She was past eighteen when I married Helen, and she chose never to live at home again. She went to colleges as far away from us as she could get—in New York and New England, in Scotland, France and Switzerland. She worked in the summer or went away with friends. Gina has been financially independent from the age of twenty. I had learned caution once, and after the money started coming in again, I set up trust funds for both Mimi and Pieragina. Mimi's money was willed to Gina, too, so though she is not rich, she will never want. At present she has an income of about twenty to twenty-five thousand a year. Does that bother you?"

Myles shook his head. "I have no chauvinistic need to control my wife through the purse strings. As a matter of fact . . ." He hesitated, then shrugged and made a full confession. "My income, aside from my job, is a good deal more than hers. My father owns the Edward Fabric Factories in Connecticut and Massachusetts. I don't take anything from him because it doesn't seem right. I'm the only son, and he was tremendously disappointed when I didn't go into the business. But I'll inherit a one-third share someday, and I have some stocks I got from my grandfather."

"I know." Vittorio Jacobi smiled at the look of astonishment on Myles's face. "Did you really think," he queried gently, "I wouldn't have you investigated after receiving your letter?" He leaned back in his chair. "One might say you were as reluctant to trust Gina with the truth about your prospects as she was to tell you the truth about her age. I wonder . . . do you still feel like murdering my daughter?"

"I'm not sure."

"Then may I make a suggestion?"

"You can try."

"Now is not the time to see her. After work she will be with me. I will tell her frankly of our talk. She will be aware you know the truth. Tomorrow I will be gone, and you will have time to cool your temper, perhaps even to think less of your pride and more of her." Vittorio took out a small pad, scribbled across one page, tore it off and handed it to Myles. "I must return directly to Europe. You can reach me here. I would be pleased if you'd keep in touch. Next month I will be back in California."

Myles would have preferred to have it out with Gina there and then, but he suspected that her father was right. Torn between self-pity, injured pride and a plainly bad temper, Myles wasn't in a state to keep his head, let alone—as Vittorio had put it earlier—to handle her with an "inspired piece of direction."

Chapter 33

Myles turned up on Gina's doorstep Sunday morning. Though undoubtedly she knew he'd be coming, she hadn't expected him quite so early.

She was dressed more for housecleaning than for battle: pale blue T-shirt, shorts cut off from a pair of jeans, terry scuffs. There was a smudge of dirt on her nose, and her hair was plaited in two thick braids tied at the ends with yellow ribbon.

"Good morning, Myles," she said in a little-girl voice.

Gina looked like a little girl, too, a damned tiresome one at that, Myles reminded himself in a fresh burst of rage.

"What the hell's good about it?" he demanded ferociously.

The leap of alarm in her eyes turned them from lilac to pansy purple. She rubbed one scuff nervously back and forth along the carpet. It made a rhythmic, hissing sound that didn't do anything to calm his nerves.

"I suppose you're mad," she offered in an angelic whisper that would have been irritating if she *were* seventeen, but was absolutely maddening from someone twenty-three.

"You suppose right."

She retreated slowly as he stalked her like a tiger about to pounce on a choice prey.

She came up hard against the edge of an end table, winced and evidently decided to make her stand there.

"Wh-what are you going to do?" she asked, sounding more like herself, but her voice quavered ever so slightly.

"What am I going to do?" Myles repeated. "Why don't you tell me? It's a choice between beating the hell out of you or rape. Suppose you take your pick."

Gina was breathing hard and biting at her underlip. Then her look of frightened defensiveness changed to one of calculated defiance. She kicked off her scuffs abruptly, and as they went flying across the room, one of them nearly hit Myles in the chest. With a single swift zip, her shorts came down, and she kicked them, too, clear off her feet. While Myles watched, baffled and bemused, she pulled the T-shirt over her head and tossed it into a corner.

Standing there in only a bra and panties, Gina eyed him unabashedly. "Take yours," she invited with the exquisite insolence that was hers alone.

Her panties were a pale cream lace, definitely see-through. The bra hooked in front and was cut so low, there seemed to be more of her out of it than in it. But Myles had seen her wearing less in the York House ladies' room.

If the effect was meant to be seductive, it failed singularly after the first few seconds. How could it not, with the fat braids, the dirt on her nose and the cranelike position of her stance, one foot on top of the other, giving her a somewhat one-legged appearance? Gina was completely unaware that the same leg, jerking back and forth, contradicted her air of bravado.

Myles's rage evaporated instantly, leaving him weak and washed out, but wonderfully calm. Once again he was looking at three girls in one—the befuddled, exasperating hitchhiker; Vittorio Jacobi's beloved, belligerent Gina; his own darling, pain-in-the-ass Pieragina. Desirable as all hell, the three of them, but not one of them a successful seductress.

Myles walked toward her and she flinched, misunderstanding. As he passed her, he saw the brief flare of surprise in her eyes. He continued on his way to the bathroom.

He put on the cold shower full force and ducked his head underneath it. After rubbing his hair with one of the towels, Myles went back to the living room just as Gina placed both feet on the floor.

He lifted her up, and she misunderstood again. He could feel Gina trembling as he heaved her over his shoulder. At the very last moment, she caught on and started struggling, but she was seconds too late. Myles had dumped her into the tub, directly under the blast of cold water, before she could wriggle free.

The water hit her directly in the face, and she began to choke, to splutter and—as soon as she got her breath—to swear.

The effects of his action lightened both his heart and his disposition. "That," Myles announced with satisfaction as he hauled her out onto the carpet, "won't be the last time, if you ever lie to me again."

He wrapped her in a bath sheet, then pulled off the pieces of yellow ribbon and toweled her hair briskly. She stood there, marvelously docile.

"Why, Pieragina?" he asked softly, and she didn't pretend not to know his meaning.

"I always did that when I hitchhiked. I look so much younger—I always have—and men are likely to be—you know—more careful if they think a girl is underage."

"But *I* wasn't just someone you hitched a few hours' ride with."

"No, but at first you made it perfectly clear you didn't want to get close to me. If not quite poison, I was danger. I kind of enjoyed—Well, even if you didn't know about it," she added defensively, "I enjoyed making a fool of you in my own mind."

"You would," Myles said grimly. "And after that?"

She swallowed nervously. "I did begin to tell you that night in your apartment when you were starting to make love to me and I laughed. I stopped when you made it plain you didn't want any part of me. After that . . . after that you let me down, and I . . . I wanted to punish you. You were agonizing so about having fallen for such a crazy, mixed-up teenager, you never gave a thought, or very little, to how much pain you might be causing me because you didn't want to get involved. So I wanted to hurt you, too."

"I'll buy that. I don't even blame you. But we did make up, Gi—Pieragina. I thought we had become friends."

"I was afraid." She began to chew on a fingernail, and Myles pulled her hand down firmly. "I had lied so much and for so long. I really wanted to tell you. But every time I got close to it, something stopped me—"

"And besides," he finished for her smoothly, "I might push a little less for marriage if I still thought you were seventeen."

"Yes," she admitted miserably after some hesitation. She pushed away his hands and dropped her head against his chest. Her arms went tightly around him as she murmured something he couldn't quite hear.

"Come again?"

"I said it wouldn't have to be rape."

"Do you mean you want me or that you're willing?" he asked dryly. "Or is this another form of penance or reward?"

She stood back from him, shaking damp strands of hair off her face. "Damn it to hell, you know you want me, and I'm willing," she gulped. "So why don't we just go to bed?"

"Because, my love, *willing* isn't good enough." Myles laughed as he saw her look of suspicion.

"What's that supposed to mean?"

"You'd like me to force the issue as well as force you. That way you could steer clear of responsibility and decision—*the man tempted me*. Well, sweetheart mine, it ain't gonna be that way. You're going to make a free, mature decision. You're never going to be able to say I forced your hand"—he grinned briefly—"or forced any other parts of your anatomy. I told you once, and I haven't changed my mind. It's marriage or nothing—responsibility and commitment, love and faith. And now," he said briskly, "go dress and let's get out of here. The effects of cold water last just so long."

"I've got things to do."

"Exactly. You can do them with me. We're going for a drive."

Myles took her to Carter's Grove, considered the most beautiful plantation house in Virginia. As they trooped with the rest of a tour group in the direction of the southwest parlor, he bent over to whisper in her ear, "How would you like to prove that I'm a better man than George Washington or Thomas Jefferson?"

"Huh?"

"You can prove it by agreeing to marry me."

Gina stared at him in puzzlement, but he merely shepherded her into the parlor, where their hostess after smoothing down the flowered panniers of her dress, began to speak graciously.

"In recent years this parlor has become known as the Refusal Room, because it was here that two of our greatest leaders, Washington and Jefferson, were rumored to have offered marriage to their first loves and been rejected."

Gina grinned at Myles in sudden understanding. "I wish I could," she murmured.

"We'll come back when you're ready to accept me," he suggested cheerfully.

They walked over the grounds later, sat on the grass and stayed content, looking down toward the river.

As they headed back to the parking lot, Gina swung around with a sudden exclamation.

"What's the matter?"

"Nothing. Nothing bad, I mean." She laughed, feeling a little embarrassed. "I thought for a moment that I saw April."

Gina was pensive when they got into the car, and even after he started driving, Myles saw her looking constantly from left to right.

"Do you want to go home?"

"No, please, no. Drive some more. . . . Would you try this road?"

He didn't know where it went, but obediently did as she asked.

Suddenly Gina cried shrilly, "Stop!"

Myles pulled up onto a muddy patch of earth. Gina stood quite still, looking off to the right, then said softly, "Yes, there she is."

Myles cautioned himself to go easy, not to say or do the wrong thing. They both got out of the car, and he came around his side to join her.

"There she is," Gina said again, and his heart gave a great leap of fright. He had followed the direction of her pointing finger, and undoubtedly there was a flutter of a flowered, colonial-style skirt just beyond the bushes.

The next minute he was telling himself not to be a fool. Gowns of that sort abounded in and about Williamsburg. This was a picnic area; benches and tables were in the distance.

As he followed Gina, Myles was sure they would find a picnic couple; even, he told himself, a romantic-minded couple not at all pleased to find another pair of lovers in their roadside paradise.

But where she went, he would go. . . . Gina was running now, running hard, her face a picture of despair because they had come into a clearing and there was no sign of anyone, female or male. He followed as she ran on toward a small grove of pines, where she sank to her knees and held her arms up and out in the age-old gesture of a woman bereft.

"It happened here," Gina said in a monotone. "Right here. The pain . . . oh, God, the pain."

Myles reached down to lift her, to shake her, to do anything to banish that otherworldly expression on her face, that unearthly light in her eyes.

Gina resisted his touch. She was looking up, but not seeing him. Then suddenly she was looking down, with her hands pawing frantically at the bed of pine needles. "Blood!" she cried. "All that blood running onto the ground. And I cried to you, don't you remember how I cried to you? *Jamie, come back. please Jamie, come back to me . . .*"

Chapter 34

1775

In the morning they would leave for Virginia. Home and Virginia. Never had sweeter words been uttered, thought Jeremy, folding his best blue jacket into a portmanteau.

The experience had been vastly interesting, but it was satisfying now to have the Congress over. The great men of the country seemed no different to him from the more ordinary folk who gathered in the Commons Room at the Raleigh. They appeared to talk much and to do little.

His dear wife also was glad to go, for with her father's death, despite her other kin, her last important tie to Philadelphia was broken. The memory of the reconciliation between Rietta and her father had been a great source of comfort to her. She had also developed a sisterly relationship with Hannah through the tender nursing they gave Mr. Rind.

Even the parting from Hannah was not *cause* for sorrow, for she had promised to visit Williamsburg next year with her son.

1776

Jeremy brought home a copy of the Declaration of Independence from Great Britain, sent to Mr. Wythe from the Congress in Philadelphia. It was a most moving document and of especial interest to Rietta, since the writing was attributed to Thomas Jefferson and seemed to be derived from his earlier pamphlet, *A Summary of the Rights of British America*, which had been published by Clementina Rind.

Jeremy watched Rietta's expressive face as his dear girl read it through several times. "Well?" he cried impatiently when she was finally done. "Is it not a most marvelous doctrine of freedom?"

"Oh, it is wonderfully well written," Rietta agreed sadly. "These are words to stir the hearts of men and send them marching gladly off to war. But don't you see the irony of it, Jeremy? It was penned by one of the largest slaveholders in Virginia . . . and signed by many others. Here and here, and there." Her fingers flicked the signatures disdainfully. "And no doubt others I do not know of." Then she fetched a deep sigh, looking up earnestly at his face. "Have you not noticed one other predictable omission? Where in this document is there any mention of the equality of women? I see nothing here to make me believe it will in any way improve a woman's lot."

He put one finger under her chin to raise her face to his. "Is your lot so hard, my love?" he queried softly.

She put the paper aside and went readily into his arms. "I am wed to you, Jamie Stuart, you paragon of men," she said in her most provocative manner. "Am I to forget my less fortunate sisters because of my own happiness?"

Even as she spoke, Rietta's hands were busy caressing him, so that he was able to forget all the world save her.

"For tonight, yes," he admitted huskily. "Right now I want you to forget everyone, everything, save me."

"Jamie, Aunt Sarey has your supper still on the stove. It will overcook."

"Let it," he said, lifting Rietta up in his arms.

"Jamie, you will—"

He stopped her mouth with a swift, hard kiss. "You are my food and drink and all I need this night."

She uttered no further word of protest as Jeremy carried her up the stairs. In their bedroom, he reached for the strings of her bodice, his hands trembling so, he soon had them miserably tied up in knots.

Rietta bent her mouth to his clumsy fingers, kissing them one by one. "Let me," she whispered.

Unable to wait once the strings were at last undone, he pulled her dress down from her shoulders to her waist, the shift soon following.

Then it was his turn—stock and waistcoat and shirt. Bared to their waist, arms possessively about each other, they swayed together, mouths seeking, bodies yearning.

"Come to bed, love." he urged her presently.

With teasing slowness, she shed her gown and petticoats. When the last garment had slithered to the floor, Rietta, naked, elegant and filled with pride, offered herself to him, the fire light turning her pale body to copper.

Jeremy joined her on the four-poster. "You are so beautiful," he moaned, leaning over her, his hand stroking the velvet thigh pulled up between his. "Your breasts—he lowered his face to them—"sweet fruit of the vine," he murmured.

"Eat, my love, drink," she invited huskily.

As his burning mouth branded Rietta, she lifted a hand to his hair, loosening the ribbon that bound it back. "I love you, Jamie," she whispered.

"I love *thee*," he vowed in the teasing, tender way he was wont to do.

In this affirmation of their mutual dependence, the lesser Declaration was forgotten.

1777

They had spent the summer months at Scot's Haven to avoid the heat of Williamsburg. One day in late August, Aunt Carrie packed a basket lunch, and Rietta and Jeremy rode to the eastern border of his father's estate, where their own modest acreage began at one of the broadest points of the river. The land was lush and the grass seemed a deeper green. When they seated themselves, the heavy, flowered branches of the trees sprinkled magnolia petals on their heads.

Laughingly, they set out rows of stones, laying down an outline of the house they would build one day. Nay, not a house, but a home. Eagerly, they pelted each other with their plans.

"High on the hill overlooking the river."

"A music room where you will play to me."

"A paneled library."

"A carved stairway."

Later they spread a cloth on the grass and laid out their lunch, though Jeremy had little appetite. For two years he had shared with her every thought and feeling of his heart, and now he was tongue-tied, completely at a loss for words.

It was she who, reaching across to touch his arm, said, "Tell me, Jamie."

"Tell you?" he hedged, feeling like the veriest of cowards and hypocrites.

"What you brought me here alone with you to say," Rietta prompted gently.

He began then, awkwardly to be sure. "For two years now I have felt myself necessary to Mr. Wythe. He had his duties at the Virginia Convention and in Philadelphia at the Congress, and I—"

"Tell me, Jamie."

He could not look at her when he said, "I can no longer convince myself it is right to wield only a pen in our cause for freedom, leaving it to others to carry the arms."

"I know, Jamie," she said softly. "I have been expecting you to tell me this for a long time. When have you arranged to go?"

"How could you know?" he asked her, amazed.

"Oh, Jamie. I know thee through and through." She smiled at him with tears in her eyes. "Did you really think I was unaware of your inner struggle this last half year and more?"

He knelt before her. "It has nothing to do with my love for you, you know that, do you not? To leave you will be like tearing my heart out. Without you I am only half alive. But it is that or to be in mine own eyes less than half a man."

"I know, Jamie. To my sorrow, I know. Go, but make me this promise. Come back, Jamie. Promise on your life, on your honor, on our love, that you will come back to me."

He promised. He rocked her in his arms, still kneeling, and she wept for the ease of the pledge and with grief for the parting to come.

"Tell me again," Jeremy whispered against her hair. "Say what I want to hear."

Rietta lifted her tear-stained face to his and repeated the pledge that had brought him his life's greatest joy when first she had said it, and which had continued to bring him happiness ever since. "You are not alone, then, Jamie, and you will never be alone again. I am yours now, too, yours forevermore." This time she added, "God go with you, my darling, as I shall, too. I love you. Love me, Jamie. Love me always."

"Only always?" he chided her lovingly. "When the fish are

fled and the James dries up, why, then I might cease to love you."

1778

The cold and hunger and extreme suffering at Valley Forge were such that Jeremy was ashamed when he had to venture out, seeing the envious glances cast at his thick coat, new boots and warm gloves.

It was still like a dream to him that Rietta should have been there. He was torn between pride in her indomitable spirit and terror for her safety when he realized how ill-protected was her journey, with only his father's man Amos to see to her. They had come laden with the plenty of Scot's Haven, and because of her, Jeremy's men were, at least for the present, the best fed and the best clothed in General Washington's makeshift army.

Jeremy's usually foul-mouthed soldiers spoke of her with love and reverence. While she had been there, they had done more than speak.

For two weeks Rietta had stayed in Philadelphia, riding to the encampment every third day with the pass wrested from the British by some of her Tory Quaker kin. On those visits Jeremy's quarters would suddenly be vacated, and one or the other of the men would make an awkward avowal. "Just to let you know, Cap'n, the men have business elsewhere. There'll be no one marching in or out this next hour. We'll post a guard a little away, but in sight of the cabin to make sure . . ."

God bless them, he thought, it was a taste of heaven after the frost of hell to have held her in his arms again. Yet his heart was lighter when the letter finally reached him, announcing her safe return to Williamsburg.

Three letters from Rietta all at once, after months with never a word. He turned them over, held them in his hands. He could have wept for joy like a woman.

"Now, why like a woman?" he could hear his dear one mock him. "What is so unmanly about tears?"

What indeed? his heart responded.

Those letters were a greater treasure than a purse of gold. Jeremy opened them all and arranged them in order of their dates. He read the first one through quickly. All was well. Bits of minor news and one very major one—that Rietta had rented their home in Williamsburg and gone to live at Scot's Haven till his return. Jeremy's heart swelled with love and gratitude, knowing this sacrifice of her private life was done for his sake. She knew how he wanted her safe with his family.

She was tutoring Tom and Billy, as well as Anne and Molly, since teachers could no longer be hired from Yale. New England, as well as Virginia, was sending all its young men off to war.

As he read the letter carefully through again, Peter Harwood asked for all the men, "Beggin' your pardon, sir, is Miz Stuart in good health?"

"In very good health, I thank you," Jeremy told him, taking up the second letter. It was much shorter, mostly to let him know that his brother George had been wounded in a naval engagement and was home, but Jeremy must not worry. She promised that George's injury was not serious. Her husband would believe her when he knew that in a week's time George was to marry the Russell girl, the pretty one with reddish hair who was kin to Cousin Sally's first husband.

Jeremy opened the third letter eagerly. Yes, George was married, but Rietta had been unable to attend the ceremony. "Your son," she wrote without any preparation at all, "chose to come into the world at a very inopportune time."

He read the sentence three or four times, not believing the evidence of his own eyes. "Do you mind that I named him Charles, for my father?" her letter continued. "For me there is only one Jeremy, and I am his forevermore. Come back, Jamie. There are two of us you must come back to now."

His men were looking at him oddly. He must appear as strange to them as he felt.

"Is anything wrong, sir?" one of them ventured finally.

"Wrong?" Jeremy roared. "How could anything be wrong? I have a son. By God, I have a son!"

1780

John Fauquier and Jeremy had been inches apart in the thick of a skirmish with an enemy patrol. The musket ball that came at the two of them might just as easily have lodged in his head instead of in John's. John died, grinning horribly, in his friend's arms.

It was Jeremy's duty as an officer to send the formal notice to John's family, but the two had been like brothers since childhood. They had been classmates at the College of William and Mary. A personal message must be sent to Mrs. Fauquier. What could he possibly say?

> Dear Madam,
> This day I was beside your youngest son when he fell in battle. I knelt beside him, grasping him in his death throes, holding his brains in my hands. Then I wiped my hands on his breeches, the gorge rising sour in my throat as I crawled away like any other frightened animal to kill in turn. Kill or be killed.

No, he couldn't write that. It was the truth, but it would offer no comfort to John's mother.

Pray God that there be glory in this cause that they were fighting for; there was no glory in war.

"Rietta, Rietta, my love, where are you?" Jeremy cried out in his grief. In all the world, she was his only reality, she and their son.

1781

It seemed more wonderful than belief that the army should have arrived at Yorktown. Jeremy had not set foot in Virginia in nearly four years.

A few minutes' walk brought him to the shoreline of the blue-watered York River, sister to his own beloved James, now being fortified with cannon for the coming battle. He could look past a vista of trees and shrubs and gay summer flowers to a road that led to Williamsburg and then on to Scot's Haven.

Scot's Haven, the son he had never seen, his father, his brothers, Sally and her girls. But it was not for them that his heart beat fast and his mouth became dry; not for those dear ones that Jeremy alternated between a fever of longing and chills at the endless delay.

Rietta . . . she, above all, his beloved wife. "Rietta," he said aloud, "though you know it not yet, I have kept my promise. I am come back to you."

George Stuart drove the wagon carefully, avoiding ruts that would cause his brother pain. It was the same wagon that, as soon as word reached Scot's Haven, had brought him from the college in Williamsburg, hastily set up as a hospital while the battle raged at York.

Rietta, sitting in the rear of the wagon, released Jeremy's hand and reached up to touch George on the shoulder. "It is here, just a few yards farther."

When the wagon stopped, George kept hold of the reins, but Big Rube, who was sitting beside him, jumped down and came around to lower the back of the wagon.

Rietta held out her hands, and he helped her to the ground. "Be careful, Rube," she whispered.

"Don't you fret, Miss Rietta. I hold him like a baby."

He lifted Jeremy from the mattress with powerful arms and carried him, while Rietta trailed behind, her arms heaped with blankets and pillows.

They settled Jeremy near a big pine so that he could half sit, half recline, looking out at the James.

"Come back for us in an hour, Rube," Jeremy directed.

"Yes, Mr. Jeremy. Now, don't you overtire yourself, hear?"

"Yes, sir, boss."

The slave shook his head indulgently as he turned away.

George brought another pillow and a small jar of herbs. But finally they were alone, and Rietta sat with her back against the pine, helping Jeremy to shift his position so that his head was resting in her lap. The scent of sweet jasmine filled the air.

They sat silently for a few minutes, content to be alone together.

"Look, Jamie," Rietta whispered eventually, "most of the stones for our house are just the way we left them."

Jeremy gazed at her tenderly. "It can still be built there, if you wish. My father has promised me he would build it for you, and you must not be too proud to accept his help. Thank God you will have enough money, but better that you husband it. You might even consider having Hannah and your young brother live with you. Perhaps now that the capital has been moved to Richmond, you might prefer to go there."

"I suppose it would be a better place to practice law," she agreed readily, "whether you go into Mr. Wythe's offices there or set up on your own."

His hand moved weakly to reach for hers. He looked steadily into her eyes. "I shall do neither, dear love. It is for you and the boy we must plan."

"Thee must stop this nonsense, Jeremy Stuart. I will not listen."

"You must listen. You shall. Everyone has faced the truth

save you, Rietta. And now, beloved, you must, too. I asked to be brought here to be alone with you, to tell you . . . to make you accept—I will not be with you, Rietta. I wish with all my heart and soul that it were otherwise, but you must accept that the life you are planning now is one I cannot share."

"No, no, I don't accept it. I won't accept it. You promised. Oh, Jamie, you promised me you would come back."

She bent over, holding him tight, and her tears splashed onto his face.

"My little love, I promised to come back, and I did. It seems I cannot stay."

"I will not let thee go," she said fiercely. "I will not live without thee, Jeremy Stuart." Rietta kissed him as though she could breathe fresh life into Jeremy with her own strength.

He whispered against her lips, "You can because you must, my own. Death cannot part us. Have you forgotten so soon? *When the fish are fled and the James dries up, why, then I might cease to love you.*"

She rocked him against her in a spasm of love and grief. "I want you now, in this life."

He smiled up mistily into her tear-stained face. "Oh, my Quaker spitfire, what an impatient wench you are," Jeremy teased with infinite tenderness. "Do you not know that we have loved before and will love again?"

They looked into each other's eyes, his gentle and at peace, hers wild and frightened.

"Say what I want to hear," he murmured, laying his cheek against hers.

"You are not alone, then, Jamie, and you never will be alone again. I am yours now, too, yours forevermore."

"Then believe it will be true for us, Rietta. No matter where I go, I will be with you. Will you remember that?"

"Yes, Jamie," she sobbed.

"Heaven could never hold more joy than I have found in your arms."

"I love you, Jamie."

"I love *thee*."

With a great effort, he smiled at her again, then thankfully closed his eyes. She looked down in fright at his pale, calm face.

"Jamie!" she cried. "Jamie!"

His eyes slowly opened to hers, but a mist came between

them. Suddenly his face constricted. His mouth opened, but no words emerged, only a fountain of bright red blood. It poured over her hands and stained her snow-white bodice, and with it came the last gasping sigh of his breath.

"Jamie," she whispered, knowing he could not hear. Slowly she lowered him to the ground, and his blood became part of the earth.

She knelt beside him and gently wiped his mouth before she kissed it. Again and again she kissed his still-warm hands.

Rietta looked out to the sun-sparkled river and then back to him, crying out in her pain and anguish, "Jamie, please don't die and leave me. Come back. Oh, Jamie, Jamie, please come back to me."

Chapter 35

Gina knelt, gazing up at Myles.
Jamie, oh, Jamie, Jamie, you've come back.
My Quaker spitfire, did I not promise thee I would?
But I waited such a long, weary while.
Thy waiting is over.

Gina reached out to him, and he knelt beside her. Holding tightly to each other, they sank onto the thick bed of pine and lay on their sides, facing each other, her hand resting on Myles's outflung arm.

He felt her trembling and whispered, "Don't be afraid, my darling."

"I'm not," she whispered back. "I want you, too."

He stared into glorious, glowing eyes that delivered a smoldering stare in return. It was his turn to shake.

Gina drew herself over him, her mouth savagely seeking his lips as she strained desperately against him. He had to push her away to scoop her into his arms and deposit her back on the pine mattress.

"Gently, my little one, gently," he teased, "or there'll be nothing left for you".

She lay quietly while Myles played with her hair, combing it with his fingers, and bent to nibble at her ears. His lips slid across her forehead and down her nose, then all around and over her mouth.

He unbuttoned her cotton blouse and smiled approvingly at her bra. "A front hook. Very foresighted of you." He felt her stiffen slightly as he nuzzled against her skin. "No tickling, I promise," he whispered, and kissed each breast firmly. "Good," he whispered again as she sighed and relaxed. "If you had laughed, I wouldn't have been responsible for the consequences."

She smiled sensuously, and laughter rose from deep in her throat.

"Gina, my Pieragina." He held her face between his hands. "Tell me that you *are* my Pieragina now."

"Heart and soul and—"

"And?"

She closed her eyes, more shaken by his tenderness than she had ever been by passion. "And whatever else of me you want."

"In that case . . ." Myles lifted himself above her, supporting his weight on his palms and elbows so as not to press too heavily on her. "All of you, my Pieragina, every lovely, luscious inch of you."

He released his weight; his hands slid under her bottom and raised her upward. As she wrapped Myles in her arms to bring him closer, he bade her softly, "Open your eyes, Pieragina."

Hours later, she opened them once again. He was beside her, his eyes staring deep into hers. A smile trembled along the corners of her mouth.

"Why, Myles, we made love, didn't we?" she murmured.

He stroked her face lovingly. "I would say so."

"I never made love before," she said in wonder. "Other things, but not . . . that."

He cradled her close, and she asked dreamily, with her head on his shoulder, "What was all the fuss about?"

"What fuss, darling?"

"I mean, why did I fight you so hard?"

"I don't know. You tell me."

"I don't know either." She moved away and sat up, brushing pine needles out of her hair as she looked at him in bewilderment. "It all seems so clear now, and so simple."

"What does?"

"Loving you. Belonging with you."

Swiftly he brought her back into his arms. "Do you?" he asked huskily.

"Do I what?"

"Love me and belong with me now?"

"Now and forevermore." Gina wondered again, confused, "Why didn't I know it before?"

"Some people learn the hard way." He kissed her ear and whispered into it, "Would it be unromantic of me to mention that the mosquitoes are eating me alive?"

"Unromantic, but painfully true. Me, too." She leaped up, brushing off more pine needles. "I must say, Myles, you picked an unusual spot."

"I picked?"

"Well, it wasn't me," Gina laughed. "I never knew this place existed. Where are we anyhow?"

"On a hill overlooking the James."

"I can see that myself." She gazed at the sun-dappled river, lined with lacy-fingered willows. "What a beautiful spot for a house," she murmured.

"Maybe someday, if you're interested. Shall I find out if the land's for sale?"

"I think I'd like that, even if we couldn't be here always. Is it because we made love that it feels so special here somehow?"

"I don't know, Pieragina, but it does for me, too."

They brushed each other off, laughing, before walking down the hill hand in hand. Just before they reached the car, they both glanced back and then continued on, not talking.

Myles came around to the passenger side of the car with her. "Will it upset your feminist heart if I open the door for you?" he asked gravely, proceeding to do so.

"As long as you don't make a habit of it," Gina answered, equally serious, as he tucked her in like a piece of fine porcelain and shut the door.

He got in on the driver's side and made no move to start the motor. "What's the matter, Pieragina?"

"You know, just because I . . . we . . . because . . . you—There'll still be plenty of problems," she blurted out finally. "I mean, it would be a mistake for you to think from here on in it will be simple."

He reached out and turned her troubled profile around full-face. "Look, my continuous little case history. I have no false illusions or delusions," he said firmly. "Easy, no; exciting, yes."

She emerged from his kiss a bit breathlessly. "I still intend to be a lawyer."

"I never doubted it for a minute. What law schools were you accepted by?"

"NYU and Cardoza in New York, and Yale and Harvard."

"New York, New Haven and Boston. Well, if your heart is set on one of those, I'm pretty sure I can get a museum job in New York or Boston for a few years. "I'd give up on Yale if I were you, unless you want to spend the first part of our marriage in the same town as your in-laws, which I wouldn't mind"—he grinned—"but I'm told it's not the best idea in the world for the bride. For what it's worth, if you're willing to apply to Georgetown, which might mean a year's delay, I can stay on at the Smithsonian. Or you might consider William and Mary, in which case I'd try to get a job with the Foundation. It's your choice, love."

"Truly?"

"Truly."

Her eyes blurred. "You'd do that for me?"

"Someday it will penetrate that I love you. Your plans are as important in our life as mine. Just never shut me out and never run away from me, even in your mind."

"You, too, with me?" she asked softly.

"Me, too."

"You know," she said unexpectedly as he steered the car onto the highway, "I've been thinking about April. It may be I'll never see her again."

Myles gave Gina a quick side glance. "Why won't you?"

"Because, oh, because I hardly ever did see her the times when I was happy. I think there was a reason, or maybe a meaning to her for me. I think she was meant to bring me to you, Myles, so now her purpose is done."

"Will you miss her?"

"I'll always miss a good friend." She reached for his hand as it groped for hers. "But if you mean, will I be unhappy, how can I be now? I have what I seem to have been wanting and waiting for all my life. I have someone to run to instead of away from. I'm not alone any longer."